BIG BOSSY TROUBLE

MANHATTAN BILLIONAIRES
BOOK 2

LILIAN MONROE

Copyright © 2023 Method and Madness Publishing PTY LTD All rights reserved.

No part of this book may be reproduced or transmitted in any form or by any means without prior written permission from the author except for short quotations used for the purpose of reviews.

Resemblance to actual persons, things living or dead, locales, or events is entirely coincidental.

Cover: Maria at Steamy Designs
Editing by Shavonne Clarke
Proofreading by Brooke Crites (proofreadingbybrooke.com)

WANT THREE BOOKS DELIVERED STRAIGHT TO YOUR INBOX?

HOW ABOUT THREE ROCK STAR ROMANCES THAT WERE *WAY* TOO HOT TO SELL?

GET THE COMPLETE *ROCK HARD* SERIES:
WWW.LILIANMONROE.COM/ROCKHARD

ONE

LAYLA

I'M LYING ON A CLOUD. A silky, pillowy, heavenly-smelling cloud.

Blinking my eyes open, a soft sort of confusion filters through my consciousness. It's not unpleasant, but... *Where am I?*

Somewhere nice. Somewhere beautiful. Somewhere better than I've ever been before.

My eyes drift shut again, and I enjoy the serenity of the moment. I haven't had a good night's sleep in weeks—months, even. But my limbs are heavy and my body is oh-so-relaxed, and I feel as if I could sleep for an eon. Stresses buzz at the distant edges of my mind, but I ignore them. Whatever problems will emerge—and I know they will—I'll deal with them later, when I wake up. When I have to leave this oasis of peace.

I feel...*safe*.

The sound of deep, steady breathing penetrates the haze in

my mind, and I turn my head toward it. My eyes slit open, and I manage to make out a shape beside me. A male shape. A muscular shape. A very distinctly *naked* shape.

Mm...a naked male chest that looks perfect to snuggle up against. Maybe I can just reach over with my hand, run it over that broad expanse of skin, and nuzzle right into the crook of his strong shoulder—

Record scratch.

Uh. Wait—what?

Reality slams into me like a bucket of ice water to the face. I freeze, wide awake. Cold jets through my veins as my skin pebbles like gooseflesh, rasping against the silky-soft sheets wrapped around my body.

I'm in a strange bed with a strange man.

A *naked*, strange man.

Except he's not a strange man at all. He's my *boss*. Well, he was my boss for the seven excruciating days that just passed.

And—hold on. I lift the edge of the sheet and peek down at myself, my body turning to stone. Every inch of me grows still as the horror of my situation settles over my ice-cold skin.

He's not the only one who's naked.

Sucking in a hard breath, my eyes widen as I stare at the ceiling, using my arms to hold the sheet tight to my bare body. A slow, deep breath fills my lungs as I attempt to calm my racing heart, but that doesn't change the fact that I'm in a bed that isn't my own, there's a man sleeping beside me, and neither of us are wearing any clothes.

Oh. My. God.

I snake my hands under the covers to make sure, moving

slowly so as not to disturb the man sleeping next to me, and yep —topless. But when I reach down, I feel the thin scrap of lace I call panties and let out a breath. And for no other reason than I need to know, I lift the sheet with one hand, sliding my gaze toward his side of the bed. Inch by inch, his arm and side are revealed. His skin is smooth and golden, dark against the white sheets.

My heart thunders, and I don't know if it's nerves at being nearly naked next to my billionaire boss, or the fact that he's male perfection made flesh.

Another inch, and I see the edge of black boxer-briefs. He's not naked. Neither of us are. My breath runs out in a rush, even if a tiny corner of my heart wilts with disappointment.

Which is insane. The last thing I want to do is have drunken sex with my boss—especially if I don't even get to remember it.

Turning my head, I take him in. Slowly, second by second, the memories from last night come back to me.

I remember leaving the hospital where my good friend Dani was entering her sixth hour of labor to welcome her new baby boy into the world. I felt a thrill pierce my stomach as Leif Sorensen, Manhattan's most famous—or infamous—blue-blooded billionaire, suggested we go out for a drink to unwind. Even under the full power of his charm, I knew I should've refused. I knew it was a bad idea to give in. But he gave me that smile, that knowing arch of his eyebrow, and honestly, how is a woman supposed to resist?

I'd resisted his magnetism for a week, but I no longer had the shield of our professional relationship.

I didn't stand a chance.

I remember letting my feet carry me through the revolving glass doors and into the waiting Rolls-Royce on the other side.

Last night, like every other time I've seen him, everything about Leif smelled of money. The way his clothes were perfectly tailored to his body, even the plain white tee he wore under his designer sport coat. The way he strode with his shoulders back, gliding through doors that were opened for him as if he were royalty.

Being next to him was like entering a parallel universe I hadn't known existed right alongside my own squalid existence.

The memories tumble through my head—memories of drinks and shots and laughter. Of low, pulsing music in the VIP section of an intimate jazz club I'd never be admitted to without Leif Sorensen by my side. Of Leif's hand on my thigh as his breath ruffled my ear. Of the dirty, flirty words that made fire slide all the way down to my core. I remember the moment I decided I'd sleep with him, when he used his thumb to swipe a bead of my drink off my bottom lip, his eyes dark and full of promises.

Something snapped in me at that moment. A thread of tension that's always kept me on the right side of trouble. Years of discipline, of responsibility, of sacrifice. Burdens piling on top of each other one after the other after the other, finally collapsing under the weight of it all.

I was *tired.* I hadn't slept right in weeks and three jobs kept me on my feet for far too many hours a day. This past week was more tiring than most, what with the extra responsibility I took on with Leif's daughter.

That's my excuse, anyway.

I've always been the reliable one. Until last night.

Last night, I let myself be swept away by the glamour. By the rich-boy smirks. By the knowledge that this would be one night of fun—and one night only.

After all, Leif Sorensen doesn't *date*—especially not mere mortals like me. I learned that a long time ago, the first time we met.

Not that he remembers.

For the briefest moment, I stare at the man whose bed I'm sharing. His body is a work of art. As he rests on his back, his chest rising and falling with every breath, I find myself itching to reach over and push a strand of unruly blond hair off his broad forehead.

His full lips are parted to reveal the edge of straight, white teeth. A billionaire's teeth. He probably spent more money on his smile than I make in a year—and every penny of it was worth it, because his smile last night nearly made my panties spontaneously combust. Male-model-worthy cheekbones give his face a regal air, with a thick fan of lashes resting against his bronzed skin.

Generations of good breeding are sleeping next to me, and I've never felt so out of place.

He's a king. A Scandinavian regent descendent from Vikings—and just as gorgeous the morning after as he was in an alcohol- and exhaustion-fueled frenzy last night. I remember the way his piercing blue eyes looked when he was on top of me, when his hand pinned my wrists above my head.

My gaze slips down the muscular planes of his torso to the

carved ridges of his stomach, and all the way down, down, down...

I squeeze my eyes shut.

Then the panic starts.

I, Layla Reynolds, am half-naked in bed beside *Leif freaking Sorensen*, and I need to get the hell out before he wakes up and realizes his mistake—or worse, asks me to stay.

Sleeping in his bed after a drunken night of debauchery is bad enough. Waking up next to him and seeing those deep, dark-blue eyes open to see me lying half-naked on his bed would be an unmitigated disaster.

I can't stay here. The memories get hazy after the whole pinning-hands-above-my-head thing. I have this awful feeling I said something mortifying. Or did I fall asleep in the middle of us fooling around?

Stifling a groan, I bite my lip. This is why I don't usually drink—and especially not when I haven't eaten or slept all day. It leads to terrible, terrible decisions.

Heart racing, head pounding, mouth tasting of death, I inch my way to the edge of the bed and slip my feet onto the floor. Slithering off the mattress, I try my best not to disturb the sheets. I land in a crouch, arms crossed over my chest to hide my nakedness.

From whom, I'm not sure. The walls might have eyes.

The room looks like it was hit by a tornado. My bra dangles from a lampshade where it landed after Leif took it off one-handed before tossing it over his shoulder. I genuinely didn't know it was possible to take off a bra one-handed. Last night, I thought it was just about the sexiest thing that had ever happened to me, especially when those broad, strong hands shaped my breasts like he owned me, when his lips touched my nipple and sent electric waves coursing through my blood.

Oh. My. Lord. I fooled around with Leif Sorensen last night. I might have fallen asleep in the middle of it.

I freaking *fell asleep* in the middle of fooling around with my boss! What is *wrong* with me?

Breathe, Layla. Step one: gather your clothing.

I scan the room. Bra is on the lampshade; jeans are next to the dresser. I can't see my top.

Dropping to my hands and knees, I find one sock under the bed. I crawl to the end of the bed, wincing at a sharp pain in my knees. When I glance down, I realize the skin is rubbed raw, and my cheeks flush as I think of the activities that led to that particular injury. "*Shit,*" I whisper to myself, then freeze when I hear movement above.

The billionaire in the bed shuffles, snorts, then stops.

My heart bangs against my ribs hard enough that I'm worried they'll crack. I stay on my hands and knees for long, interminable seconds, staring at the lush, abstract-design rug that probably cost more than my entire miserable apartment across the river.

I don't belong here. Last night was a mistake.

When I hear nothing for what feels like an eternity, I shuffle to the other side of the bed and reach underneath to grab my sock. Then I crawl to the leather-upholstered chair sitting beneath the picture window. There, I find my top. I have to reach under a side table for the second of my socks, grasping it with the very tips of my fingers. When I try to back out, I bang my head against the underside of the table. Objects rattle. I freeze at the sound of more movement in the bed.

I can only imagine the view Leif has of me right now. Who knew full moons happened in broad daylight? My thong sure as hell isn't hiding anything.

When all I hear are deep, rhythmic breaths, I back out from under the side table. Gathering my clothes under one arm, I hold my breath as I make my way to the sleek, modern lampshade and pluck off the bra dangling from it.

This is a new low.

Even for me.

Finally reaching the bedroom door, I turn the handle.

I don't know why, but right before I slip through the door, I look over my shoulder—and pause.

He's too gorgeous for his own good. For *my* own good. He's turned onto his side and his body looks carved from bronze, all muscle and taut skin. Three parallel red marks mar the smooth expanse of flesh where my nails dug into his shoulder in the darkest hours of the night.

I scratched red marks into my boss's skin while he tugged my nipple with those wicked teeth, *and then I fell asleep.* How utterly mortifying.

What have I done?

Last night was a *very* big mistake. A terrible lapse in judgment.

His hand reaches toward my side of the bed and—wait, no. It's not *my* side of the bed. I need to get out of here.

Completely naked except for the valiant panties that somehow survived last night, I slip out the bedroom door and ignore the pang in my chest when the latch snicks shut behind me. A long breath slips through my lips as I lean my forehead against the door. I feel like I just sprinted the hundred-meter dash.

Last night was an aberration. It can't—it *won't*—happen again.

Firstly, I have responsibilities. I can't spend nights away from home when what I should be doing is trying to find a permanent job. If I'm going to keep my family afloat, I have to start making more money. This gig with Leif was always going to be temporary, and I'm glad it's over.

Liar, liar...

Secondly, Leif Sorensen is a different breed. I've known this for a long time—six years, to be exact. After our first meeting, I googled his name and came up empty but for a short Wikipedia page on the Sorensen fortune. Generational wealth, it said, first made a century ago when the family first arrived in America.

I didn't sleep next to a man last night; I slept next to an *heir*.

To make matters worse, Wikipedia informed me that Leif caused a stir in his twenties by defying his parents to start his own real estate development business. It has since grown to be one of the largest companies of its kind in the northeast.

He's an heir *and* a CEO, and according to the *Forbes* articles I've read over the years, he's a ruthless one at that. His company's success has been explosive, and most analysts agree it's because of the single-mindedness with which Leif attacks every business deal. He's much the same in the way he pursues women. Lots of women.

Oh, but in his private life, he's a picture-perfect father who dotes on his daughter—a fact that I didn't quite believe until I saw it with my own eyes.

In the years since our first meeting, I've seen his name in the papers countless times. If he's not acting debauched and reckless, he's cutting multi-hundred-million-dollar deals and growing his fortune. The man has a nose for business like no one else. He's unmerciful, bloodthirsty, and attractive enough to have women lining up to be corrupted by him.

I didn't think I would be one of them.

The best thing for me to do is get out of here and never look back. I live in the real world, where people have jobs instead of multi-million-dollar inheritances and even bigger net worths. A world where others depend on me. Where my sister's future rests squarely on my shoulders. Where my grandparents' home might get taken away from them unless I pull a rabbit out of my hat and save it.

People like me don't sleep with people like him—and if they do, it's just for one night. Just a bit of fun.

I didn't even get that, because I *freaking fell asleep.*

With shaking hands, I slip on my bra first, then tug on my top. My clothes are wrinkled and smell vaguely of alcohol and Leif. But there's not time to think of that. I need to get out of here, get home, forget this ever happened.

Tiptoeing on polished hardwood floors, I make it down the hallway into a vast, cavernous space. My chest constricts at the sight of the clean, white lines of the contemporary furniture, the huge windows overlooking the chaos of the Manhattan streets, the splashes of colorful art displayed on pristine white walls.

I'd kill to own a space like this. Hell, I'd kill to plan a party in this space. It was made for entertaining, but judging by what Leif has told me, it's basically where he rests his head after working too late to go home.

Or, reading between the lines, where he brings women to hook up with.

A group which now includes yours truly, the Queen of Bad Decisions.

When I exhale, I know this place will never be mine—neither this four-bedroom penthouse, nor the six-bedroom townhouse on the Upper West Side that Leif calls home with his daughter. Because if there's one thing I've learned about billionaire real estate moguls in the past week, it's that they own multiple Manhattan properties. One isn't enough, apparently, when the rest of us struggle to give our slumlords enough money for rent every month.

Focus, Layla. You're trying to escape.

On the huge, smooth stone countertop, I see my purse. It's a knockoff Michael Kors shoulder bag that I got from a vendor in Chinatown. The fake leather is worn and flaking, the strap hanging on by a thread. Amidst all this understated opulence and evidence of wealth, it looks completely out of place.

Half its contents are spilled out onto the gleaming marble countertop. Last night, Leif tore the bag off my shoulder and tossed it halfway across the room right before hauling me over his shoulder to carry me to bed. It was an appropriate prelude to the whole one-handed-bra-removal thing. Very macho and funny and sexy—or at least it was to my addled brain.

Now, as my throat tightens and I stuff the contents back into my purse, it doesn't seem so hot and hilarious. He could have cracked my phone screen. That might be inconsequential to someone with commas in their bank account, but it would be devastating to me.

Once I have my things, I stab my feet into my sneakers and angle for the door. I remember thinking the bouncer wouldn't let me into the club last night in my stained and torn Nikes when it looked like sky-high stilettos were a part of the dress code—then I realized Leif Sorensen had his arm around my shoulders. I could have worn faded Crocs and that velvet rope would've still opened for me.

I pause, wondering if I should leave a note, then quickly dismiss the thought. The best thing for me to do is slip away and never speak of this to anyone. I'll lock the memories of last night into a vault, only to be taken out and looked at in the darkest hours of the night.

I open the door.

...and there's someone on the other side.

A little girl with perfect blond ringlets tilts her head. "Hi, Layla. Are you my nanny this week again?"

"I—uh... No. I'm—" I stop myself when my brain fails to provide the right word for this situation. Unfortunately, the organ inhabiting my skull seems to have turned to mush.

I met Isla, the precocious seven-year-old, at a birthday party a few months ago, and then again exactly seven days ago, when this entire disaster began. I've been looking after her while her regular nanny, Harriet, had a family emergency.

"Hi, Isla. No. I just needed to grab a few things from your dad's apartment," I lie. "Mrs. Harriet is starting again today. Her husband is home from the hospital."

"They're not home yet," Isla tells me, slipping inside the door. "Marcus and I went to check before we came here, because Marcus has things to do and he said he can't watch me anymore. Daddy wasn't answering his phone," Isla informs me.

The name Marcus makes me freeze. If Isla is here, that means Leif's best friend will be somewhere nearby...

The elevators across the lobby open, and a frazzled-looking man rushes out, accompanied by a big, fluffy brown dog. Marcus is tall—six-foot plus—and so gorgeous he's hard to look at. I'm not exactly sure of his ancestry, but whatever it is, it works in a big way. He has uptilted eyes of emerald green, drool-worthy bone structure, and the body of an Olympic swimmer. The genetic lottery went *ding-ding-ding* when he was conceived.

Oh, and I'm pretty sure he hates me.

The dog shoves his nose into my crotch as if to say, *This place smells like someone I know!*

"Bear, stop that," Marcus says, grabbing the beast's collar. His beautiful eyes narrow on me.

I back up and gently push the dog's snout aside as he tries to sniff me again, then I sidestep away from the door. "Hi, Marcus."

"What are you doing here?" Marcus asks.

"Layla works for Daddy," Isla informs him. "Don't you remember? She planned my birthday party. She was my temporary nanny for the week. She says she's not my permanent nanny anymore, but she should be, because I like the way she does my hair. That would be fun, right, Layla? You could be my new nanny forever."

Please, Lordy, no.

Not because of Isla. She's a great kid.

But if Leif asks me to work for him permanently, I won't be able to say no, because this job pays better than all my other jobs combined, but then I'll have to speak to him again when I'd rather just crawl into a hole and die.

I cringe internally at the look Marcus gives me. Those green eyes miss nothing.

My boss, Linda Delmar, boasts the best nanny agency in the city and caters to an exclusive clientele. If she hears about this, she'll have my head. Maybe I should lop it off myself and save her the mess.

As Isla saunters into the luxurious apartment behind me, I hike my purse higher on my shoulder and give the man studying me an awkward nod. "I was just leaving."

He pauses in the doorway as we shuffle to pass each other, his eyes searching my face. The smudged makeup. The rat's nest hair. The crooked clothes.

"Marcus," Isla calls out as she opens the refrigerator. "Why are you looking at Layla so funny? Don't you remember her? She used to be Benny and Jane's nanny, but only for a little while. Layla organized the baking class I went to where I made those cupcakes for you. I decorated one to look like Bear. You said no one had ever made a cupcake that looked like your dog before and you felt almost sad to eat it." She turns her head to look in the refrigerator. "Then you said it was the best dog-decorated cupcake you'd ever tasted. You talked to her at my birthday party."

When Isla turns and blinks at the two of us, I get an awful, sinking feeling in my stomach. This little girl's memory is a vault, and there's no way she'll forget the fact that I'm here at the crack of dawn for absolutely no professional reason at all.

I'm too shellshocked to answer. Isla, totally unbothered by our lack of response, angles her body toward the hallway and inhales deeply to yell, "Daddy! Get up!"

At the sound, I snap out of my stupor. Time for me to get the hell out of Dodge.

"It was, um, nice to see you," I mumble, then I turn on my heels and literally run for the elevator. Mashing the down button, I glance at the door to the apartment that's still held ajar by Marcus's hand. He's staring at me, his jaw set in stone, his eyes narrowed.

I bare my teeth in my best imitation of a smile while my finger beats a harsh staccato against the elevator button.

"*Come on, come on, come on,*" I say through my grimace. I press the down arrow again, and oh, screw it. Pushing the doorway to the stairwell open with my hip, I rush through just in time to hear Leif's voice rumble to life behind the closing apartment door.

This whole mess started eight days ago, and I knew I should have refused the job. Anything involving Leif Sorensen can only end in trouble.

But let me start at the beginning. Rewind to last week, when Leif Sorensen crashed into my life and turned everything on its head.

TWO
LAYLA

A TEENAGER with acne-covered cheeks and a bored expression on his face reads out the total cost of my groceries, then points at the machine when I lift up my debit card. Inserting my precious rectangle of plastic into the reader, I punch out my PIN with one hand and subtly cross my fingers with the other.

I'm pretty sure I have enough to cover groceries this week. I *should* have enough—I checked right before I came to the store. Ten minutes ago, I had the money to pay for food for my sister and myself for the week, but I can't help it. I'm still nervous.

Maybe it's the look on the face of the middle-aged lady standing in line behind me that makes the space between my shoulder blades itch. She has perfectly styled hair and a huge rock on her finger, and she's looking at me like I'm scum.

She knows I'm worried about the cost of my meager groceries. I can tell by the way her eyes flick to my crossed fingers, then down to my hole-studded and stained shoes, then up to my messy ponytail.

I bet her sneer would increase tenfold if my card was declined and I had to do that whole shameful dance of deciding which items I don't really need to buy. I scan the bags and decide I'd lose the chicken. It's the most expensive item I picked up this week, and I've been meaning to eat less meat anyway. Win-win, right?

The card reader keeps thinking, that little screen taunting me with the word "AUTHENTICATING," seeming to take an eternity. Maybe the machine is authenticating *me*, determining whether I'm worthy of my groceries this week.

It's not my fault I'm broke.

The scowling lady's diamond-clad fingers drum on the handle of her cart, her brow arched in impatience. I shift my weight from foot to foot, waiting for that damn machine to put me out of my misery and tell me if my payment went through or not.

It beeps once, and I can't help the sigh of relief that escapes my lips when I see the word "APPROVED" written in black, block letters.

See? Nothing to worry about. I knew I had enough.

"Receipt?" The spotty-faced teen hands me a long strip of white paper, which I accept with a nod, then shuffle out of the store without looking back.

Groceries shouldn't be so stressful. Standing at a till

shouldn't make me feel like I'm standing at the pearly gates being judged by St. Peter himself.

I haul one bag over each shoulder and start the cold, six-block trek back to the apartment I share with my little sister. I could have gone to a closer store, but I had a coupon for buy-one-get-one-free cleaning products. Plus, a little extra walk never hurt anyone, right?

Huffing and puffing, I hike the bags a little higher on my shoulders, put my head down, and try to ignore the January winds piercing through my too-thin jacket. My sneakers are soaked from snow and slush, toes curled against the cold. I really need new boots. New Jersey winters are harsh, especially when I have three jobs that require me to crisscross the Hudson River multiple times a week. I put a lot of miles on my shoes, and I already know these old sneakers won't last through the cold months.

That, however, is a problem for another day. Maybe a day when I have more than six dollars left in my checking account.

Wiggling my frozen toes as I wait for a streetlight to turn green, I feel the vibration of my cell phone against the interior pocket of my inadequate jacket. The light changes as I unzip my jacket and reach into my pocket, and a man beside me bumps my shoulder.

It wouldn't be a big deal normally, but the tread on my shoes is almost completely worn down and I hadn't noticed the little patch of ice under my left heel. The bags of groceries have me slightly unbalanced while the cold is making my muscles stiff.

In other words, it's a perfect storm of winter fuckery.

That's why I lose my balance.

In the age of smartphones, it's a wonder that nobody catches me on video. My legs sweep out from under me in a classic *America's Funniest Home Videos* gag and I land flat on my tailbone, crying out in pain and surprise at the impact. The worst part, though, is the crunch I feel in one of my precious grocery bags, and I know I've lost my carton of eggs.

Tears cloud my eyes as my cheeks burn in embarrassment, my phone still buzzing merrily against my chest. The man who bumped me is long gone, but a kind-looking older woman bends over, her huge purple puffer jacket and matching woolly hat making her look like an elderly Violet Beauregarde.

"Are you okay, dear?" She's even chewing gum. She smacks her lips and nods at my bags. "That was a spectacular fall."

"I'm good," I lie, groaning as I shuffle to a standing position. My eggs are already leaking through my reusable cloth grocery bag, and my tailbone feels like it was hit with a sledgehammer. "I'm fine," I tell Old Ms. Beauregarde, who nods and rushes across the road before the light changes.

I'll wait, I decide, and stretch out my back. Maybe by the time the light changes again, everyone will have walked on and I'll be anonymous again.

"Layla!"

I freeze, halfway bent over my broken eggs and spilled groceries. Tilting my head to peer in the direction of the voice, my heart starts thundering.

No.

I can't—I'm not—I don't...

Oh, no, no, no.

Leif Sorensen jogs toward me, his charcoal-grey peacoat

flapping open to reveal a tailored three-piece suit. With his cashmere scarf sailing in the wind, pedestrians part around him like a school of fish around a very attractive shark. His blond hair is tousled, cheeks ruddy from the cold, long limbs eating up the distance between us as I shove my ruined groceries back in their bags and straighten my creaking, sore body to face him.

The man is hotter than sin.

I officially met Leif Sorensen when I was the temporary nanny for Benny and Jane Eldridge, two precious kids from the Upper East Side. The job only lasted three months while their regular nanny was on maternity leave, but they were the most stable, calm three months of my adult life. I've been begging my boss, Linda, to find me a permanent placement like that for months. If I were a full-time nanny, I could quit my café job *and* my waitressing job, and I might even have enough money for winter boots.

Leif came to the birthday party I threw for the twins. It was the second time we met, but he didn't remember the first—and I wasn't going to remind him.

I learned my lesson six years ago, thank you very much. I know that people like me mean nothing to people like him. I was forgettable then—but apparently this time, when I'm making a fool of myself, I'm memorable.

And now he's jogging up to me looking like he just walked out of a high-end cologne commercial while I just fell on my ass in the middle of the street.

Yeah, he's definitely out of my league. I stand to face him, bracing myself for the assault of his attractiveness on my poor little female soul.

"Layla," he repeats, his breath coming out in a huff. "I saw you fall. Are you okay?"

Before I can stop him, Leif reaches toward me. Broad hands clad in fine-leather gloves grip my shoulders, then one of them moves to my jaw as he inspects my face. I don't know why—shock, maybe—but I let him tilt my head this way and that, his thumb pressing into my chin before sweeping gently across the curve of my lower lip. Heat gushes through my veins, and my jacket doesn't seem so inadequate anymore.

He touched me six years ago, not so differently from how he's touching me now. Like I was precious. Like he *cared*.

Then he forgot me—and why wouldn't he?

I squeeze my eyes shut and remember all the reasons Leif is out of my league.

He's rich. He's successful. He's an *heir*. He went to private school and probably an Ivy League college and he looks like masculine perfection. He started one of the fastest-growing real estate development companies on the Eastern seaboard. He's a shark in the boardroom. He *has* a boardroom, for that matter.

I, on the other hand, am more broke than the eggs at the bottom of my grocery bag. I have no future, no familial connections, and more responsibility on my shoulders than he'll ever know in his life. Between my sister's college tuition and my grandparents' care, I don't have two red cents to rub together. I certainly don't have time to indulge in useless fantasies about a man who will forget about me by the time he crosses the Hudson back into Manhattan.

But he remembered my name this time, and I haven't seen him in months.

I shove the thought aside and mentally smack myself across the face. *Bad Layla!* He's like a white-hot flame. Get too close and I'll burn up into nothing. Girls like me don't belong in his world.

But Leif's hand slides from my chin to my cheek, the leather soft as he lets his fingers drift over my cheekbone. His eyes meet mine, crystalline blue that makes my breath catch. I didn't know eyes could be that piercing. His irises shatter from dark to icy blue at the edges, deep and complicated and beautiful, just like the man they belong to.

Still lost in the quagmire of my attraction to him, I let Leif slide his other hand down to take my bag of groceries from me. His brows tug together, eyes roaming over me as if to make sure I'm still in one piece.

I am, indeed, in one piece. One piece that's about to be consumed by the fiery-hot flame of bone-deep embarrassment.

"Leif," I croak. "What are you doing in Newark?"

"I had a meeting," he answers, gripping my old green grocery bag in his hand. Egg guts drip down from the bottom of it onto the pavement beside him. "Where are you going? I'll get my driver to bring you."

He has a *driver*. I don't even have a car, never mind a whole other person whose sole job it is to drive me places.

"That's okay," I say, reaching for the bag to take it from his hand.

He angles his body so the bag is out of reach, and my hand touches the edge of his coat and my face almost comes into contact with the soft wool of his jacket. He smells delicious, and he clearly doesn't want to give me my groceries back. "Then I'll walk you."

"That's really okay," I repeat, gritting my teeth. "I'm sure you're busy."

"Layla," he growls softly, the sound sending heat shivering through my veins. For a brief moment, I wonder how it would feel to have him say my name like that with his lips next to my ear, his body on top of mine, my legs wrapped around his waist—

"I'm either driving you to a doctor, driving you home, or walking you to where you need to go," he finishes, his voice still holding that growly edge that makes my lady-parts quiver in a way I haven't felt before. His blue, blue eyes meet mine, brow arching. "So which is it going to be?"

My eyes dart to the eggs still dripping through the bag. I'd make a mess of his doubtless expensive car interior. Eggs dry like glue, and I'd probably cause permanent damage to his vehicle. "Let's walk."

He grunts in what I guess is approval or agreement, and another shiver tumbles through my body. Something about his voice—even his growls—reaches deep in the pit of my belly and makes heat flame to life. My body clearly hasn't gotten the memo that I'm not supposed to be attracted to him.

We stand in silence until the lights change, then start walking. We're at the next set of lights when he speaks again. "Did Linda call you?"

I frown. "Linda?"

"Linda Delmar. She said she'd call you this afternoon."

"Oh!" I reach into my jacket and pull out my phone to see a

missed call on the screen. "Yeah. I was trying to get to my phone when I fell. I'll call her back when I get home."

But wait. Why would Leif know that my boss called me?

As if he could read my thoughts, Leif explains, "My daughter's nanny has a family emergency." The light changes and we both start walking. "You'll be working for me."

The pavement rears up beneath my feet, tangling with my sodden shoes. Stumbling, I throw my hands out in front of me, but not before a strong, male arm darts out to wrap around my waist. In a moment, I'm crushed against the hard, warm surface of Leif Sorensen's chest as my legs remember the job they're supposed to be doing keeping me upright.

His closeness jolts something from my memory. Another time when his arm was around me like this. When he saved me from another danger... When my unfortunate infatuation with Leif Sorensen started.

THREE
LAYLA

THE FIRST TIME I met Leif Sorensen was six years ago. I was twenty-one years old, and perpetually on the brink of disaster. Money was tight, so tight. Bills were in arrears, rent seemed to be always due, and my eleven-year-old little sister looked like she was in desperate need of a good meal.

I have no idea how I looked. Worse than Emma, probably. A stick insect with desperate eyes, scrabbling to make ends meet while pretending that everything was going to be fine.

It'd been five years since Mom left, since my world imploded and I was forced to grow up. Five long, hard years since I kissed my teenage years goodbye and took responsibility for myself and Emma.

All the while, my grandparents were struggling. Grandpa needed a new kind of heart medication while the insurance company gave him the runaround, and their house somehow acquired a carpenter ant infestation.

Then I got The Job. You know the one—the type of job that takes you from relying on loose change from the couch for at least a meal a month to a bank account that isn't overdrawn. The type of job that feels like a gift from God, because it means you'll be able to feed the people that depend on you *and* pay the bills *and* pay rent. The type of job that leaves extra at the end of the month, that would even allow me to pay for my grandfather's medication as well as an exterminator.

All I had to do was wear a bright smile and ferry drinks from the bar to VIP tables in a dark, pulsing nightclub. I bluffed my way to the job, lied about my experience, and wore a teeny tiny skirt to the interview, and I'm not ashamed of any of it. I know I was hired for my looks, because VIP waitresses in dark nightclubs are supposed to look pretty and available and expensive.

Fine by me. My grandparents, Emma, and I needed the money and I was ready to do almost anything to get it.

The lucky thing about my face, I think, is that it's generically pretty enough to be able to transform into something more. With some clever contouring, eyeliner, and false lashes, I was able to become a different person. I wasn't Layla Reynolds, desperate big sister pretending to know what she was doing. I was a flaxen-haired babe who batted her lashes and flirted, then relieved drunk, horny men from the weight of all that cash in their pockets.

Glamorous? Of course not. But I didn't care. I had a hard-earned high school diploma and no additional training to speak of, with my best asset being my looks. I would've been a fool not to use them.

The makeup and hair were my armor—along with the push-up bras. My modest cleavage looked fantastic with the help of not one, not two, but *three* double-padded bras. I hid behind my Hot Waitress persona, then I'd go home, strip off the layers of padding, scrub my face, and be the big sister Emma needed to get her to school on time.

For three whole weeks, Emma and I had more stability than we'd had in all the years since my mother walked out on us. I had *money*. Wads of it, rolled up in neat cylinders, stuffed in my underwear drawer. A couple hundred bucks doesn't seem like a lot to some people, but to Emma and me, it was everything. It was stability.

Stupidly, I allowed myself a thin, golden thread of hope. I nurtured it in the depth of my heart, hid it from view, but secretly let it grow into something shining and strong and real. With The Job, I could save some money. I'd be able to get my sister and me an apartment so we wouldn't have to crash in our grandparents' cramped spare room. I might even be able to afford some of those summer camps she was so desperate to go to—and maybe, one day, put aside some money for her college education. Even at eleven years old, Emma was a brainiac. She wouldn't be held back in life the way I was; she was going to get every opportunity I could scrape together for her—and The Job was going to make it happen.

Hope made everything taste sweeter. It made me enjoy putting on pounds of makeup every night. It made me not care that I had to wear three bras to work. Hope, ultimately, is what broke me.

Because at the height of my hopefulness, Leif happened.

That night is written in my mind with crystal clarity, as if it happened yesterday instead of over six years ago. I remember getting ready for work and having a Good Eyeliner Day. Both eyes were perfectly outlined in sultry black, a little flick at the outer corner angled perfectly to suit my face. Red lips, shimmery and enticingly wet-looking. Hair in big, loose curls, pinned back from my face to show off the too-sharp cheekbones that betrayed the fact that I was in need of a good meal.

I looked good. I felt good. I was ready to paint that bubbly, brainless smile on my face that was so useful in making me seem friendly and unthreatening and worthy of all the tips in the world.

And, of course, the bras. Three double-padded bras that took my modest bust to something Hooterific. The moneymakers, I called them.

I blame the bras for everything that happened. If I hadn't been wearing them, things wouldn't have gone so horribly wrong. I would have reacted quicker. Or at all.

The club was set up in two sections. The bottom level was mostly a big, sticky dance floor with two bars on opposite ends of the room. There were high-top tables and a few chairs along the edges, but mostly the area was reserved for drunken, debauched dancing. I worked in the mezzanine level, with the VIPs.

The VIP section was set up in multiple nooks of low couches, arranged to afford as much privacy as possible in a nightclub. Seeing it at the end of the shift—when the lights came on and the place was a mess—was enough to strip any illusions of glamour, but wealthy young people with egos and money loved to come sip a drink and regard the dancing masses like they were royals overseeing their subjects.

One set of couches in particular was on its own on one side of the mezzanine and gave a perfect view of the floor below. That night, halfway through my shift, I was tasked with removing a group from that section to make way for people higher up in the hierarchy of VIPs.

Easy, right?

Not so much.

The thing about people who go to fancy nightclubs and pay stupid amounts of money to be waited on in an exclusive VIP section is they don't like being told what to do. So when I asked the group to move, telling them the couch had been reserved by other, more important Very Important People, I could tell there would be trouble.

The big man nearest me had hands like ham hocks which clenched into tight, white-knuckled fists when I asked him to vacate the space. His hair was dark and cut short, revealing a few white scars on the side of his head. A crooked nose sat above thin, angry lips.

A brawler. And by my count, he'd had five or six drinks in the time he'd occupied that particular sofa.

"Fuck off," he said to my breasts.

"Sir, this table is reserved," I answered, leaning over to be heard above the pulsing music. This put my breasts even more directly in his eyesight, with the added benefit of having the neckline of my shirt dip down to reveal a bit more skin.

I didn't do it on purpose. Typically, my breasts didn't bulge out so much, and sometimes I forgot what the three bras did for me. But when his eyes dipped down and his tongue darted out to lick his lips, I immediately straightened.

Brawler lifted his dark, dark eyes to meet mine, a dangerous expression in his eyes. "I said, *fuck off*. And get us another bottle."

My fingers curled around the edge of the tray I held under one arm as I straightened, resisting the urge to pinch my nose. Brawler was clearly the leader, with his cronies cackling along with him. For once, my bubbly Hot Waitress persona was a disadvantage. It didn't exactly engender respect.

The woman next to him flicked her hair over her shoulder and arched her brows. "You heard him, girlie. Run along and get us a round."

"This table is reserved," I said, a bit louder. "I'm happy to show you to your new table, but you have to leave this one."

"I don't *want* to leave this one," Brawler said as petulantly as a child. Then, inexplicably, he took a bucket of ice I'd brought over for their drinks and upended it all over the table, to the delight of his friends. They cawed and cackled like a pack of hyenas, kicking ice cubes toward me.

Unbothered, I stood waiting. This was the thing about drunk people: they were like children. They just needed a firm hand.

Face blank, I lifted my arm and gestured to the open table a few paces away and waited for the group to get up. Brawler rolled his eyes, muttered something that made his girlfriend sneer at me, then heaved himself off the couch.

I took a step back to let them pass—and banged right into a wall.

Except this wall was warm, hard, and it smelled like heaven. Two hands slid over my hips as a deep, deep voice said next to my ear, "Well done, gorgeous."

Warmth flooded my belly and for a single, shimmering moment, I felt the urge to melt into those strong arms and let that deep, sinful voice carry me somewhere new. I forgot I was at work. I forgot I was supposed to be helping the customers to their new table and making sure everyone was supplied with enough alcohol to make them overlook the fact that they were upset.

All that existed was the strong, broad chest behind me, the big hands wrapped around my hips, and the soft, minty breath tickling the edge of my cheek. For that moment, I wasn't worried about money, about my sister, about carpenter ants, and certainly not about angry customers. The man's touch did something to my body—electrified it, turned my knees to jelly. My brain started dissolving the moment he touched me, and it took all my strength to take a single step forward, away from the warmth and safety of his body.

Then I turned.

Leif Sorensen stood before me, tousled blond hair and strong, warrior-like features. Ocean-deep eyes danced with barely concealed amusement as his gaze landed on mine, then moved lower. He stared at my lips for a long, torturous moment, then flicked his eyes down my body and back up again.

I'd been working in this club for weeks, and I was used to men checking me out. It was part of the job. It was the reason I wore three double-push-up bras.

But Leif was *different*.

His gaze set my body alight. It felt like a physical touch and it made my skin tingle from my scalp down to my toes. I wasn't just an automaton with big boobs and a bright smile carrying drinks to various tables. I was a woman, and all I wanted to do was close the distance between us, wrap my arms around his neck, and let him do whatever he wanted to me.

Of course, that's not what I did. I mumbled something unintelligible and got a mop to clean up the mess from the upended ice bucket. Then I got them all a round of complimentary drinks for their trouble and went to the brawler's table to soothe his precious ego.

All the while, I felt his gaze. The hairs on the back of my neck prickled and an awareness settled over me like a blanket. Even though I only looked over once to see him watching me, I could *feel* his gaze pressing up against me, his presence filling the room like a storm cloud. My hips burned from his touch, and the space between my legs felt painfully empty. My cheeks flushed and my heart pounded for long minutes afterward, until I darted into a back room to gulp down shaking breaths.

Of course, at the time, I didn't know he was Leif Sorensen. I didn't know he was the heir to a fortune, or that he was a genius businessman, or that he had a two-year-old daughter. I'd learn his name later, when my manager's face turned reddish-purple as he yelled at me for my supposed unprofessional behavior.

All I knew was the danger in his gaze, those sapphire-bright eyes piercing through every shield I'd ever erected.

With a deep breath, I stepped back onto the floor and ran more drinks to their table. I thought I'd recovered, but he sat in the sofa like a Viking king reclining on a throne of furs, his arm draped casually over the back of the seat as his eyes scanned the room, missing nothing.

A woman sitting to his right leaned into him as I deposited drinks on their table, feeling Leif's gaze on me like a heavy weight. Furtively, I threw him a glance and met his gaze in time to see the woman run her hand up his thigh, dangerously close to the bulge at his crotch.

He leaned his head toward her to listen while his eyes followed me, and I knew he was trouble. Big, blond trouble. A berserker dressed in an expensive suit. A dangerous, blood-thirsty Viking masquerading as a civilized businessman.

Then his eyes slid away from me toward the woman at his side, and my chest gave a sharp twist.

I was jealous of her, which was stupid. I was jealous of the sky-high heels that didn't make her totter. Her expensive, revealing dress. The diamonds shimmering like a collar around her neck. I was jealous of her hand, and the way it slid over Leif Sorensen's leg like it was her right to do so.

Thoughts and feelings built up like a maelstrom inside me, demolishing everything in their way. My hands shook as I gathered empty glasses, my vision became hazy as I straightened and headed for the bar.

I was still in a daze when I went to the brawler's table. That's probably why I didn't notice the hand. Well, that and the push-up bras.

The thing about wearing three double-push-up bras is that there are at least four to six inches between skin and shirt. My breasts were so much bigger than I was used to that I'd bump into things without noticing, brush up against people and objects, even spill drinks if I wasn't careful. A small price to pay for double or triple the tips and enough money to feed, clothe, and house myself and my sister.

But on that particular night, I didn't notice the brawler's hand reach out toward me as I leaned over to pick up an empty glass. I didn't even feel him touching my breast until he squeezed.

Then all hell broke loose.

An arm banded around my waist and yanked me back into that same warm, hard wall. I had another minor brain-melt moment as the length of my body pressed up against the length of Leif's. Then he was depositing me to the side and pulling the brawler up by his shirt collar.

I have no idea how Leif moved that quickly. I still don't know how long the brawler was fondling me before I noticed. All I know is within moments, Leif had the other man on his feet and was pummeling his fist into the bigger man's face.

Someone screamed. Security rushed the two men. I just stood there and stared.

If I'd noticed the fact that I was being groped, maybe I could have shied away. I could have batted his hand away before things turned ugly. I could have even dodged his touch. But those stupid three push-up bras were a shield that did their job a little too well, and Leif Freaking Sorensen rushed to my rescue.

No one—and I mean *no one*—had ever defended me like that. No one had ever fought for me, or even cared. I'd been on my own for so long, with my life and my sister's life resting on my narrow shoulders, and in that moment, I felt seen. I wasn't just an invisible waitress who used her padded bras to draw more tips out of Neanderthalic men. I was a *person*. I was worthy of being defended, of being protected.

I think, for those few, brief moments, I was in love. It was a bright, hot feeling that pierced the middle of my chest. My feet no longer ached and my heart didn't know if it wanted to stop dead or pound harder.

Leif Sorensen, the Viking king who was equal parts terrifying and thrilling, fought for *me*.

But then security was dragging them apart, the brawler and his crew were being ejected, and the moment was over. Leif shook off the security guard and in three strides, he was in front of me. His big, broad hands cupped my cheeks so gently it was like I was made of glass. His unforgettable eyes stared into mine for a moment, an eternity.

"Are you okay?" His voice was a low growl that reverberated in all the places I wasn't supposed to be thinking about right then.

I nodded, my voice deciding to take that moment to malfunction.

"Leif," a female voice shrieked. "Let's go!"

He held me for another long second, then glanced over his shoulder. The beauty who'd been stroking his leg stood with her arms crossed, her foot tapping on the dirty floor.

I felt the tension in the air between us. It was like breathing in soup. His energy crackled, anger and rage and adrenaline and pure, male virility. For a moment, I thought he'd stay here—with me. I thought he felt what I did, that he knew what he did to me and he wanted more of it, like I did.

How utterly, desperately stupid.

Leif Sorensen, heir, billionaire, businessman, dropped his hands from my face. "Take care," he said.

Then he turned around...and left.

I stood there like a lump: crushed, confused, horny, and alone.

Later that night, my boss fired me. I still had two more months in my probationary period, and he said I was more trouble than I was worth. I lost The Job. That thin, brilliant thread of hope snapped, and I knew that stability was an illusion. Safety was out of reach. Men would never rush to my rescue and fight for my honor. If I was to care for my grandparents and help my sister achieve all she could, the only person I could rely on was myself.

Leif Sorensen didn't see *me*. He probably had a temper, was spoiling for a fight, and the man fondling my bras gave him a convenient excuse. It was never about me, and I was a fool to think it was.

A painful lesson, but a necessary one.

I scraped together enough money to cover my grandfather's medication until the insurance got sorted and worked at a call center to pay the rest of the never-ending bills. The Job slipped from my fingers.

As much as I told myself I'd learned my lesson, I still kept a tiny, flickering flame of desire alive. I fantasized about Leif Sorensen riding to my rescue and lifting me out of the grips of despair. I gobbled up any news or gossip about him and his family, trawled every inch of his social media accounts late at night, and imagined what it would feel like to have those strong arms wrapped around me again.

In short, I was an idiot. I clung to the one bright moment from my life in those years, and I made it into something it wasn't.

Six years later, the fact that that fateful night meant nothing to Leif was confirmed when I saw him at Benny and Jane Eldridge's birthday party and knew from the blank look on his face that he didn't remember me at all. And why would he?

Today, all those memories rush through my mind as Leif's arm clamps around my waist. His cheek brushes mine as he pulls my back to his front, his other arm reaching to catch the grocery bag trying to tumble once again off my shoulder.

Just like that, Leif transports me to that one, single night when I felt safe, protected—and the horrible moment when I realized it was all an illusion.

Working for him will be a disaster. No matter how much I'll try to keep my distance, Leif will sweep through my defenses like they're nothing more than cobwebs. All it will take for me to crumble will be his confident stride and his deep, deep voice. I'll feel things I have no business feeling, and then he'll leave and forget all about me.

It'll break me.

To me, he's the most attractive man in the world. To him, I'm nothing more than another replaceable woman.

As his hand eases from around me and he sets me on my feet again, time freezes. Things haven't changed so much since that day at the nightclub. I'm still broke, still desperate for money, still shouldering too many responsibilities. But what choice do I have?

If Leif is offering me a job, I'm not in any position to say no.

FOUR

LEIF

IF I HADN'T BEEN WATCHING Layla, I would've missed the stiffness stealing over her shoulders. Would it really be so bad to work for me?

She brushed me off when I met her at that children's birthday party, too. I saw her as soon as I walked into the room. I remember exactly what she was wearing: a pretty yellow sundress that nipped in at her waist and set off the warmth in her skin. She looked like bottled sunlight, from the spun gold of her hair to her skin to the bright, happy smile on her face.

She looked familiar.

I stumbled on the threshold at the sight of her, and I wanted to grab her by the waist and drag her to whatever dark corner would allow us a modicum of privacy. I wanted to slip that dress off her slim body and see what delights were hidden underneath.

In the fragmented, compartmentalized existence I called my

life, I wanted to drink up her sunshine and see if it would make everything better.

But when I tried to approach her, I couldn't get more than a few words out of her, and she ran away at the first opportunity. I had to deal with my friend Emil's ribbing comments for my strikeout.

I watched her get into the car and drive away from me, and just like that, she was a splinter lodged under my skin. The second of such splinters—the first of which happened six years ago on a night that was supposed to be like any other. A night that ended with a sprained wrist and the feeling that I'd lost my chance with the first woman who made me look at her twice.

I've managed to ignore those splinters, of course. I've gone on dates as I always do, flirted, teased, fucked. I've acted like myself, but she's been there at the back of my mind. The woman made of golden sunlight that wouldn't give me a minute of her time.

And now, even when I'm going to pay her for that time, she won't even give me a second. Am I really that repulsive? Is it because her friend Dani is dating my friend Emil? Is it because my last name is Sorensen? What the *hell* is so terrible about me?

It's...unusual.

Conquests have always been easy for me. I see a woman I like, and I go after her. They melt, they wilt, they bend to my will, and then they leave.

It works for me. I like to keep women in a special, insulated corner of my life, separate from my business, separate from my daughter and the rest of my family. Everything in my life has its place, and nothing ever crosses from one box to the other.

Except Layla.

Layla knows my daughter, and if she works for me, it will make her utterly off-limits to anything relating to sex and romance.

It should be a good thing. I can keep work and family and sex separate, as they should be.

But I want her. The problem is, she doesn't seem to want me.

So, if she's going to refuse the offer of a temporary, one-week position in my household that pays way more than the market rate, I need to know *why*. I need to know what it is about me that makes her want to run away, and I want to drag her back to my bed and show her all the reasons she's wrong.

But before I can open my mouth to ask Layla why she's so intent on avoiding me, the tension leaves her body and she lets out a shallow breath. "Oh," she says. "When do I start?"

Pleased, I stand up a little straighter. Then I realize my arm is still banded around her front. I take one long moment to enjoy the touch, then drop my arm and step away. She turns to meet my eyes when I answer, "Tomorrow—Saturday—if you can. We'll do your orientation and get you prepared for Monday. You can have Sunday off in the meantime." We reach another street corner and Layla turns left to follow the sidewalk. "I need you for a week. My regular nanny had a family emergency."

"Oh! Is Harriet okay?"

I nod. "Yes, but her husband is sick." We dodge around a few pedestrians as I glance at the surrounding buildings. Peeling paint and a few overgrown patches of grass, but otherwise tidy. A working-class neighborhood. Lining the street are a few townhouses leaning up against a tall apartment building, with cars parked on either side.

This is exactly why I've been interested in Newark. The block I'm trying to develop is a few streets away, closer to the local elementary school and steps away from a small enclave of cafés and shops. Currently, there are a few single-family dwellings taking up the space, but with a new subway station planned nearby, the potential profits for a development project are huge.

The city was enthusiastic about my company's proposal to develop the block into a tower of luxury condominiums. We'd replace six family homes with over sixty dwellings, skyrocketing the surrounding property values. It's a win-win for everyone.

Well, everyone except the residents of the six homes I'm trying to buy. Three owners accepted our initial buyout offer, while two held out with hard negotiations. A family of four—a lawyer couple with two young kids—negotiated double our initial offer. The other house was owned by a middle-aged couple who wanted to downsize anyway, but who knew the value of their land. They also negotiated hard but ultimately accepted.

Only one couple has held out against all our buyout offers. My lawyers tell me they're in their seventies, an old husband and wife who built the house and have raised all their family in it. The man still mows the lawn every Saturday if the weather permits, and the woman is an active church member.

They don't want to move.

No matter—if they don't accept our generous offer, we'll use the long arm of the law and force them to sell. The city will put pressure on them. This development opportunity is too lucrative to give up. Real estate is in my blood; I know when to be aggressive. I'm doing these people a favor, offering more than a fair price and willing to go even higher.

They'll cave. They always do.

"This is me," Layla says, stopping in front of a decrepit apartment building. It lists slightly to the side, with balconies studded at regular windows on the way up revealing snow-covered planters and barbecues, and dirty curtains behind streaked windows.

This is exactly the type of building I'd buy—along with the surrounding townhouses—tear down, and rebuild into luxury condominiums. There's money to be made here. I can almost smell it in the air.

"Looks nice," I hear myself saying, all the while calculating the cost of the tear-down and development I'm imagining.

Layla snorts, her eyes glimmering. A strand of golden hair has escaped her hat, and everything inside me wants to twist it around my finger and watch it fall away. "Don't lie to me, Mr. Sorensen."

"Leif," I correct.

"If you're going to be my boss, shouldn't we keep things professional?" There's a flash in her eyes that makes my gut clench. Just like that kids' birthday party, I feel some thread of familiarity. I've met her before—but where?

"Fine," I concede, lips twitching. "I look forward to working with you, Miss Reynolds." Extending my arm, I pass the green grocery bag over to Layla, who slips it onto her shoulder. Her jacket crinkles under the weight of it, and I frown. It's too thin for the winters here. She'll freeze.

Layla's eyes climb up to mine, throat working as she swallows thickly. Full lashes fan over her cheeks as she blinks a few times in quick succession, then she shakes her head as if to clear her thoughts. "Right. I'll call Linda and get the details. Thanks for walking me home."

"Anytime," I answer, surprised to realize I mean it. I'd walk her home—but I'd prefer to pack her into my car and take her somewhere nicer, which makes no sense. Sure, she's beautiful—so what? I date beautiful women all the time.

One thing I do not do is date employees, and I certainly don't bring any women around my daughter. Those two compartments of my life are far, far apart, with an impenetrable steel barricade between them.

Layla's eyes dart up to mine, then she's shuffling in the door. She only makes it up two steps when her shoes slip out from under her.

I'm there in a flash, arm around her back, catching her before she cracks her skull on the icy steps. Scowling, I look down at our feet. "Your shoes aren't winter appropriate," I growl. "And your super should be clearing these steps and putting salt or gravel down. It's dangerous." I only realize I'm still holding onto her when she pulls away, face flushed.

Three times she's stumbled today. Twice I've been there to catch her, but what will happen to her when I leave? I glance down at her feet and frown again. She's wearing old sneakers with holes near both big toes. Hardly appropriate winter footwear. Between her jacket and her shoes, she's asking for a serious injury.

Discomfort races up my spine. I have to clench my hands into fists to stop myself from dragging her back down the street to my car, taking her home, and making sure she's safe and warm and fed.

"I know," she says, her voice husky. "Thanks for the rescue."

I wait until she disappears up the narrow staircase before turning around. My driver, Elton, has parked his car right behind me. He gets out and opens the back door for me with a nod. As soon as I'm ensconced in the warmth and comfort of the clean leather interior, I let out a breath, my eyes still on the decrepit building Layla calls home.

It's not nice enough for her. Not even a little bit.

FIVE

LAYLA

BREATHING a sigh of relief when I duck out of Leif's view, I lean against the cigarette-smoke-stained hallway wall and close my eyes. My heart beats a rapid tattoo against my ribs as I try to regain control over my rioting body.

And I'm going to be *working* for him?

Disaster.

Godsend.

Trouble.

He's had the same effect on me every time I've been near him. First, at the nightclub when I thought he was some sort of savior, then quickly realized I was pathetically stupid. Again, I had the feeling at Benny and Jane's birthday party when he unleashed that charming, arrogant smile and dissolved my knees —then I realized he didn't remember me at all.

Both times, my body has reacted violently. A pulsing in my

gut, reminding me that I'm not a nun, a stuttering of my heart, and a heaviness in my tongue that makes it hard to make sentences—and makes me trip over my own feet, apparently.

And along with the physical feelings, the aching embarrassment of being *forgettable.*

Leif is the kind of man you see from a distance and think, *I'd do him.* But then you get closer and you can't hold his gaze because of the sheer magnetism of him. His presence presses against my skin and makes me simultaneously want to be near him while also feeling the urge to run and hide.

Hence my running up the stairs and hiding around the corner.

He's the type of man that is photographed with supermodels and socialites, who can pluck any woman from a crowd and make her feel like a queen—if only for a night. And from what I know, it would only be for a night. Not only because of the gossip magazines, but my own experience with him. He was all too eager to play the savior and walk away, proving that I was beneath him. I wasn't a stiletto-and-diamond-wearing model who had the right to touch his thigh. I was just the poor, pathetic waitress who got fondled and then forgotten.

Even Dani says he's a player. She met him the same night she met Emil, and she said he looked at her like she was fresh meat, like he'd love to eat her up.

"Don't get me wrong, Leif's hot as hell," she told me last week when she got back to town after staying in Vermont for a few months. There was a photo of him in the tabloid on the coffee shop table where we sat. A suit-clad Leif had his arm around a besotted pop singer, a jagged line in the middle of the photo proclaiming the couple had officially broken up after only two heavily publicized dates. Dani sipped her herbal tea and rubbed a hand over her pregnant stomach while pushing the newspaper away. "But I wouldn't trust him as far as I can throw him."

"Mm-hmm," I'd replied knowingly, pretending I wasn't hanging on every word. My eyes darted to the photo again, a stupid, foolish kind of satisfaction coursing through me at the sight of that jagged line.

Yes, it caused me deep satisfaction that a billionaire whom I'd met exactly *two times*—months and years ago—was now single.

I never claimed to be smart. That's my sister's domain.

"He came over for dinner last night with a new date, and I caught him texting another woman at the same time." Dani clicked her tongue and gave me a loaded look. "No man is hot enough to justify that."

True enough, but no other man has ever had that kind of effect on me. I didn't tell Dani, though.

Today, while my heart settles to a more manageable pace, I creep to the window at the end of the hall. I glance outside in time to see him getting into a sleek silver car that doesn't belong on this street—or this neighborhood. Leif Sorensen's driver is dressed in a crisp black uniform. He jogs around the front of the vehicle after making sure his master is safe inside. I lean a shoulder against the window frame and feel the vibrations of the car purring to life below, then watch them drive away.

Dani is right. No man is worth the kind of heartache Leif would deliver. If I were the type of woman who could separate sex from emotion, I'd go for it—but I'm not. The safest thing for me to do is stay away from Leif.

I snort. Fat chance of that happening when I work for him. Since I'm desperate for money and can't afford to turn down a week of steady work, the only other thing I can do is erect a wall between the two of us and do my best to ignore my body's reaction to him.

Easy peasy.

Straightening my spine, I head back toward the staircase. Maybe this job is a good thing—and not just because I'm broke. It'll give me a shield of professionalism to ignore my body's needs. I can hide behind the paycheck and treat him as a boss should be treated.

Plus, I'll probably get to know him and see all the warts he's hiding under his billionaire veneer. This stupid crush will fade once I get to know the real him.

Yes, this is a fantastic idea, I decide. Working for Leif will cure me of this attraction, and I'll be able to move on.

Because no one is that sexy in real life.

When I make it to the apartment I call home on the third floor of this derelict four-story building, I find my younger sister lying on her stomach in the middle of the living room, books and papers fanned out in front of her. A scowl carves deep grooves between her brows as she chews the end of a pen like her life depends on it.

"You'll get ink all over your lips again, Em." I walk across the small space and drop my slightly-worse-for-wear grocery bags on the end of our galley kitchen counter.

"Blame it on organic chemistry," she says, tossing the pen aside and flopping onto her back. She throws her arm across her face and groans like the dramatic seventeen-year-old she is. "It makes no *sense*."

Sometimes I forget how young she is. Even when she was a kid, my sister had this *age* about her. An old soul. Not to mention her brain. There's a reason Emma graduated high school a year early and was accepted into NYU's Prehealth program at the tender age of sixteen.

Her hair is blond, like mine, but hers is a darker strawberry-blond to my pure gold. I'm the taller of the two of us, but I wouldn't put it past Emma to have another growth spurt in the next year or two. She has long, long legs and is the type of person who forgets to eat, so she's skinny as hell.

I'm glad she's so focused on school, because whenever she discovers that she's gorgeous and she notices that men are already prowling, I'll have to invest in a machete. Or a gun. Or a flamethrower. Or all three.

While I strip off my jacket, Emma jumps up off the floor in a display of teenage agility and starts unpacking the groceries. When she gets to the eggs, she frowns. "Um, Layla..." The crushed box looks pitiful as she holds it up, brows arched high.

"Did any of them survive?" I ask, starting to unpack the second bag.

My sister carefully opens the box and bunches her lips to the side. "We've got three. I can probably save two more of them if you give me a bowl to dump them in."

I sigh. Five eggs out of twelve, all because of a patch of

stupid black ice and the smooth bottoms of my shoes. I hate winter. And I hate being broke.

But on the bright side, Leif caught me the second (and third) time, and I definitely would have crushed the remaining unbroken eggs if I fell on them again.

"Grandma just called. She's making roast beef and she said we could bring dessert. Can I make brownies?"

"Sure, Em," I say, nudging her shoulder with mine as I pull my phone out of my purse. "You know they'll love that." Dinner with Grandma and Grandpa might not be everyone's ideal Friday night, but it sounds like heaven to me. "I have to call Linda. You mind unpacking the rest of the groceries?"

My sister's eyes brighten. "She has a placement for you?"

"I think so."

"For how long?"

"A week, I think."

Emma's shoulders drop. "So not a permanent one."

I ruffle her hair until she squeals and ducks out of reach. "Don't worry. I'll get a permanent position soon."

"You work too hard, Layla. You have three jobs and you don't get enough sleep. Don't think I don't notice."

"The only thing you need to worry about is passing organic chemistry, okay?" I wave my phone. "I need to make this call." I dial Linda Delmar's number and wait for her cool, sophisticated voice to answer.

She confirms what Leif said—one week of work. It's better than nothing, I suppose.

"Harriet's husband is in the hospital," Linda tells me. "He had a minor heart attack and Harriet needs to care for him, and she called me directly to recommend you after seeing how you handled the Eldridge twins. You should thank her, Layla, because you jumped ahead of some more senior girls with that recommendation."

Throat thick, I nod. "I will. What hospital is her husband in? I'll send flowers." *Once I scrounge up enough money to buy them.*

Harriet doesn't work for Linda, but the two of them know each other from way back. When I first met Harriet, I was in awe of her skill with kids. Little Isla Sorensen was the most well-behaved seven-year-old I'd ever met, and that was all down to Harriet's loving iron fist.

"Already done, darling," Linda says. "I sent a care package from all of us at the Delmar Childcare Agency."

When I hang up the phone, my sister is leaning against the end of the kitchen counter, brows arching high.

"A week," I say in answer to her unvoiced question. "Half-day tomorrow to meet Isla and get acquainted with her schedule, then I officially start Monday."

Her shoulders drop and she voices what I'd been thinking: "It's better than nothing, I guess."

I smile and wrap my arms around her, squeezing tight. "Make some brownies, Em. I'm taking a shower, then we'll head to Grandma's."

OUR GRANDPARENTS' house is a handful of blocks away from our apartment. Fifteen minutes' walk, and we're heading up the pavers leading to the front door. It's a small, two-story house with three dormers overlooking the street, complete with white siding and black shutters.

My grandmother is extremely house-proud. Even in winter, the walkway is cleared of snow and the entrance is kept tidy. She and Grandpa put Christmas lights up every year, but this year, I notice they haven't yet taken them down even though we're nearing the end of January. Putting the lights up was a big job that required help from one of the neighbor's sons. Taking them down will be the same. Grandma and Grandpa are getting older.

Emma pushes the door open without knocking, warm brownies held in her other hand, and calls out into the house. I inhale familiar scents as we walk in, and I know I'm home.

"I'm in the kitchen!" Grandma calls out. "Dinner is almost ready."

Emma drops the brownies on the counter and a kiss on Grandma's cheek, then she's heading off to find Grandpa—probably in his favorite La-Z-Boy chair, watching whatever sports happen to be on television. I wrap my arms around my grandmother and inhale deeply, letting the comfort and love of her hug settle into my bones.

"Rough day?" she asks when I pull away.

I snort. "No worse than usual."

Grandma nods, then checks the potatoes boiling on the stove. Her mashed potatoes are the best I've ever tasted. Everything she cooks is divine—I don't know what I'd do if she didn't live nearby. Any time I need an injection of family, love, and laughter, all I have to do is come here.

Emma and I lived here for a few years after Mom left, but

the house is small, cramped, and I knew we were putting a strain on Grandma and Grandpa. The spare room has only a narrow single bed—which I insisted Emma use—so I alternated sleeping on the floor and the living room sofa for years. I moved out as soon as I could afford it but made sure to stay close.

"I'll set the table," I tell my grandmother, and she chucks my cheek before turning back to her pots and pans. The dining room is just behind a shared wall with the kitchen, and I find a neat stack of paperwork on one end of it that needs to be cleared before I can put out the plates and utensils.

Intending to stack the papers and set them on the sideboard, I pause when my eyes snag on the top sheet of paper. It's from a lawyer's office, and when I read further, a cold fist tightens around my stomach.

My grandfather clears his throat, his knobby fingers wrapped around the back of a chair. His eyes are clear, but the lines around his mouth are deeper. Sadder.

"What's this, Grandpa?" I lift the paper. "Some developer is trying to force you out of the house?"

"Trying, but they won't succeed," Grandma says from the other room. "They've been harassing us for months."

"What?" I glance toward the kitchen, then back to my grandfather. "Why didn't you tell me?"

"Nothing for you to worry about, Layla-darling." He hobbles closer, and my heart squeezes as I watch him. He looks *old*. "Some developer wants to build fancy condos here, but they can damn well wait until Grandma and I are in the ground. No one is pushing me out of my house. I built this place with my own hands, and the only way I'm leaving is when I'm in a box."

"Have you spoken to a lawyer?" I scan the letter, not liking the implied threats written in convoluted legalese. "This says they can compel you to take a deal that's much lower than what you've been offered. The project has been approved by the city, they say."

"Crooks, every one of them," Grandpa huffs. "Lawyers and politicians. All the same."

"While I agree with the principle," I start slowly, scanning the letter for the third time, "I think it might be a good idea to get a professional opinion. What if you lost the house?"

"That's not going to happen." He pulls his chair out as Emma comes up behind him to help, meeting my eyes across the table.

She's thinking the same thing I am: this letter from the lawyer could turn into a serious problem. But before I can do anything about it, the two of us clear the table, put out place-mats, plates, utensils, and all the other things we'll need to eat. I make sure Grandpa has a fresh drink, then I help Grandma bring everything to the table.

In our family, food is love, and Grandma feeds us until we're ready to roll home. I mop up the last of the juices on my plate with fresh, warm rolls, a bit of tension eking out of my bones. This place is as much a home to me as it is to my grandparents. They can't lose it. Not for some fancy luxury condos that will probably just make a rich developer richer.

After dinner and brownies, we call my mother, who lives in Colorado with her new husband. She's in good spirits, in love, and as flighty as she's ever been. Sometimes it hurts my heart to know that she dumped us on Grandma's doorstep the minute she met her new man, especially considering I was only sixteen and Emma was six, but she's my mother, and I can't help but love her.

I've learned not to rely on her, though.

Malice wasn't the reason my mother left. She was just...selfish. I still don't think she realized what a burden she placed on my shoulders, and she probably never will. When we hang up the phone, Emma's lips are pinched and I feel completely drained.

We don't talk about the lawyer's letter until I have my jacket wrapped around my torso and my feet stuffed into my old, wet sneakers. "I'm going to find a lawyer, Grandma," I tell her, bracing myself for a fight. "We need to have someone look at that letter and tell us what our options are."

Instead of protesting, my grandmother surprises me by softening her shoulders before glancing back toward the living room, where Grandpa is snoring in his favorite chair. She looks back at me, and her eyes look *tired*. "Thank you, honey." She leans in, voice quiet. "I'm worried." Before I can answer, she paints a smile on her face and thrusts a bag full of leftovers toward me. "Take care of your sister. Night-night! Love you both."

Fat, slow snowflakes drift down from the sky outside. I step onto the sidewalk and glance up at the thick layer of clouds, letting out a puff of white breath as my grandparents' door closes behind me. The air is cold, piercing through my thin jacket, but the world has that hushed, muffled feeling that always comes with fresh snow. I glance over my shoulder to look at the tidy, homey place that has been my sanctuary for most of my life and try to ignore the knot in the pit of my stomach. They can't lose the house. They *can't*. Never mind the emotional attachment; Grandma and Grandpa are too old to move. Losing the house would weaken them, and the expenses of moving and buying a new place would make them as destitute as I am.

Grandpa might be in denial, and he might be right about lawyers and politicians, but that doesn't mean we can't fight back. Giving my sister a nod, we start walking back together.

Emma and I are halfway home before she speaks: "They're in trouble, aren't they?" Her voice is quiet as she extends a mittened hand to catch a particularly large snowflake in her palm before bringing it to her mouth to touch her tongue to it. Sometimes I forget that she's still a teenager and then she does something like that—childlike, innocent. I'm so used to thinking of her as a brainiac that I forget she's still a child in many ways.

And right now, she's speaking with a child's voice. So, being the responsible big sister I've always been, I put an arm around Emma's shoulders and squeeze her close. "I'll figure it out, Em," I tell her with more confidence than I feel. "They won't lose the house just because some rich asshole wants to put up a bunch of fancy condos. Grandpa wants to live out the rest of his life on that old leather La-Z-Boy, and I intend to make that happen."

Snorting, Emma gives me a grin. "Remember when Grandma tried to get him to replace it with a newer one?"

"World War Three," I say, squeezing her close once more before releasing her. My grandfather's face was set in that grim, stubborn way of his when she proposed the idea of replacing his chair. He crossed his arms and set his jaw, and both Em and I had taken cover in the next room before the explosions started between the two of them.

That stubborn, steel-hard spine is something my grandfather passed on to me. He'll fight for his chair, and I'll fight for his home.

Come Monday, I'm finding a lawyer. No matter what it costs me, I'll make sure my grandparents keep their home.

SIX
LAYLA

BEFORE I CAN START the undoubtedly long and expensive process of finding a lawyer for my grandparents, I have a shift at a local coffee shop followed by a half-day with the Sorensens. My shift at the coffee shop is only four hours, from the dark pre-dawn of four-thirty in the morning to a grey eight-thirty. Being Saturday, the rush of early-morning commuters is more of a trickle, but there are enough customers to keep me busy.

Hanging up my apron and washing a few coffee grounds off my fingers at the end of my shift, I nod to the barista taking over my station at the hulking espresso machine.

"Have fun rubbing elbows with billionaires!" Rachael calls out, her nose ring glinting under the bright lights above. She turns the knob for the steam wand and starts frothing milk, all the while wiggling her eyebrows at me.

Rachael is a tall, broad woman with deep dimples in her full cheeks. We clicked from our very first shift together. She showed me how to make latte art and made me laugh endlessly while we endured the drudgery of a minimum-wage job. She's got chin-length brown hair with a silver streak down one side, which she tells me started growing when she was eighteen. She thought it was funky and left it, adding in a few bright strands throughout her hair to set off the silver. With her delicate nose ring and tattoos poking out from under her short sleeves, she is the epitome of cool.

She's also a damn good cook. Almost every day we've worked together, Rachael has brought me samples of her cooking to try—I suspect because she knows I'm struggling for money and she likes to feed people. She and my grandmother would get along.

Rachael has been trying to start her own catering business for three years, and she gets casual jobs here and there, but, like me, supplements her income with the café job.

She's…a friend. I don't have many of those, but Rachael is one of them.

"You all gossip too much for your own good," I grumble, even though my lips twitch.

"You're no better," Rachael answers with a grin. Her dimples make an appearance, and I can't help but smile back. "I expect a full report tomorrow morning. With pictures."

Laughing, I wave at the people behind the register, then grab my bag from the back room and slip into the bathrooms to change into an outfit appropriate for a billionaire's nanny. Sort of.

Black jeans, long-sleeve shirt in a soft cream color, and hair up in a no-nonsense ponytail. For no reason whatsoever, I brush on some mascara and dab a bit of concealer over a stubborn red zit in the middle of my chin. Whoever said acne was only for teenagers going through puberty was a dirty, awful liar. I'll be thirty years old in eighteen months, and I still have to deal with blemishes all the damn time.

Leif's skin was flawless, my brain informs me.

Bet it would taste good to lick, my lady-parts add.

He was clean shaven to show off his strong, square jaw, with the gold undertones in his skin making his blue eyes even more brilliant. There are no angry zits taking up valuable facial real estate when you have a billionaire skincare regimen, apparently.

Tapping out the concealer, I straighten my clothes and throw on my jacket. Emma insisted I wear her new shoes this morning—all-black sneakers that don't have any holes in them and aren't still soaked from my traipsing through the snow last night—so at least I look presentable from head to toe.

Then I head to my second of three jobs for the day, ignoring the tangled nerves in my stomach. I'm not nervous. There's nothing to be nervous about. I know Isla, the precocious seven-year-old who has Leif's eyes and hair. We saw each other nearly every day for months last year when I met Harriet and Dani at the park for our daily coffees and playdates.

As I bury my chin in my jacket and brace myself against the cold wind on my way to the subway, I know I'm lying to myself. It's not Isla that makes me nervous. It's her father.

With minutes to spare for my nine-a.m. start at my new nannying gig, I make it to Leif and Isla Sorensen's home. The townhouse is located in the Upper West Side, a stone's throw away from the David H. Koch Theatre in the Lincoln Center. I bet Isla loves that. When I knew her, she was always twirling like a ballerina in the park, practicing her positions, and dancing her way across the grass.

Standing in front of the townhouse, I bite back my surprise. It looks so...*normal*. I was expecting some gleaming penthouse, a glittering jewel overlooking Central Park. From the outside, this place looks almost...modest.

But then I ring the doorbell.

Expecting a maid or a member of staff, I'm surprised to see Isla herself in the open doorway. She's wearing a frilly peach skirt on top of a leotard with her hair in a sleek ballerina bun on top of her head, and her face splits into a broad smile at the sight of me.

"Layla!" she cries. "Daddy told me it would be you. You're supposed to take me to ballet, but first you have to sign some papers for Daddy. Mrs. Harriet is with her husband. We sent her some flowers at the hospital, and I'm going to go see her and her husband later. Daddy said he'd take me, so I'm making a card when I'm done with ballet."

All this is said while she stands in the doorway. Then she takes a step aside to let me in, and my jaw drops.

I take back what I said about this place being modest. It's like one of those enchanted bags that's larger on the inside than it is on the outside. It looks like Leif actually bought two (maybe three?) townhouses side-by-side and knocked down the wall between them, with the front half of the space completely open-plan. Gleaming hardwood floors are covered in luxurious rugs. To my left, a massive sofa faces a central fireplace that can be seen from either side, with blue, gas-powered flames dancing in the central core. Vibrant artwork is displayed on two walls, with matching armchairs and tasteful, luxurious finishes.

Oh, to have money. What would it be like to live in a place like this every day? What would it be like to have enough room for an actual desk for Emma to study at? Maybe even have two bathrooms? A separate shower and bath? *Space* for the two of us.

A small hand slips into mine, completely oblivious to the heartbreak occurring inside me. Isla drags me inside with exaggerated huffs before closing the door behind me, but I hardly notice her.

Because the truth? The truth is that I live in an apartment a tenth of the size of the ground floor alone, I share it with my sister, and I have to work three jobs just to keep food on the table for the two of us.

Movement makes me turn toward a staircase on the right side of the room. Leif prowls down the steps, his eyes meeting mine in an instant. He's wearing charcoal-grey suit pants and a white shirt that's open at the collar. His sleeves are rolled up to reveal corded forearms, the muscles writhing and bunching as he raises his hand to comb his fingers through his blond hair.

I've never seen such a refined Viking. He looks like a battle-worn warrior dressed up to fool hapless maidens into thinking he's not a dangerous predator.

Feeling very much like a hapless maiden, I gulp.

"Layla," he says, and the sound of my name on his lips does something criminal to my insides.

Clenching my thighs together, I nod. "Mr. Sorensen."

His blue eyes flash, something like amusement glinting in

them. Instead of answering, he shifts his gaze to Isla. "Is your bag packed for ballet?"

Isla rolls her eyes in a display of undiluted sass. "Yes, Daddy. I've been waiting for you *forever*."

"We'll be going soon." He turns. "Layla, follow me."

Clearly, Leif Sorensen is used to being obeyed. He doesn't pause for an answer before striding across the gorgeous living room to a door on the far wall.

Even though I bristle at being told to come like I'm a lapdog trotting after him, I do as he says. Never bite the hand that feeds, and all that. If I'm going to help my grandparents fight to keep their home, I need every penny I can get. Sassing Leif Sorensen into firing me would not be conducive to achieving my goals.

He walks with purposeful, confident strides toward the back of the room, and I can't help but notice the way his white shirt clings to his muscular shoulders and the way his pants outline his very gorgeous, very bitable butt. Mentally slapping myself, I snap my eyes up to stare just over his right shoulder.

I learned this lesson six years ago. Leif doesn't care about me. A nanny would be the same as a waitress—beneath his notice. He can save me from being assaulted or from tripping over my own clumsy feet, but I'm not an actual *person* to him.

Sure, he's attractive, but he might as well be a different species for the good it does me. The two of us are incompatible. It's never going to happen, and the sooner I accept that, the better my life will be.

Employer-employee. That's what we are. That's all we'll ever be.

Still, when Leif opens the door to the office beyond, standing in the doorway as he motions for me to enter ahead of him, I can't help sipping in a little bit of his scent as my shoulder brushes his chest. He smells *divine*. All I want to do is stop where I am, turn into his arms, and bury my face in the crook of his neck. What would it feel like to have those strong arms wrapped around me once more? To feel safe, protected, *supported* for just another short moment?

Shoulders stiff, I force the thought from my mind. What I need to do right now is focus on work. If I can get a good reference from Leif, it might be exactly what I need to get a permanent placement from Linda Delmar. All these rich people know each other, and I just need an in. As a full-time nanny, I can make a decent living and take care of my sister and grandparents. This week is just a stepping-stone to stability.

So all thoughts of how sexy Leif looks with the top button of his shirt undone need to leave my mind. He's my boss, nothing more.

But when the door clicks shut behind me, desire wraps silken, heated fingers around my core—and squeezes.

SEVEN
LEIF

LAYLA STANDS stiff in the center of my home office, her shoulders bunched near her ears. She's still wearing that too-thin jacket, but at least her shoes look newer. My brows tug together. She should be wearing boots. The snow and slush and ice are no match for sneakers at this time of year.

Picking up a bag my assistant set beside my desk, I hand it to Layla.

She frowns. "What's this?"

"You tripped three times yesterday. You need proper winter boots." Not waiting for an answer, I take my seat behind my desk and motion to an armchair. My lips twitch at the vibrating temper I feel pulsing from her.

She doesn't like my gift, apparently.

"Leif," she starts, fists clenched.

I ignore the fact that my name on her tongue sends heat

spearing through my gut. "Mr. Sorensen," I correct. "Or have you changed your mind about our professional relationship?"

"You're an asshole," she spits, then clamps her mouth shut.

This time, my lips visibly twitch. "Although I know that's true, I'm curious what has brought you to that conclusion. Was it the boots?"

"I don't need you to buy me boots."

I arch a brow, which I can tell infuriates her. "I beg to differ. I won't have you tripping and falling all over the place while you care for my daughter."

Layla blinks, and I wonder if she forgot she was here for Isla. I wouldn't blame her. Being near Layla makes me forget everything, too.

She pauses, staring at a spot on the floor, and I wonder if she's counting to ten. When she lifts her gaze, she gives me a curt nod. "Thank you. The boots are very generous of you." She glances inside and frowns. "How did you know my size?"

"My assistant handled it." *Sort of.* I might have also helped by digging through Layla's social media every time I had a free moment last night and stumbled upon a post of hers trying to sell a few pairs of stilettos three years ago. But my assistant *is* the one who bought the boots, so that much is true. I wave a hand at the seat across from mine. "Please."

Without answering, Layla gathers her bag in front of her and sits primly on the edge of the chair, her shoulders back, chin high.

I hide my grin. That fire coursing through her veins gets more attractive with every moment I spend with her. I feel like a little boy holding a stick, looking at a big beehive knowing I shouldn't poke it—but unable to resist. I meet her eyes, then drop my gaze to her lips. A lush, pink bow that looks soft and kissable, her mouth has probably been the inspiration for countless male fantasies. With her hair in a tight ponytail like that, I can just imagine wrapping my hand around it and guiding her toward my—

"Thank you for coming in on such short notice," I say, my voice rougher than I intended. I slide into my chair and roll forward to hide the evidence of her effect on me, my cock a rigid length pushing against my zipper. "When Harriet told me about her husband's heart attack, Isla immediately asked for you."

Layla's brows jump up.

I grin. "I think the Eldridge twins' birthday party was a highlight of her summer, and she knows it was your idea."

"Cupcakes have hidden powers, apparently." Her voice is husky and sensual, and it doesn't help the blood pooling in my groin. She's not affected by me the way I am by her; that's just her voice. Just like her lips, it's a voice crafted for male fantasies. For *my* fantasies.

Clearing my throat, I grab a manila folder and pull it toward me. "Ms. Delmar emailed through the contract you signed last night. Thanks for that. I've just got a few more things to go through. Harriet thinks she'll be back next week, but I wanted to ask if you would be able to stay on, in the event that things work out between you and Isla, and if Harriet needs more time with her husband."

Layla's head bobs up and down, so vigorous a strand of golden hair falls against her temple. "Yes, that would be fine. I have a couple of other jobs, but this one would be the priority, of course. My schedule is fairly flexible, and I won't let anything interfere with my work for you."

I freeze, brows lowering. "A 'couple' of other jobs?"

"Two," Layla clarifies, then shifts in her seat while clearing her throat, clearly uncomfortable. She motions to the folder in front of me. "Is that for me to sign?"

"You've already signed the contract and the NDA," I answer. "This is Isla's schedule and some information from Harriet. Phone numbers, meal preferences, location of all of Isla's things that you might need. She always keeps a handover document up to date." I push the folder toward Layla.

She scans it, brows jumping. "Wow. This is thorough."

"You have large shoes to fill," I say with a grin. "Harriet is part of the family."

"She's a formidable woman," Layla answers, eyes still on the documents in front of her. Her throat works as she swallows, and I find myself tracing the graceful length of her neck down to the edge of that damn jacket.

I can't make sense of this woman. She didn't give me the time of day when I first met her and now she's all professionalism. But yesterday, she was rosy-cheeked and flustered, and I was sure there was a spark between us.

But then there's the fact she lives in that shitty building across the river, she has old, worn clothes that need to be replaced, and she has not one but *three* jobs, counting this one.

What is she hiding? How could a bright, beautiful woman like her end up struggling so much? Surely she could have any career she wants?

"What did you study in college?" I blurt.

A red flush creeps over her cheeks, and Layla closes the manila folder with delicate, precise movements. "Um, I didn't," she says, not meeting my eyes. "I studied event management at a local community college but had to drop out after a year for... personal reasons. I trained with the Delmar Agency and got my childcare certifications, and my first aid is up to date. I can send everything through if you need to see it."

I wave a hand. That's not what I was asking. I know she's trained and qualified; Linda only hires the best. That's why the Delmar Childcare Agency is the premier childcare agency catering to a particular high-net-worth swath of Manhattan's population.

What I want is a hint of who Layla is. How she ended up here. Why she looks like she's clinging onto her dignity and her pride like it's the last thing she has left. There's something about her that rings a bell somewhere in my memory. I know her from somewhere.

A knock on the door makes us both turn, and Isla pokes her head through the door. "We're going to be late, Daddy. You know Miss Oliver doesn't like tardiness."

The strict, silver-haired ballet teacher is scary enough to make me pause, so I push my chair back with a nod. "We'll go now, kiddo."

Isla's lips pinch. "I'm not a kiddo."

"Munchkin," I amend, hiding the twitch in my lips.

Isla pushes the door open wide, plants her feet, and crosses her arms. "I'm not a munchkin either."

"Sugarplum? Sweetheart Treatheart?" I come around my desk, seeing the laughter dancing in my daughter's eyes even as she lets out a little feral growl. I arch my brows. "Pudding-cakes McGee?"

The last one proves to be too much, because Isla drops her arms to her sides and rolls her eyes so hard they make her whole head travel in a circle. "Whatever, Daddy. Come on."

"Okay, Miss McGee." I grab a jacket off a hook by my office door while Isla betrays herself with a giggle. I grin, only to remember Layla is still in my office. She's standing next to the door, a strange, soft expression on her face.

"You're not what I expected," she says quietly.

I arch a brow. "No? What did you expect?"

She shakes her head, shrugging. "The parents I've worked with have all been a bit...cold."

"Let's *go!*" Isla calls out from the front door, and I give Layla an apologetic grin.

"The boss has spoken." I sweep a hand for her to exit the office in front of me, taking a moment to admire the twitching smile on her lips.

Layla's eyes flick to Isla, who is literally tapping her foot as she gives us a meaningful glare. My daughter's temporary nanny glances at me. "I'm in trouble, aren't I?" Her arm brushes mine as we head across the living room. Neither of us move away from the contact.

I nod. "Yep."

A delicate, tinkling laugh, a sound of pure delight. "Good," Layla answers. "I like trouble."

· · ·

ONCE ISLA IS at her ballet class and Layla's been introduced to the teacher, the two of us head back to my townhouse. Layla's quiet in the car, looking out at the rows of townhouses we pass on our way home.

Her presence is a flame at my side. I feel rather than see the way she shifts in her seat, the mere inches of space that separate our thighs and knees. When she turns to look at a particular house or car or person we pass, her knee comes dangerously close to touching mine.

Blinking, I look away.

Why would I care if her knee touches mine? Haven't I done worse—done more—with any woman I chose? Why would Layla Reynolds's presence twist me in knots like this?

It's because she doesn't seem interested in me that way, I decide. She presented me with a challenge that I can't refuse, even if I know it's a bad idea. There's a reason I only pursue unattached women and leave them as soon as I can: simplicity.

I learned my lesson with Isla's mother, and I'm not going to make the same mistakes again.

Personal and professional matters don't mix. Family and love life don't, either.

"How long have you been working at the Delmar Agency?" I ask just to fill the silence.

"A couple of years," she answers, hands curling around the purse on her lap. Her shoulders stiffen at the sound of my voice, which bothers me. Why does that bother me? "Linda is a great boss. Her sister Bonnie is hilarious. I met her at the company Christmas party last month."

"Dani's friend, right? She stayed at Bonnie's place in Vermont when she was running away from Emil."

"She wasn't *running away* from him." Layla's voice is tight, clipped.

I stifle a smile. "Seemed like running away to me. He had to go traipsing around the countryside to drag her back to Manhattan."

Layla lets out an indelicate snort. "Of course you would think that way. Like he's some caveman that threw her over his shoulder and dragged her back to his cave."

"Isn't that what happened?"

"He *won* her," Layla responds with infinite patience. "He *wooed* her."

"Wooed her," I repeat, brow arched. I meet her eyes then, endless blue in her beautiful face. "I don't believe in wooing."

Her full, pink lips purse, and it makes me want to kiss them until they soften again. "Of course you don't. Women fight each other for the privilege of sharing your bed, don't they? Wooing isn't necessary when you're Manhattan's handsomest, most eligible bachelor."

She thinks you're handsome, the preening, male part of my mind says, not at all worried about the scoffing tone Layla used to give me the compliment. I beat that voice down, because why would I care what Layla thinks? Her noticing my looks should make it *easier* to bed her, but instead she makes it sound like my being handsome is a crime.

And why am I thinking about sleeping with her at all? She works for me and she knows Isla, and is therefore completely off-limits.

Before I can answer, we pull up outside the house and my heart sinks. "Oh, no."

"What?" Layla follows my gaze to the car idling in front of my door. "Who's that?"

"Sir?" Elton meets my gaze in the rearview mirror. "Should I take you somewhere else?"

"I'm not going to hide from my great-aunt, Elton," I answer, unable to keep the surliness out of my tone. The truth is, running and hiding from Great-Aunt Hilda is exactly what I want to do.

Elton knows better than to protest, though, and he slips out of the car to open the door for Layla. Vaguely, I hear her thank him, but my eyes are on the front door. It opens as if it can sense my gaze, and a young, dark-haired man fills the void.

"Who's that?" Layla says under her breath as she comes to stand beside me. The warmth of her body next to me makes me want to shuffle closer, but I hold myself apart with every last scrap of my will.

"That's my Great-Aunt Hilda's lackey, Jeremy. He goes everywhere with her, which means she's hiding on the other side of that door."

"What's taking so long?" a scratchy, elderly voice calls out from behind Jeremy. "We're not trying to heat the outdoors, Jeremy, so either let the fools in or close the door."

Sweeping up the walk, I square my shoulders and set my jaw. Great-Aunt Hilda can sense weakness at a hundred paces. Nothing but the most iron-hard will can stand up to her.

After a morning spent panting after Layla while telling myself I can't have her, I'm not sure I'm up to facing Hilda.

Still, I nod to Jeremy, who opens the door wider. Layla enters behind me, and I scan the room to see my great-aunt sitting in a hard-backed chair next to the fireplace. Her gnarled hand is curled over the top of her cane, a silk pashmina scarf wrapped around her shoulders.

I'm a grown man. I can deal with this.

"Who's she?" Great-Aunt Hilda says by way of greeting, jerking her chin to the woman standing half a step behind me and to my left.

Layla steps forward. "I'm Layla Reynolds, ma'am. I'm Isla's fill-in nanny for the week."

"And now Harriet isn't even here!" Hilda throws her hands up before bringing the cane down hard on my expensive hardwood floors. I had that wood imported from Japan, and Hilda treats it like she *wants* to dent it.

"Is there a problem, Hilda?" I ask. My eyes drift to the side table next to her, where her gloves and hat are neatly placed. "Has Jeremy gotten you a drink yet?"

"He has not," Hilda's gruff voice answers. "I wouldn't say no to a hot cup of coffee."

Before I can do anything, Layla is moving. She gives me a nod and sways her hips on her way to the kitchen. I want to follow her, but I know it would be cowardly. Instead, I pull a chair up next to my great-aunt and take a seat.

"What can I do for you, Hilda?"

"Your daughter's birthday is this week," she starts.

I nod. "Yes. I'm planning on taking her to her favorite restaurant on Thursday to celebrate."

"Unacceptable," Great-Aunt Hilda answers. "She'll have a party."

Resisting the urge to pinch the bridge of my nose, I listen to Layla opening and closing cabinets in the next room. It would be easy to get up and go help her, give myself time to think—but that would only antagonize my great-aunt, and that only spells trouble.

"She doesn't want a party, Hilda."

"Nonsense. She'll be eight years old. Of course she wants a party."

"She told me she wanted a quiet dinner with just me."

"That's because she's perceptive and sensitive, and she can see you're stressed about whatever big business deal is boiling your brain." Sharp, clipped words that hit me like gunshots.

Is that true? Is my daughter sacrificing a birthday party because she doesn't want to trouble me? Something hot and uncomfortable snakes through my chest.

"Your mother called me because she tried to organize a venue and a caterer, but she hasn't had any luck. She doesn't know any of the girl's friends, and she needs you to cooperate."

"She brought out the big guns right away, I see," I say, nodding to my great-aunt.

A ghost of a smile tugs at the wrinkled corners of my great-aunt's lips. They're rare, Hilda's smiles, but they do make an appearance once in a while.

The sound of clinking cups makes me turn my head, and I see Layla arriving with a tray. She didn't just make coffee, she found the nice set of cups and saucers I keep in the corner cupboard, and even unearthed some cookies that must have been hidden in the pantry. A delicate bowl is filled with perfect cubes of sugar, which I didn't even know existed.

With the grace of a dancer, she slides the tray onto the side table and kneels, putting a cup and saucer beside my aunt. "Cream? Sugar?"

"Drop of cream, girl," my great-aunt answers, hawk-eyes studying my daughter's new nanny. I'm surprised by her use of the word "girl," because my great-aunt never uses pet names of any kind.

"I'll lean your cane against the edge of the chair so it's within reach," Layla says, arranging everything around Hilda with brisk efficiency. She makes sure my aunt is happy with her coffee, then moves to me. When she places my coffee on my own side table, I catch a hint of her tantalizing, sweet scent. I nod my thanks, but I don't want her to leave.

"The problem," Hilda continues, "is that we can't get a venue on such short notice."

"How big a party are you wanting for my eight-year-old daughter?" I ask, eyes drifting to Layla as she takes the tray back to the kitchen.

"Oh, a small gathering. Fifty, sixty people. Your mother mentioned she was invited to Paula's granddaughter's birthday, and she only wanted to return the favor."

This time, I do pinch the bridge of my nose. "You want me to throw a party for my daughter...so that my mother can continue this strange feud with her frenemy Paula York?"

"Well, you wouldn't want that hag to get the upper hand, would you?"

"No," I answer, slicing my hand through the air. "No party.

There's no time. How could I possibly organize an event for fifty people in less than five days? I assume you want it to happen this weekend?"

"Friday is a half day at Isla's school," my great-aunt answers.

"How the hell do you know that?"

Hilda just shrugs.

I suck in a hard breath. "Hilda, I'd need a caterer. A venue. Staff. Food. Drinks. Alcohol for the adults. Not to mention invitations and RSVPs, all on short notice. No one will come!"

"*Everyone* will come. Who could resist an invitation from the Sorensen heir himself?"

I groan, massaging my temples. After a pause, I lift my gaze to my great-aunt's. "You're sure Isla wants a party?"

Hilda's eyes soften ever so slightly. She sips her coffee and takes her time putting the cup back down, then folds her hands in her lap. "Last time she came to visit me, she nattered on about some twins' birthday party that happened months ago. She said she'd love to do something, but she'd wait until she was nine or ten. She said her daddy was busy and she didn't want to make things difficult."

My heart gives a hard, sharp tug. I sigh. "Fine. Where do you propose to have this party?"

Hilda shrugs. "I was hoping you had ideas. Your mother's made inquiries at all the nearby venues, but there haven't been any openings. People are loving winter weddings, apparently, and every place is booked for months."

"You could have it here," a soft, feminine voice says from behind my shoulder. I turn to see Layla standing behind my chair, a strange, calculating expression on her face.

She points to a far wall. "I'd move that couch out of the way and set up a bar there. It's near enough to the kitchen that staff can go back and forth to get ice and limes and whatnot. I'd clear this space for dancing and standing room, and have the next room arranged for seating." She points to the space on the other side of the central fireplace. "Small tables grouped for easy conversation. Since it's a children's party, you need activities. I'd lock your office but open that door that leads to the courtyard. Fairy lights and heat lamps should give it an intimate feel, and you could have the usual games. Pin the tail on the donkey, face painting, that kind of thing. But you'd need a theme, since she's eight." Completely oblivious to her audience, Layla takes a few steps to look at the courtyard, then whirls around with a beaming, bright smile on her face. "*Swan Lake!* Ballet! You could hire dancers to mill around the room, and even get Isla's ballet class to do a demonstration. She'd love that."

My heart gives an unsteady beat at the sight of Layla's smile. It's more than a smile, really. It brightens her entire face, like she's lit by some internal glow. Rubbing the ache in the center of my chest, I shift my gaze to Great-Aunt Hilda.

The older woman has the same calculating look on her face, her eyes scanning the space. "Having it in your home would make it more intimate, exclusive. People will want to know where you and Isla live, since you're the bachelor of the century. It's not a terrible idea."

My head moves from my great-aunt to Layla and back again. "Catering? Drinks? Where the hell am I going to find dancers and staff?"

"Well, a friend of mine owns a catering company," Layla

says, her back turned to the two of us. She's pacing out the side of the room and doing a slow turn. "Alcohol is easy enough, and children's games don't need to be complicated. There are companies that rent out furniture for events, and all we'd need to do is move all this expensive furniture out of the way. Simple." She turns that beaming smile on me again, and my heart gives another lurch.

Great-Aunt Hilda, cane in hand, raps the end of it on my hardwood floors again. "It's settled, then. Miss Reynolds, you're in charge. I'm glad we got that settled."

I blink.

My eyes drift to Layla, who's frozen on the spot. Her face, which had been so bright and beautiful a moment ago, drains of all color. It's like she just realized what she's done. Great-Aunt Hilda saw an opening, and she's not the type of woman to hesitate.

I could fix this. I could tell my great-aunt that Layla has her hands full with Isla, that I haven't hired her to be an event planner, too. I could brush the whole idea aside and take Isla out for a birthday dinner and call it a day.

But the truth is, if Isla told Great-Aunt Hilda that she'd hold off on birthday parties because she didn't want to burden me, I know my daughter would love a party. And a ballet theme? Even better. I can just imagine the bouncing, bubbly laugh that my daughter would let out if we did all this for her.

And then there's Layla. The way she lit up from the inside when she spoke about the party. How she easily dismantled all my hesitations and came up with an easy, elegant solution to the venue and catering problems.

She impressed me. And maybe I want to know what she'll do next.

"I'll walk you to the door," I tell Great-Aunt Hilda, extending my arm. "Then Layla and I will talk about particulars."

Hilda lifts her cane and points it at Layla. "You'll need to send invitations tomorrow or Monday at the latest. People will want to rearrange their schedules. Good luck."

Then she ambles to the door and I transfer her into Jeremy's care. When I turn around, Layla's still standing in the same spot, looking stricken.

She closes her mouth, gulps, then lifts her eyes to mine. Endless blue, so blue I could lose myself in them. She blinks. "What have I done?"

EIGHT
LAYLA

I, um, got carried away.

See, I couldn't help but overhear Leif and his great-aunt talking about Isla's party, and my mind started churning. All those Pinterest boards of events, cute little details and party favors, the *potential* that unlimited funds could bring... It made me speak before I could think.

I did one year of an event planning course at a local community college before I had to quit to work full-time, but the truth is, I *love* parties. In theory. I haven't exactly gotten to plan many of them, unless you include church potlucks with my grandmother.

Now Leif is staring at me from the other side of the room, his lips twitching. "You heard the woman," his deep, deep voice rumbles. "You're in charge."

"No," I answer.

"No?"

"No. I'm not in charge. I wasn't thinking. I don't know what I'm doing. I can't plan an event for literal billionaires."

His smile widens. "You just planned the whole thing in less than ten minutes, Layla. Of course you can."

Gah! My name on his tongue shouldn't twist me up in knots like that. Now, not only do I have to contend with blind panic seizing my muscles, I also have to deal with wobbly knees.

Why couldn't I get a job with people like the Eldridges? When I worked for them, they barely gave me a second glance. I took care of the twins and followed the rules and did everything I had to, and Mr. Eldridge treated me with cold courtesy. Mrs. Eldridge was mostly just cold.

It was perfect!

None of this heat lashing my core. None of the electric anticipation every time Leif moves. None of the prickling on my skin.

I should never have accepted this job.

But, but, but...

Emma's college fees. Rent. Bills. Grandma and Grandpa's upcoming legal battles. I can't turn down a week of steady work when it pays as much as Leif Sorensen does.

Turning away from his too-sharp gaze, I survey the room. I sense him coming closer, his presence pressing in on me like an electrical storm. He comes to stand next to me, shoulder brushing mine.

"What are you thinking?" he asks quietly.

"There's a lot to do before Friday."

"Great-Aunt Hilda seemed to think invitations were a good place to start."

"That's your domain," I answer. "How am I supposed to know how to create a guest list?" An alarm goes off, and I swear under my breath. "I need to go."

"What?" Leif stiffens next to me. "Where?"

"I have a shift at the bar," I answer. Why now? Why me? I should have cleared my schedule entirely this week. I should have known that rich people expected more time than normal clients.

"You can't go. We have a party to plan."

"Work on the guest list," I answer, turning to the closet where I hung my jacket. "I'll work on invitation design after my shift, and we can send them out tomorrow. Is this going to be a surprise for Isla, or do you want her to help with planning?"

"Surprise," Leif answers automatically. "I want to see her face when she walks in."

I nod, pulling my jacket on. "Fine. I won't come tomorrow, then, but I'll talk to the caterer I know and work on other logistics. What's the budget?"

Leif waves a hand, because of course he does. Why would someone with the net worth of a small country worry about the budget for a kids' party?

"Here," he says, reaching into his pocket to pull out a credit card. "Buy whatever you need. Elton will be at your disposal this week to take you where you need to go. I'll expect a full proposal by tomorrow evening, though, with a projected budget." He clears his throat. "Thank you, Layla."

I pause as I pull on my hat, then nod. "No problem at all, Mr. Sorensen. Isla's a great kid. She deserves to feel special." I grab my new boots and purse, turn to the door, then pause.

Turning to face him once more, it takes me half a second to regain my senses, because he's so beautiful it almost hurts my eyes. "You should talk to Isla's ballet teacher today, ask her if she can organize for the kids to come and do a small performance. She might even know dancers that we can hire for the event. If your mother wants to impress a rival, there should be entertainment for the adults as well."

"Yes ma'am," Leif says with a little salute. He moves toward the door and opens it for me, but doesn't move out of the way. We pause, staring at each other, and the moment stretches.

I wonder what it would feel like to run my palm over his cheek. He's usually clean-shaven, but there's a hint of stubble there now. It would be rough against my skin, my cheek, my lips. If I kissed his stubble, would he turn his face to take my lips in his? Would he taste as masculine and strong and irresistible as he looks?

"I'll send you the guest list tonight," he says. It might be my imagination, but his voice sounds ever so slightly huskier than usual. But his face is a mask of professionalism, and Leif Sorensen takes half a step away from me to let me pass.

I slip out the door and into the cold Manhattan winter, using every ounce of my will not to turn my head and see if he's watching me go.

THE NEXT HOUR or two hardly give me time to stop and breathe. If I do, I might panic about all the extra work I've taken on.

But the panic would be laced with excitement, too. Event

planning is always something that has interested me, and the prospect of doing it on an unlimited budget? All I can say is —*squee!*

All I know is I can't mess up. If I do a bad job of Isla's party, not only will it reflect badly on Leif, but it'll also completely ruin my chances of getting a permanent nannying placement. I'll be the one who planned the horrible children's party, and why would you trust someone who couldn't even do something so simple?

But if I do a good job...

Well, it's better not to think of that. Instead, I rush home and get ready for my shift at the sports bar, also known as Job Number Three. My evenings most nights are occupied working at a sports bar near my apartment, and tonight is no different. Even this coming week, I'll be working at the bar most evenings after I leave Leif and Isla's, unless I can miraculously get all my shifts covered. Truthfully, I can't really afford to take the week off, even if I could find someone to pick up my shifts.

Now that I have an event to plan as well, I know I'll be run off my feet. Tomorrow morning, I'll stop in at the café and talk to Rachael about her catering business. She's been struggling to find clients these days, her busy season being summer. If she's booked out on Friday, I don't know what I'll do instead, but there's no time to think about that.

I have to find suitable furniture to rent and figure out where to store Leif's current oversized, comfortable pieces. They won't do for a large party. I need to source drinks, cutlery, dishes, decorations, children's games, design and print invitations, think of lighting and heat lamps and tablecloths and, and, and...

These are the things I think about while I do a late shift at the sports bar near my apartment, running drinks to tables and halfheartedly smiling at patrons as they try to flirt with me. I've been doing this for years—using my smile and bubbly persona to make sure I get decent tips at the end of the night. I'm not bad at it, exactly, but it always feels...fake. I hear the same jokes from patrons over and over again. I make the same jokes back. I make sure to remember customers and memorize their regular orders, and I ask about their families and hobbies.

It pays the bills, but the truth? The truth is, the thought of planning Isla's party fills me with so much energy and excitement that it doesn't even compare. I could plan a thousand events on short notice, run myself down to the ground, and enjoy it a lot more than painting a false smile on my face and tolerating half-drunk men leering at me.

One day, maybe. One day I'll pursue something I want. For now, I need the money waitressing provides.

So tonight, even as my mind tries to unknot all the problems I'll have to solve for Isla's birthday party, I put my patented Vapid Waitress Smile on my face and do my job.

One of my regulars is a man named Joe. He always comes in on weeknights, makes sure to sit in my section, orders a couple of baskets of wings and a few beers, and tips generously. He wears this old, worn baseball cap that's fraying around the edges, and he smiles every time I come up to the table. He works at the port as a teamster, and he's built like a linebacker.

I know a lot of the other waitresses think he's cute. We've had lots of whispered, giggling conversations where they lamented the fact that he always searches out my section. One of the younger waitresses, Kylie, seems to be particularly infatu-ated with him.

It's unusual for him to be here on Saturday, and Kylie is making moon eyes at him from across the bar.

She can have Joe. Tonight, I find myself comparing him to another man—a man who is utterly off-limits. Joe has a soft kind of musculature. He's built like a teddy bear. He doesn't have that lethal kind of strength that pulses in Leif. Joe's scruff is always a bit untidy. He's always nice, but he's never said anything interesting.

In other words, he's cute—but boring.

Tonight, his hat is nowhere in sight and he's wearing a button-down shirt.

"You got a hot date tonight, Joe?" I ask, dropping off his beer with my usual smile. Truthfully, I don't feel like smiling. I feel like going home, opening my laptop, and starting on one of the thousand items on my to-do list for the party. I'm energized in a way I haven't been in a long time, and it feels like torture to have to work in this bar until one or two in the morning.

Streaks of red appear on Joe's cheekbones, his eyes sliding away from mine. "A man can't wear a shirt?"

I laugh. "Of course you can. You look very handsome." Another patented bright, bubbly Waitress Smile. "Who's the lucky lady?"

Joe clears his throat, reaching for his beer. He takes a big gulp, wiping his mouth on the back of his hand. "Well, that's the thing, Layla. I was wondering..."

My stomach sinks. I know that look. He's about to ask me out, and it's going to be horrendously, painfully awkward, because he's taken my waitress persona as interest, and I'm going to have to find a way to reject him.

"Um, ex*cuse* me?" A lady at the next table over snaps her fingers at me. "We've been waiting for our food for *ten* minutes while you're standing there flirting. We haven't even received our drinks yet. Can't you do your job?" She raises her eyebrow at me, her too-tight top bulging with excess cleavage.

I give her a slight variant of my Waitress Smile, this time with a hint of an apology in my eyes—all while raging on the inside. I *hate* when people snap their fingers at me, and I know for a fact that it hasn't been ten minutes since I put in their orders. Two minutes, at most.

Leif has been nothing but respectful, even though he's used to ordering people around. He's my boss, my superior, but when I stupidly blurted out my ideas for Isla's party, he didn't dismiss me. He *listened*. He'd never snap his fingers at me or sneer like this lady.

Then again, she did just save me from rejecting Joe, so maybe I should be thanking her. "I'll go check on the bar. Shouldn't be long!"

Scurrying away on aching feet, I lean over the bar and ask the bartender to rush the drinks for the rude lady. The back of my neck itches, and I can almost feel Joe's eyes on me.

As I wait for the bartender to pour the lady's drinks—ahead of other customers that have been waiting longer, I might add—I bite my lip.

This infatuation with Leif is ridiculous. He forgot about me when we first met. No matter what my stupid heart wants to believe, Leif doesn't *see* me. Holding on to this crush will only hurt me in the end.

Maybe I shouldn't turn Joe down. Maybe I should date him. Isn't he in my league? Wouldn't he be the exact perfect type of guy for me to date? He's nice. He has a job. He cares about his family.

For no decipherable reason whatsoever, my thoughts snap to Leif's face when he said goodbye to me earlier today. His eyes were soft, but there was heat there. His shirt tugged at his shoulders, and I ached to feel the smooth hardness of his muscles. My body felt like fire and ice all wrapped in one.

Joe has never made me feel like *that*.

Then again, Leif is a fantasy. If I did sleep with him—which would be a mistake, of course—he would forget about me immediately. And I don't mean he'd set me aside and never pick me up again, like a toy. I mean he would literally *forget*. The way he did before.

The rude lady's drinks are ready, so I push all thoughts of Leif and Joe aside. I arrange them on my tray and bring them over to her, apologizing for the wait and resigning myself to a low tip from her when she rolls her eyes and snorts. When Joe gives me a sympathetic look, I wink at him. And later, when he pays his bill and asks me if I'd like to grab dinner sometime, I tell him I'd love to even though it feels like a lie.

NINE
LEIF

I SHOULD BE at work already. On a normal day, I would've
been gone an hour ago.

As I sit on a barstool at the kitchen island with an empty
mug in front of me, the housekeeper dusts the living room end
tables and my assistant taps an email out on her phone. The
house manager is gathering bills from last week and heading to
the office to reconcile the expenses, and my daughter is
swinging her legs as she eats a bowl of cereal.

My mind, however, is on someone who should be arriving
any minute.

I thought of Layla all weekend—purely because of the party,
of course. I sent her a guest list yesterday, and a few hours later,
she had three options for invitations. When I chose one, she
promised to have them printed by this afternoon. Her emails
were brisk and businesslike, just like mine.

But still...

There was *something*. Something in the way my heart thumped when I saw her name pop up on my screen, in those seconds before I clicked to open her emails. Something in the way I read her name and scoured her messages for a hint—anything—that would tell me she noticed me the way I noticed her.

Shaking my head, I turn back to the tablet in front of me. I have a meeting in two hours with the lawyers in charge of acquiring the properties in Newark for our new development. I should be preparing for that, but my mind keeps slipping away, to shimmering golden hair, to long, long, *long* legs, to big blue eyes that see more than they should.

The doorbell rings, and my heart takes off at a mad gallop.

"I'll get it!" Isla is already off her stool and sprinting to the door. She pulls it open before I can say anything, before I can get my heart to slow down to a reasonable pace. I turn toward the front door, looking across the vast expanse of my formal living room—

And there she is.

Endless legs clad in tight, dark-blue jeans, that ratty old jacket wrapped around her slim shoulders, and blond hair tied up in a high ponytail.

She's wearing the boots I bought, and I almost let out a purr of satisfaction.

Layla greets my daughter with a brilliant smile. A strange pain pierces my chest again, like a sharp twist in the area of my heart. Frowning, I slip off my barstool and straighten my clothes.

Layla smiles at something my daughter is saying, but I can't quite hear any of it. All I see is the way my daughter holds out her hand for Layla's jacket, and the slow, delicious way she strips it off to reveal a white peasant top. It's loose and a little sheer and it makes me want to pull it down past her shoulders to run my lips over every inch of her creamy skin.

Blinking, I clench my hands into fists until my nails bite into my palms. Then I can come back to myself—and that's when Layla looks at me.

"Mr. Sorensen," she says with a nod. "I wasn't expecting to see you this morning."

"I'm on my way out," I say, a bit more roughly than I'd intended. "We have a few things to discuss, though. Are you free this evening to stay back for an hour or so?"

She nods, lush lips curling into a polite smile. I don't want polite. I want the smile that lit her face when she talked about fairy lights and furniture and caterers.

"Of course," Layla says. "I'll be here."

"Will you pick me up from school?" Isla asks. "I have swimming lessons tonight so I'll have to go there before I go home. Harriet usually has a snack ready for me because I'm always hungry after school. Will you make me a snack too?"

Layla's smile softens into something more real, and a bit of tension unwinds in my chest. She nods. "Of course, Isla. I hear you like cheese and crackers most of all."

"And apple slices!" My daughter turns to me, bright-eyed. "Layla already knows what I like for snacks!"

"Harriet made sure your replacement was well-informed," I tell my daughter. "Now give me a kiss. I need to go to work."

Isla runs to me, throws her hands around my neck, and

plants a loud kiss on my cheek. "Bye!" she says, then turns to Layla. "Will you braid my hair?"

That same soft smile appears on her face, but this time it's a little brighter. "Sure. A French braid?"

Isla freezes, eyes going wide. "You know how to French braid hair? Harriet didn't know how to French braid hair. She just did pigtails."

"I used to do it for my sister all the time. I could do two French braids tied into a bun at the nape of your neck if you want. If you have a pretty clip, we can use that too."

Isla practically vibrates with excitement. She rushes to Layla, grabs her hand, and starts tugging her to the stairs. "I have the *perfect* clip. It's sparkly. I'll show you. Let's go!"

The sound of Layla's laughter wraps around me like a velvet rope, causing all kinds of sensations to erupt over my skin. I watch them head to the stairs, where my daughter gives me a wave and starts describing, in great detail, every single one of her hair accessories.

My assistant, Regina, looks up from her phone with that look that sees everything. She arches one single eyebrow.

"Is Elton out front?" I ask, my voice harsh. "We need to leave."

"He's been double-parked for twenty minutes." Regina strides across the lower level and shrugs on her jacket. "Now that I know what we were waiting for, it all makes so much more sense."

My housekeeper, Mary, snorts. I even hear a chuckle from the office where Darren is reconciling the household accounts.

"What the hell is that supposed to mean?" I look at Mary,

who continues dusting, unbothered by my question. My gaze shifts to the open door to the office, where Darren remains bent over the desk. Finally, I look at Regina, who still has that insolent eyebrow arched. I point a finger at her. "You're lucky you're good at your job, Regina, because you have no idea what respect means. None of you do."

"Please," Regina says, her hand on the doorknob. "If you wanted to be surrounded by yes-people, you wouldn't have hired any of us. You certainly wouldn't have hired that pretty new nanny, either."

"It's temporary. Harriet will be back in a week, and Layla will be gone."

"Sure she will." Regina opens the door. "Come on. Your lawyers charge us for their time whether you're in the room or not. I'd rather not line their pockets for twiddling their thumbs."

"I get no respect around here. None."

Mary lets out another snort, her eyes twinkling when they meet mine. "Have a good day, Mr. Sorensen."

"Are you sure you don't need either of us to stay back tonight, too?" Darren says, appearing in the office doorway. "Maybe as chaperones?"

"I should fire every single one of you," I grumble, pulling on my wool peacoat and wrapping my favorite cashmere scarf around my neck. There's no heat in my words, though, and I find myself glancing at the stairway one last time before I leave my house and go to work.

. . .

THE LAWYERS TELL me they haven't made any headway with the elderly couple in Newark. They've refused all our generous offers to buy them out, and now there's a rumor they'll be hiring their own law firm to fight. Apparently the old man actually answered the phone this morning and said as much, between insults and accusations of corruption.

"Not to worry," Barry, the partner at the law firm, says. "There's no way they can out-litigate us. They'll waste a lot of money and time on legal fees, and we'll end up buying the house at a bargain. It could actually turn out to our advantage."

"To your advantage, I'm sure," I answer, glancing pointedly at my watch. "How much are you charging per hour again?"

Barry just laughs. He picks up a stack of papers in front of him and taps them on the table to straighten them. "We have it all in hand, Mr. Sorensen. All you need to do is keep the city council happy and you'll be starting the demolition as per schedule, in March."

My blood feels hot—the thrill of the hunt. This development is the first my company is pursuing outside of the state of New York. If I can make it work in New Jersey, it'll give me a template to expand the business to other states. The growth potential is huge, and I can almost taste success on my tongue.

The elderly couple should take what we offer. They could retire in Florida and live out their days under the sun.

This is what I live for. Or at least, it's what I live for in my professional world. When I'm not with Isla, I'm the aggressive businessman who's built this company from the ground up. I love closing a deal. I love hard negotiations. I love winning.

It sometimes feels strange to go home to my daughter after a day being the CEO. I have to turn into a completely different man to be a father to my daughter. And if I'm going on a date with a woman, I slip into another compartment in my life to seduce and charm her, completely separate to the father or the businessman I am elsewhere.

With Layla, it feels different. She sees me as a father, but I act like a CEO. I want her like a man wants a woman, but I love seeing her soft smile and the way she speaks to my daughter.

It's...confusing. I'm so used to separating the various aspects of my life that seeing Layla blend them makes me uneasy.

That discomfort sticks with me all morning. Once gone from the lawyers' offices, Regina tells me of various other business meetings and engagements. It's a day like any other, but it isn't. I'm no longer excited by the prospect of making money, of negotiating lucrative deals, of finding opportunities where other people see only loss.

Today, my thoughts drift to my home. To the woman who's there, planning a surprise party for my daughter. The one who has already designed invitations and promised to have a caterer organized by this afternoon. The woman who could look at my living room and see a completely different space—one where a kids' party with a *Swan Lake* theme could happen.

"Leif?"

I blink, then look up from my desk. Regina's standing across from me, tablet cradled in her arm, stylus held aloft.

"I'm sorry," I say, "my mind wandered. What did you say?"

"I asked about the Lusso project. The project managers tell me that they'll be ready for a final unveiling within six weeks.

That's three weeks ahead of schedule. All but one apartment has already been sold."

Lusso means luxury in Italian. We built the Lusso tower on the south end of Central Park, refitting and expanding a tired old commercial building. Even with one of the units yet to be sold, I stand to make a tidy profit. To finish ahead of schedule and under budget is a victory—but I feel nothing.

Nodding, I wave a hand. "Good, good." My eyes drift to my screen again, where a new email from Layla has arrived. This time, she's attached a proposed menu from her caterer friend, and all I can say is I'm impressed. Small bites, cocktail foods, as well as larger plates and a whole array of desserts, all paired with various wines.

"Typically, you meet with the project managers and congratulate them, Mr. Sorensen," Regina says, drawing my attention back to her. "Last time a project finished ahead of schedule and nearly fully sold, you took your management team out for dinner and drinks and gave them bonuses."

"Set up whatever you need to set up, Regina. Just put it in my calendar and I'll be there."

Frowning at me, Regina pauses for a moment, then nods.

"And clear my schedule for Friday. I'm celebrating my daughter's birthday." With that, I turn back to the menu on my screen and make notes, a deep, drumming excitement welling up in my core at the thought of the woman waiting for me when I get home.

TEN

LAYLA

THE DAY PASSES QUICKLY. I've always loved working with kids, and when you add all the tasks I need to do to make sure Isla's birthday happens, I'm so busy I can hardly think.

Between the time I drop Isla off at school and pick her up again, I have precious few hours to make phone calls and start ticking things off my very long to-do list.

Firstly, catering. Rachael was thrilled when I asked her about catering yesterday. She came through with a menu that looked delicious and sophisticated. Leif never answered the email I sent, which is fine. He wants to talk tonight—we'll go over it then.

Secondly, furniture. There are rental companies that can provide tables and chairs, but I'll have to put together table-cloths, napkins, dishes, centerpieces, glassware—all the things that will make the rental furniture look appropriate.

Thirdly, decorations. *Swan Lake* is the theme, and we need

ethereal, beautiful decorations. Fairy lights, gauzy fabric, elegant touches.

Finally, entertainment. Great-Aunt Hilda made it clear that this event had to impress, and that means making sure the adults are as entertained as the children.

By the time I pick Isla up, give her a snack, and go with Elton to her swimming lessons, I'm in a mire of tasks and details and to-dos.

And I love it.

I haven't felt this energized in years. I've never been afraid of working hard, but this is different. It doesn't feel like work, because it's fun. All the thousands of Pinterest boards I've crafted over the years, the ideas I've had for events, the things I've imagined when I have a few minutes to myself... I'll finally see it all coming together.

I'm actually *doing* something. I'm not running drinks from a bar to a table and listening to the same old jokes I've heard a hundred times. I'm not working in a daycare with a dozen kids, running after them from dawn till dusk. I'm not making coffees and scrimping together all the dollars from the tip jar to make it all worth it.

There are a thousand things to do, but I feel ready to take them all on. I feel *capable*.

By the time Leif gets home from work, Isla has finished her swimming lessons, been picked up, bathed, and fed, and she's sitting quietly in her bedroom with a book. I hear the door open when I'm brushing out her hair, and my heart thumps.

"Your father's home," I note, making sure to keep my voice level.

"He wanted to talk to you," Isla answers, turning a page in her book. "Don't you remember?"

Soft footsteps sound in the hallway, and I know it's Leif. I can feel the air in the room change, turn heavier. Harder to breathe. Harder to think.

Turning my head, I see him lean against the doorframe and cross his arms over his broad chest. The top two buttons of his shirt are undone, and his hair looks like he's run his hands through it a few times. Tousled. Ruffled. He looks like how I imagine he'd be in the morning, waking up after a long sleep-in. My eyes drift down his strong arms, his trim waist, his long, strong legs...all the way down to his feet. He's only wearing a pair of black socks, I note, and I can see the outline of each toe.

It feels wrong to see his feet. Intimate, somehow.

Clearing my throat, I run the brush once more through Isla's hair and give Leif my best professional smile. "Hi, Mr. Sorensen."

"Did you have a good day?" His eyes are on me, but I know the question is aimed at Isla.

His gaze—his gaze does something to my insides. Everything feels warm and cold and sharp and fuzzy all at once. It's hard to think when he looks at me like that.

"Yes," Isla answers. "I passed my swimming test." She beams at her father, who pushes himself off the door and comes closer.

Inhaling sharply when he bends down near me, I catch a hint of his tantalizing scent as he brushes his lips over Isla's freshly washed hair, pressing a kiss to the top of her head. "I need to talk to Layla. Is that okay?"

"It's fine," Isla says, turning back to her book. "I'm reading."

Lips twitching, Leif shifts his gaze to me. He jerks his head and I follow him out and back down the stairs to the home office. I enter in front of him and see him hesitate at the door. After a moment, he closes it completely, then turns to me.

The full force of his masculinity hits me like a high-speed train. I inhale sharply, bracing myself against his desk, unsure how to react.

I'm at work. This is work. Leif Sorensen is my boss. He's an heir. He's a businessman and a player, and he would break my heart without a second thought—then forget it ever happened.

"You look...tired." There's a note in his voice. Something unfamiliar. Concern?

I blink, straightening. "I'm fine."

He studies me for another moment, then shakes his head slightly. He rounds the desk and sits down, opening the laptop there and turning it for me to see. "I have some notes about the menu."

Squaring my shoulders, I nod and pull out my extensive notes for the party. For the next hour, we go over details of the menu, of the furniture I've secured, and the plan I have for where to store his expensive couches in the meantime. I've gotten quotes for short-term storage, but Leif suggests the TV room off the main living space. Storing the furniture on-site is even better.

"The rental company said they could do the setup of tables, chairs, and bar furniture. They'll set everything up in three hours or less, which should give us enough time while Isla is at school on Friday."

"You did all this in one day," Leif says, voice neutral.

I can't read his expression. No wonder he's good at business —he gives nothing away. I can't tell if he's impressed or disappointed. "Well, a day and a half, technically. And a bit on Saturday night when I got home from work. I know there's a lot left to do. I'm waiting on confirmation from the ballet school. Miss Oliver said she'd talk to some former students of hers who can provide entertainment throughout the night. With the menu finalized, I can confirm it with Rach—with the caterer— and then we can move forward. That will allow me to also procure all the linens and dishes and bits and pieces needed for that." My gaze moves down the list in my hands. "I'm waiting on quotes for gas-powered heat lamps for the courtyard as well as fairy lights, which we can rent for the day. Then there's the cake. I found a bakery that can make it in the shape of a balle-rina, but I need to know what flavor Isla likes. They'll charge extra for a rush order, of course, but the reviews are all really good."

I'm babbling, but I can't stop. When I lift my eyes from my long list of notes, Leif is studying me like I'm a strange bug he's never seen before. He leans back in his chair, tenting his fingers in front of his chest. He keeps his eyes on me for another moment, then spreads his hands. "I didn't think this was going to come together, but I have to say, I'm impressed."

Warmth spreads through my chest as I fight to keep the smile off my lips. I've always been a good worker. Except for the little hiccup at the nightclub where I first met Leif—not that he remembers—I've always left jobs with solid references.

Still, this feels different. I've always known I'd be good at event management, but this is the very first time I've gotten to really test myself.

"I also got the invitations printed," I say, getting up to go to the bag I'd brought in with me. I pull out a small cardboard box, opening up to reveal the gilded, gold filigree-edged birthday invitations. Handing one over to Leif, I finally let my smile spread across my face. "They turned out really well, I think."

He looks at it, face blank, and turns it over briefly before returning it to me. When he meets my gaze again, a strange stuttering fills my chest.

I shift my weight. "Say something, Leif."

Something flares in his eyes. His gaze drops to my lips for such a short moment that if I'd blinked, I would've missed it—but even that brief look makes fire flood my belly, turns my knees to jelly.

"Have a drink with me," he commands, his voice smooth and deep and irresistible.

"Sure," I hear myself say before my brain can begin to function. What I should have said was, *No thanks, I have to go,* because getting any closer to Leif Sorensen is a bad idea.

I know this. My brain is aware. Logic and reason scream at me that I need to keep my distance.

But Leif's big, tall body is rounding the desk and he's placing a hand on the small of my back. All thoughts flee from my head. He leads me to the kitchen with nothing more than a slight pressure from his hand, and a small voice in my head screeches at me to *Run!*

But one little drink won't hurt, will it?

ELEVEN
LEIF

SITTING behind my desk listening to Layla prattle on about all her plans and ideas was the sweetest torture I've ever experienced. She's passionate, organized, smart, ambitious. Everything I'd want in a woman and more.

That light emanating from her was so bright as she spoke, her delicate finger trailing along her notes as she explained everything in great detail. Truthfully, I only heard half of it. I was too focused on the shape of her lips as she spoke, the slight flush on her high cheekbones, the yellow light of the office glinting gold on her hair. As she spoke, she sat up straighter, her body lithe and slender and womanly.

It was like the twins' birthday party. She turned into bottled sunshine before my very eyes.

At some point while she spoke, a strange pain entered my chest. I kept my face blank to hide it—hide how much it scared me.

Women don't have that effect on me. They haven't for years. I learned my lesson with Isla's mother—or at least I thought I did. I keep women separate from business and family, because life is easier that way. Isla is my priority, and my love life cannot touch her, ever.

And here I am, fantasizing about stripping every stitch of clothing off my daughter's *nanny*?

Despicable. Low. Even for me.

"Have a drink with me," I told her a minute ago.

Idiot.

I should be keeping my distance. Any woman who can muddle all my boundaries should be kept at arm's length. Still, I find myself unable to resist touching her as I lead her to the kitchen, her back a warm, shallow curve under my palm. She smells fresh and womanly and perfect, and all I want to do is wrap my arms around her and bury my head in the crook of her neck to inhale her scent deep into my lungs until she's imprinted in my memory.

What the hell is wrong with me?

As we both enter the kitchen, Layla moves to the cupboard to pull out two wine glasses while I get the bottle. We move around each other like we've done it for years. There's no awkward bumping, no shifting out of each other's way. For once, I'm not upset about having someone else in my space. She belongs here.

The wine glugs out of the bottle into the glasses, and then I hand one over. Layla's fingers brush mine as she takes it from me, and a spark jolts me at the touch. Her eyes fly to mine as she pulls the glass away, and I know she felt it too.

This is bad. This is very, very bad.

On Friday, I wanted her. I was content to wait until the end of the week, when she wasn't my daughter's nanny anymore, to seduce her, sleep with her, and move on from this strange infatuation.

Now, though?

Now I see her passion, and I want more of it. I've grown addicted to the husky notes in her voice and that low, seductive laugh in little more than a couple of days. At the end of the week, she won't be Isla's nanny anymore, but I'm not sure I'll be able to get her out of my system, even if we do end up in bed together. There are too many layers to her I want to uncover. Too many secrets she keeps showing me about herself and her life.

"This is good wine," Layla says, gently swirling her glass after a sip. She sniffs it delicately and lets out a little noise that sounds like a moan.

That noise goes straight to my cock. Turning toward the counter to hide the evidence, I take a sip from my own glass. The rich, complex notes of the red wine dance on my tongue and instead of clearing my head, only make me wonder what that wine would taste like if I drank it from her lips.

To my surprise, Layla's shoulders relax. In my office, she was stiff and formal and nervous. Now, she puts her glass down on the counter and lifts herself up to sit on it before plucking the wine up and taking another sip. She crosses her feet at the ankles, leaning her head against the upper cabinets as she glances out at the slice of living room we can see from here.

"You have a beautiful home," she tells me. "I thought you'd have some kind of sleek penthouse like Emil's place."

"Oh, I have one of those, too," I tell her absently, tracing her profile with my gaze. "I sleep there some nights when I work too late to come home, when Isla is at my parents' house or a friend's place. It's closer to the office." My fingers itch to draw a line along her jaw, down her throat, along the delicate blade of her collarbone. I wonder if her skin tastes as sweet as I imagine.

She snorts, throwing me a sideways glance. "Of course you do."

The light dancing in her eyes makes my lips curl. "What's that supposed to mean?"

"Only a very rich man would off-handedly mention the Manhattan penthouse he has as a *pied-à-terre*, as if it doesn't cost more than most people make in their lifetime."

I straighten. "Do you speak French? Your accent sounds very good."

Layla's gaze is flat and unimpressed when it meets mine. "Really? You're not acknowledging anything else from that sentence?"

"You didn't answer my question either." I shift closer to her, my hip leaning against the counter next to her knee.

Another blush sweeps over her cheeks, and the sight of it makes my heart stutter. She shrugs. "I took French classes a couple of years ago, when I was doing the event management course. It was before my sister decided on NYU for college and I had a bit of extra money. I used to have this fantasy of going to Paris and eating croissants at a café overlooking the Seine, then taking a train down to the south of France to see the fields of lavender in Provence." The flush turns brighter red, and I move even closer. "It's silly and cliché."

"It doesn't sound silly."

She arches a brow. "But it is cliché."

Her knee moves, gently touching my hip. She moves it back, but not before the contact jolts through me. Here's a beautiful woman who's good with my kid, who has dreams of eating French pastries in Paris, who can plan an elaborate girl's birthday party in little more than a few days.

She's so much more than I thought she was. So much more than I gave her credit for. Yes, she struck me dumb when I saw her at the Eldridge kids' birthday party, but that was just the physical. This is...different.

Her wine glass is nearly empty, sitting on the counter on the other side of her legs. I grab the bottle and refill it, shifting my body in front of hers. She spreads her knees to give me room between them, but when I move closer, the catch in her breath makes me realize she didn't mean to do it.

Setting the wine bottle down next to her glass, I put my hand on her thigh. My hips are cradled between her knees, my chest level with hers.

"Leif," she whispers.

I move my hand up higher along her thigh, relishing the short, sharp breaths she takes. "What?"

"This is a bad idea."

"What is?" My hand moves to her hip, fingers sliding up under the loose peasant top I've wanted to tear off ever since I saw it this morning. When my fingers touch the skin above the waistband of her jeans, Layla's breath stutters. Her hands move to my biceps and she closes her eyes as her fingers rove slowly, tenderly, up to my shoulders.

If she'd grabbed my neck and kissed me, it would have done less to turn me on than that delicate touch. My heart hits a harsh, violent beat against my ribs as her eyes slit open, regarding me with an unreadable expression.

"This is a bad idea," she repeats, voice huskier than it was a moment ago.

My other hand has moved to her hip, and I pull her to the edge of the counter. Her center presses against my groin, the heat of her sending a wave of lust crashing through me.

She's right, of course. This is a bad idea. If we do sleep together, it should be after she's done working for me. After the birthday party. When things will be simpler. When we can go our separate ways—a clean break.

But those hands, those hands. They move from my shoulders to tangle into the hair at my nape, her touch so delicately feminine it makes me want to growl.

"Daddy?" a soft voice calls out from the other side of the living room.

In an instant, my lust is doused with ice. Layla goes stiff as she slides off the counter, and I readjust my pants and run a hand through my hair, clearing my throat before calling out, "Yes, kiddo?"

"You're supposed to come tuck me in. I can't sleep otherwise."

Layla has a hand over her eyes. I give her a quick glance, swearing under my breath. I round the corner and see Isla at the base of the stairs, her hair still damp from her bath, her pajamas fluffy and covered in little white sheep. Guilt crashes into me.

What the hell was I thinking?

I don't bring women around my daughter. I don't mix my professional and personal lives. My staff are treated with respect, they're paid well, and they have firm boundaries.

Boundaries that I do not ever cross.

Painting a smile on my face, I pick Isla up and cradle her in my arms, her little arms coming around my neck in the same way Layla's did a moment ago. Layla, my daughter's nanny.

I'm a despicable man.

My daughter rests her head on my shoulder as I bring her to her room, tuck her in, and read her favorite bedtime story. By the time I come back downstairs, Layla's wine has been dumped down the sink, the red stain still visible around the drain, and her glass tucked away in the dishwasher.

All other evidence of her presence is gone, and so is she.

TWELVE

LAYLA

I'VE ALWAYS KNOWN Emma was the smart one. Even when she was a kid, she understood homework and school and complicated concepts more quickly than I ever did.

I didn't know I was *this* stupid.

I lambast myself all along the subway ride and the frigid, icy walk to my apartment. I curse my stupidity, my lack of discipline, my weak, spineless self.

Leif is paying me a stupid amount of money to be a nanny for a week. Money that I can use for an initial consultation for a lawyer for my grandparents' problem. Money that can buy groceries and rent and power bills. Money that can support me and my sister when no one else can.

And I'm ready to throw it all away—for what? For a kiss? For sex? For a few moments in the arms of a man who will doubtless forget me within a week?

When I enter my apartment, I smell something sweet and

buttery and fresh, and Emma appears from the kitchen wearing an apron and a smear of flour in her hair.

"I made cookies!" she announces. "Chocolate chip. Your favorite." She presents me with a warm, gooey, delicious cookie, and I eat it to soothe the ache in my chest.

"If you don't want to pursue medicine, Em, you could always open a bakery." I sink down in a chair as Emma grabs me another cookie.

She gives me an impish grin. "A backup plan. I like it. How was work? You look worn out."

You have no idea. Whether the exhaustion comes from the balked lust, the whirlwind of thoughts and emotion, or the hour of self-flagellation I just endured on my way home, I'm not sure.

"Did he like the invitations?" Emma asks, sitting across from me. She leans her chin on her hand and blinks those big, innocent eyes at me.

I frown. "The invitations?"

My sister arches her brows in a distinctly teenage way. "Um, for the party? Hello?"

"Oh." I shake my head. "Yeah, he liked them. He liked all my ideas."

"*Oooh,*" Emma says, bouncing on her chair. "Exciting!"

I give her a tired smile. "I might just get ready for bed, Em. You don't mind, do you?"

She shakes her head. "I have to study, anyway. I just made cookies as an excuse to take a break, but I have to finish an assignment before midnight. My professor is *such* a hard ass. He takes one point off your grade for every minute the assignment is late! How unfair is that?"

"Better not be late, then," I tell her, forcing a smile. My body feels a hundred years old as I get up from the kitchen table, shuffling to the bathroom to brush my teeth before collapsing in bed. But sleep doesn't come easy. I curl up into a tight ball, feeling lost and alone and unable to stop thinking about the way it felt to have Leif's hands on my thighs, my hips, to feel him pull me to the edge of the counter like he owned me.

I felt his cock against the seam of my pants, hard and hot and *right there.*

If I thought I was in trouble before, I had no idea what I was in for. This is bad—and only going to get worse.

LIKE ANY REASONABLE, mature young woman, I decide to solve the problem of Leif Sorensen by completely avoiding him. For the next two days, we cross paths in the morning and the evening, but I treat him to a blank, professional smile and as few words as I can manage. I communicate through email for the party and do everything I can to avoid being alone with him.

In the evenings, I work at the bar. Joe is there, as usual, eating wings and drinking beer, and his hopeful, shy smiles make me feel like the most horrible person who ever lived.

I also hear back from a few of the lawyers I contacted over the weekend. Lawyers are expensive—a fact I learn by the end of the day on Wednesday, after I've gotten a few emails back about consultation fees. Flicking from the emails to my online bank account, I pinch the bridge of my nose.

I'm no genius, but even I know the math isn't adding up.

Even with the injection of cash I'll get from the week of

working for Leif, I'll only have enough for a consultation and maybe one hour of work. Nowhere near enough for any sort of extended legal battle with the army of lawyers the developers surely have. So basically, I'm screwed.

Maybe Harriet will need more time with her husband and I'll have the Sorensen job for more than a week.

As the thought crosses my mind, I drop my head in my hands. Sitting cross-legged on my bed with my laptop in front of me, bitter despair starts seeping through the cracks around my heart.

If I work for Leif for more than a week, I won't be able to keep dodging him. There's a pull in the depth of my gut that makes me want to be near him, and fighting it every day is wearing me down. The more time I spend in his house, with his daughter, near *him*, the more I wish we had something between us.

How ridiculous.

There will never be anything between us other than stolen kisses on a kitchen counter—and I didn't even get to do that.

Leif doesn't date anyone for longer than a few days, and he certainly doesn't date people who aren't in the upper echelons of society. Working for him is torture, slowly tearing my mind apart strip by strip.

But what's the alternative? The café, with a measly tip jar? A sports bar with a few regulars on weeknights?

My grandparents will lose their house unless I pull myself together and deal with it. And I can do it. I *can*. All I need to do is put my attraction to Leif in a little locked box, stuff it down deep, and never, ever think of it again.

I tell myself that with so much force, I almost believe I can do it.

"Layla?" The front door slams behind my sister. "Are you home?"

I close my old, clunking laptop and swing my legs off the bed, heading out to meet my sister in the living room. "I made stew," I tell her, pointing to the slow cooker on the counter. The good thing about stew is you can make it tasty with really inexpensive cuts of meat, as long as you have time to cook it low and slow. A slow cooker can also be left on while I'm away all day, which is doubly good.

Emma lets out a groan and makes a beeline for the cupboard housing our chipped and mismatched bowls. "I'm starving."

"You're a teenager. Of course you're starving."

She ladles a few big scoops of rich stew into her bowl before leaning against the counter. "Org chem is the bane of my existence," she announces. "You know what my professor did today, when he was telling us about the midterm exam?"

"Tell me." I scoop some stew into a bowl of my own, making sure to leave most of it for my sister. This should feed us for tomorrow and possibly the next day, too, as long as we watch our portions.

"He's this old, white-haired man, right. I'm pretty sure he's been lecturing at NYU since the seventies." She blinks, meeting my eyes. "The *eighteen* seventies." When I laugh, Emma takes another bite, groaning in approval as she chews. "And he says, 'Look to the person on your left. Now look to the person on your right.' *Dramatic pause*," Emma says with a sweep of her hand that sends a bit of stew sloshing against the edge of the bowl.

"'At least one of the people you just looked at will fail this exam.' He *said* that. Why would you say that? What purpose could that possibly have in teaching people about stupid organic chemistry?"

"Is this the guy who docks a point for every minute an assignment is late?"

"*Yes!* Come *on!*"

My shoulders shake with laughter at the outrage painted on my sister's face, the worries about my grandparents fading to the background as I listen to the mundane yet important problems of my little sister's life.

"I'd probably fail organic chemistry, so I believe him." My thoughts dart to Leif's question on Saturday morning. He didn't ask *if* I went to college. He asked what I studied. As if it was a given that I'd have had the opportunity to go to college and it wasn't a huge privilege to assume that. The truth is, I didn't have the grades to go to college. Everything fell apart at home when I was barely sixteen and Emma was six. I had her to worry about, then. Trigonometry didn't seem so important.

It's exactly the same thing that's happening right now. I could be enjoying planning Isla's birthday party—and I am—but there's my grandparents' house hanging over it all. There's my rent, there's making sure that Emma has enough food to fuel that big brain of hers. Anytime something good happens in my life, anytime there's a hint of an opportunity, a calamity happens and I find myself fighting fires.

It's not *fair*.

Spooning more stew into my mouth, I try to eat past the lump in my throat. Self-pity never helped anyone, and I'm not going to start now. Yes, I'm tired. Yes, I'm attracted to a man I can never have. Yes, my beloved grandparents might end up homeless before the year is out. I just need to put my big-girl pants on and deal with it, because no one else will.

Putting down my bowl, I head to the pantry to grab some half-stale bread that might fill me up.

My sister makes a very unladylike grunt, her spoon clinking on the side of her bowl. "Layla, you're smarter than you give yourself credit for. You could pass org chem for sure. You could do any college degree you wanted; you just never had the chance. Mom left when you were a junior in high school and you had to take care of me. I know your grades dropped because of it. And you did really well when you were studying event management. If we'd had the money, you'd probably be running a super-successful business by now."

My heart squeezes, eyes blurring, and I busy myself dunking my bread into my stew. "How do you know anything about my grades, Emma?"

"I saw your old report cards in Grandma's attic one time. Connected the dots."

Of course she did. If there are dots to connect, Emma will be there to link them together. My little sister is a bona fide genius, hence her early graduation and acceptance to NYU. I'm so proud of her I could scream, and all I want to do is make sure she has the opportunities I never had.

She keeps eating, unperturbed by the violent emotions swirling through me. "I know you sacrificed a lot—still sacrifice a lot—for me to study and live with you. The reason you didn't go to college isn't because you aren't able, it's because you had bigger things to worry about when you were younger than I am. That's why when I'm a rich, fancy doctor, I'll buy you anything you want. I'll pay for *your* college, and then you can be one of those annoying old people that interrupts the professor a dozen times every class to talk about their life experience."

I snort-laugh, putting the old loaf of bread down to wrap my arms around my little sister. "Don't worry about me, Em. I'll be fine."

"You could finish your event management course!" Emma beams at me, pointing her spoon my way. "You know you'd love that."

A familiar pain squeezes my chest. "Maybe I will," I tell her, not believing a word of it. "But first, you have to pass your midterms."

"*Ugh.*" With that quintessentially teenage noise, my sister and I finish our food, and when Emma starts washing the dishes, she glances over at me. "Did you hear from any lawyers?"

A knot of tension forms in my gut so quickly I flinch. I cover it with a nod. "Yeah. I'll meet with at least one later in the week. They need to review the offer the developers gave Grandma and Grandpa, as well as the deal the city made with the developers. It's not a guarantee that Grandma and Grandpa won't be forced out of their house, but we'll fight it with all we have."

"I still have scholarship money," Emma says casually. "I never used everything from last semester. Lawyers are expensive, right?"

"Em, that money is for your education."

She leans her hands against the edge of the sink, glancing over at me with eyes that are far, far older than seventeen years.

The cheerful enthusiasm of a minute ago gives way to something much more serious. When my sister speaks, her voice is low. "Let me help for once, Layla. You pay for everything, but you forget that we're in this together."

"No."

"Layla."

"No," I repeat.

"Why do you have to be the one to save the day all the time, Layla? You didn't even eat half a bowl of stew and I know it's because you wanted there to be enough leftovers for me. I *see* what you're doing every day for me, and it kills me that you won't let me help. Would you let Grandma and Grandpa lose their house because you won't let me pay for anything?"

"You'll need that money for school, Emma," I answer. "You don't know if they'll change the terms of your scholarship, and you need to save up for medical school. Anything extra now should be put aside for that."

My sister faces me fully, puts her hands on my shoulders, and stares me straight in the eyes. "Let. Me. Help." She shakes me slightly with every word, and each of the shakes weakens my resolve.

I shouldn't accept. I know by the time she's finished medical school she'll have a mountain of student loans, and it'll be years before she's a doctor. But the truth is, I'm *tired*. It's taken so much energy to stay away from Leif, to stop myself thinking about him all day every day. I work sixteen, eighteen hours a day, and it's still not enough.

Maybe just this once, we can dip into Emma's scholarship money.

Shoulders dropping, I nod. "Fine. You can pay for the initial consultation, but we're not making a habit of borrowing your college money for things that aren't education-related."

Emma's shoulders straighten, a triumphant gleam in her eyes. "Good. Make an appointment right now. I'll help you write the email."

I give my sister a flat stare. "It's almost like you don't trust me to go through with this."

Emma ignores me, tapping on her phone. "I just transferred three hundred bucks to your account. That'll cover the consultation, right?"

I purse my lips, a tight knot of emotion budding in the middle of my chest.

Emma glances up, sees the look on my face, and wraps me up in a hug. "It's okay, Layla. Share the burden for once. I'm not a little kid anymore. I can help."

"I hate taking your money for this."

She squeezes me tightly. "Maybe I just want to be able to take credit when we save Grandma and Grandpa's house."

Laughing, I hug her back, then I pull away and make an appointment. When it's done, I give my sister a hug, and I realize that it feels good to lean on someone else, for once, even if it feels wrong for that person to be my seventeen-year-old sister.

THIRTEEN
LAYLA

LAST NIGHT, Leif sent me home early and took his daughter out for her birthday dinner. She still has no idea we're planning this birthday party for her today, and I can't wait to see the joy bursting out of her when she finds out.

I get to the townhouse to see Leif standing in the kitchen holding a cup of coffee and Isla twirling in front of him. For a short moment, before he notices me, Leif's face is soft, open. He smiles at his daughter and murmurs something that makes her laugh so hard she clutches her belly, then she wraps her arms around his waist and squeezes tight.

Then he looks up, sees me, and the softness remains for a moment before a cool mask descends on his features. For a second, it almost looked like he was happy to see me. Like he...cared.

We haven't talked about what happened in that same

kitchen. Why would we? We're both adults, and we realize that it was inappropriate. I'm more than willing to move on.

My body hasn't gotten the memo. The sight of Leif's long body leaning against the counter causes heat to build in the pit of my stomach. My skin grows more sensitive, my nipples tightening against my bra.

The man had his hands on me *one* time and I can hardly think in his presence. We didn't even kiss. We did nothing more than touch—mostly over clothes, if you don't count his fingertips diving beneath my top.

But now he watches me as I approach the kitchen and I feel naked. Gloriously, shamelessly naked. Heat flushes through me, all the way up to the top of my head.

"Layla," Leif says in that low tenor of his.

"Mr. Sorensen." I nod.

Amusement glints in his eyes. "I need to get to work. I'll see you tonight, Isla. Be good this afternoon."

"Can I invite Talia over to play?" She blinks her immense eyes at her father, clasping her hands at her chest. "Pleeeaasee?"

"We'll see. Dani's due date is coming up, remember? The baby will be here any minute. Talia might not be allowed to go far."

A stab of guilt pierces my stomach. I haven't spoken to Dani all week. We saw each other nearly every day when we were both nannying our respective kids and we've kept in touch, but this week I've completely forgotten about her—apart from the invitation I sent over to her place. She's going to be giving birth to Emil Van der Berg's baby, and I should be there for her. My head is a muddled mess, though.

Leif lays a soft kiss on top of his daughter's head, barks out a few orders at me and the other employees scattered around the house, then leaves. When he passes me, his arm brushes mine, the faint touch sending my body into cartwheels.

I really, *really* need to get a grip. Once Leif leaves, everything will be easier, including breathing and forming coherent thoughts.

It doesn't help that I've barely gotten more than a couple hours of sleep every night this week. It takes me an hour to commute to the Sorensen house every morning, and I've worked late at the bar every night. Adding in the party planning and the pressure of impressing a bunch of billionaires attending a kids' party—well, I haven't had much time to rest.

But after today it'll all be over, and I'll sleep tonight.

I ignore the stab in my gut at the thought that today is my last day in this household. My last day with Isla. My last day with Leif.

"What do you want for breakfast, Isla?" I ask.

"French toast!" She beams at me, hopping from one foot to the other.

I glance at the clock on the wall and shrug. "Sure. But you have to get your bag packed for school so we can leave right after you eat."

"Okay!" She takes off like a bullet to gather her things, and I make her a special breakfast.

ONCE ISLA IS AT SCHOOL, I make a few phone calls, and the townhouse turns into a hive of activity. Carrying my notes under an arm, my hair in a bun atop my head, I direct the movers to shift the furniture as I've planned. There's an army of employees ready to string up lights and set up tables.

Rachael arrives midmorning with a broad smile on her face. She wraps me in a big bear hug, squeezing tight. "I can't believe you got me this catering job, Layla. If these people like my food, it could change my business forever."

Rachael is always bright and boisterous, but I see something different in her face this morning. A vulnerability and a kind of tenuous hope that I recognize. For her, this is The Job.

Heart squeezing, I wrap my arms around her. "Let's make sure they like your food, then."

Directing a young man to grab the other end of a portable bar, I set it up near the mouth of the kitchen and start arranging the tablecloth, linens, and glasses that will be used during the party. Rachael goes outside and reappears with trays and trays of food, along with another helper.

The house is a disaster, but there's a buzz in the air. A thousand people have questions for me, requests, problems, and we only have a couple of hours to sort everything out before Isla's half day at school is done and guests start arriving.

But...I love it.

The tiredness that clung to me this morning disappears and I find myself buzzing with excitement of my own. I love the pressure of a tight timeline. I love seeing all my plans come together. When I'm ticking this off my list, I look around and realize we have no cake.

Frowning, I call the bakery. The ballerina cake should have

been delivered by now. There's no answer, and I call again. Nothing.

While I'm staring at my phone wondering if I should call a third time, the bakery calls back.

"I'm sorry, Miss Reynolds," the woman on the other side of the line says. "A pipe burst in the kitchen overnight. Must have frozen in the cold." She sucks in a breath, and I know she's near tears. "We lost the cakes. We lost everything. I would make another one, but I have no oven, nothing. I'll refund you, of course, but I...I..."

Speechless, I listen to the despair in the baker's voice, close my eyes, and take a deep breath. "No problem. Thank you for letting me know."

I hang up the phone and let out a curse.

Rachael looks up from her spot in the kitchen, brows arching. Her hands are still moving in front of her, chopping chives into teeny tiny pieces that she then scoops into a waiting bowl. "Everything okay?"

"We have no cake."

Her knife stops moving. She bites her lip, brows drawing together. "I can't bake, Layla. I'm a good cook, but I can't whip up a cake in an hour."

"I know," I answer. "I'll have to get a cake at a different bakery. A ready-made one. It'll have to be generic. I'll scrap the ballerina idea."

As I open my web browser to look up local bakeries, my phone starts ringing. My sister's name pops up, and I hesitate. I don't have time to do anything but sort out this cake problem.

But this is my sister. I never reject a call from my sister.

"Hey, Em."

"How's the party set-up going?"

"Good," I answer, then hesitate. "Well, good, except for the cake."

"What's going on?"

I tell my sister the problem, and she lets out a low hum. Then, she squeals. "Oh! I have an idea. You could do cupcakes. I was looking for frosting recipes the other day and came upon a photo of this tower of cupcakes. What if you put a ballerina doll at the top, draped some fabric over some kind of tiered cupcake stand, then arranged the cupcakes on top of the fabric? That way her skirt is made of cupcakes. Plus, cupcakes are way easier to find on short notice from bakeries, and kids love them. You can buy some fancy gold-and-silver sprinkles if they look too generic."

I'm staring at the wall, trying to picture what my sister's describing. "You said you saw a picture of this? Can you send it to me?"

"One sec." Emma's voice goes distant, and I know she's tapping on her phone. A moment later, my phone buzzes with a photo from her. "Did you get it?"

"Yeah. Hold on." I take the phone away from my ear and with a few taps on the screen, I see exactly what Emma described. In the photo, a cupcake stand with three tiers is covered in shimmery blue fabric acting as the doll's skirt. A doll is propped at the top of the cake stand, the fabric tied around her waist. On top of the fabric, dozens of cupcakes are artfully arranged. The princess in the photo is a Disney princess. It would be easy enough to swap that for a ballerina if I could find an appropriate doll...of which Isla has dozens. Cake stands and fabric and cupcakes I can definitely find on short notice.

"Emma, you're a genius."

"It'll work?"

"It'll look great. I have to go. I have cupcakes and cake stands to find."

Emma lets out a little squeal. "Okay. Send me a picture of the whole setup and the cake. Good luck! Love you!"

"Love you too." I hang up and spin around, then yelp when I bump into a big, broad chest that's standing too close to me. Warm, strong hands curl around my elbows as I stumble back, and I look up, up, up to meet Leif's gaze.

It's unreadable, as usual. "Everything under control?"

"Mostly," I croak. "A little wrinkle with the cake. Specifically, an emergency at the bakery means we don't have one. But I have a solution."

"Which is?"

His hands are still on my elbows. They slide to my upper arms, and the almost irresistible desire to melt into his chest threatens to overwhelm me.

But I don't have time for that. I don't care if he's handsome and strong and tall and a Nordic god come to life with a soft spot for his daughter. I have a cake emergency to fix.

Pulling away, I shake my head. "No time to explain. I need to get a cab and head to the nearest store to grab a tiered cupcake stand."

I make to dart around him but Leif turns with me. "You'll take my car," he informs me. "Elton is parked outside."

"Oh," I answer. "Thank you. That will save a lot of trouble."

Leif nods, his steps keeping pace with mine. It's not until we're at the front door and my jacket is on that Leif speaks again. "And I'm coming with you."

FOURTEEN
LEIF

MY HOUSE IS a disaster of people and tables and chairs and tablecloths and decorations, but instead of staying and supervising, I realize the thing that interests me most is the mission Layla is going on for my daughter's birthday cake.

Also, the final bit of the conversation I heard, when she told the person on the other end of the line that she loved them.

A boyfriend? Is that why she ran away after our time in the kitchen?

I grit my teeth against the sharp stab in my chest. Not wanting to investigate that emotion too closely, I just follow Layla to the door and watch as she directs a few workers to reposition tables, decides where decorations will go, and answers half a dozen questions that come up from various people. The location of lights needs to be approved. There aren't enough power points and the cords won't reach, so Layla directs the person to a box of extension cords that she had the foresight to prepare. The tables don't fit exactly as planned, but there's an easy solution—that Layla comes up with, of course. One of the workers cut their hand and needs a first aid kit.

Layla answers every question with no hesitation. She puts her jacket on and wraps a scarf around her neck while directing the proceedings, and I can't help but watch the way she handles the chaos with ease.

She's *good.*

It's not often that I'm impressed. I hire good people to do hard work and I expect the best. But Layla seems to be spinning dozens of plates, all while dealing with some kind of cake emergency. Her cheeks are flushed, her eyes are bright, and that tired, drawn look I noticed on her face this morning seems to have disappeared.

"Oh!" She glances at the stairs. "I need one of Isla's dolls." Before I can say anything, Layla darts to the stairs. I'm only halfway up behind her by the time she reappears at the top, holding a doll dressed in a ballerina outfit in one hand. "Got it!" She smiles at me. "Step one of the Cake Crisis is complete."

"Are you going to explain any of this to me?"

"Maybe if you're nice." Her eyes glimmer as she brushes past me on her way to the stairs. When we step outside, she takes a deep breath. I watch her chest rise and fall, aching to put my arm around her shoulders and tuck her close to me.

But she's Isla's nanny, and I don't bring women anywhere near my daughter. My love life does not intersect with my family life which does not intersect with my business life. Ever.

Still, I can't quite stop the words from coming out of my mouth. "I'm surprised you had time to take a personal phone call in all that chaos. Your...boyfriend...must be very important to you."

Layla gives me a strange look as Elton jumps out of the car and hurries to open the back door. "My boyfriend?"

"You were on the phone when I walked in, huddled in the corner away from everyone. You told him you loved him."

Layla laughs. *Laughs*. At me.

Women don't laugh at me. They laugh at things I say while they trail their fingers over my arm in overwrought flirtation. They don't turn their back on me and walk away, waiting for me to follow.

She slides into the car after thanking Elton, calling him by name. For a moment, I'm distracted by that simple action. How many women have I taken on dates and driven through the city who didn't even acknowledge my driver's existence?

But Layla just slides into her seat and puts her seatbelt on, tapping on her phone while Elton gets behind the wheel. "Elton," she says, "we need a tiered cake stand and a bit of nice fabric that will match this ballerina. I'm thinking somewhere like Target would have both. But before we go there, I need to stop at these three bakeries to check for cupcakes." She rattles off the name of three bakeries, along with their addresses.

Elton nods. "No problem, Layla. There's actually a bakery a few blocks closer, a kind of hole-in-the-wall place. I got my niece a cupcake from there and she said it was, quote, 'The best ever *ever* ever.'"

Layla smiles at his reflection in the rearview mirror, asking if it's the same niece who made his braided bracelet, which Elton confirms, lifting his wrist to show off the bit of colorful string.

He's driven her around a couple of times and she knows about his family?

I have the strangest impression that I'm intruding—that Elton is *her* driver. That this is *her* car. And I'm not sure I like the familiarity Elton has with her. I'm not sure I like this first-name basis. Anger builds inside me, hot and red and writhing—but where the hell did that come from? Why am I angry that two members of my staff talk to each other cordially?

Why didn't *I* know of a good bakery to suggest? Impotent frustration adds to my anger.

"You're the best, Elton." Finally, her eyes turn to me. "My sister gave me the idea," she says, turning her phone to show me a picture of a doll with a skirt made of cupcakes. "She loves baking and she happened to call at exactly the right time just now."

Realization dawns, my anger leaking out of my pores. "Your sister."

"The one and only," Layla says with a gleam in her eyes. "I love her." She turns back to her phone, seeming to ignore me. But I can see the corner of her lip twitching.

"Not a boyfriend," I answer. My voice is still tense from restrained temper.

Her blue eyes land on me again, a fine brow arched high. "Leif, I have three jobs, a sister and grandparents to support, and as of this week, a birthday party to plan. Where do you suppose I'd find time for a man?"

There's a subtext to her words. *Where do you suppose I'd find time for you?*

The sass makes me want to pull her onto my lap and kiss her

senseless. It makes me want to touch every inch of her, stake my claim on her inside and out. I can show her that I can make her forget about everything that puts shadows under her eyes.

But I can't, can I?

She's my employee. She knows my daughter. She's off-limits.

And that pisses me right the hell off.

FIFTEEN
LAYLA

THE TENSION in the car is thick as soup, but I just decide to ignore it. I live with a teenager, after all, and I know how to let moodiness roll off my back. Even when Leif is gruff at the bakeries, or when he stands with his arms crossed and a scowl on his brow as I buy a cake stand, I just pretend he doesn't exist.

It's easier that way.

And when we get back to the townhouse, progress has been made. The room is almost completely set up, Rachael has the food well in hand, and I focus on the cake. With some clever draping of gauzy white fabric I pilfered from a children's princess dress from Target, a doll duct-taped to the cake stand, and beautifully arranged cupcakes, I end up with something that looks elegant and appropriate for an eight-year-old ballerina.

Speaking of ballerinas, Miss Oliver arrives with four former students in tow, and we talk about where they will perform and how long we'll need them.

All the while, I feel Leif's eyes follow me around the room. I'm not sure what happened, but I can feel his anger pulsing against my skin.

Just ignore it.

Today is my last day, after all. I'll help with clean-up tomorrow, and then it's bye-bye nannying job.

After what seems like only a minute, my alarm goes off. "I have to go pick Isla up from school," I say. Then the doorbell rings, and the first guests arrive.

Dani, my extremely pregnant friend and the soon-to-be wife of billionaire Emil Van der Berg, enters the house and looks around, wide-eyed. Her gaze lands on me, and she wraps me in a big hug—or as big a hug as we can manage across her baby bump.

"This looks incredible, Layla. I can't believe you pulled this off in a week."

"Isla is going to *love* this," Talia says. The little girl is Isla's age and the two of them are the best of friends. Talia's hair is near-black, and she's her little brother's protector and defender. Frankie is hanging onto his father's neck while Emil looks at Dani with stars in his eyes. The two of them are in love; it's obvious for anyone to see.

I don't know why that causes my stomach to knot. I've never been in love, and I've never had a man look at me the way Emil looks at Dani. Maybe I'm just jealous.

"You are *definitely* planning my next party," Dani says with a shake of her head. "This place looks beautiful."

"She's impressive," a deep voice says from behind me. It makes my skin prickle even though I felt Leif approach a moment ago, as if my body is finely attuned to his presence.

Shrugging off the compliment as the doorbell rings again with more guests, I make my excuses and head out to pick the birthday girl up from school.

AN HOUR AND A HALF LATER, after having taken Isla shopping as planned to give guests more time to arrive, Isla and I climb into the Rolls-Royce that I've somehow become accustomed to, and Elton takes us back to the townhouse.

"Do you think Daddy will like my new dress?" Isla smooths her hands over the skirt of her dress, her feet kicking back and forth as the car rumbles beneath us. When she picked out the princess dress with the long tulle skirt ("Like a ballerina!"), I told her she should wear it and surprise her dad. Then we went to a café, got hot chocolates, and I redid Isla's hair into a complicated set of braids tied into a bun at the crown of her head.

"I think he'll love the dress," I answer. "You look beautiful."

Isla turns to look at me. "Are you going to come back next week, Layla? I like how you did my hair for school. Everyone was impressed, even my teacher."

A twist in my chest makes it hard to speak for a moment. I pat Isla's knee. "Mrs. Harriet will be happy to be back, Isla. I'm sure you'll have lots of fun with her too."

Isla shrugs. "Yeah. She's nice, but she's strict." Her eyes brighten. "Maybe you can show her how to French braid my hair."

The car turns onto our street and I almost say something placating—but I know from experience with Emma that with kids her age, it's best to be gently honest. "I'm not sure that will happen, Isla. Mrs. Harriet and I probably won't see each other. I'll be in New Jersey at my other job."

"You should quit your other job."

I snort. "I would if I could, believe me."

Isla giggles, her feet still kicking. We stop in front of the townhouse and Elton helps us out, his eyes twinkling as he opens my door. "The boss just texted me. Almost everyone is here and ready for you to go in."

Heart fluttering with excitement at the thought of my first big event coming together, I extend a hand toward Isla, who has wandered to a nearby car. "Come on, Isla! Let's go inside. I think your dad is home, we can show him your new dress."

"That's Miss Oliver's car," she says, pointing to a white car parked on the other side of the street. She turns to look at me. "Why is my ballet teacher here?"

Elton and I exchange a glance, and I bite my lip. "It might be someone else's vehicle."

"Nope," Isla says, marching toward me. "She has a scratch on the door just like that car. It's hers. Do you think I'm in trouble?"

I arch a brow. "You think you did something that deserves trouble?"

Isla gives me an impish grin, then shrugs, grabbing my hand to head to the door. We climb the few steps to the landing, then Isla turns the handle and enters.

"*SURPRISE!*"

The shout is so loud that even though I was expecting it, I jump. Isla stands in the doorway, mouth open, staring at all her classmates, ballet buddies, their parents, and all her family members. The ground floor of the townhouse is packed, with uniformed caterers already milling around with little bites and trays of drinks.

Above us, the ceiling is a web of twinkling fairy lights. Gauzy fabric is draped along the walls to match the tablecloths I got to cover the rented café tables on the far side of the room. The centerpieces on the tables have little ballerinas twirling among glittery puffs of cotton that look like smoke. A big banner proclaiming, "Happy Birthday, Isla!" hangs above the central fireplace bisecting the room.

It's better than I could have imagined. I was fairly confident my choices would all work together, from the lighting to the food to the choice of centerpieces, but it's different to see it in real life. When I left just over an hour ago, the fairy lights were off and the place was still a manic hive of activity.

From the crowd, Leif detaches himself and bends in front of his daughter. She runs into his arms and he twirls her around, causing her to giggle and giggle and giggle.

"Happy birthday, kiddo," he says in a low murmur.

"I'm not a kiddo," she answers, but she squeezes her arms around his neck again. "Love you, Daddy."

"Love you too, baby girl." Leif sets his daughter down, and she strips off her jacket and tosses it aside before running toward Talia and Dani, who are the first to approach with birthday wishes.

Picking up Isla's jacket, I hang it up in the hall closet when a familiar male presence moves closer. Glancing over my shoulder, I see Leif regarding me with a strange expression.

"Thank you, Layla," he says quietly. "Isla's face when she saw the room was..." He shakes his head, throat working. "I should have known she'd want a birthday party."

"You have a lot on your mind," I answer with a polite smile.

Before he can answer, one of Rachael's employees approaches. "Sorry to interrupt," she says, "but Rachael asked me to get you, Layla. She needs you in the kitchen."

I nod, slipping away from Leif. I feel his eyes on me until I turn the corner into the kitchen.

From there, I do my best to stay out of the way. I help the catering team gather dirty dishes and glasses, I make sure drinks are chilled and ready to be served, I put out fires and organize kids' games, and make sure everyone has everything they could possibly need.

After an hour, Miss Oliver starts the show. A male and female dancer twirl in the middle of the floor to the delight of all the little girls in the audience. The older generation looks on appreciatively, and I even see Great-Aunt Hilda nodding in approval. She's sitting in the corner next to a younger woman who has to be Leif's mother.

Rachael transferred my hodgepodge cake stand onto a wheeled trolley of hers and added a tablecloth, fresh flowers, and sparkly decorations to the edges to make it look sophisticated, ethereal, and utterly beautiful. A smaller, six-inch cake I bought to have Isla blow candles out is placed beside the ballerina cupcake extravaganza.

With one last adjustment to the flowers on the edge of the

trolley, Rachael smiles at me. "You did good, Layla. She's going to love this."

I adjust the doll's arms so they're above her head in an approximation of a ballerina's pose, then nod at one of the waitresses. "Bring it out. It's time."

I follow into the main room as Leif asks for silence, then starts the "Happy Birthday" song in a surprisingly deep and beautiful singing voice.

Of course the man can sing. He's beautiful and rich and charming—what's one more panty-melting skill to add to the bunch?

Unable to resist watching this part of the proceedings, I stand next to the wall and join in the singing, trying to catch a glimpse of Isla's face. She has her hands clasped at her chest, her face beaming with pure childish joy. Throwing her arm around her best friend Talia's shoulders, she points at the doll and says something in her ear.

When Leif holds out the smaller cake for her to blow out candles, the entire room erupts in applause.

"My son tells me you planned all this in less than a week," a female voice says from my right.

It takes all my self-control not to jump out of my skin. I turn to see the woman that had been sitting next to Great-Aunt Hilda. Mrs. Sorensen is as tall as I am, dressed in a beautifully tailored cream pantsuit. Her neck is ringed with an emerald necklace, hair tied back in a French twist. Rings glitter on her fingers as she folds her hands in front of her stomach, her piecing green eyes studying me.

Finally, I find my voice. "It was Hilda's idea," I demur.

"Oh, she made sure to tell me," Mrs. Sorensen answers with a laugh. "But you're the one who pulled it off. Good work."

And with that, she drifts through the crowd to talk to another woman, who—judging by the frenemy vibe between the two older women—has to be Paula, the one who needed to be outdone by this party.

I let out a sigh, closing my eyes for a moment and gripping the wall for support. I need air, or silence, or just a moment to gather my wits. I haven't had more than a few hours' sleep this whole week, I've worked crazy hours, but a terrifyingly elegant woman just told me she was happy with my work—and then went over to another woman to gloat.

I did it.

Slipping through the crowd, I enter the first door I can find, which is the spare room opposite the kitchen. It's an intimate TV room where we stored the extra couch from the living room, which now dominates the space. I close the door behind me and lean my hands on the back of the sofa, dropping my chin to my chest.

I only have a moment's respite, though, because the door opens behind me. The noise of the distant party gets louder then quiets again when the person closes the door.

By the thickness of the air in the room and the prickling of my skin, I already know who it is.

Turning slowly, I meet Leif's eyes as he turns the latch on the door.

"Layla," he growls.

"Mr. Sorensen."

His eyes flash at the sound of his name, and I know it's because he wanted me to call him Leif. There's a storm in his eyes, an emotion I can't decipher.

Then he crosses the distance between us, hooks an arm around my waist, and kisses me like the world is ending.

SIXTEEN
LEIF

I'VE WATCHED Layla all afternoon, need growing inside me like a bad toothache. She's worked diligently, fielding problems as they arose and making sure everyone has anything they could ever need. She thought of everything.

It's a simple party, really. Nothing like the lavish affairs my parents throw or the galas I've attended in the past. But the simplicity of the afternoon doesn't detract from the pure joy Layla has brought to my daughter.

Isla's face when she walked into the room nearly broke me. How could I think my eight-year-old daughter was happy to have a birthday dinner with me and nothing else? How could I miss the fact that my little girl loves feeling like a princess?

The dancers were a genius touch, too. I watched Isla staring at them intently, mimicking their movements as they used a small space to twirl and dance, her mouth open and her eyes wide.

Then there was the cake. That was the last straw for me, I think. Isla did that thing where she wiggles her butt and hops from one foot to the other—a sure sign that she's so excited she can hardly contain it. She whispered something in Talia's ear, unable to keep her eyes off the tower of cupcakes and the ballerina atop it all.

Layla barely knows my daughter, but she was able to give her an afternoon of pure joy. She was able to transform the bottom floor of my house into a wonderland for my daughter and make Isla feel special.

I've felt so full I could burst ever since they walked in the door. No one but me has ever done something like this for my daughter. My mother buys her presents and spends time with her, of course, but sometimes I feel like she's trying to mold Isla into something my mother wants, instead of seeing my daughter for the amazing girl she is. My father dotes on Isla, but he's always been distant. Harriet has been part of our family for years and she's like a mother to Isla, but this is different.

It's like Layla saw to the core of my daughter, saw what Isla would love, and then did everything in her power to make it happen.

So, when I saw Layla slipping into the other room, I had to follow. It was like a magnet dragging me across the floor. A hook anchored in my gut that I was powerless to resist. I walked in and there she was, bowed over the back of the sofa dragging in deep breaths, the exhaustion written on every line of her body.

Layla did that for *Isla*. For *me*.

Kissing her was inevitable. To have a woman give so much for my daughter and me made me unable to resist.

So that's how I ended up where I am, with one arm wrapped around Layla's body, my other hand cupping her jaw. After a mere moment of surprise, she softens in my arms like she belongs to me. Her lips part, letting me in. The taste of her jolts through me, sweet and soft and delicious and *mine*. I slide my fingers to tangle into the hair at the nape of her neck, a low growl riding in the back of my throat as I deepen the kiss, wanting to etch her taste and her touch into my mind forever.

When Layla slides her hands up my arms and wraps them around my neck, something yawns open inside me. A torrent of feelings rushes out, and it's all I can do to grip onto her to survive the onslaught. Her kiss melts my brain, sends all my blood rushing south, makes me forget all the reasons we shouldn't be touching each other at all.

It's *right*. Her arms around my neck, her lips on mine, her sweet, beautiful body pressed up against the length of my own. Through the whirlwind inside me, the realization builds—this is exactly where I should be. This is where *she* should be.

I break the kiss, breathing harshly, to stare into her eyes. Her kiss-bruised lips are swollen and glistening, her eyes hazy and wild.

She looks beautiful. Irresistible.

Then her hands press the back of my head and her chin angles up toward me, and who am I to resist that kind of sweet demand? I crush my lips to hers again, sliding my arm from her waist down to her bottom. Pressing her against the front of me, I know she feels my arousal when she gasps against my lips.

It's not enough. It'll never be enough.

I want this woman like I've never wanted anyone before. It's beyond the thrill of a challenge. It's beyond the fact that she's beautiful and attractive and sassy.

She *fits*. Her curves and hollows press against my body like she was made to be there. She fits in my life. In my family.

When Layla starts gently rocking her hips, I groan and move my lips to her jaw, her cheek, her neck.

"Leif," she pants, hips still writhing, hands curling into my hair.

"Shh," I manage to say, tugging her shirt aside to run my tongue along her collarbone.

"Don't shush me," she pants, her breath catching when I pull her hard against me.

This is more than a kiss. It's more than sex. This is my whole world tilting onto its side, everything I knew about women and dating and rules shattered in an instant. This is some door in the darkest corner of my mind opening up to reveal wants and needs and desires I told myself didn't exist.

Her hands move from my neck to my shoulders and down to my chest. I groan, copying the movement as I press her hips against the back of the sofa, using both hands to shape her breasts, feel the sweet hollow of her waist, the graceful curve of her hip.

Her *body*. Goddamn.

"Leif," she repeats, eyes closed, head tilted back to reveal the creamy column of her neck. It's irresistible, so why would I resist? I bury my head in the crook of her neck and press my lips to her skin, letting my tongue dart out to taste her there, just like I want to taste her everywhere.

Her breasts are small, but they fit perfectly in the palm of my hand. I knead one while my other hand slides down to cup that hot space between her legs.

It's my daughter's eighth birthday party, and I'm in the other room debauching her nanny. I'm despicable. I'm a piece of shit. I don't deserve Layla, but she's giving herself to me, and I don't care what I deserve anymore.

The button of her jeans releases in a soft whisper of fabric, and my fingers touch a lacy edge. Pulling back enough to look between us, I see white lace with a little satin bow framed perfectly by the open fly of her jeans. My cock throbs painfully at the sight. It's innocent-looking, almost virginal, and it makes me want to rip her clothes off and plunge inside her.

Forcing myself to slow down, I let my fingers coast down the center seam of her jeans. She shivers, whispering my name in a husky voice that travels straight to my cock. Hips moving against my hand, I watch the way she searches to sate herself, to use my touch how she needs it.

My breaths are harsh. Pinning her to the sofa with my hips, I keep one hand between her legs where it belongs, then tug her top down. Her breast spills out, pink nipple hard and waiting for my mouth.

Like a man starved, I pull her breast into my mouth, grind my hand against her core, and revel in the sweet, needy sounds she makes.

"You're going to forget every name but mine," I tell her as I nip at the stiff peak of her breast. I brush my lips over it, then lave it with my tongue. "You'll stop avoiding me, Layla. Do you hear me?"

"Yes, I hear you." Her fingers tunnel into my hair, hips grinding against my hand.

"You're going to let me give your body what it needs."

"I will." Her grip tightens on my hair. "Give me what I need, Leif."

Growling, I can't wait any longer. I need to feel the soft wetness between her legs. I need to be inside her. I slide my hand up to those sweet, white panties, dip my fingertips underneath the waistband—

Then someone screams in the other room.

Layla freezes, her hands clenching on my biceps, but my mind is still in a fog. Thoughts are sluggish, coming at me in fragments and pieces. All I can see is that white bit of lace framed by dark-blue denim. All I can think about is what's hiding underneath, how hot and wet and sweet it'll feel to thrust inside.

My lips capture her breast then move up to trace the pulse point on Layla's neck, and she taps my arms. "Leif, wait. I think something's wrong outside."

"Someone else will deal with it," I growl, barely recognizing my own voice. I sound like an animal. Savage, guttural. I press my palm to her stomach, dipping my fingers below her panties to feel the very edge of the split between her legs. Another half an inch, and her sweet little clit will swell against my fingertips—

She grips my wrist to stop me.

Slowly, second by second, my brain comes back online. Layla pushes at my shoulders and I back up a step, glancing toward the closed door like it's an enemy that needs to be demolished.

Then I hear it too—the hubbub on the other side. The panicked shouts, the sound of Emil's voice telling someone to call 9-1-1.

Like ice water pouring over the heat of my desire, consciousness returns to me. My best friend is asking for an ambulance, and he sounds like he's panicking, which means—

"Dani," Layla says, eyes wide when they meet mine. Her hands tremble as she fumbles with the button of her jeans. I readjust myself, straighten my clothes, and within moments, we're tumbling out the door and into the chaos beyond.

A pack of children are crying. A crowd is pressed around the far corner of the room. The caterers and staff watch on with wide eyes and frozen expressions.

Emil roars.

"Will you be quiet?" Dani's voice snaps, then she gasps. I elbow my way through the crush of people to find Dani doubled over, her knuckles white as they grip Emil's forearm, her face bleached of color. She glances at me as I push myself to the front of the crowd, breathing heavily as she clutches a hand to her bulging baby bump. With a wry grin, she manages to say, "Sorry to interrupt Isla's party, Leif. Apparently the baby wanted to join."

SEVENTEEN
LEIF

PANDEMONIUM REIGNS until Dani and Emil head to the hospital in the back of my car with Elton at the wheel. Once they're gone, Layla gently directs party attendees to remain, eat more cake, and enjoy themselves for another hour or two.

My mother catches me watching her and arches a brow at me. "You're sniffing at her like a dog in heat, Leif. It's not like you."

I stiffen. She's right. It's not like me, and it's completely inappropriate. I should be detached and professional with Layla, just like I am with all my other staff.

Then again, I don't take any other members of my staff into the side room and bend them over the back of a sofa.

"She's a remarkable young woman," my mother continues, pensive.

Freezing, I replay my mother's words to make sure I heard her right. Then I clear my throat. "She is."

"Your great-aunt told me she organized this entire party within a couple of days."

"It's impressive," I answer, unable to say more than a couple of words at a time. My mother is watching Layla, and a deep feeling of discomfort steals over me.

Layla is my little secret. She's the dark desire I keep tucked away, the woman who bleeds through all the boundaries I've set for myself.

But my mother of all people—a woman who is as exacting as she is elegant—looks at Layla and seems to see everything I do. Someone beautiful and intelligent and...remarkable.

My mother surveys my living room like it's her kingdom. Great-Aunt Hilda has her gnarled hand on Marcus's forearm, her head bent near his. My friend meets my gaze across the room and gives me a wry grin over my great-aunt's head.

In the opposite corner, Isla's ballet friends are giggling around the cake trolley. Parents hover, with fathers sitting around tables while they sip beers and mothers gossiping across from them. It's amazing how similar adulthood is to middle school.

Like a moth to a flame, my gaze moves to Layla once more. She's picking up plates from a table, sweeping up cake crumbs and gathering empty glasses. When the caterer says something, Layla lets out a laugh.

A strange, sharp pain passes through my chest at the sound of her laughter. It makes everything inside me expand and collapse at the same time—then my mother clicks her tongue.

"Get a grip, Leif."

"Mother, I have no idea what you're talking about."

Before she can answer, my phone rings. It's Emil. "Dani's having my baby," he says when I answer the phone. "Right now."

"I know, Emil. I was there when her water broke. It happened in my living room, remember?"

"I'm freaking out, man."

"You already have two kids."

"I know! But you know how it feels. You were there when your daughter was born."

It takes all my self-control to keep my face steady. I was there, yes. I watched Isla come into the world, her red, scrunched face showing everyone just how angry she was about the interruption. It was the best moment of my life, shortly followed by the worst.

Emil lets out a breath, and I hear Dani's voice in the background. He says something I can't hear, then brings the phone back to his ear. "Dani's hospital bag is packed, but I left it at the apartment. The baby wasn't supposed to come for another week. I gave my staff the day off, and my mother's out of the city. You're the closest one to the apartment. Would you mind going to get it? How are Talia and Francis? Do you mind watching them for a bit longer?"

I glance at the pack of feral children still swarming the cake table. Talia has a protective arm around Francis's shoulders, as usual, and my own daughter is bouncing excitedly in front of them. "Your kids are fine. Marcus mentioned he was babysitting his niece tonight. I'll ask if he has room for a couple more. I'll be there soon. Text me your room number." I hang up the phone and turn to my mother.

"Duty calls. My best friend is freaking out about being a father."

My mother rolls her eyes. "Men. Fine, go. I'll make sure Isla stays out of trouble."

"Thanks, Mom." I give her a kiss on the cheek and head to the pack of children. Isla's at the eye of the storm, as usual, and she squeals in delight when she sees me. Jumping into my arms, she wraps herself around me.

"This is the best birthday ever, Daddy! Thank you, thank you, thank you!"

My heart gives another lurch. To see Isla so ecstatic about something so simple—a party in our living room—makes me realize that I haven't given my daughter enough time. I've seen her every day, but I've been so caught up in making this real estate business work that I've lost sight of my own family.

I heard Emil a few minutes ago overcome with emotion because he's going to be a new dad, and I need to remember what a privilege that is. When Isla was born, her mother handed her to me and walked away, and I made a commitment. My daughter would be my world.

When I put her down, I catch a sweet, feminine scent and turn to see Layla at my elbow. She smiles. "I just got a text from Dani with all the things she forgot to pack in her hospital bag. She told me you were heading over to her place; do you want the list or would you like me to come help pack everything up?"

"Come with me," I answer before I can think clearly. But even if I'd given myself time to think clearly, I'm not sure I would have said anything different.

She smiles softly, nodding. "Should I kick everyone out?"

Isla gives a little plaintive squeak, and I put my hand on my daughter's head. "My mom and Hilda can hold down the fort. They can stay as long as they like. Let me go talk to Marcus about babysitting."

"I'll grab my jacket," Layla says, then kneels in front of Isla to give her one last happy birthday hug.

I watch my daughter's face break into a bright smile. When she pulls away, she puts her hands on Layla's shoulders. "This was the best birthday ever," she tells Layla solemnly. "I want you to plan every party from now until forever!"

Layla laughs, gives Isla one last hug, then nods at me and heads for the closet to grab her coat and bag. With a final few words to Marcus, who agrees to take on Isla as well as Emil's kids for a few hours, then a polite goodbye for my mother, my great-aunt, and a few other guests, I follow her to the front door and find Elton waiting outside, already briefed and waiting to take us to Emil's place.

So, for the second time today, I find myself in the back seat of my car with Layla by my side—and there's nowhere I'd rather be.

BABIES BRING out the best and worst emotions in people. I'm in a hospital waiting room with a small group of close friends, waiting for Dani to bring her first child into the world. The atmosphere is tense and jubilant and worried and exultant, the air a thick soup of emotion. For no reason that I can explain, I find myself drifting close to Layla. We sit next to each other on hard hospital chairs and somehow her fingers end up intertwined with mine, her hand clasped on my knee.

Her touch isn't electric and all-consuming like it was in the TV room at the party. This feels comforting. Like I'm home.

The tired lines of her face are back now that the thrill of the party is over. She slumps on the chair and in the sixth hour of waiting, ends up falling asleep with her head on my shoulder. I listen to her breathing and feel strangely...at peace.

Hours later, when it becomes obvious the baby isn't coming anytime soon, Emil convinces us to head home.

"The doctors say it'll be a while. Dani doesn't want to take any Pitocin to bring on any stronger contractions yet, and the doctor agreed to wait and see if things start moving on their own. You two should head out. I'll call you when the baby gets here."

"Let me know if you need anything," Layla says, squeezing Emil's arm. He turns and wraps her in a tight hug, and a wave of heat and anger washes over me at the sight of Layla in another man's arms.

I'm...jealous? Of my best friend? Whose fiancée is literally in the other room having his baby?

Maybe my blue balls have sucked all the blood from my brain and I'm no longer capable of rational thought.

Shaking my head, I move to give Emil a hug of my own. Then Layla and I drift down the hall toward the elevator, and I glance at her. "Marcus agreed to babysit Isla overnight since she's already asleep," I tell her. "What do you say we go get a celebratory drink before I drop you off at home?"

There's a moment of hesitation. I see the wheels turning in

her mind, the doubt screaming at her to refuse. Which she should, of course. I'm her boss—or I was, up until the end of today's workday. We should just go our separate ways.

Emotions are high today. From the pure joy of Isla's party to the heated kiss—and more—we shared, to the long labor that isn't over for Dani yet, I feel strung out and on edge, and the only thing that will make it better is having a quiet drink with a beautiful woman.

"Sure," Layla finally says to the beat of my lurching heart. "One drink won't hurt."

EIGHTEEN
LAYLA

IT'S A MISTAKE.

Of course it's a mistake.

What I *should* do is gather my things, bid everyone goodbye, and go home to my bed. Tomorrow, I'll finish the clean-up for the party, go check on Dani, pick up my paycheck, and put Leif out of my mind. Forever.

But my bed is across the river and it'll take me over an hour to get back. I've worked every day this week while hardly getting more than three hours of sleep per night. The party was a success and the day ended in suspense. I'm worried about Dani, I'm happy about the party, and I feel so strung out I know I won't be able to sleep despite my exhaustion.

I deserve a drink. Even if I end up falling asleep on my feet, but at least this way I'll get a ride home in Leif's nice car, with heated leather seats and soft music. Much better than the subway.

That's what I tell myself, anyway.
That's how I let myself run headlong into trouble.
Big, blond, Leif-shaped trouble.

NINETEEN
LEIF

IT'S her laugh that does me in. As soon as we leave the hospital, with its bright white lights and antiseptic smell, I know Layla and I should go our separate ways.

She knows my daughter, for one, and my daughter likes her. She's breached that innermost sanctuary of my life, where I haven't let any woman enter since the one who gave birth to Isla. That's my golden rule, isn't it? Women and Isla don't mix. Women don't get close to the core of my life, to the things that really matter.

Not only that, but Layla works for me. Maybe not technically right now, but how long will Harriet's husband's health hold? How long until I need to call on the Delmar Agency for a replacement nanny, knowing that Isla will want Layla back?

Finally, Layla is exhausted. I can see it in the rounding of her shoulders, in the small sigh she makes every time she sits down. I see it in the way she leans against the car's headrest as if she doesn't have the energy to even keep her head upright. And who could blame her? She told me herself she has about seven million jobs, works a thousand hours a day, and took on the planning for Isla's surprise birthday party to boot.

What I should do is take Layla out for one drink to debrief on this trying day. Then I should take her home.

But when I've resolved to do that, everything turns on its ear.

We go to a jazz bar, tucked in the basement of a tall building with nothing but a fizzing neon sign and a big bouncer to mark the entrance. In the dark, sensuous room, Layla and I order drinks and sit at the bar, talking about Isla's party, the cake, and the unexpected arrival of the new Van der Berg baby.

Then Layla goes to the bathroom, and I decide the night should come to an end. I pay our tab and sip the final dregs of my drink, waiting for her to reappear so I can be a gallant gentleman. I'll driver her across to New Jersey, make plans for the final clean-up tomorrow, and say goodnight. End of story. I'm Leif Sorensen: Mr. Responsible.

But she doesn't just slip into her seat beside me. She walks by me and smacks me on the arm, giving me an exasperated look. "You should have told me my makeup was running halfway down my face, Leif. I looked like a raccoon. I shrieked when I saw myself in the mirror just now. It took three drunk women I met in the bathroom all that time to touch up my makeup until I looked presentable." She gestures at her face with both hands. With a huff and a shake of her head, she slides onto the barstool and gives me another sideways glare.

I frown. "Your makeup?"

"Don't pretend you didn't see what a mess I was. I can only imagine what people thought when they saw us walk in here together. You—handsome, dapper, in control. Me—a disheveled hot mess."

Handsome? Dapper? In control? Is that how she sees me, when on the inside I'm perpetually on the edge when I'm near her? "I never noticed your makeup."

That comment makes her turn to face me fully, and I notice the dark circles under her eyes aren't quite so dark. Her under-eyes are still purply and shadowed, but not quite as badly as before. So that was smudged makeup?

Hope flames in my heart, because the reason I counted on to take her home disintegrates. She's not so exhausted, so maybe we can stay out for a second drink.

"You can't be serious," she scoffs. "I had the worst raccoon eyes in the history of makeup, Leif. My undereyes were completely black."

"They've been dark all week. I just assumed you were as exhausted as you looked." I blurt out the words, belatedly real-izing I've just told a woman she's looked terrible all week. Where is my usual smoothness? Where are the soft, seductive words I can usually call up to compliment a beautiful woman and coax her into my bed?

Layla stares at me for a beat, blue eyes wide, as if she's trying to read down to my soul. She's going to get up and leave. Who wouldn't? I just insulted her and told her she's looked like shit. Mind scrambling for something to say to dig myself out of this hole, I clear my throat—

And Layla doubles over with a laugh. Hard, racking shakes

of her body make her grip the edge of the bar as she laughs, drawing the gaze of every man in the room. It's not the type of laugh women affect to look cute and flirty. It's *real*. It's raspy and seductive and it makes everything inside me tighten.

She's unlike any other woman I've met. She's not trying to preen and position herself on her stool to show her body off to its best advantage. She's not wearing sky-high heels and a designer dress. Her hair hasn't been professionally styled and blow-dried and whatever else women think they need to do.

And she's gorgeous. In smudged makeup and messy hair and old jeans, she looks deliciously undone. It makes me want to drag her onto my lap and mess her up even more.

Despite myself, my lips curl and I find myself chuckling along with her. She wipes her eyes and clicks her tongue, throwing me another exasperated stare before waving the bartender over to order another round.

So, we stay for a second.

From there, we move to a booth in the corner. She sits next to me and tells me about her sister, pride shining in her eyes when she tells me about Emma's early acceptance to NYU's Prehealth program. She tells me about her grandparents, and the way her eyes soften tells me they were the single source of happiness and warmth and support in her teenage years.

"Your parents?" I ask.

"Never knew my dad," she says, lifting her drink to her lips. She takes a sip, then shrugs. "My mother left when I was sixteen."

Her voice is casual, but there's something in the tightness

around her eyes, the set of her shoulders, the way she won't meet my gaze that tells me this memory hurts her.

"She left?" I ask.

Layla lets out a huff. "My mother has always been...flighty. She loves us, I think, but she's selfish. Not maliciously so, but she just...doesn't think about other people. When I was sixteen, she met a guy and decided she didn't want to be a mother anymore. Left us with my grandparents and took off. It didn't make sense for a long time, but it made me the person I am now, so I can't blame her." There's strain in her voice, and I marvel at how much she's borne on her slim shoulders. Layla is *strong*.

My throat is tight, and I can't help but put my hand on her knee. My ex left, too. She didn't wait sixteen years, though. She did it as soon as she was discharged from the hospital after giving birth.

"I don't understand how people can leave their kids behind," I hear myself saying. "Isla is everything to me. She's the coolest kid, too. How could you not love her?"

Layla smiles at me, genuine warmth in her gaze. "She's special. She reminds me of Emma when she was that age. Really precocious and too smart for her own good." When I nod, Layla tilts her head. "Isla's mother... She left?"

I nod. "Said she didn't want to be a mother. I haven't seen her since Isla was less than a week old."

Layla blows out a breath. "Wow."

A kink in my heart unknots itself then, and all it took was Layla to sit there and *understand*. She gets it, because she's been through something similar. Arguably something worse. She watched her own mother leave, had to care for her sister, her grandparents.

We move closer to each other and order another round, then another. A pleasant buzz fills my body, and I don't care whether it's the alcohol or the company. All I care about is her thigh touching the length of mine and the way it feels to put my arm around her shoulders.

A band starts playing on a small, circular stage in the corner, and we move closer so we can hear each other talk. I watch her lips move, remembering the way they tasted just a few hours ago. I inhale the floral notes of her shampoo and the unnameable scent that is Layla. Her body fits perfectly against mine, and when she turns her head to look up at me, I only have to move my head an inch to bring my lips to hers.

Just one kiss, I tell myself as I slide my palm over her jaw and tilt her head to take her lips. Just one taste.

But I should know that one taste will never be enough.

An earthquake could bring the bar down around my ears, and I wouldn't notice it. That's how much I lose myself in Layla's kiss. She puts her hand on my chest and I have no doubt she can feel the thundering of my heart beneath her palm. When she curls her hand into my shirt to tug me closer, my whole body lurches with desire.

It's the laugh that did it. Ever since she laughed like that, unselfconsciously doubled over at the bar, it was inevitable that we'd end up in each other's arms. She can't show me that side of her and expect me to turn away—something so real and intrinsically seductive that it called to me like a siren's song.

With a few deft flicks of my fingers, I tug her hair loose and let it fall down her back in a golden wave. I've wanted to bury my fingers in her hair since the day I saw her at the Eldridge twins' birthday party all those months ago. The soft silk of her hair twines around my fingers as I pull her closer, crushing my lips to hers and wishing this moment would never end.

"Want to see my *pied-a-terre?*" I ask, breathless as we pull apart, my lips moving over hers.

"Is it so swanky and pretentious that I'll hate it immediately?" Her eyes gleam in the low light, lips tugging at one corner.

"Most definitely." I kiss her again, wanting her taste embedded in my memory, wanting her soft lips open and yielding to me.

"Fine, then." She gasps as my hands roam down her body, over her breasts and down to the sweet hollow of her waist.

From there, it doesn't take long to get home. Elton meets us outside and I put up the privacy screen between us before dragging Layla onto my lap. Where she belongs.

"This isn't safe," she says between kisses. "If we get in an accident, we'll both die."

"We're moving at about ten miles an hour."

A little giggle while Layla's fingers undo the top few buttons of my shirt. Her fingertips brush the skin of my chest, sending fire rushing down to my groin.

My mind is so clouded by lust that I can't think of all the reasons we shouldn't do this. I can't think about anything except the soft, lithe female body in my arms and the overwhelming feeling of rightness at having her here.

Then we're stumbling through the lobby and I'm crowding her in the elevator. The second it takes to press the button to the top floor is too long away from her, and I hook my arm around her waist to bring her hard against my chest.

This is right. So, so right.

My body screams with pleasure at the feel of her in my arms, like everything that was wrong with my life has suddenly been made good. I'm dizzy with it. My blood pounds in my ears, in my hands, in my cock. When we reach my apartment, I take her purse and fling it across the room, scattering all her things across the kitchen.

She laughs that laugh again. The one that drives me crazy. Husky and low and Layla.

Throwing her over my shoulder, I stalk to the bedroom, scarcely seeing anything in the apartment around us. All that matters is getting her to the bed and relieving her of all these clothes. All that matters is thrusting inside her sweet heat and feeling her shudder around me. Making her mine, once and for all. Showing her that she belongs to me.

I tear at her clothes, savage and unrelenting. I toss them over my shoulder while she claws at me until she's wearing nothing but a bra and very lacy panties.

Groaning, I force myself to slow down. In some distant echo of my reasoning mind, I realize this could be my only chance to have her. Today was intense, and we'll both wake up tomorrow back in our right minds.

But her bra—her bra is in the way. I unclasp it with one hand, tear it off, and toss it over my shoulder.

She laughs again, and I lose my mind.

My lips trail down her neck, her chest, down to the soft

handful of her breast. I suckle the pink tip, feeling her soften in my arms—and I know I was an animal before.

This is a woman who hasn't been worshipped. I heard it in her voice when we sat at that booth, the tension and the guardedness and the strength she's built up to withstand life's assaults. She hasn't been treated like she should, and I've just torn her clothes off like a man incensed. With every scrap of my self-control, I force myself to slow down. Enjoy. Revere.

Layla deserves to be treated like a queen.

Arranging the pillows behind her, I lay her down and take in her body, bare but for a bit of lace around her hips. She wraps her arms around my shoulders and pulls me down for a kiss, sighing against my lips when I let my hands roam. Her body trembles, then softens. I run my palms over her breasts and feel her arch into my touch, then a soft moan travels through her body as she relaxes.

Yes, she needs to be loved properly. By me.

I move my lips to her jaw, to her ear, to the skin at the side of her neck. She curls her fingers in my hair when I kiss her there, so I spend a few more seconds kissing and touching and loving.

This is right. Nothing could be more right than having this woman in my arms.

I trail my tongue over her skin as she lets out another soft sigh. I move down her collarbone, her chest, laving attention on her perfect breasts. Her belly is soft and beautiful, and I press kisses in a line down the center of it, then move to her legs. Her feet, her knees, the soft, soft skin of her inner thigh.

Her body was made for me. Every little mole, every old scar, every mark and smooth expanse. *Mine*, my heart screeches as I memorize every inch of her. She softens some more and I close my eyes, inhaling the scent of her skin and memorizing every inch of her body.

I brush my lips over her panties and she...

Does nothing. No arch of her back. No sigh. No soft moan.

Frowning, I flick my gaze up—and freeze.

Layla Reynolds is asleep. Lashes fanned over her high cheekbones, soft mouth open, she has one arm curved above her head and the other resting on her stomach.

I sit back on my haunches, staring at her prone body, feeling a strange mix of warm tenderness and bone-deep embarrassment.

This has never happened before. Women are usually trying to show off just how sensual and willing they are in bed. They don't fall asleep right before I eat them out.

If anyone has a cure for an inflated ego, it's Layla.

Still, the tenderness inside me grows, and I can do nothing except gently gather her in my arms and flick the covers on top of her. From there, I go brush my teeth and splash water in my face, looking down at the throbbing length of my cock.

"Not tonight, buddy," I tell it. Then I head back to the bed, wrap myself around her, and fall asleep.

TWENTY
LAYLA

SEE? Trouble.

All it took was eight short days for me to mess up my own life.

Not only did I ruin my chances of ever working with Leif again, but I also pretty much torpedoed my chance of getting a permanent placement with anyone else. Who wants to hire a nanny who sleeps with the boss?

No one, that's who. And they're right.

There's no way I'll get a permanent job as a high-profile nanny. I'll be forced to work minimum wage at a café and a sports bar for the rest of my days.

All because my stupid brain decided to stop functioning and my body was all too happy to take charge.

Well, it won't happen again. Not in a million years.

TWENTY-ONE

LEIF

I WAKE up to an aching head and the sun's long golden fingers stretching through my gauzy curtains. The Morning After. Also known as time to get rid of my bedmate—except this time, I find myself not quite wanting this night to end. Reaching across the bed, my hand slides over, over, over...and feels nothing but the cold expanse of empty sheets. I pause.

I'm alone.

Sitting up, my eyes scan the room. The carnage from last night has mostly vanished, apart from my own clothes strewn around the place.

Layla's gone.

I flop back down on my pillows and let out a low groan.

Last night...*ugh*. I scrub my face then let my hands fall to the side, staring at the ceiling.

Last night was *good*. From the moment I guided Layla down

the hospital hallways to the time I asked her to come home with me, I felt alive. It was the first time in months—years, maybe—that I was with a woman and I didn't feel like I wanted it to end once the main event was over.

Not that we ever got to the main event.

When I close my eyes, I can still see her standing nearly naked before me. I can smell the sweet scent of her skin, I can feel the softness of her body against mine, so perfect and warm and mine.

But she's gone.

I walk through yesterday's events, from the hectic planning, to the cake fiasco, to the party itself, to the wait at the hospital, to our first drink that was supposed to be our last. Then, what happened after.

What *didn't* happen after.

I learned a lot about Layla in those few hours we spent together, and all of it was good. She's complicated and intelligent and she loves her family fiercely. The way she spoke about her sister and grandparents made me think of what I feel for Isla, and how I'll do anything to keep my daughter safe and happy.

Layla has that same core inside her. Protective, loving, and loyal. She's nothing like the other women I've dated. Nothing like the women who wanted me for status or money or bragging rights.

Nothing like the woman who left without looking back.

That's why we ended up in bed together.

I couldn't *not* bring her here. It was an eventuality. And

when I leaned over and asked her to come home with me, I saw the way her body shivered, how she pressed into me before looking at me through thick lashes and saying yes.

And then she fell asleep on me. Well, technically she fell asleep when I was on *her*, but still. We shared hot, deep, drunken kisses and tore the clothes off each other. She rewarded me with smiles and laughter and sighs and moans, and I felt like the king of the world.

Apparently I was the king of lulling a woman to sleep with my boring lovemaking.

Talk about a blow to the ego.

It's for the best, though, isn't it? In the bright light of day, I remember all the reasons we can't get involved. She worked for me. She has a busy, exhausting life. And most importantly, she knows Isla. I refuse to bring women around my daughter when the woman who was supposed to be there forever so callously walked away. I refuse to expose my daughter to that kind of rejection. That's a hard rule for me... Or it was, until Layla.

As I lie in my empty bed, looking at the imprint of her body in the sheets next to me, I find myself wishing she was still here.

The smell of sizzling bacon wafts toward me, but my mind stays stuck on Layla. I remember inhaling the scent of her skin and kissing her neck, her jaw. I remember feeling her hands shape my shoulders, my arms, and nearly coming in my pants when she wrapped her legs around my hips.

Maybe it's a good thing she fell asleep. When I have her for real, I want to be sober and present, and I want her to be right there with me. I want it to mean something.

The thought clangs through me. My brows tug together.

I want it to mean something? Since when does sex mean anything? Sex is just sex. It's scratching an itch, a biological need. Nothing more.

I sit up, bringing my hands up to massage my temples.

No, I don't want sex to mean anything. Especially not with a woman who is supposed to work for me. A woman who has spent time with my daughter. A woman that can't just be jettisoned from my life without complications.

This is bad. Very, very bad. Sex is meaningless. Women are replaceable, and Layla is nothing special.

Right?

Ripping the sheets off, I swing my legs over the edge of the bed. Layla means nothing. Last night meant nothing. It *can't* mean anything. I've been down that road once before—I let a woman in, and she gave me a beautiful daughter and a beautifully shredded heart. I'm not going through that again. I'm not letting a woman rip apart my carefully constructed life.

Layla's gone, and that's a good thing.

... Or maybe she's in the kitchen cooking bacon?

Standing up so fast I give myself a head rush, I stare at the closed door. Isla's here. I hear the high pitch of her voice now. Who is she talking to?

Wait—Isla? What the hell is my daughter doing here? She's supposed to be with Marcus.

Could she be talking to Layla? I start moving, tangling my feet in the sheet, and hop on one foot then the other to regain my balance. Finally, I make it to the walk-in closet without tripping over and cracking my head open. Yanking my drawers open, I throw on sweatpants and a tee, then practically run to the door.

My feet slap on the hardwood floors as I force myself to slow down on my way to the main room, heart pounding.

The sight of Layla cooking breakfast for my daughter might be too much to bear. That's the stuff dreams are made of. A beautiful woman laughing as she listens to my daughter, whisking eggs while the sun makes her hair shine and her face glow—

I stop dead.

It's not a gorgeous blond bombshell in the kitchen. The dark head bent over the stove belongs to my good friend Marcus. I scan the room before they notice me. There's no sign of Layla anywhere.

Tightness grips my chest and I rub the spot with the heel of my hand, unsure where that pain came from. Surely not from Layla's absence. She's just a woman, and women don't matter. Not in that way. It's a good thing she's gone. Whatever fantasy I had about her cooking breakfast for my daughter and me was just that—a fantasy. Women and Isla don't mix. Not in my life.

"Daddy!" Isla launches herself at my waist. Hot on her heels, Marcus's dog, Bear, comes trotting toward me.

I ruffle her hair then give the dog a quick ear scratch. "How was your sleepover at your uncle Marcus's house?"

He's not actually her uncle, but he's been in her life since she was born. He has four sisters and about four thousand nieces and nephews, and Uncle Marcus's house is a favorite among the brood.

"Fun. We watched a movie and ate pizza for dinner. We

went to bed an hour past my bedtime and he said it was a special birthday bedtime even though my birthday was Thursday. Marcus told me not to tell you, but I knew you wouldn't be mad."

My lips twitch. Apparently my daughter is well aware that she has me wrapped around her little finger.

She moves back to the kitchen island, onto one of the barstools lining the edge. Her feet kick out back and forth as she rests her chin on her hand. "When do I get to meet Dani's baby?"

"Well, I haven't heard from Emil, so I think the baby hasn't arrived yet. You might have to wait a couple of weeks, kiddo," I answer, pouring myself a cup of coffee. "They have to get settled at home before they have anyone over."

"*Weeks?*" Isla answers, horrified. "That's like, forever!"

"We have to give Emil and Dani time together as a family, Isla." I sip my coffee. "And time for Talia and Francis to get to know their new sibling."

Isla gives me the longest, most dramatic sigh I've ever heard. "Fine," she says, dragging out the word.

Marcus places a plate in front of Isla with a slice of buttered toast, a sunny-side-up egg, and two slices of bacon. Isla immediately forgets about her hardships and starts eating. Bear sits obediently at her feet. My daughter breaks off a piece of bacon and feeds it to him with a secret grin. When she catches me watching with an arched brow—she knows she's not supposed to feed the dog while she's eating—Isla just shrugs.

My plate is next. It slides across the counter as I take a seat.

Bear comes shuffling over to my feet and I just shake my head. "Don't even think about it, buddy."

The dog huffs and returns to my daughter's end of the island. Marcus fixes his own breakfast last, and his dog doesn't even try to come beg for scraps. When Marcus turns around to put his plate on the island to eat standing up, his eyes meet mine for a long moment.

He knows about Layla.

I don't know how, but he does.

Ignoring my friend's stare, I have breakfast with the two of them and try to drown myself in coffee. "What movie did you watch, kiddo?" I say, dragging my gaze away from my friend's.

"*The Emperor's New Groove,*" Isla answers before chomping on a triangle of toast. "It was funny. But Daddy, I'm eight years old now. I'm not a kiddo anymore."

I smile into my toast. "My mistake, Miss McGee."

Isla just rolls her eyes. Once her breakfast is eaten, she puts her plate away in the dishwasher and announces that she's going to practice her ballet routine and to come get her when we're ready to leave again. Then she heads for the other side of the cavernous open-plan room, to the blank space on the hardwood floors she always uses to dance. Bear follows obediently, circling his tail three times before flopping on the floor with a sigh.

I watch her prance away, already half-dreading her teenage years. She's willful enough as an eight-year-old. I don't want to know how she'll act when she's sixteen.

When I turn around again and face my friend, I already know what's coming.

"Layla was here this morning," he says in a low voice.

I clear my throat. "Yeah."

"Isla thought she was here to be her nanny again. Layla denied it. Then your daughter asked me why Layla was wearing the same clothes she was wearing yesterday at the party."

My stool creaks as I shift, reaching for my now-empty mug. I stare at the brown ring at the bottom and let out a sigh. "She's very perceptive, my daughter."

"Leif."

"Marcus."

"You fucked her, didn't you?"

The mug clinks against the marble when I put it down with a little too much force. My spine stiffens. "Even if I did, is that any of your business?"

"It's messy. Isla likes her. Are you just going to kick Layla out of your life when your daughter is attached to her? You need to *think*, Leif."

"I didn't know I'd wake up to a lecture from the biggest libertine in Manhattan. Who are you to tell me what's messy and what isn't? You'll fuck anything that moves. You're probably just jealous I got there before you did."

My words come out sharp, and I narrow my gaze at my friend. Does he want Layla?

Marcus meets my gaze. "I sleep around, sure. But I don't have a daughter."

His words hit me like a slap across the face, because they echo exactly what I've been thinking. I should never have asked Layla out yesterday. I should have had one drink as planned, offered her a ride home, then said goodbye and forgotten all about her.

"Nothing happened," I tell him. It's a blatant lie, obviously. But if I tell myself that we didn't technically have sex, maybe I can pretend none of the prelude to it happened, either.

"I don't believe you," Marcus answers.

"I don't feel like being lectured by a man who just a few days ago was telling me he slept with seven different women in seven days," I growl, glancing across the room to make sure my precocious little sponge isn't eavesdropping.

Isla has started some music and is going through ballet positions, oblivious.

I turn back to Marcus. "It was nothing. We had a few drinks and came back here to sleep it off."

"To sleep it off," he answers flatly. His uptilted emerald eyes regard me from under coal-black brows. Marcus comes from mixed ancestry, with a Spanish grandmother on one side, Chinese grandfather on the other, and various European bloodlines mixing to create the chiseled perfection he calls a face. That perfect face is currently looking utterly unimpressed with me.

"Yes. Sleep. You know, when you close your eyes and wake up the next morning."

"Don't be an asshole."

I snort, moving to fill up my mug again. "Me? You're the one who barged in here and started lecturing me about my private life."

There's a taut pause, and finally Marcus lets out a low chuckle. "So you didn't sleep with her," he says quietly. "Otherwise you wouldn't be nearly so high-strung."

"I'm not high-strung," I answer through gritted teeth.

He just blinks those green eyes at me, his perfect face blank. "No, of course not."

"This is a pointless conversation. Nothing happened. Nothing will happen."

"That's good, because your mother mentioned hiring Layla to do another event for her."

I whip my head around so fast my brain rattles against my skull. Or at least that's what it feels like when pain explodes across my temple. "She what?"

"After you left to get Dani's hospital bag. Your mother told me she was impressed with Layla and had already resolved to never hire the event planners who bailed on her. She wants to plan a party for her thirty-fifth wedding anniversary, and she wants to hire Layla."

Elbows on the counter, I drop my head into my hands and groan.

"You can't get involved with Layla, Leif." His voice is quiet yet unyielding.

Marcus knows my history. He knew Isla's mother, and he predicted the train wreck before it happened. If I were a wise man, I'd listen to him. I'd heed his words, because Marcus sees things with surprising clarity.

He knew my ex, Abby, was having doubts about the baby, and he tried to warn me. All throughout her pregnancy, Marcus told me he wasn't sure about the woman I thought I loved. He said she was fickle. He said she'd run the first chance she got.

The truth is, Abby didn't have to run. She did something infinitely worse—she walked away. She gave birth to Isla, looked at the perfect little girl she'd just brought into the world, and decided motherhood wasn't what she wanted.

I didn't get it. I still don't get it. Isla is the best kid I've ever met. She's smart and funny and sweet, really good at ballet, a dedicated student, and a great daughter. Who wouldn't want to be her mom? Who would choose to turn their back on a little girl like that?

Marcus saw it before it happened. He tried to warn me, but I brushed it off. When Abby told me she didn't want to be a mother mere hours after she'd given birth, I thought it was some postpartum problem. I thought she'd come to her senses eventually.

But she left. She *left*. Eyes wide open, mind clear, Abby turned her back on us and walked away.

Truthfully, it broke me.

That's why women and Isla don't mix. That's why I don't bring my dates near my daughter—because I won't let anyone do that to Isla again. Not when she's old enough to remember. Not when it's my job as a father to protect her and care for her.

But Layla... Layla is different. The party was proof. She *knows* my daughter. Sees her. I can feel it—you can't fake that kind of care. It's like the way Layla speaks about her sister or her grandparents—there's bone-deep love there. Layla isn't the type of woman to walk away from a difficult situation.

She's been on the receiving end. Layla's mother walked away, and Layla knows how much it hurts. She wouldn't do it to anyone else.

"Layla is nothing like Abby," I say through clenched teeth,

glancing over at Isla to make sure my daughter is still occupied with her practice.

"You barely know her."

"And you don't know her at all."

"Leif."

"Marcus."

"I've seen this look on your face before. It was more than a night of fun. You're infatuated. It won't end well." He sighs, running his fingers through his black hair. "I'm not saying this to be a dick, Leif. I'm saying it because it's true. I get that you want to meet someone worthy of you and your daughter, but I don't want to see you hurt again. It took you years to recover. Years, Leif."

His words rankle. Yes, it took years to recover from the broken husk Abby left behind. I threw myself into my work, pouring all my hurt and frustration into tough negotiations and impossible odds. I attacked opportunities for new developments and built the business into what it is today.

But I feel...fragmented. My business is wholly separate from my home life, which is separate again from my love life. Layla blurs the lines. When Layla's eyes sparkled with laughter, I felt some seismic shift in the way my heart functions. I saw a flash of a future I could have where the woman of my dreams was part of my life the way a partner should be.

"I just don't want you to end up hurt. It'll only hurt Isla in the end." Marcus's voice is neutral, but I see red.

Anger whips through me, lashing against my ribs. Those words clang through me like a church bell, bringing up every lasting scar marring the mottled lump of my heart.

Does he think I *want* to hurt Isla? Does he think I'm pursuing Layla without thinking of all the implications?

Instead of answering, I follow Isla's lead and clear my plate. Marcus's eyes are like a brand on my back, tracing my movements through the kitchen until I let out a sigh and turn around. I lean against the counter and cross my arms.

That's when I see something resting on the floor in the corner of the kitchen. Bending down, I pick up a worn wallet no bigger than my palm.

I glance at Marcus, who sighs, resigned. "It's hers, isn't it?"

Opening the wallet, I pull out the first card I see—a debit card so beat-up the corners are peeling apart. "Layla Reynolds," I say, reading the name on the card. "Yeah. It's hers."

"She left it on purpose?"

I shake my head. "I threw her purse across the room. It must have fallen out."

"You *threw*—" Marcus interrupts himself, closing his eyes to massage his temples. "Leif, you need to take a step back and *think*. You're acting like a hormonal teen."

"I can't help the fact that she lost her wallet, Marcus," I protest. I meet his gaze and see nothing but hardness in his eyes. Dropping my arms to my side, I give him a tired sigh. "Say it. Say what you want to say."

"You shouldn't get involved with her. I know you're thinking of returning her wallet in person. You should just courier it over to her place and be done with it. Your mother will hire her, and you should treat her with polite courtesy and nothing more. You know I'm right. You know you're playing with fire."

"Why do you care?" My voice has a sharp edge to it that I don't even bother hiding.

"Isla needs you to be strong, Leif. You're all she has. What happens when things between you and Layla fall apart? What happens when you go back to that dark place where all you can do is work?" Marcus's shoulders soften and he puts up his palms. "Look," he starts again, voice gentling, "I want you to be happy. I do. And hooking up with the nanny worked with Emil, but Leif, that was one in a million. If you bring Layla around, Isla will get attached. Are you ready for that? Have you thought about the consequences?"

I gulp my coffee as an alarm goes off in the bedroom. "I need to get Isla to her ballet class. Isla!" I call out. The dog lifts his head and blinks at me while my daughter twirls. "Time to get ready for ballet!"

She stops spinning. "I need help with my hair!" she screams, way louder than necessary. She sprints toward me with Bear on her heels. "Can you call Layla back? She does the bun way tighter than you do and it never comes apart. Plus, she can do a French braid. Even Harriet can't do a French braid."

"Layla's busy, kiddo. You're stuck with me."

"I'll do your hair," Marcus says. "I have four sisters and twelve nieces. I know how to do a bun."

Isla lets out a long-suffering sigh. "Fine. But you have to brush it back so it's *smooth*." She runs her hand over the top of her head to demonstrate. "Otherwise it doesn't look right. And make it tight so it doesn't fall out. You have to tuck the ends in."

"I'm going to go shower and get dressed," I tell them, lips twitching.

"Okay but hurry up, Daddy," my imperious daughter commands. "You should be dressed already."

Smiling, I drop a kiss on my daughter's hair and walk toward my room.

When my back is turned, my smile slips off my lips. I know Marcus is trying to be the voice of reason. He doesn't want me or Isla to get hurt.

But really... Would it be so bad to see where things go with Layla?

TWENTY-TWO
LAYLA

MY PHONE BUZZES when I exit the subway station in Newark. I pause, stepping to the side to avoid the flow of people on the sidewalk and glance at the screen. There are two messages.

The first is from an unknown number.

Unknown: Mrs. Sorensen was impressed with Isla's party yesterday. She'd like to meet to discuss another event. Please reply if you're interested. This is her assistant, Patty.

My heart pounds and I have to lean against the grimy wall to stay upright. Leif's mother wants to *hire me?* I let out a little squeal, clapping my hand over my mouth. A stream of people flows past me, oblivious to the excitement coursing through me.

Maybe this morning isn't such a disaster, after all.

But the second message is from someone I know.

Joe: Hey Layla! Missed you at the bar last night. Are we still on for dinner and a drink tonight?

I bite back a groan. I forgot about Joe. Last time I was at the bar, on Thursday night, I told Joe I was free today. I told myself that I'd be done working for Leif and it would be a good thing to move on.

I didn't know I'd end up spending last night in Leif's bed.

I stare at the message, fighting with myself. I'm not interested in Joe, so I should refuse. But am I uninterested simply because I'm hung up on my billionaire boss?

Of course I am. It's pathetic, really.

I need to move on as quickly as possible. As they say, the best way to get over someone is to get under someone else.

Except I absolutely do not *want to get under Joe.*

Ignoring that little detail, I type out a quick message. I tell Joe to meet me at the local Italian restaurant by my place at seven o'clock. As soon as I hit send, my stomach drops. I might have just made a horrible mistake, but I immediately push that niggle aside. Joe is cute. He has a good job, he's nice, and he would surely make a good boyfriend.

I should be happy to go on a date with him. There's nothing wrong with him at all.

Instead of dwelling on all the reasons I'm not interested in Joe, I focus on the first text I read—the one that could quite literally be life-changing. *That's* what I want to think about.

So, my mind on the good news, I hurry down the streets and take a deep breath of crisp, late-winter air.

Soon, the weather will warm. Summer will come, and I'll be able to enjoy the city at its best. And who knows? Maybe I wasn't meant to be a nanny. Maybe I can become an event planner—after all, rich people all know each other, don't they? This could be my big break.

This could be The Job, but for real this time.

By the time I make it to my four-story walkup apartment, I can't keep the smile off my face. Things will work out. I'll talk to Mrs. Sorensen's assistant, I'll keep food in the fridge, my grandparents will get to keep their house, and everything will be A-OK.

Leif will be a distant memory, as he should be.

When I enter the apartment, Emma is once again sprawled over the living room floor with books and scribbled papers spread out in front of her. I feel a pang in my chest when I think of Leif's gorgeous properties and how I'd love to give my sister a proper study space.

Emma doesn't seem to mind. She rolls onto her back and throws her arm over her face with a groan. "I'm going cross-eyed, Layla. I can't study anymore. I'll go blind."

"That bad, huh?" I drop my bag onto the floor and flop into the worn sofa near Emma's feet. "Organic chemistry again?"

She shifts her arm and peeks underneath it, grimacing. "College is so much harder than I thought it would be."

I nudge her toes. "You can do it."

"You don't get it, Layla. It's *hard*. I have three assignments due tomorrow and three hundred pages of case studies to read by Tuesday. I don't know if I *can* do it."

I slump down and lean my head against the back of the couch, giving her a sympathetic smile. Despite her grousing, my sister is on track to get to medical school by the time she's allowed to drink legally.

My resume, on the other hand, includes one year of an unfinished event planning course. Is it any wonder I've been trying to make sure Emma makes it, even if I never do?

"What are you learning about?"

"I don't even want to talk about it," Emma answers with a scowl. She pushes a textbook with her elbow as if the mere sight of it disgusts her.

I grin. Emma is so responsible and studious, sometimes I forget she's barely seventeen.

But like any other teenager, she's perceptive and not afraid of being nosy. She lifts herself up on her elbows and tilts her head. "Where were you last night? How's Dani's baby?"

I clear my throat. "The baby hasn't arrived yet, actually. I'm going to shower and head back to the city to check on her."

Maybe if I just ignore the other question, Emma will drop it.

No such luck. My sister arches her brows. "And last night...? You sent me a text that you'd be back this morning, but you never told me what you were doing. And you look..." She frowns.

Like I had a night of hot, dirty, feral sex? If only. I need a shower.

"Disheveled," my sister finishes.

"I went out with a few friends to celebrate," I answer placidly. Needing to change the subject, I blurt out, "The party was a success. Your cupcake tower was genius—a big hit with the kids." I paint a hopeful smile on my face. "Mrs. Sorensen's assistant texted me this morning. She said she wants to hire me for another event."

Emma sits up, eyes bright. "Awesome. She'll pay you to plan it?"

"I certainly hope so." My fake smile widens.

She brings her long legs in to sit cross-legged. "Whatever you're thinking of charging, you should triple it."

I start. "What?"

"Rich people value things that cost a lot. If you charge more, she'll respect you and assume you're worth it."

A laugh slips out of me. "Emma... I'm not sure that's how it works."

"Of course it is," my sister answers. "If you undercharge, she won't hire you. Plus, she's loaded, right? Get everything you can out of her!"

"I don't even know what the event is," I answer, squirming uncomfortably. "All I've ever planned is an eight-year-old's birthday party. I don't even know if I can do anything bigger."

"Of course you can," my sister replies. "Don't be silly."

Unshakeable confidence in me—that's what Emma has. My

heart thuds, and my sister gets up as if she didn't just give me the biggest compliment ever.

But...tripling my fee to plan a billionaire family's event? I don't know... I don't even know how much event planners cost!

"Okay, I just googled typical event planner fees. Weddings are more, of course, but here, I'll email it over," Emma says as she bends over her phone's screen, apparently reading my mind. "You can do a flat fee, a percentage of expenses, an hourly rate... Hmm..." She bites her lip, lifting her head to meet my eyes. "You should go for a percentage of expenses. I bet she'll want the best of everything. Say, twenty percent of expenses? If she spends a hundred grand, you'll make *twenty thousand dollars*. For one event." Her eyes shine. "Awesome."

I nearly choke. "Emma, stop. This is ridiculous. I'll charge her an hourly rate and triple what I make at the café just to make you happy."

"Absolutely not," my sister—my *seventeen-year-old sister*—replies. "You make minimum wage. That's way too little. Do the percentage."

"That's taking advantage of her."

"It's *business*."

I just came from a penthouse in Manhattan where I had to sneak out of a billionaire's bed. I am *not* in the mood to get lectured by my seventeen-year-old sister about money. The sheets I slept in are probably worth more than the sum total of all my belongings.

Still... What if Emma was right? If I could make that much money from one event, I could pay for a lawyer for my grandparents' problem. Rent would be covered. I'd finally, *finally* have a bit of stability.

Standing up, I walk over to the kitchen. Our apartment is basically one small room with a peninsula-type counter separating the living and kitchen spaces, so Emma's eyes follow me the whole way. I turn on the coffee machine and start brewing a pot.

"Layla."

"Yeah?" I turn to open the refrigerator, even though I know it'll be empty. Well, not completely empty—there are two soft, floppy carrots, some mustard, and a jar of pickle juice with half a pickle floating in it. Even with my creative meal skills, I can't do anything with this.

"Look at me," my sister says, and I hear the rustling of clothes and papers as she stands up.

I turn around and lean against the counter separating us. "What?"

The coffee machine gurgles as Emma meets my gaze. "You're worth twenty percent."

"No one would pay that," I protest, even though I'm not sure it's true. "Aren't rich people usually cheap? If I come on too strong, she'll laugh in my face and I won't get the job."

"And what if you do?" Sass drips off her words as my little sister tilts her head. She scoffs. "You need to start valuing yourself more. You did a fancy kids' party in less than a week, and you spent probably fifty hours planning it. You haven't slept. You've barely eaten. How much money would you have gotten if you'd charged twenty percent of expenses?"

I bite my lip. Between the catering, the drinks, the furniture rental, the ballet dancers... I would have made a few grand. Leif would have paid it without blinking.

I huff. "I don't want to talk about it, Emma." Maybe all those wealthy kids at her college are putting ideas in her head. Valuing myself more? How can I value myself when the whole world keeps screaming at me that I'm worth nothing?

I don't even want to know how Leif freaking Sorensen would have treated me if he'd woken up in time to see me off this morning.

Turning back to the coffee maker, I make my voice as hard as possible. "Emma, I can't afford to be greedy. Your next scholarship disbursement won't come until the fall semester. You insisted on paying for the lawyer's consultation next week, and we need to save up for any legal fees after that. We need rent, food, bills."

"Yeah? I'm not really seeing your point. Wouldn't it be better to have twenty thousand extra dollars?"

Grr. I hate when Emma uses that sassy teenage logic on me. I don't even know what the event is! I have no idea how much Mrs. Sorensen would want to spend. I don't even know if she was serious about hiring me. "You just let me worry about that. You do your assignments, do your reading, and get that degree. I want to be calling you Dr. Reynolds in a few years, and I'm not going to let you worry about things that are my responsibility. We have a deal, don't we? You worry about school, and I worry about everything else."

Emma's face screws up. "Layla..."

"No. I won't hear it." I pull a chipped mug from the cupboard and fill it with coffee. It smells strong and bitter and I gulp down a scalding mouthful. "The deal is you stay here, you study, and I take care of the rest. Once you're a doctor with a fat salary, you can repay the favor."

"I can get more loans," Emma says. "Then you won't be working yourself to the bone to support the two of us. You could find a job you actually enjoy. You could even finish your event planning course! You could do something *you* want."

I almost laugh. Something I want? When was the last time I did something that I actually wanted to do—other than last night?

My heart aches.

I woke up in a gorgeous apartment with a gorgeous man, and it only highlighted how obvious it is that I don't belong in that world. My little sister, barely seventeen years old, thinks I'm undervaluing myself, but she doesn't know the stakes. If I fail, we'll be on the street, and so will our grandparents.

How am I supposed to value myself beyond survival when all I know is how to scrape by?

Both our futures—and our grandparents'—rest on my shoulders. Emma's more than mine. My life is already passing me by, but I won't let Emma put her future at risk.

Event planning? A future? For me? Please.

"We don't need you to get a loan out, Em. Keep your debt as low as possible until medical school. I don't want you paying back hundreds of thousands of dollars for the rest of your life. We have enough with the grants, my job, and the scholarships to get by. We'll figure it out. We always do."

"What about you?" Emma's eyes are wide as she stares at me.

"I'll be fine, kid," I tell her. "I'm going to call Mrs. Sorensen's assistant, and after that I'll talk to Linda about any open nannying positions. It's all under control."

Liar, liar, panties on fire.

"But what about you?" Emma says softly.

"I'm good, Em." I put a brave smile on my face and wrap my arms around her. "Hey, how about we go out for breakfast?"

Emma brightens. "We can make a game plan for your call with the Sorensen assistant! Twenty percent will seem like nothing once I've got you convinced."

I give her a flat stare. "You're like a dog with a bone."

My sister laughs, winking.

"Let me just make sure I have enough cash for breakfast." I reach for my purse, look inside, and frown. I dig through the bag and curse under my breath. Then, heart pounding, I grab the whole thing and dump the contents on the counter.

"*Shit.*" I stare at the contents of my purse in horror. There are six lip glosses, four tampons, old receipts and candy wrappers, my phone with my MetroCard strapped onto the back of the case...but no wallet.

Emma leans over the kitchen's peninsula counter. "What's wrong?"

"My wallet. It's not here." I turn my purse inside out and check the lining, my stomach sinking lower and lower with every second.

Groaning, I drop my head in my hands.

My wallet is either at the club, on the floor of a Rolls-Royce...or at Leif's place.

When I think of my things scattered all over the kitchen

counter this morning, I have a fairly good idea where my wallet happens to be...which means I'm going to have to see Leif again, and soon. I won't be able to scurry to his townhouse, direct the cleanup, then run away.

"Are you going to tell me where you were last night, then?" Emma crosses her arms and arches a brow. "Or will you keep deflecting?"

"Don't you have assignments to finish?"

"Deflection it is, then," Emma says with a grin.

We both freeze when the apartment buzzer sounds. I stare at the intercom by the door for a few seconds before crossing the space. "Yeah?" I say into the microphone.

A deep voice answers, "It's me," Leif says. "I have your wallet."

TWENTY-THREE
LAYLA

THE SECONDS that pass between Leif's words and the moment I buzz him up last an eternity. In that moment, I feel a thousand different emotions.

I feel elation that all he had to say was, "It's me," as if we share that kind of bond already. Sheer terror that he's going to see my tiny, rundown apartment. Horror that I still haven't showered. Excitement that I'll see him again so soon.

"Uh, Layla?" Emma calls out. She's standing on the balcony, staring down. "There's a freaking Rolls-Royce outside the building. It's the shiniest car I've ever seen."

That whole mess of emotions boils down to a hard ball of sheer panic that sits like dead weight in my gut. I spring away from the door and sprint to the bathroom, yelping when I see my own reflection. Attacking my rat's nest with a brush, I tame my locks into a messy bun, then run my fingers under my eyes to wipe away most of the mascara smudges.

This is even worse than last night, which I didn't know was even possible. Raccoons would shudder at the sight of me.

No time to get changed, but I don't want Leif to see me in the same clothes as I was wearing last night. Hyperventilating, I grab a robe off the back of the bathroom door and toss it on just in time to hear the hard knock of a fist against our apartment door.

I tear the bathroom door open only to see Emma standing at the front door, stepping aside to let a literal billionaire who drives around town in a half-million-dollar car into our apartment.

Leif's eyes cut straight to me and he raises his hand, my old, stained wallet held between his thumb and forefinger. "You left this at my place."

Emma is standing behind Leif, and her eyes grow wide. She mouths the words, *You left it at his place?* and I pretty much die inside.

"You didn't have to bring it over," I say, gripping the robe closed with my fist as I force my lips into a smile. "But thank you."

Leif shrugs. "Maybe I wanted an excuse to see you again."

Emma puts the back of her hand to her forehead and pretends to faint. I'm going to kill her.

Moving quickly, I shuffle across the room and accept the wallet that Leif extends toward me. My fingers brush his as I take it from him, and a jolt of pure, white-hot desire travels through my core. Leif's eyes flick to our hands and he holds on to the wallet for a moment before letting go.

Emma, still hiding behind him, fans herself.

"Well, thanks," I say, giving him a polite smile. *Operation: Kick Leif Out of my Dingy Apartment Before I Die of Embarrassment* is officially underway.

"You left before I could talk to you," Leif says.

"I'll give you some privacy!" Emma finally speaks, hopping toward the stack of papers strewn over the floor.

"That's okay, Em—"

"I'm going to my room!" My sister vaults over the couch and starts running away. The daggers I shoot at her with my eyes bounce right off and clatter onto the floor.

Leif's lush lips—lips that were all over my body approximately eight hours ago—slide into a smile. "There's no need. Emma, right?" He lets the word hang.

My sister pauses near her room. "Yeah." A bright-red blush washes over her cheeks, which I think might just be karma for her little performance a minute ago. "Layla's sister."

"I'm Leif," he replies.

Leif walks further into our apartment and picks up a heavy textbook. "Organic chemistry?" He mock-shudders. "I think I still have scars from when I took it. I did one year of science in undergrad and immediately switched to business. I don't know how you do it." He smiles at my sister, whose blush deepens. "Layla tells me you're at NYU."

My sister, usually snarky and self-assured, looks positively flustered. She flicks her hair over her shoulder and shrugs. "Studying Prehealth. I just started this year."

Leif arches his brows and nods, his eyes flicking to mine. "Impressive."

"She got all the brains in the family," I say, throat tight. "Well, anyway, it was nice of you to stop by—"

"Love the apartment," Leif interrupts. He glances around at the shabby secondhand furniture I've collected over the years with an assessing eye. His gaze travels to the far wall which has a gallery of punchy, colorful photos I've found in various thrift stores.

Then he glances at the corner of the room, where mold has once again started to bloom. I've called my landlord about it, but he's been as proactive as the super with the icy steps outside. As in, not proactive at all. This apartment building is falling apart around us, but what can I do?

Leif's gaze travels from the mold to the peeling paint around the window frame to the deep, jagged crack on the front wall, then thankfully back to the photos.

Emma helped me arrange the frames on the wall. It took us hours to set them up in a random-yet-elegant arrangement, each photo in its own black frame. Now, looking at it through the lens of the apartment I just left this morning, the whole apartment looks cheap, tacky, and on the verge of falling apart.

I cringe.

Leif walks over to the wall and inspects the photos one by one. His gaze shifts to a selfie of Emma and me sitting at the top of the Ferris wheel at the Jersey Shore. Curling my fingers into my palms, I resist the urge to grab him by the arm and toss him out the door. Or the window.

This feels...intimate. Like he's seeing some part of me I don't want him to see.

The photo he's looking at is a vivid memory. I scraped together all my money and took her to the Shore for her ninth birthday. Those years were hard. I'd just graduated and had even less money than I do now. Grandpa's heart was bad, and they couldn't afford to support us. I was sleeping on my grandparents' guest room floor so Emma could have the bed, trying to scrape together enough money to get our own place. When I told Emma I was taking her out for her birthday, her eyes lit up like nothing else. We ate ice cream and laughed and rode the Ferris wheel until I ran out of money. It was one of the best days I can remember from my teenage years.

Leif stares at the photo for a long while, our ruddy cheeks and wide smiles, before straightening up. His eyes meet mine and he gives me a soft smile, then he shifts his gaze to contents of my purse still strewn across the countertop, receipts and tampons and candy wrappers and all.

Why do I keep literal trash in my purse? What is wrong with me?

I close my eyes.

Not only is there a billionaire inspecting my home with a magnifying glass, but he happens to be the billionaire I nearly slept with last night... Except I *fell asleep when he was on top of me.*

Kill me now. Seriously. If a sinkhole appeared beneath my feet, I'd thank my lucky stars.

"Have you eaten?" Leif blurts. "There's a hole-in-the-wall brunch place not far from here that used to have the best potatoes I've ever eaten."

I shift my weight from foot to foot. *Operation: Kick Leif Out of my Dingy Apartment Before I Die of Embarrassment* has just turned into *Operation: Get Rid of Leif Before I Do Something Stupid. Again.*

"Nope," Emma interjects. "Layla hasn't eaten a thing. I'm worried about her, actually. She's definitely low on micronutrients. You should make sure she has something healthy." My sister gives me an angelic smile, and I mentally slap duct tape over her mouth as I send more eye-daggers her way.

My mind whirls as I try to come up with an appropriate excuse as to why I can't have morning-after brunch with Leif.

It's not that I don't want to. Of course I want to! The man is sex on legs. Six-foot-four, broad shoulders, a mess of blond hair begging to be stroked. He was basically plucked from my wildest fantasies—and that was *before* he kissed me like the world was ending. And did...everything else.

If I have brunch with him, one of two things will happen. Either it'll be awkward as hell and I'll die of embarrassment all over again, or it'll be magic and it'll leave me wanting more.

So, no. I can't go to brunch with Leif. Or breakfast, or lunch, or dinner, or drinks. I can't have him standing in my apartment in his custom-tailored clothing and expensive-smelling cologne. I can't feel the heat of those deep blue eyes sweeping over my body, and I can't listen to him asking my sister polite questions about her studies.

Leif needs to *leave.* And I need to get back to the reality of my life. I'll help him clean up the party, I'll go to the hospital to visit Dani, meet his mother's assistant, and that will be the end of it. Bye-bye, fantasy man.

"I'm sorry, Leif, I can't go to brunch with you." Leif needs to walk away, and I'll keep the memories of last night frozen in amber, preserved for the rest of time.

Then a buzz starts in his pocket, and I motion to it. "You can take that."

He pulls out his phone and glances at it. "Shit. It's my daughter. I hadn't realized the time. Her ballet class is almost over. I don't have time for brunch, I have to get back to Manhattan." Those beautiful blue eyes flick up to mine. "Want a ride into town? I was going to visit Dani and Emil later. Raincheck on brunch?"

Did he not hear the part where I told him I couldn't go to brunch? Not now, not ever?

"Yep, she'll take a raincheck," Emma says, giving me a very meaningful stare. "And she'd love a ride. She said she needed to help you clean up after your daughter's party too, so you can just go ahead and drive her to your place."

Honestly, I think my sister is the devil incarnate. There's no other explanation for the way she acts.

"Good." Leif nods. He strides to the door and opens it. "I'll wait for you downstairs."

I'm still standing on the same spot on the floor when the door closes behind him, wondering what the hell just happened.

He'll wait for me downstairs? He'll give me a ride?

Oh, no. No, no, no.

I don't want to see his face when he realizes I'm not as special as he thinks I am. I don't want to feel the heartbreak when I wait for him to call after he's moved on from me. My life is hard enough as it is; I can't take any more heartbreak.

Emma needs me to provide for her. I need to get a job, keep

my head down, and make sure the two of us make it through the next few years. After that, I can date. Once I'm not responsible for my little sister's future, then I can think about finding love.

What am I even talking about? Love? Last night wasn't love. Last night was hot, messy sex—or it would have been if I hadn't lost my chance and *fallen asleep*.

No, I need to nip this in the bud. Priority number one is getting another job, hiring a lawyer for my grandparents, and making sure Emma and I can keep ahead of our rent and bills. The fastest way to do that is to call Leif's mother and make sure she hires me. Anything beyond that is on the back burner.

Ergo, spending time with Leif is a Bad Idea.

Groaning, I slump against the wall and drop my head into my hands. I don't lift my gaze until I hear Emma approach. She stands in front of me and clears her throat.

I peek through my fingers at her. "What?"

"'Out with friends?' Isn't that what you said?" She crosses her arms. "I may be seventeen, but I'm not an idiot, Layla."

"Leif is a friend, and we were out."

"Uh-huh." She scoffs. "Where can I get a *friend* like him?"

"Nowhere until you're at least eighteen. Or eighty."

Emma rolls her eyes. "Right."

"You should be studying. I need to shower. Then, thanks to you, Leif is giving me a ride back into the city. I could have had a nice, quiet subway ride. But no. My little sister wanted to stir things up."

She grins a devilish grin. "Yes. It is thanks to me, isn't it?"

"You're evil."

"I'm a genius."

"An evil genius."

Emma laughs. "Go shower. But be careful—the showerhead is loose again. I used duct tape on it this morning, but I'm not sure it'll hold."

"Wonderful. I'll add that to the ever-growing list of problems. What I wouldn't give for an apartment where the landlord actually fixes things that are broken."

"You can pretend you're mad all you want, Layla, but I know you're excited on the inside."

I scowl. She's right—and that's the problem.

"While you shower, I'll choose your outfit," she calls out, heading for my room. "I'm thinking sophisticated but sexy. You want to look like you're trying but not *too* hard, you get me?"

I roll my eyes and finally relent. "Nothing too risqué. He's still my boss. Sort of."

"Don't worry, Layla. I'm an evil genius, remember?"

Throwing her a halfhearted glare, I pull out my phone to dial Mrs. Sorensen's assistant's number, then pause. "Hey, is my black lace bodysuit clean? You borrowed it last week, right?" I call out to my sister. "I'm going out with Joe tonight."

Silence answers back. After a beat, Emma appears in my bedroom doorway. "Joe? Did I hear that right? You said Joe? Not Leif?"

I roll my eyes. "Leif was my boss up until yesterday, Layla."

"Which means today you could totally date him." She arches both brows as if to say, *duh!*

"I'm not discussing this with you."

"Joe is nice and all, but... Layla, come on. You talk about

him like he's a weird cousin you have to endure at family reunions."

I blink at my sister, then huff a laugh. "Where do you come up with this shit, Emma?"

"Me? You're the one who's going on a date with a man you feel precisely zero sexual attraction to. But sure, *I'm* the one who's talking crazy."

"Is the bodysuit clean or not?"

"Yes, it's clean and hung up in your closet." She crosses her arms. "I'm probably going to spend the night in the library tonight, so feel free to bring Joe back here after your date."

Despite my best efforts at keeping my face steady, I rear back as my lips curl. The thought of me and Joe...here...in my bed...

"See?" Emma's sass is bone deep as she purses her lips. "Weird cousin vibes. You're not into him at all."

Yeah, because he's not Leif.

"I'm not talking about this. I have to call Mrs. Sorensen's assistant back."

"Whatever." Emma disappears in my room again.

I push the thought of Joe and me getting intimate to a corner of my mind labeled *Destroy ASAP* and dial the number for Mrs. Sorensen's assistant, Patty. She answers on the first ring.

"Layla," Patty says without preamble. "Thank you for returning my text."

"Of course. What can I do for you? You mentioned an event for Mrs. Sorensen?"

"She and Mr. Sorensen are celebrating their thirty-fifth

wedding anniversary next month. She'd like to meet to discuss hiring you to plan the event. Are you free later today?"

I stand up straighter. "I—yes—of course—I'm not"—I take a deep breath—"I have the final party cleanup to do at her son's place, but I'll be free any time after two o'clock."

"Perfect. I'll send a car to Mr. Sorensen's house to pick you up at a quarter past two." She hangs up, and I just stare at my phone.

Emma pokes her head out from my bedroom. "Twenty percent of expenses, Layla," she says. "Trust me."

I let out a huffing laugh, shake my head, and walk to the bathroom to get ready. Looks like my crazy week isn't about to slow down anytime soon.

<h1 style="text-align:center">TWENTY-FOUR</h1>
<h2 style="text-align:center">LEIF</h2>

BOSS/EMPLOYEE. That should be enough for me to keep my damn distance. It doesn't matter that Layla's last day was yesterday. It's still not appropriate.

Never mind everything Marcus was saying.

Apparently my brain has disengaged from the discussion, though, because I wait in the car outside Layla's apartment until the door opens and she sweeps out in that worn-out jacket and painted-on jeans.

Elton is out in a flash, opening the door for her. A cool blast of air comes in with her, and she sits down on the seat with a sigh. "Thanks for waiting."

"We're going to make a stop first," I tell her. When Elton gets behind the wheel, I tell him to make a stop at the nearest department store. Layla sits quietly, her hands folded on her lap.

When we get to the store, I ask her to follow. It's not until we're in the women's clothing section that a suspicious look etches itself on her face.

I grab a fluffy down jacket and hold it up in front of her body. "Try that on."

"That's a Balenciaga jacket, Leif."

I glance at the display. "So it is. Try it on."

"I'm not trying on a jacket that costs"—she grabs the tag and her eyes bulge—"*three thousand, eight hundred and fifty dollars?*" She drops the tag and steps away like the jacket in my hands will jump up and infect her with some deadly disease. "No way."

"You need a new jacket."

"So I'll get one at a thrift store! I can wait until summer when everything is on clearance. My jacket is fine, and I definitely don't need a jacket that costs that much."

"Are you two finding everything okay?" a sales associate cuts in, her face a mask of politeness. Her eyes roam over me, flick to Layla, then cut back to me. Her smile brightens a bit. "Can I get a changeroom started for you?"

"Where's your sale section?" Layla blurts while I say, "We're fine."

The woman arches a condescending brow at Layla, and it makes me want to rip her head right off her shoulders. No one should look at her like that—like she's some kind of insect that's beneath them. No one.

"We're fine. My—" What is Layla to me? "Layla was just going to try on this jacket."

Layla crosses her arms and huffs. "I am not putting that on."

"Fine. I'll buy it and if it doesn't fit, I'll buy you another one." I bundle the down up and hand it to the sales associate.

"Leif, no." Layla drops her hands at her sides and gives me an exasperated look—the same way she looked at me in the jazz bar, except this time it's tinged with rage instead of humor.

It makes my cock harden to steel. I want to wrap my arm around her waist and drag her close for a punishing kiss.

Somehow, I resist. "So try it on, otherwise I'm buying as many as I need until we find one that fits." I take the jacket back from the sales associate, who's not even pretending not to enjoy the show. I unzip the jacket and hold it open.

Layla growls, gives me a death glare, and pulls her own zipper down. "You are without a doubt the most insufferable man I've ever met."

"I'm honored. Now try this on."

She huffs, then drapes her old, stained jacket over the display of multi-thousand-dollar jackets, to the horror of Ms. Sales Associate. I bite back a smile, then a groan, because Layla looks like magic in a tight white tank and a cropped cardigan. Her breasts stretch the white fabric and the cardigan falls off one shoulder, and all I want to do is unwrap her like a present.

I swallow, throat thick, and shake the jacket I'm holding in her direction.

"Calm your horses, Mr. Sorensen," she grumbles, then spins around so I can slip the jacket over her shoulders. Before she can move, I spin her around and work the zipper myself. Once it's done up all the way to her neck, I give her a once-over.

Layla answers with a flat stare. "So?"

"Looks good." I turn to the sales associate. "We'll take it."

"Leif, this is about two sizes too big." She bends her arm at the elbow to show me the four inches of excess fabric past her hand. "You're saying this looks good?"

"It looks warm."

"This is ridiculous."

"Might I suggest this style? The collar is oversized which is great for keeping warm." The sales lady holds up a bright white puffer jacket.

I tug at Layla's zipper and she bats my hands away. "When did you get so overbearing? I'm perfectly capable of dressing myself."

"This is more fun," I answer, and am surprised to realize it's the truth.

She purses her lips but allows me to pull the zipper down. She tries on the other jacket and turns to me. "What's the verdict, Your Highhandedness?"

I cross my arms and squint, then turn to the sales lady. "Does it come in black?"

"Of course." She smiles brightly and grabs a black version, sweeping it out to display it in a graceful move I'm sure she's done a thousand times.

"We'll take them both." I start walking to the cash register as Layla sputters behind me.

She stomps up to me, holding her ratty old rain jacket crumpled in one hand. "You can't spend nearly eight thousand dollars on *jackets*, Leif. I won't allow it."

I lean on the counter as the sales associate starts scanning the jacket, then reach over to unzip the one Layla's wearing. "You're not in charge here, Layla."

"I won't wear them." Her jaw clenches, chin jutting out, and it makes me want to bend her over and smack her ass to teach her not to sass me like that.

"You will, because we're going to burn that sad excuse of nylon you call a coat."

Layla vibrates beside me as I tug the jacket off her shoulders, using the excuse to get nearer to her and brush my hands down her arms. Her eyelids droop as her pulse flutters in her neck.

In a rustle of puffy down, the second jacket goes on the counter and I hold out my credit card, eyes still on Layla. Her cheeks are awash with red and her eyes are shooting flames. I've never wanted anyone so badly in my entire life.

Once the payment is processed, I nod to the jackets. "Which one do you want to wear?"

Teeth grinding, Layla glares at me for a moment, and I just reply with a placid, blank expression on my face. Finally, my heart leaps when her shoulders soften. She jerks her chin. "The black one."

When she's safely ensconced in the puffy down monstrosity, something settles in the depths of my heart. It feels good to take care of her, to know that I'm the one who has the privilege to do it. I'm the man who should be providing for her, protecting her, cherishing her. Me.

If only she'd let me buy her a new apartment. I could even get her one in the new tower we're building a few blocks over from her place if that elderly couple ever decides to do the right thing and accept our offer.

"Can we get to work now?" she sasses, arching a brow at me.

"Or did you want to visit the jewelry section on the way out? I wouldn't mind a nice diamond tennis bracelet for all the galas I attend. Maybe a designer gown while we're at it. I can wear it while I wash your toilets. Oh, and how about an all-expenses trip to France?" She turns to the sales associate, who's still hovering nearby pretending not to listen. "You wouldn't happen to know what's fashionable in Paris this time of year, would you?"

My lips twitch. "Your wish is my command, Layla, but be quick, because Isla's ballet lesson ends in twenty minutes and traffic is pretty heavy. I'll ask Regina to book some flights for you."

Layla just rolls her eyes and stomps toward the exit. I don't even try to bite back my grin.

WE PICK UP ISLA, who natters on about ballet positions and hairstyles and leotards, and I can't keep any of it straight. All I can do is notice the way Layla burrows into her jacket whenever we're outside. She doesn't tremble with cold anymore.

I should have bought her the jacket days ago.

The three of us head home again, just in time for Layla to call the rental company to pick up their gear. Harriet arrives in the meantime to watch Isla this afternoon, and Isla sits at the kitchen island while Harriet fixes us both some lunch.

It should feel like life is getting back to normal with Harriet here, but it feels like the opposite. Like life is about to get worse.

When my daughter is fed and busy reading in the TV room, I watch Layla coordinating the cleanup and furniture moving. She's *good*. There's this energy about Layla when she's in the midst of party planning that isn't there at any other time.

As much as I'd love to keep Layla close to me, to have her as my daughter's nanny full-time, it's plain as day that her calling isn't taking care of children.

Heart in my throat, I retreat into my office to bury myself in work. The plans for the Newark development still have a few issues, so I busy myself looking over every detail. Work never fails to sober me up, to strip away the emotion that seems to have invaded every other aspect of my life. With work, I can hold myself apart from all that and be a logical, successful man who built an empire.

A while later, I exit my office to find Layla gone. She's left to meet my mother about my parents' wedding anniversary party, and it feels like all the separate parts of my life are mixing together. The perfectly separate compartments I've so carefully constructed are being melded together one by one.

A week ago, I was upset about it. Now it feels...right.

"Looks like you had an interesting week without me," Harriet says, her face a perfectly blank mask.

I snap my eyes away from the front door and give her a flat stare.

She just shrugs, a little smile playing over her lips.

Harriet might see something between me and Layla, but she doesn't know how easily Layla twists me up in knots. She doesn't know that Layla has torn through my defenses like so much tissue paper. Everything is muddled. Family, relationships, women...

The only thing I have left that's truly separate is my business. That, at least, is easy.

So, as Harriet takes care of my daughter and my household staff buzzes around me, I once again throw myself into my work. The uncomplicated contracts, schedules, and staff issues that need to be handled. Waiting in my email inbox are dozens of messages that just came in, including a notification from my legal team that the elderly couple blocking the Newark development have indicated they'll fight us.

Instead of being upset about the news, I feel excited. Finally, something normal, typical. My home life is being turned around by a blond-haired woman with a smoky, seductive laugh, but business is still business. I can fight for the condo development and battle it out with this stubborn old couple until they fold under the pressure.

Work makes sense when nothing else does.

My lawyers sent through a long report including all the areas we might be exposed to legal action and how they plan to fight it. We're in a strong position, they say. This could even work out to our advantage.

I assume, judging by the fees they charge, that my lawyers mean this whole mess will work out to *their* advantage, not mine. But I'll pay them, because building this condo building in Newark is exactly the type of expansion my company needs.

Plus, it's exactly the distraction I need to remind myself that there's more to life than a beautiful woman who confuses all the rules I've set for myself.

I work until Isla knocks on my office door and tells me dinner is ready. Blinking, I realize hours have passed. Layla must be home by now, and I wonder if my mother decided to hire her. If she's wearing the jacket and boots I bought her. If she was serious about the diamond bracelet and new purse. If she's thinking of me, missing me, needing me.

I shut my computer down and follow my daughter to the kitchen, then give in when she asks me if she can sleep over at one of her ballet friends' houses tonight.

Harriet already packed Isla's bag for the night, so clearly she realizes just how easy it is for Isla to get what she wants in this house. I watch the two of them leave with Elton, then I sink down onto my sofa, which is back in its original position. My living room is pristine, with not a speck of dirt or glitter or cake crumbs to betray the fact that a party happened here just yesterday.

I look at the door to the TV room and feel a pang in my chest. That's where I kissed Layla. Where I dragged her to my chest and felt that voice in my head screaming that it was right. It was good. It was exactly where she was supposed to be.

And I can't stand not feeling that way right now. I can't stand the fact that she's on the other side of the Hudson River, that she's in that shitty apartment, that she's not safe and warm here by my side.

I want her to take care of my daughter. I want her to live with us. I want her to be in my life, and for her to blur as many lines and demolish as many compartments as she needs to.

The realization hits me hard. I want *Layla*, and I don't care what I have to change to get her to stay.

I don't have time to wait for Elton. I grab my jacket, wallet, and the keys to my Mercedes S-Class sedan and head to the back of the townhouse where my single-car garage backs onto a narrow alley. From there, I stomp on the accelerator and head for the Lincoln Tunnel. Using the car's Bluetooth, I dial Layla's number.

I don't care that she was my daughter's nanny. I don't care that she'll work for my mother. I need to see her. Kiss her. Trudge through the confusion in my mind until she's in my arms and things make *sense* again.

The call rings out, and I dial once more. Again, no answer. I swear, gripping the steering wheel tighter as I make my way to New Jersey. The car purrs beneath me, gliding down the darkened streets as my heart thuds. I'm not letting Layla get away. Not tonight. Not again. She can ignore me all she wants, but I'll knock down her door if I have to.

Layla belongs beside me. I can't let her drift out of my life like every casual relationship I've had. I can't let her leave like Abby did. Layla is the one who should *stay*.

Miraculously, there's a parking spot open in front of her building. I glance up at the grimy balconies studded up the front of the old brick building, cut the engine, and march to the intercom.

"Hello?" a young voice says after I buzz.

"Is Layla there?"

"Who's this?"

I close my eyes, frustration mounting. "It's Leif Sorensen. We met this morning, Emma. I need to talk to your sister."

"Oh." There's a silence. "She's...not here."

My fingers curl into my fists, but I manage to keep my voice calm. "She's not answering her phone. Do you know where she is?"

"Um. One sec. I'll be right down."

Every second that passes makes me feel like Layla's slipping through my fingers. Irrational, but isn't that par for the course with Layla? She confuses everything—and I can't get enough of it.

Heavy clomping on the steps inside makes me look up, and I see Emma Reynolds coming down. She's wearing the white puffer jacket I bought today, and for the first time since Layla left my house today, I feel the edge of a grin coming on.

I knew she'd want to give the jacket to her sister. That's why I bought two. Layla isn't the type of woman who would let her loved ones go without.

"Hey, Leif," Emma says, hiking her backpack higher on her shoulder. "So, um..." She glances at me, then away. "Layla is, uh, busy."

"Busy?"

"Yeah. She's out." Emma clears her throat, adjusting her backpack strap again. She won't look at me.

"Out? Out where?"

"Out on a date," the girl answers, glancing at me through her lashes. Her gaze is sharp, though, and I have the strange feeling she can read my every thought on my face.

Like the pure, white-hot rage that floods my veins. Or the throat-crushing jealousy that threatens to suffocate me.

"A date?" I manage to squeeze out through clenched teeth. "A date with a man?"

A man who isn't me?

"Um, yeah." She shifts her weight. "Well, anyway, I'm going to the library. I have a midterm tomorrow, so I'll probably pull an all-nighter. Thanks for the jacket, by the way. It's really warm. Layla said she'd kill me if I spill coffee on it tonight, so I'll have to be careful." She clears her throat. "I'm babbling. Sorry. Well, goodnight!" With a bright smile and a wave, Layla's sister starts walking down the steps.

"Emma."

She stops, turns, and meets my gaze. Big, guileless eyes blink up at me. "Yes?"

"Where's Layla now?"

The girl scratches the side of her head, glances over her shoulder before turning to face me fully. She purses her lips. "She'll kill me if I tell you, Leif. It'll get blood all over this nice jacket and everything."

"Fuck the jacket," I growl. "Tell me where your sister is." *And tell me what asshole she decided was better than me.*

With a long, dramatic sigh that reminds me of Isla, Emma jerks her head down the street. "She's at the Italian restaurant on the corner. La Trattoria."

I'm down the steps between one heartbeat and the next. I'm halfway down the street when I hear Emma's voice shouting, "You owe me, Leif. Big time! I'm going to need witness protection now and everything. She'll kill me!"

Despite the stress and rage and jealousy pumping through my veins, a laugh falls from my lips and I glance over my shoulder to see Emma grinning at me. She gives me a wave, then crosses the street in the opposite direction.

If I were thinking clearly, I'd offer to drive her to the college library. It's still relatively early—barely seven-thirty—but it's dark out, and she's young. Damn it, I should be taking care of Layla's family. I *want* to take care of them, because I know it would make Layla's eyes go soft. It would show her how much I care.

But Layla is on a date.

With a man.

Who isn't me.

The sign for La Trattoria appears in the distance, and I start running.

LOOK, I have nothing against fantasy football, but when Joe asked me out on a date, I didn't think he'd walk me through every decision he made from September to January for his pretend football team for pretend points and pretend glory. I certainly didn't think he'd expect me to actually comment on his decisions like I knew what the heck he was talking about.

Sighing with relief as the waiter appears with our food, I let him place the steaming plate of pasta in front of me and smile before gulping down half my wine and asking for another glass.

"This looks good," Joe says, grabbing his fork to dig in.

"I love this restaurant," I answer.

"Next time we go out, I'll take you to my favorite pizza place. You'll love it." His eyes are glued on his plate, so he doesn't see me freeze.

Next time we go out.

Oh, no. Emma was right. This was a mistake. I said yes to

going out with Joe because it felt like Leif was out of reach and my attraction to him was—is—completely inappropriate.

But I can't do this again. I can't sit through a dinner with a man who—okay, fine, Emma was right about this too—feels like a cousin I have nothing in common with.

He's not a bad guy. He's just...

Not Leif.

"I think if I were to rank pizza," Joe says, "I'd put Neapolitan pizza at the top. Then New York style. Chicago deep dish would be way down at the bottom of the list. What do you think?"

I don't care! I want to scream. *I don't care about pizza styles or fantasy football or teamster politics or unions or ANYTHING YOU CARE ABOUT!*

I stuff my mouth full of pasta to keep myself from saying something rude. Sauce dribbles down my chin as noodles hang out of my mouth, and I chew violently while gesturing to my mouth in apology and explanation as to why I can't answer his inane questions about pizza styles—

And the front door of the restaurant bangs open. I jump, pasta hanging out of my mouth. And my heart stops.

Leif Sorensen, billionaire, single dad, business owner, and all-around hunk, is standing in the doorway looking hot as hell and awfully, terribly angry.

His eyes flash as they cut to me, and then he starts moving. His chest is heaving, but he walks slowly, deliberately across the dining room.

No, not walking. *Stalking.*

His windswept hair somehow still looks elegantly styled.

His peacoat is hanging open, scarf draped over his shoulders. His hands flex and release as they take me in where I sit. My body feels hot and cold at once. I can't move. I can hardly breathe.

And for the first time tonight, I feel unbearably turned on. My panties soak through in an instant, nipples tightening to hard points beneath my black lace bodysuit and matching black bra. My blood thrums to the beat of Leif's slow, steady steps.

Conversation dies in his wake. People's utensils stay suspended halfway to their mouths, and I just sit frozen with a huge bite of food stuck in my mouth, quickly congealing to unchewable glue.

If I try to swallow this, I'll choke.

"Layla?" Joe finally looks up from his plate and frowns at me. "Are you okay?"

"She's fine," a deep voice replies. Leif turns to the older couple beside us and politely asks if he can use one of the chairs at their table. The woman, cheeks flushed, lashes batting, waves a hand in permission.

Smooth as anything, Leif flips the chair around and arranges himself on it like he's a king.

I still have food in my mouth.

One finger at a time, Leif tugs off his leather gloves and deposits them lightly on the table in front of him. I watch him, unable to move, unable to think, unable to do anything but breathe through my nose and blink, hoping this is all just some weird, awful hallucination.

"Who the hell are you?" Joe puffs his chest out.

Nope. Not a hallucination.

Leif just blinks at him and interlaces his fingers, resting them on his crossed knee. "Oh, don't mind me. Carry on." He waves a hand at our food, his eyes moving to meet mine. "I wouldn't want to interrupt your *date*." The emphasis on the last word makes it sound like a sharp, pointy dagger aimed right at my chest.

I need to say something, but I have food in my mouth. Do I chew it for ages, swallow, and then try to defuse this situation, leaving the two men to discuss things while I finish my bite? Do I spit it out into my napkin? Do I run to the bathroom and sneak out through the window, change my name, run all the way to Mexico, and start a new life somewhere far, far away from Leif Sorensen?

"You need to leave," Joe says. "The lady and I were having a good time, and you need to go."

"Were you?" Leif's eyes are still on me. He arches a brow. "How good a time were you having, Layla? Would you prefer it if I left?"

"Yes, she would." Joe's practically vibrating with outrage on the other side of the table, but there's confusion in his gaze. Leif has such an undeniably strong presence that Joe doesn't know what to do. Everyone knows who the alpha male in this situation is.

When Leif holds up a hand to silence him, I can almost feel the temperature in the room drop, and the pressure cooker of Joe's rage crank up a few notches.

"I want to hear it from Layla. Tell me how much you're enjoying your date with a man who isn't me."

Joe starts speaking, then stops. I don't want to meet his gaze, but I can feel him staring at me. "Who is this guy, Layla? Is this your boyfriend or something?"

I have no choice. I need to spit out my food, because there's no way I can swallow past the constriction in my throat. Grabbing the cloth napkin from my lap, a part of me dies of shame as I turn my back to both of them and spit out the half-chewed food that was supposed to save me from answering an awkward question.

Bundling the napkin up, I square my shoulders and dab the corners of my mouth with an unsoiled corner of the cloth, then turn to face the interloper. "Leif," I say, painting a courteous smile on my face. "What a pleasant surprise."

His eyes darken. They're not clear blue anymore. They're dark as the ocean depths. They're stormy and dangerous and they make me want to strip down and present my body to him like an offering.

I think Mexico is a good option right about now. Or maybe an asylum. Clearly I've lost my mind.

"Wine, sir?" The waiter appears, hands clasped behind his back, face a mask of professionalism.

I've worked in restaurants. I know he's not actually asking if Leif wants wine. He's gathering intel for the hordes of kitchen and waitstaff who are staring at us and gossiping about what could possibly be happening.

Leif rattles off the name and year of a wine I've never heard of, because clearly he knows the best vintage and expects a decent restaurant to carry it. Which apparently they do, because the waiter gives him a deferential bow and scurries away.

"Layla," Joe hisses. "Who the hell is this guy?"

"This is Leif. Leif, Joe."

After a pause, the men shake, as if this isn't the most horrifying situation ever.

Joe looks furious and confused. Leif looks totally at ease, but I can sense the anger pulsing off him. When the waiter reappears and does the whole song and dance about tasting a splash of wine before nodding to accept it, Leif takes his time and acts like nothing at all is amiss.

It makes me squirm, because inexplicably, I'm turned on. I'm turned on by his arrogance and the way he swirls his wine. I'm turned on by the way he arranged his gloves on the table, and how he sat like a king on his throne. I'm turned on by the silken strands of his scent that waft over me whenever he moves.

I'm also furious. How dare he waltz in here like he owns the place? How dare he sit down like he was invited? How dare he interrupt the first date I've been on in ages, just because he feels like he owns me?

What. A. *Dick*. An arrogant, attractive asshole that I never ever *ever* should have kissed.

But Emma was right. I should never have gone out with Joe, either. I was lying to myself when I said he'd be good boyfriend material. I was grasping at straws when I told myself he was cute like a teddy bear. It was cruel of me to go out with him when I knew deep down that it would never work out.

Finally, I lift my eyes and meet Joe's gaze. He stares at me for a moment, then wilts. He clicks his tongue and crumples his napkin, tossing it on the edge of the table. "This is bullshit," he grumbles, then pushes his chair back to get up. He stares down at me and shakes his head.

"I'm sorry," I whisper. "I can explain."

But what would I say?

"Don't bother, Layla." He reaches into his wallet and tosses few bills on the table. I try to protest, but Joe is already grabbing his jacket and walking away.

The faint clinking of utensils is the only sound in the restaurant. People glance at me, then at Leif, then at the door. My cheeks burn, shame and anger and embarrassment warring inside me.

And Leif just sits there, sipping his wine, looking as bored and aristocratic as Anna Wintour at a subpar fashion show.

"You," I start, my voice a low hiss. "You have a lot of nerve."

Leif blinks, swirls his wine, and takes a sip. He places the glass down precisely where it was when he picked it up. "I could say the same about you."

"Me?" My voice is loud enough for the next table to glance over. I lower it again. "What the hell did I do wrong?"

"What was it, twenty-four hours it took you to go out with another man? I would have hoped I was worth forty-eight, at least."

"Oh, I'm sorry. I didn't realize a drunken makeout session with the great Leif Sorensen precluded me from ever dating again."

"Shall I clear the gentleman's plate?"

I jump at the waiter's question, not having noticed him return, but Leif just nods. "Thank you," he says. Then he has the nerve to order himself a meal. I gape at him, not understanding, jaw hanging all the way down to the floor, until the waiter bows again and walks away, at which point Leif finally meets my gaze.

"What are you *doing*?" I grit out.

"I'm hungry," he says, "so I ordered the risotto of the day." He calls the waiter back, and nods to my crumpled, soiled napkin. "Can you replace the napkin, please? That one seems to be dirty."

"Of course, sir," the waiter replies, grabbing my napkin before I can protest. Not that I'd have any reason to stop him from taking it, but I'm feeling very much like I need to protest about something. Anything. Everything.

"You have a lot of nerve." I lean back on my chair and grab my wine. A glint of amusement enters Leif's eyes as I take a sip, scowling over the edge of the glass.

I should grab my things and stomp out of here. I should tell Leif's mother to shove her job up her elegant ass because I want nothing to do with her family. I should tell Leif that he has no right to interrupt a date that has nothing to do with him.

Yesterday, my job with Leif ended, and good riddance. He's trouble. He'll chew me up and spit me out like I did with a glob of pasta a few minutes ago. The only person who will end up hurt is *me*.

But I stay right where I am, because Leif's nearness makes me buzz with energy and lust. I take another gulp of wine before setting it down, not wanting a repeat of last night. I'm not getting drunk tonight. I'm not making any bad decisions.

"You look beautiful," Leif says, his eyes sweeping down my body. His face hardens for a moment before I watch him force himself to relax. "When I walked in, I was...displeased...to see that you'd dressed up for another man."

I set my glass down and pop a brow. "Displeased? I think the word you're looking for is irate. Incensed. Wildly jealous and possessive of a woman you have absolutely no claim over."

Instead of answering, Leif reaches a hand toward me. I freeze where I am while his fingertips touch my face, tracing the line of my cheekbone over to my hairline. He runs a finger over the shell of my ear and across my jaw, and I can't hide the shiver that courses through my body.

"I'm sorry," he says.

"No you're not." I'm trying to stay angry, but the heat is leaking out of me with every touch, every look, every word.

This man is dangerous. He makes me forget all the reasons I should push him away. He makes my body take control. He makes me feel like I'm drunk just from being near him. Even now, I have to resist the urge to lean toward him. I want his hands on me—everywhere. I want to kiss him the way we kissed yesterday.

"Fine," Leif replies with a knowing grin. "I'm not sorry."

His risotto arrives, and he waves at me to keep eating my dish before digging in to his own. After a moment's hesitation, I start eating again.

And that's how I end up on a dinner date with the man I was trying to avoid.

TWENTY-SIX
LAYLA

LEIF ORDERS TIRAMISU for dessert and we get a couple of coffees to finish the meal. He insists on pretending like nothing is wrong, and I end up in a weird limbo between enjoyment and white-hot anger.

So, when we leave the restaurant and Leif walks me to my building, I turn to face him and give him a curt nod. "Thank you for dinner. Goodnight." I turn away, but Leif isn't having any of it. He grabs my hand and spins me around, tugging me until I crash into his chest.

"Layla," he growls.

"Let go of me," I say, but it comes out breathy and needy.

"No."

Then he slides his hand over my jaw, tilts my face, and kisses me—and damn me, but I melt into it. I want this. I want Leif's arms around me, the smell of him surrounding me, the warmth of him protecting me from winter's chill. Even through my anger and outrage tonight, I couldn't hide the truth from myself—that I felt grateful he broke up my date. I *wanted* it to be him I shared a meal with.

Whenever Leif is near, I feel safe. I'm no longer standing in a hurricane, trying to keep my life together with sheer force of will. I'm no longer the only person that can provide for my sister and keep my grandparents in their house. When Leif is beside me, I finally, *finally* have someone to lean on.

And how stupid is that? I know he'll leave. He'll get bored of me. He'll move on. Men like Leif Sorensen—*heirs* like Leif Sorensen—don't end up with working-class women like me. I don't have a college degree or a retirement account or anything even vaguely resembling an asset. I'm perpetually on the edge of financial disaster.

But maybe for right now—for tonight—I can pretend I'm the type of woman Leif could want. I can tell myself he enjoys taking care of me as much as I enjoy being taken care of by him.

As soon as the thought crosses my mind, something softens inside me. Leif growls in response, deepening the kiss and pulling me impossibly closer to his hard, hot body. My new designer puffer jacket condenses under his hand, my arms moving to circle around his neck.

"Open the door, Layla," Leif says against my lips. "I'd take you to my place, but I need you right now. I can't drive like this. You make me lose my mind."

I do? I do that to him?

"Yes," I answer, because of course I want to open the door and take him upstairs immediately, right this second, without delay.

My hands shake, but I manage to get the front door open. I don't even see the stains and wear in the stairwell and hallways before getting to my apartment. Within moments, we're tumbling through the door. Leif kicks it closed behind me and reaches back to turn the deadbolt, then his lips are on mine again.

He strips my jacket off and tosses it carelessly onto my worn, hand-me-down sofa. Then his hands are on my arms and he's kissing my neck, my shoulders, all the way down to the Bardot neckline of my bodysuit. The long sleeves are tight to my arms and I know it's molded to my body like a second skin. Leif's hands move to my hips, then slide up to cup my breasts.

He groans. "I wanted to rip his head off," he growls, lips tracing my collarbone. His hands knead my breasts as he backs me toward the nearest wall. "It took every ounce of self-control for me to walk toward you and sit down instead of pulling him up from that chair and pummeling his face in." Leif's voice is a rasp, and it makes my skin prickle with awareness.

It shouldn't turn me on, but it does.

My back hits the wall and my hands fly to his shoulders. He shoves a knee between my legs, grips my hips, and hikes me up so my core is pressed up against his thigh. I'm on my tiptoes, pinned against the wall, feeling like I'll die if he decides he wants to stop.

Heaven help me, but I might come right now from being manhandled like this. Being possessed like this.

My hips start moving without me realizing, my body searching for the friction I need. Leif makes an appreciative noise at the back of his throat, his hands moving to my breasts as he kisses my jaw, my cheeks, my lips.

"The only man you should be dating is *me*." He kneads my breast, sending electricity sizzling through every nerve ending. The tips of his fingers touch my bare skin above the neckline of my top, that slight touch almost enough to make me lose my mind.

"You're an arrogant asshole," I gasp, hips grinding, mind reeling.

Leif moves a hand to my hip, guiding my movements to be rougher, harder. "Here's what's going to happen," he tells me in a voice that promises sin and danger. "You're going to ride my leg until you come. Right here." He punctuates the words by moving my hips to grind harder against the solid muscle of his thigh. "Then I'm going to use my hands and my mouth until you forget about every other man apart from me. Then, I'm going to fuck you, and you're going to scream *my* name. Understood?"

His eyes are dark. Stormy. But his hands—oh, his hands are magic. With one hand on my hip, guiding me inexorably closer to orgasm, his other hand tugs my top and bra down. He palms my breast, burying his head in the crook of my shoulder. My nipple is hard against his palm and I gasp when he tweaks it between his thumb and forefinger, heat flooding every sense.

"Leif," I gasp, the tight knot in the pit of my stomach growing tighter, hotter, more insistent.

He growls in response, pinning me harder against the wall. Moving both hands to my hips, he rocks me against his leg, pulling his head back to watch me through heavy-lidded eyes.

I should resist this—right? He marched into my life like he owned it, and now he's acting like he owns *me*. But oh, it feels good. My orgasm rushes toward me as my core grinds against the hard plane of his leg, the friction of lace and the seam of my jeans hitting exactly where I need it. I can't think about anything except how good it feels to be surrounded by his heat and his scent and the feel of his body pressed up against mine.

And it feels dirty, somehow, to be fully clothed and feel like I'm having sex. To have Leif's eyes on me, knowing exactly how close I am to orgasm.

"Come for me, Layla," he orders, and I do.

My orgasm rips through me like a bolt of lightning, arching my back as my hips rock faster, my body searching for every last bit of pleasure. I fly apart in his arms, fully clothed, pinned against the wall with nothing but his thigh shoved between my legs.

Through the bright intensity of my pleasure, I realize I'm chanting his name, and he's making a harsh, approving sound that makes another thrill of pleasure gush through me.

"Good," he says, his tone almost businesslike. He extracts his thigh from between my legs and my feet hit the ground again —because apparently at some point, he hiked me up so high on his leg that I wasn't even touching the floor. I collapse against him and his arms come around me softly, almost tenderly.

Bending over, Leif sweeps me into his arms, and it's all I can do to rest my head against his shoulder. He walks across the apartment, and the sound of his shoes against the floor makes me realize that Leif is still fully dressed. He hasn't even removed his jacket.

He places me down on the bed and I watch him through heavy eyelids as he peels off his jacket and lays it down across my chair. There's no hurry in his movements. As he unbuttons the cuffs of his shirt, he glances sideways at me and clicks his tongue. "Don't think I'll let you fall asleep on me tonight, Layla. I'm not done with you."

With his cuffs undone, Leif pulls the bottom of his shirt out of his pants. Instead of unbuttoning it all, he just undoes the top two buttons and pulls the whole thing over his head, shaking the shirt out and laying it on the back of my chair.

It's a bid to maintain control, I realize. It's like the slow walk into the restaurant or the deliberate way he removed his gloves. He moves slowly because if he lets himself go as fast as he wants to, he'll snap.

The realization makes a hot, heavy awareness knot in my stomach. My breasts feel heavier and my nipples peak beneath my bra. Leif is very, very close to losing control.

I watch the muscles in his chest and shoulders bunch as he moves, and I know I'm at no risk of falling asleep now. My body is coming to attention again, breath catching at the sight of all that beautiful male flesh on display. Crawling up the bed to sit up for a better look, I yelp when Leif grabs my ankles and pulls me back down.

"Don't move," he rasps, watching me, his thumbs sliding under the hem of my jeans to touch the soft, sensitive skin behind my ankle bone. It sends a jolt of pleasure traveling up my leg.

"Hurry up, then," I say, curling an arm behind my head. My

other hand moves to the button of my jeans, and Leif's eyes follow the movement like a predator watching its prey.

Just because I'm feeling dangerous, I circle the edge of the button with my fingertip—then pop it open. Leif's hands are on me in an instant, unzipping the jeans and tugging them off my hips. He tosses them unceremoniously aside, that precious control disintegrated.

His hands slide up my legs to the edge of my bodysuit, and a line appears between his brows. He traces the edge of the bodysuit over my hips and down between my legs, the touch making me shiver.

Because I'm done pretending I'm not as desperate for this as he is, I spread my knees wide. "It's a bodysuit. There are snaps in the gusset area."

With one harsh movement of his hand, the snaps fly open. He covers the space between my legs with his palm as my breath catches, my greedy hips once again rocking against the touch.

But Leif moves his hand away, tracing the edge of the panties I wore under my bodysuit. A thong, which I wore in a bid to avoid double panty lines.

"You wear such tiny panties," he says, fingertip sliding under the elastic of my thong to snap it against my hip. I gasp at the small hurt, pleasure quick on its heels. "You wore this for him."

"I wore it for *me*, you thickheaded jerk."

With one curled finger, Leif runs a knuckle along my seam. I close my eyes and gasp, wondering if this teasing and waiting is better or worse than the mindless lust I felt when he had me pinned up against the wall.

Yes, this man is trouble. He's reeling me in, making sure I'll never forget what it's like to be in bed with him—because no other man has ever turned me on this much.

His knuckle moves over and back along the gusset of my panties, circling my clit before moving back down. It's not enough and I whimper, but Leif doesn't seem to be in a hurry. He continues to make those maddening strokes, slow and steady, over and over again.

"Leif," I beg, hips jerking as he oh-so-gently touches my clit over my panties. It's not enough. It's too much.

"Tell me what you want."

"You," I gasp. "I want you."

He meets my gaze, a slow smile spreading over his lips. Then his hands are scooping under my waist to flip me over before tugging me up to my hands and knees. He uses one strong hand to push my chest back down to the bed, the other hand pulling my thong down to mid-thigh.

Then his hand is right where I want it, stroking through the wetness of my arousal up to the sensitive bud at the apex of my thighs. He kneels behind me, his belt buckle cold against my ass, one hand holding me down while the other wreaks havoc in the space between my legs.

He slides a finger inside me and I want more. Mindless, I tell him exactly that, so he gives me another finger, stroking me until I'm at a fever pitch. I'm grunting, groaning, moaning, gripping the sheets as my hips search for more, Leif giving me rough words of encouragement.

It's shameless. Wanton. Completely lewd, and I love every minute of it. I come harder than the first time, crying out his name in a breathless chant as my body clenches around his fingers, wanting something bigger.

When he pulls his fingers out and lets them drag up to tease my rear, I arch into the touch. He groans, sliding his fingers over and back along the puckered entrance. No one has ever touched me so intimately, so brazenly. Everything is turning me on. My body is out of my control and my brain has left the building. Vaguely, through the haze of my lust, I hear the sound of a belt buckle, followed by a zipper.

"I need you, Layla," Leif says, his voice harsher than I've ever heard it. "I need you, please."

"Me too," I gasp. I move my hips toward him and try to spread my knees, but my panties won't let me get any wider. My brain is a haze, a great muddle of lust and hormones and desires. There's something I'm forgetting. Something important.

Leif's cock slides against my wetness and I let out a moan. I want him inside me *now*. My hips rock against him and he lets out a harsh groan, then swears. His wallet hits the bedside table a moment later.

"I don't have a condom." The words are guttural.

Condom. Right. That was the important thing. Okay, no condom. I try to think it through. I don't have any, because I haven't had sex in ages and it's not like I bring anybody home to the apartment I share with my little sister. I blink, fingers twisting into the sheets as my body keeps moving over and back, his cock stroking up and down my slit. It feels so good, but not good enough. My brain is mush. All I know is I want him inside me like I've never wanted anything before.

"Um," I say, mindless with pleasure, his cock rocking against my clit in a way that makes me lose the ability to speak. "Uh..."

"I'll pull out," Leif says, his breath harsh as his hands tighten on my hips, his cock speeding up to a maddening rhythm between my legs. "Okay? I'm clean."

I should protest and stop this, because I'm responsible. I know where babies come from. But the velvet-covered steel of his cock is sliding through my arousal and I haven't had sex in ages and he made me come *so hard*, twice, and how good is it going to feel to be filled up with him? I've never felt so safe and loved and cherished and turned on, and don't I deserve a bit of pleasure in this drudgery I call a life?

"Layla?" He pulls back, his cock moving away from me.

Between one moment and the next, I can no longer feel his zipper against my skin. I can't feel his thighs against mine, I can't feel his cock against my swollen lips. His hands start sliding off my hips, and I can't help the sob that escapes my lips. "Come back," I cry. "I want you inside me. Please. Now."

"Fuck," Leif groans, hands tightening on my hips again— and then he thrusts inside me. His cock splits me in half as he buries himself to the hilt. We both freeze, in surprise or pleasure or both.

"Oh," I breathe, a mix of wonder and shock. I'd forgotten how good it felt—but I don't think it's ever felt *this* good.

And then he starts moving. Hard, sharp thrusts that make me bounce against him, letting out little gasps with each penetration. He grunts with every thrust, as if the two of us are so far beyond words we turn into something feral, something animal.

His hand slides up my spine to grip my shoulder and he uses the leverage to thrust deeper, harder.

It's intense and fast and it feels so fucking good I can't do anything but grip the sheets and hang on. I realize I'm screaming when drool drops from my mouth to my hand, but I can't wipe it away because I'm flying up to the stratosphere. It's more intense than anything I've ever felt. Heat explodes in my body as I convulse, unable to breathe, to think, to do anything but ride out the pleasure that lashes my body.

Leif's hand tightens on my shoulder, his grunts turning rougher as he grinds out my name—and then I cry out in disappointment and surprise as he pulls out of me a moment before his seed lashes across my behind, my core, the backs of my thighs.

Then I collapse, dazed, stunned, with the sinking realization I'll never, ever recover from this.

TWENTY-SEVEN
LEIF

IT TAKES me a few moments to come back to myself. My body buzzes as I kneel on the bed, trying to understand what just happened.

Sex has never been like that before. So intense. So pleasurable. So...*much.*

As thoughts start to trickle into my head, I look down at myself—and at Layla. From there, it only takes me a moment to pull my underwear back on, find the bathroom, and get a washcloth to clean up the mess I made of her. She lets out a dazed little moan as I run the cloth over the backs of her thighs, and I have the odd realization that nothing will ever be the same.

I want this. Her. Us.

Once the cloth is set aside and I've shucked off my pants, I climb into bed beside Layla and gather her in my arms. She snuggles against my chest and drapes an arm over me, her breath soft against my collarbone.

"Well," she says, her lashes tickling my shoulder as she blinks repeatedly.

"Yeah," is the only answer I can manage.

"I should go on dates with other men more often."

A dart of black jealousy, then it's gone. My chest starts shaking as laughter washes over me. Layla giggles along with me, her fingers drifting across my chest in casual intimacy.

"I'm going to pretend you didn't say that."

"What? That I should date other men?"

"Layla." It comes out as a low growl.

She lifts her head, her expression one of angelic innocence. "If you didn't like seeing me with Joe, you shouldn't have rewarded me so thoroughly."

In one swift move, I tumble her onto her back and pin her arms beside her head. She lets out that big, carefree laugh, eyes twinkling beneath me, and my body comes alive again. My heart thumps while lower, other things come to attention as well.

This is nothing like my romps with other women. With other women, once the main event is over, I lose interest almost immediately. But this... Every second with Layla just makes me want more.

She feels my arousal and arches her brows. "That was a quick recovery."

"You make me crazy."

"The feeling is mutual," she says, her lips curling into a soft smile. "But I like it. Although..." She glances down between us. "If this is going to be a repeat occurrence, we really need to figure something out besides the pull-out method."

"Yes," I answer, but my body doesn't seem to care, because my cock swells even more. Visions of her thighs and behind covered in my seed flash in my mind and all I want is to do it again. Mark her. Own her.

Layla's knees spread to cradle me between them, her hips gyrating softly against me. Her lids drop down to half-mast, breath catching in her throat.

"I should go out and buy some condoms now," I tell her, my hips moving against hers.

"Yes." She arches her back, offering up her breasts for me to kiss—and I do. With one rough tug of her top, I expose her pretty pink nipple and take it in my mouth. As soon as her fingers tunnel into my hair to hold me to her breast, I know I'm not going anywhere.

This isn't like me. Ever since my ex got pregnant with Isla, I've been careful to the point of paranoia. Today, though, my brain seems to have lost all capability of reasoning, because all I can think about is Layla's soft, supple body beneath mine, the taste of her skin, and the intense pleasure of being inside her.

When her hands smooth down my back and push at the hem of my boxer-briefs, I've already lost the battle with good sense. This time, I get to see her face when I enter her—the slight widening of her eyes, the way her lips drop open. It's another assault on my heart, one I don't have the strength to fight.

"You're beautiful," I pant between thrusts, dropping my chin to my chest as ecstasy rips through me. She feels so good. Too good. Better than anyone I've ever had.

Her fingers trace my chest, my shoulders, my jaw. "So are you."

I kiss her then, our bodies joined, and sex becomes something more than it was before. It's a tangle of limbs, fervent touches, deep kisses, and a kind of intimacy I've never experienced before. I kiss her like it's the only thing that'll keep me alive, and when she lets out a soft cry beneath me, her body growing taut as a bowstring, I nearly forget myself.

By the thinnest of margins, I stop myself from exploding inside her. I pull out to lash her thighs, her stomach, the glistening space between her legs—and it's not enough. A twinge of disappointment vibrates in my chest, because all I want to do is mark her inside and out.

Barbaric, contemptible, animalistic. The urges that course through me are as unfamiliar as they are strong. I want to fill her with my seed. I want to put a baby inside her. I want to tie her to me, irrevocably, forever mine.

But as the haze clears, I come back to myself. I stare at the mess I made of her, wanting to do it again and again and again.

Layla lifts herself onto her elbows and surveys the damage, bunching her lips to the side. "I don't think a washcloth is going to do the trick this time," she says. "I need a shower."

"Sorry," I pant, flopping onto my back.

"No you're not."

I meet her gaze and grin. "Not really, no."

She laughs, then saunters out of the bedroom. A moment later, I hear the shower start, and I lie back on the bed and stare at the room around me. Layla's closet is half-open, clothes hanging neatly from hangers while the floor of the closet is covered in a tangle of shoes. There's a waitress's apron hanging on the back of the door, a hair dryer on the floor, and a few bottles of perfume on top of a dresser. It's tidy but worn. There are worrying cracks on the walls, and the windows don't block much of the winter chill.

I want to give Layla more. I want to show her how good life can be and shower her with the best that money can buy. Last night, I learned that Layla carries her family on her shoulders. She should have someone to carry her right back.

Whether it's a selfish desire to be the only man who provides for her or something more admirable, I want to show her that she can rely on me. The feeling hits me hard in the chest, like a weight falling from the sky to crush me against the bed. I want to stand by Layla. I want her to laugh and smile in that beautiful way of hers every day for the rest of her life—and I want it to be because I've made her happy.

We shared something today, something I thought didn't exist. An intimacy, a connection that makes me realize how cold and dreary my life has been.

Maybe with Layla, I don't have to keep her apart from my family life. She knows Isla, and they already love each other. She wouldn't have to work seventeen shitty jobs just to get by. Her sister's college wouldn't be a crushing debt—I could pay for it all. I could make her life easy. After all, at my net worth, a hundred grand or so is basically a rounding error.

I've compartmentalized my life too much. My world at home with Isla is completely separate from my work life, which is completely separate from my love life. I keep tall, iron barricades between each world—and in the process, I've split myself into a thousand different people.

With Layla, I can see a different future. One where I share a life with a beautiful woman who cares for my daughter, with whom I can talk about work and decompress at the end of a long day. I could take all the disparate parts of my life and bring them together—maybe make myself whole in the process, too.

Because that's the truth, isn't it? I haven't been whole since Abby left me. My ex chose to walk away from her baby daughter, from me. It broke me, and I thought I was unfixable.

What if things could be different?

My rumination is interrupted by an abrupt scream and a crash—both sounds coming from the bathroom. I'm on my feet and out of the bedroom in an instant.

TWENTY-EIGHT
LAYLA

THE SHOWER IS A BEAUTIFUL PLACE.

Well, not *my* shower specifically—this one is quite ugly, with its 1970s, faux-marble tile that looks more like odd orange fungus than any sort of natural stone, and the pea-green tub beneath my feet—but it's still a place that feels serene.

Especially when I just had the best sex of my life.

When I first enter the shower, I look at the duct tape Emma wrapped around the base of the showerhead and decide it's a problem for tomorrow. Today, I'm just going to take a scalding-hot shower, wash my body and hair, and let this pleasant, post-orgasmic sensation permeate my entire being.

The first part of that plan goes great. I turn on the shower and tilt my head, closing my eyes under the stream. I think of every-thing that happened today, from Leif showing up at my door, to the final party cleanup, to my meeting with Mrs. Sorensen.

I smile under the shower stream. Christine Sorensen is terrifying. I was practically shaking in my four-thousand-dollar puffer jacket, hands clenched on my lap as I waited for her. Patty was friendly—a woman in her forties that clearly takes pride in her job as a personal assistant.

Mrs. Sorensen strode into the living room wearing a pencil skirt of soft khaki brown and a silky top. Her hair and makeup were tasteful and elegant—subtle touches that emphasized her natural beauty.

No wonder Leif is so pretty. With genes like those, there was no other option.

She sat down across from me and gave me a leather-bound folder with all the requirements for her anniversary party. She wanted an elegant event that felt intimate, similar to her granddaughter's birthday party. The event planners she fired all tried to sell her on wedding-like events, which was all wrong, according to her.

When I suggested a private dinner party, perhaps something like a degustation menu with a theme that was meaningful to her and her husband, Mrs. Sorensen beamed.

Why she thought a part-time nanny who had planned one single birthday party was qualified to take this on, I'll never know, but the excitement of having a chance to prove myself made my whole body buzz.

But I pretended I could do it, and just like Emma asked, I worked up the nerve to sound mostly confident when I told her my fees were twenty percent of total expenses—plus an initial fee of one thousand dollars.

Christine didn't need to know that extra thousand would pay for my grandparents' initial legal fees.

It sounded ridiculous when I said it, and it took everything in me not to let my voice tremble.

Those few seconds when she paused to consider my price were the longest in my life—but she finally dipped her chin and agreed.

Just like that.

I smile under the stream of water, already knowing that Emma will give me an impertinent teenage arch of her eyebrow and an I-told-you-so smirk. As she should. My sister *is* a genius, after all.

I have four weeks to plan the party, which means I'll have to put all my time into it. Tomorrow, I'm going to speak to my managers at the café and the bar to see if I can take a few weeks off. If not, I'll quit. The money I could make from this event should more than make up for it, and if I do a good job, it might lead to more event planning. I could have a future. A future! Me!

Finally, I open my eyes and think about what happened after the meeting.

The dread I felt when I got ready for my date with Joe. The feeling that blossomed in my gut when Leif interrupted. Everything that happened after we got home.

A twinge of guilt makes me resolve to apologize to Joe when I next see him. I should never have agreed to go out on a date when I knew I wasn't interested in him. It wasn't fair to him.

And what happened in my apartment...well. That wasn't exactly responsible either, but I'm not feeling too upset about it.

How could I, when I just had the best sex of my life? I'm too high on endorphins to flog myself about not using protection.

I grab my loofah and start washing—and that's when my hand knocks the showerhead. It wobbles, and water starts shooting out of the bottom of it. I drop my loofah and try to cup my hands around the water, but that just creates more pressure around the base.

Don't ask me why I don't just turn the shower off. I think sex with Leif permanently boiled my brain, because as I try to somehow stop the flow of water with my bare hands, the showerhead comes off the wall and into my grip. Water shoots out of the wall and hits me in the face. I scream, flailing.

Off-balance, I put my foot down on the loofah, which slides right out from under me. My right hand grabs for the wall, finding nothing but slick tile. My left hand, still holding the showerhead, reaches for the curtain and comes into contact with the shower rail instead.

I go tumbling out of the bath as water shoots out of the wall, the shower curtain and rail clattering down on top of me in a tangle of plastic and metal.

Bare-assed, soaking wet, and stunned, I look up as the door crashes open.

Leif blinks at me, eyes flicking to the showerhead, then the jet of water coming out of the wall. Calm as anything, he steps inside and turns the knob to stop the water, then he looks down at me.

I extend a hand (the one not gripping the showerhead). "Help. Get me off this shower curtain. I hate touching it. It's grossing me out."

Lips twitching, Leif hauls me up and wraps his arms around me. He gently pries my fingers off the showerhead and deposits it on the edge of the sink. "You okay?"

"Uh-huh." Except for the embarrassment.

"You need a plumber."

"That's what I've been telling my landlord for months, but does he listen?" I look at the hole in the wall where the end of a pipe sticks out, water still dripping in a slow stream. Then I look down at my feet, my rubber-ducky-covered shower curtain crumpled beneath me, the shower rail diagonal across the toilet down to the ground. "Well," I say, planting my hands on my hips, "I guess Emma and I will be showering at the gym for a while."

"You'll be showering at my place," Leif answers. Before I can protest, he scoops me up into his arms and marches back to the bedroom. "Pack a bag. We'll come back tomorrow morning to get Emma. You'll stay at my apartment in the city until your place is livable. *If* it ever becomes livable."

Water drips everywhere. I stare at him. "What? No."

"Yes." He tightens his hold on me, not putting me down until we're in front of my closet. "Now pack."

I turn toward him, hands on hips. We're both still naked. "Leif, no."

"Layla, *yes*."

"You're ridiculous."

"Your shower just came off the wall. If you'd hit your head on the way down, you could have died. There's mold on the walls, and those cracks look structural. Now pack. I'm taking you home."

"I *am* home." I cross my arms, which draws Leif's eyes to my breasts. Goosebumps prickle over my entire damp body, and I look down at the trail of wet footsteps Leif left on the carpet. Then I look at the water stains on the ceiling and the places where mold has started growing near the windows. Last time I told my landlord about the mold, he just painted over it.

I sigh. "Fine. But it's only temporary."

"Whatever. Pack." He grabs his underwear and pulls it on, followed by his pants and shirt. When he meets my gaze and arches his brows, I realize I've been staring at him getting dressed. Sue me; he's pretty.

"You're really overbearing, you know that?" I ask, but I still reach for my underwear drawer and start dressing.

"I do know that," he says. "That's what makes me a good father and a great boss."

"Yeah, well, I'm not your daughter or your employee, remember?"

He just grins. "I'll wait in the living room."

And that's how I end up moving into a penthouse in Midtown Manhattan owned by Leif Sorensen, billionaire extraordinaire.

TWENTY-NINE
LAYLA

EMMA IS MORE than happy to move into Leif's apartment. It cuts her commute down to ten minutes via subway, she says, but there's a glimmer in her eyes when Leif and I pick her up from our place in New Jersey the next day. Somehow, I don't think the commute is the main reason she's happy about this development. She's probably hearing wedding bells in that addled, too-big brain of hers.

"We should have Grandma and Grandpa over for dinner," she says when we walk into the vast space. She walks to the huge plate-glass windows overlooking bustling, hectic streets. "They'd love this. You could introduce them to Leif too."

"Sounds great," Leif says before I can come up with some excuse why introducing this man to my entire family is a terrible idea.

It's not that I don't want Leif to meet my grandparents, it's just that this all seems like too much, too fast. I'm not technically working for him anymore, but I'm working for his mother. We'll be living rent-free in an apartment that probably costs... Actually, I don't even have a concept of how much this place would cost. More than I'll ever have, that's for sure.

Because I have to stop working my other jobs in order to plan Mrs. Sorensen's anniversary party, it means not only are my finances completely reliant on the Sorensens, now my housing is, too.

As someone who's always been independent, it makes me squicky to be this reliant on someone else—especially a man.

But as Leif shows Emma to her room, I take a deep breath. It's just temporary. My apartment isn't exactly livable, and this works for everyone. Plus, it'll help to have more room. I can set up a little office in the corner, and Emma will have a dedicated space to study in the library.

Oh yeah, because this place has *its own library*. I didn't notice that when Leif was tearing my clothes off the other night.

"You ready to head to the hospital?" Leif asks, sliding his hand over my lower back.

I nod. We both got texts from Emil and Dani announcing the arrival of their little one just after five o'clock in the morning, including invitations to come meet the baby. I gather my bag, call out a goodbye to Emma, and follow Leif out the door.

Elton drives us to the hospital, and a twinge of fear makes me pause. What if I get used to this kind of luxury? The driver, the fancy car, the gorgeous home? What if when it ends— because it *will* end—it makes me realize how hard my life was before, and it all becomes unbearable?

I've always been independent. I've always made things

work. But being here makes me realize how dismal my life has truly been. I'm rich in relationships and love and friendship, but there's so much...drudgery. Life for me has been *hard*. What if once I see how good things could be, the hardship just becomes too much?

Leif's hand slides over my thigh as we drive along busy Manhattan streets. "I can relax now," he says in a low rumble.

"Because Dani had the baby?"

He huffs a laugh. "No. Because you're living in a safe place. Somewhere I can take care of you properly."

There's a note in his voice that makes me turn to look at him, something tender, wistful. His eyes meet mine, and the softness in his expression makes my heart seize.

Desperately, I want this. Him. Us. But I know it'll be a disaster. If I give him my heart, when this all ends, it'll break me.

Hell, it hurt me when he forgot I was his waitress for one short night once upon a time. How will I survive when he forgets about me after taking care of me so well?

I give him a tight smile. "I can take care of myself."

His hand squeezes my thigh, and we drive the rest of the way in silence.

DANI'S SON, Ambrose Liam Van der Berg, is gorgeous. Well, he's very squishy and scrunched up, but he's so tiny and precious that I can't help cooing over him like everyone else in the room. My heart gives a sharp lurch at the sight of the tiny newborn, and for the first time in my life I...want that. A baby of my own.

But how can I think of that when I can hardly take care of the people that already need me?

Marcus is there and he gives me a strange, hard look before arching his brows at Leif. Emil's parents come with his other kids, and the mood in the room is euphoric.

When Leif and I leave together an hour later, he drives me back to the Midtown apartment and kisses me tenderly. Hope flutters its delicate wings inside me, because I think things might finally get better for me.

THE NEXT DAY, Monday, I have a meeting with two lawyers who are interested in representing my grandparents. Grandma and Grandpa meet me at the lawyer's office, and we sit in a glass-walled conference room while we review the particulars of the case.

The lead lawyer, a woman in a brown suit with harsh, straight eyebrows, looks me square in the face and tells me it'll be very difficult to win this case. If the city is siding with the developers, there are only limited avenues we can take to fight them.

I glance at my grandfather, who has his arms crossed and a bullish expression on his face, then I turn back to the woman. "We have to try."

She nods. "Then we will."

My bank account cries fat, angry tears.

When the meeting is over, I hug my grandparents and invite them over for dinner. My grandmother's jaw drops when she walks into Leif's apartment, and she immediately makes a beeline for the kitchen. I text Leif to invite him and Isla over for dinner (at Emma's insistence), and that evening, the six of us sit around the huge dining table and share one of my grandmother's delicious home-cooked meals. She makes a roast chicken with stuffing, gravy, mashed potatoes, and roasted veggies. Everything is succulent and delicious. After dinner, Emma pulls out little coupes of chocolate mousse she made earlier "during a study break."

Isla charms my grandparents within minutes of arriving, of course. So does Leif. When he compliments my grandmother's stuffing, her smile gets so bright I can't help but let my lips curl in response. After we've wound down for the evening—with no talk of lawyers of developers, as decreed earlier by my grandfather—Leif has Elton drive them back home.

Emma disappears into the library and Isla follows her, and Leif and I are alone. He slides his hands over my jaw and tilts my head, pressing a soft kiss to my lips.

"Thank you," he says.

"For what?"

"For tonight."

"My grandmother and Emma cooked. I didn't do anything."

"You invited me." He kisses me again, rubbing his nose against mine in a touch that feels somehow more intimate than anything before. "It felt like a real family dinner. I loved it. This apartment has never had that kind of energy in it."

My heart squeezes and I wonder if maybe Leif's life isn't so perfect as it seems on the outside. Maybe I can provide something to this relationship—some sort of normalcy, an intimacy he's been missing. Maybe this complicated mess of being his employee and his lover and his mother's event planner... Maybe he's right. We'll figure it out.

Hooking my arms around his neck, I deepen the kiss until the sound of little footsteps makes us draw apart. Isla appears at the mouth of the hallway, informing us that it's time for her to go home if she's going to make it to her before-school swimming lessons tomorrow morning.

Leif checks his watch and his brows jump, then he gives me an apologetic smile. "My eight-year-old daughter is more responsible than I am."

"That's news to no one," I quip, and Leif laughs.

After a hug with Isla and one last kiss with Leif, I watch them leave. All the dishes are washed, but I find myself in the kitchen with a tea towel, drying everything and putting it away.

My mind runs through the last week or so, replaying all the events that led me here. This thing between Leif and me... It feels *real*. It feels like maybe there's a future here for us. Maybe all this luxury and luck won't end. Maybe Emma will have a stable home, and my grandparents will get to keep their house, and I'll become an in-demand event manager, and I'll live happily ever after.

"What are you smiling about?" Emma says from the other side of the cavernous room. She pads toward me on bare feet, her hair piled on top of her head in a messy heap.

"I was just daydreaming," I answer.

"Scheming, you mean." She slides onto a barstool on the other side of the kitchen island. "Wondering how you can stay here forever."

I laugh. "Maybe." I put the roasting pan away and turn back to my sister. "How'd your midterm go, by the way?"

Emma shrugs. "It'll be a week before my professor posts the grades, but I think I did okay." Her eyes glimmer. "Maybe better than okay."

Opening the refrigerator, I grab two of the extra chocolate mousses sitting on the middle shelf and slide one across the counter toward my sister. "Let's celebrate with extra dessert, then."

"The only way to celebrate." She grabs the spoon I pass her and digs in. I lean against the counter while I eat my sister's delicious creation, looking around at the fancy fixtures in this beautiful apartment, and I realize that even though we're surrounded by beautiful things, the reality of our life isn't that different.

I have a great family who loves me, a smart-as-hell sister, and a fridge and pantry permanently stocked with the results of my sister's stress baking.

I'm lucky, in other words. I have a lot to be grateful for.

It's too bad I'm a few short weeks from finding out it's all about to change.

THIRTY
LEIF

IT'S amazing how one week can change your life. I didn't realize how much I was missing until Layla arrived and shook everything to its foundations.

For the next two weeks, my life is a dream. I throw myself into my work—both the final throes of the Lusso apartment block and the new development in Newark. We're so close to breaking ground, with just one final, stubborn old couple standing in the way.

I send a plumber to Layla's old place and ask one of my construction supervisors to take a look at those cracks. When he reports back with a grim shake of his head, it only takes me a moment to put in a call to city officials. I won't have Layla and her sister living in an unsafe place.

After work, I spend time with Isla, Harriet, and most days with Layla, too. When Harriet goes home for the evening and Isla goes to bed, Layla and I snuggle on the couch, talk about her plans for my mother's wedding anniversary, watch TV, and do everything a normal couple would do together.

I make love to her often and hungrily. The TV room at my townhouse becomes an unholy place. The first time Layla gets on her knees and puts my cock in her mouth is in that room. The first time she straddles me and rides me to orgasm is in that room. I'm slowly but surely losing my mind, and I couldn't be happier.

For the first time since Abby walked away without looking back, it feels like I have a family. A real family.

Best of all, Isla thrives. When she draws pictures, she always draws Layla with her long legs and golden hair. When she needs her hair tied up, she asks Layla to do it. The three of us end up going to the ballet together, going to movies, going for walks in the park. When Emma can join, it makes four.

My life feels...rich. Richer than any money could provide.

The one thing we don't often have are sleepovers. In those two weeks, I only get to wake up next to Layla once, when Isla is at my mother's house and Emma is at the library until late. I want more, but I know not to push. We've only known each other a short time. Still, I want to wake up next to her, kiss her, love her.

So, we fall into a routine that makes me realize how much I've been missing.

My mother notices, too. When I visit her two weeks before her party, she shows me the plans that Layla has come up with, but her eyes are sharp as she looks me over.

"You look better, Leif."

"I wasn't aware I looked bad before."

My mother just rolls her eyes. "That's not what I meant and you know it. You're smiling more. You look...happy."

I feel happy. Three words I never thought I'd say again.

"Would this have anything to do with my new event planner?" My mother grabs her tablet from the coffee table between us and flicks her finger over the screen to unlock it. "Isla told me she's been living in your Midtown apartment."

"Did she, now," I answer, leaning back on the leather sofa to stretch my arms across the back. "My daughter loves to talk."

She turns to her tablet. "Layla sent through a proposed menu, and somehow she's managed to make every course an ode to my marriage to your father." She spins the screen around. "Look. She drew from the trips we've taken over the years to inspire every course. The first course is a tiny bite of what I ate at my wedding."

I nod, impressed.

My mother leans toward me. "She's good, Leif."

"I know. She planned the best birthday party Isla's ever had in only a few days."

"I'm going to offer to invest in her. I think she should have her own business."

I sit back, staring at my mother, unable to formulate words.

My mother holds my gaze, that steely expression unshakeable. "Do you have a problem with that? I know you and she have...something going on."

Snapping out of my stupor, I shake my head. "I'm upset I didn't think of it first."

My mother's lips quirk. We talk for a few more minutes until it's time for me to leave. When my mom wraps her arms around me and squeezes me tight, a strange, unfamiliar ball of emotion clogs my throat. She pulls back, holding my shoulders, and looks me in the eyes.

"It's good to see you happy, Leif. I've been worried about you. You carry your pain on the inside, but now..." She smiles, pushing a strand of hair back from my forehead. "It feels like I've finally gotten my son back."

THIRTY-ONE
LAYLA

I STARE AT CHRISTINE SORENSEN, unable to make sense of what she just told me.

"We'll see how the event unfolds, of course, but I like to think I can spot potential from a distance." She straightens papers on her desk, then gives me a wry grin. "My husband and son aren't the only ones who have a keen business brain, as much as they like to think otherwise."

"So." My voice comes out gravelly, so I clear my throat. "So when you say you want to invest in me, you mean…"

"I want you to start a company. I'll provide funding for marketing and administration expenses. I can provide strategic business advice and help you get on your feet. You'll have to cultivate all the relationships and manage the business. I can introduce you to my network, of course, but it'll be your job to close the deal."

My heart leaps. This isn't happening. This can't be true.

Leif's mother is offering me the opportunity of a lifetime. She wants to invest in *me*.

No one has ever seen potential in me. No one has ever seen me and thought, *Layla could do more.* No one has ever seen talent.

Emma is the smart one. The one with a future.

But now...

"I don't know what to say." I'm going to puke, right here on this priceless Turkish rug.

Christine's shoulders soften. "You don't have to say anything. Do you have a lawyer? I'll send through a proposal, but you should have someone look it over. I'm asking for fifty percent ownership."

Mind reeling, I just nod dumbly.

Three weeks ago, I mourned the loss of a carton of eggs that got crushed by my clumsiness. Now, I'm living in a billionaire's penthouse apartment and I'm being offered my dream business.

This isn't real life.

It can't be.

"Thank you," I finally manage to croak out. "Thank you, Christine. I don't—I can't—I..." I shake my head. "I wasn't expecting this."

"Well," the older woman says, standing up and extending a hand, "I'm glad you're open to the idea."

Open to it? I want to jump for joy. I can hardly believe what's happening in my life. In less than a month, I've met the man of my dreams and been offered a home and a relationship and a *future*.

If I can start my own business—and if Christine is backing

me—it'll open so many doors for me. For Rachael. For everyone else that has struggled alongside me.

I'll be able to take care of my grandparents. They'll keep their home, get all the medication they might need, and live out their days happy and as healthy as possible. I'll see Leif and Isla and I won't be the temporary nanny—I might actually be an equal.

Emma will get her college paid for. She'll go to medical school and she won't have to worry about a thing other than exams and assignments.

In a daze, I let Leif's mother lead me to the front of the house and I stumble to the waiting car. Mrs. Sorensen's driver is waiting to take me back to the penthouse apartment I call home. The wind whips around my new puffer jacket, but I'm ensconced in the warmth and safety within. When I slide into the back seat and feel the car rumble beneath me, I let out a laugh before clapping my hand over my face.

This isn't real life. It can't be.

It's too good.

WHEN I GET HOME, I'm relieved to see the apartment empty. I shuffle into the bedroom and fall onto the blankets, groaning into my pillow.

It's probably the excitement of Christine's offer, but I feel completely worn out.

To be honest, I've felt this way all week. Bone-tired no matter how long I sleep. Maybe it's stress, or excitement, or the fact that I've gone through so many big changes over the past month.

Maybe I have a mineral deficiency. That would explain why I suddenly feel nauseous around the smell of bacon cooking...right?

It's just all the change. I'm as busy as ever, and my body needs time to adjust. Unless...

A thought darts through my head, too quick for me to latch onto. There's something I'm not considering, but my brain seems to have forgotten how to function properly.

Thoughts blur as my eyelids grow heavy. I'll just take a little nap. Just twenty minutes, and then I'll figure out what it is I'm missing.

THIRTY-TWO
LEIF

WITH HARRIET WATCHING Isla for the evening, I put on a fresh shirt and make my way to my apartment—Layla's apartment. Layla opens the door for me and immediately leaps into my arms.

"Leif, oh my goodness, Leif. Your mom. I'm—I don't know what to say. She wants me!" Her breath ruffles my neck as she squeezes me tight, and I can't help but laugh.

My arms wrap around her and my heart settles into a steady beat. Shaping her curves with my palms, I let myself bask in the feeling of having Layla wrapped around me. Pulling back to kiss the tip of her nose, the corner of her mouth, I tighten my hold on her and back her into the apartment.

"The other shoe is about to drop, isn't it?" she says, her voice dazed, her eyes at half-mast. "Things are going too well. It's going to fall apart."

"Or maybe it's about to get better," I answer, reaching into my back pocket to pull out a long velvet box.

Layla inhales sharply, eyes bulging.

I spin it around and open it, revealing a sparkling tennis bracelet studded with diamonds.

"Leif," she breathes. Her eyes snap up to mine, and she shakes her head. "No."

"Yes." I pull out the bracelet with one hand, set the box aside, and lift her wrist with my other hand.

"Are those real diamonds?" She stares as I drape the bracelet over her wrist.

I just laugh. "Of course they're real. You said you wanted a diamond tennis bracelet, didn't you?"

"I was kidding. I didn't mean... Oh, Leif."

I fiddle with the tiny clasp, then slide my hands over her hips as she lifts her arm and turns it about to watch the light dance on the gemstones. Meanwhile, I watch Layla's face.

She looks shocked. A faint blush sweeps over her cheeks, her lush lips open in awe. If all it takes is a few sparkly baubles to put that look on her face, well, she'd better get ready for a very big jewelry collection.

This is the woman for me. Kind, strong, generous, hard-working—she deserves to bathe in diamonds if that's what she wants.

Her eyes flick to mine and she shakes her head. "This is too much."

"I'm taking you to dinner to celebrate," I say, ignoring her protests. "You're going to be the best event manager in the city, and I'm the lucky man who gets to stand by your side."

"Leif." Her eyes shimmer and she blinks rapidly, her throat working all the while.

Something softens in my chest. I slide a palm over her jaw and bring my lips to hers, loving the way she melts against me.

This is the woman for me. Not because she loves diamonds, and not because my mother believes in her as much as I do.

Layla is the woman for me because she makes my life whole. She breaks down all the barriers I'd erected and makes me want a real, fulfilling life. With her by my side, I see a future for me, for my daughter, for my entire family.

My feelings are so strong, I'm afraid to think of them too closely. We haven't known each other long and it's crazy how quickly things have moved, but the emotions are there. Stronger than I've ever felt before. Truer than I ever knew was possible.

"I have to change," she says, smoothing her hands over my shoulders to straighten my shirt. "You're all dressed up and I'm wearing jeans and an old tee. Give me a few minutes."

Instead of letting go, I pull her close and close my lips over hers. "I'll help," I mumble, letting my hands slide up underneath her top. She raises her arms and I remove the shirt. I lift her up and groan when she wraps her legs around my waist.

It feels like the first night, when I was frantic and out of control. Except this time, Layla is in no danger of falling asleep. She's been tired lately, but nothing like when we first met.

The bedroom is too far. The nearest surface is the dining room table, so I set her down on the edge and slide a palm over her breast. She arches into the touch, lids heavy, a daring smile on her lips.

That's all it takes. No matter how much I get to taste her, I can't help wanting more. Our clothes disintegrate in an instant. My hungry hands touch her, mark her, possess her. I slip my fingers through the sweet wetness between her legs and groan, cock throbbing, reveling in the fact that she's mine.

When I taste her, she gasps my name. I groan against her center, enjoying this as much as she is. Maybe more. This woman is my *life*. She tastes like sweet heaven, temptation, and sin all wrapped into one. When I suckle on her clit and feel her writhe against me, I can't help smiling against her flesh.

"Leif," she pants. "I want you. Now. Please, now. Now, now, now."

Her hips ride against my tongue and I groan, unlatching my belt with my other hand. Despite what happened that first night, we've been responsible. I reach into my pocket and pull out a condom, groaning when she takes it from my hands and slides it on.

Then all thought disappears from my head, because Layla is leaning back on the table and letting her knees fall open. Offering herself up to me.

Groaning, I lose the last thread of control and thrust inside. It feels as good as the first time. Better. I plunge inside her again and again, loving the way she runs her nails down my back, how she bites my shoulder, how she screams my name and clenches around me.

My woman. *Mine.*

WE LEAVE FOR DINNER EVENTUALLY, but Layla is wearing a gorgeous red gown that dips low between her breasts and I almost ask Elton to drive right back to the apartment. Her cheeks are still flushed, a temptress's smile toying on her lips.

She shifts her wrist to let her new bracelet fall against her hand.

"You like it?" I ask, intertwining my fingers with hers as we enter the restaurant.

"Stop, Leif. I love it."

We drink champagne and eat delicious food, celebrating my mother's offer. I'm surprised to hear she already has a lawyer who can look over the contract but nod, forcing myself to let her handle her business herself. As much as I want to check every-thing over and make sure Layla has the best, I know I need to let her spread her wings.

"I heard back from the city officials," I finally say after the waiter clears our plates. "They're worried about your old building. It'll take another while to get their engineers to look at the building, but they think it might have to be condemned."

Layla's brows jump, then her eyes narrow. "This wouldn't be some ploy to get me to stay at your penthouse longer, would it?"

"You make it sound like some sort of torture to stay at my place," I laugh. I lower my voice and lean forward. "You didn't seem to mind so much an hour ago."

Primly, Layla folds the napkin on her lap and sets it on the table. "You fight dirty."

I chuckle, then grow serious. "I don't want you living in an apartment that has mold and structural cracks and showerheads that fall off the wall, Layla. It's not safe."

"I was there for three years and survived. It's how the ninety-nine percent live, Leif."

I grit my teeth. "Still. I want you to stay at the penthouse until we get word about the building."

"And if it's unlivable? What then? Where am I going to live?"

I give her a pointed look, and Layla bites her lip, laughing. "You're so overbearing it's not even funny." She clicks her tongue but relents.

Satisfaction curls inside me. My woman will stay at my apartment. She'll be safe. Provided for.

When we finally head home, I take my time unwrapping her like a present. Her red gown has driven me crazy all evening, so it's only fair I do the same in return. It's not until we're sweaty, wrapped up in each other's arms, moving like only lovers can, that I growl in her ear, "I want you to stay here for good, baby. Right here in this apartment."

I punctuate the words with a thrust of my hips, and Layla gasps. "You're fighting dirty again, Leif."

"Say you'll stay." I let my lips coast over her neck, biting down in that way that always makes her moan. I grab her wrists and pin them above her head, loving the way her back arches into me. "Say you'll stay here and you won't run away."

"I won't run away, Leif. You know I won't."

Growling in satisfaction, I piston into her until I know she's satisfied, until her eyes go blind and her moans turn into wordless cries.

And when she's asleep in my arms, her ass tucked up against my lap, I feel like I can finally breathe easy.

THIRTY-THREE
LAYLA

MY PERIOD IS LATE.

My alarm just went off for the fourth time, interrupting a vivid dream about talking tampons. That's what made me check my calendar and realize it's been six weeks since I last had my cycle.

Leif took me out to dinner a week ago to celebrate. The Sorensens' anniversary party is in only seven days, and I'm stressed out of my mind. I've been working like crazy, falling head over heels for Leif, and running around town trying to plan the perfect party. There's a lot going on. I haven't had time to think of my menstrual cycle.

I rub my eyes, the gears in my mind grinding ever so slowly.

It's just stress...right?

Stress and mineral deficiencies. I just need to eat more vegetables and start sleeping more, then my cycle will normalize again. Probably.

I swing my legs over the side of the bed and stare at the wall.

Definitely just stress. I've been going through a lot.

Except for that first time when he pulled out, Leif and I have used condoms every time. So I know I'm not pregnant. Maybe all this sex I've been having has messed up my hormones somehow.

Yes, that's what's been going on. I've been napping all the time and I feel run-down, but what else is new? I always feel that way. I fell asleep right before Leif was going to eat me out for the first time, for crying out loud.

This morning, I'm meeting Rachael to go over the final touches to the menu. Then I have to go to the Sorensens' Long Island estate to get some measurements for the rental furniture, then I have a meeting with my grandparents' lawyers.

I don't have time to be tired.

So, ignoring the case of the missing period, I get to work.

THAT EVENING, I fall asleep on the couch while Emma bakes in the kitchen. She prods me with a finger to wake me up, then ushers me to bed. A wrinkle appears between her brows when she asks me if I'm feeling okay.

"I feel fine," I mumble, then collapse into bed.

Rinse and repeat. The days before the party are a blur of exhaustion, faint nausea, and inexplicably sore boobs. I keep expecting to see blood when I go to the bathroom, but my PMS seems to be lasting an eternity this time.

I spend a lot of time with Leif and his daughter, watching

Harriet do her job with the quiet efficiency of someone who is truly gifted. I've never been as good a nanny as Harriet, and I probably never will be.

Maybe I'll never have to be… If this party goes off without a hitch, I could be looking at a partnership with one of the wealthiest women in the state.

The night before the party, my eyes grow blurry as I go through the final to-do list and my plan for tomorrow. I rub my eyes and let out a heavy sigh, then turn my head when I hear Emma shouting from the bathroom.

"Do you have any tampons?" my sister calls out. "I'm all out."

"One second!" I head to my bathroom and check my cabinets, but I already know I don't have any. I haven't had to buy any feminine hygiene products since we moved to the penthouse, which was four weeks ago—and seven weeks before my last period.

But I'm not going to think about that right now. Stressing about my period will only make it even later…right? Assuming all these symptoms are due to stress?

Moving outside Emma's bathroom door, I lean against it and speak to her. "I haven't got any," I tell her. "I'll go out and grab you some. Need anything else?"

"Chocolate," she says with a groan. "Lots of chocolate."

"Coming right up." I grin, then head out the door.

As I walk to the nearest pharmacy, my heart starts to thud. There's another explanation for the missing period. One that doesn't seem so far-fetched, considering Leif and I had unprotected sex. Twice. We used the pull-out method, but...*ugh*. I remember sex-ed enough to know it's nowhere near perfect.

Bells tinkle above my head as I walk into the store and head for the correct aisle. I grab Emma's tampons, then pause. Right beside the shelves of feminine hygiene products are condoms, lube...and pregnancy tests.

I'm not pregnant. I'm just stressed. Everything is changing, I've moved, I've been having sex...um, not enough vegetables...

I close my eyes. What the hell do vegetables have to do with anything?

Before I can lose the nerve, I grab a pregnancy test and shuffle to the cash register. Grabbing chocolate bars at random from the space below the counter, I throw them onto the conveyor and reach for my purse. I pay without making eye contact with the middle-aged woman behind the register, then cradle the bag containing my purchases next to my chest and rush home.

I'm being ridiculous, of course. But isn't it better to be sure? I'll pee on the stick, it'll be negative, and then I can focus on the party tomorrow.

Easy peasy.

But when I get home and give Emma her stuff, I can't quite bring myself to take the test. Plus, when I hide in my room and read the instructions, it says it's best to do it when you first pee in the morning.

I'm not chicken, I'm just following instructions.

But the next morning comes far too quickly and I find myself staring at the unopened pregnancy test box, as exhausted as ever with no menstruation in sight. My doubts grow.

"Just do it, you coward," I whisper to myself.

So I do. Pee, wait, check.

And then I panic.

THIRTY-FOUR
LAYLA

THE SORENSENS' private conservatory on their Long Island estate looks like a dream. Lush green plants line the walls in front of huge windows that arch overhead. A collection of circular tables is dotted around the vast space, with delicate tableware set out for the guests. At the far end of the glasshouse, the tuxedo-clad members of a string quartet tune their instruments.

I test the lights, turning on the lanterns that have been strung up from the ceiling, and smile. This looks like a fairy wonderland, with the cold, dreary outside making the glasshouse feel like a green safe haven.

It's finally time for the Sorensens' thirty-five-year wedding anniversary party. After four weeks of planning—and four weeks of absolute bliss, hectic work, and dreamlike happiness—the day is finally here.

This is the final test. After tonight, all going well, Mrs. Sorensen will invest in me. I'll be a real event planner.

We've installed temporary flooring to accommodate the heels and fancy footwear that will soon be treading on the floor, and some of the more delicate plants have been moved to a safe place. The Sorensens' gardener flits about the space, checking his babies with tender care.

Babies.

A lurch in my chest makes me grip the back of the nearest chair to stay upright.

Nope. I'm not thinking about that right now.

This morning was a mistake. I bought the cheapest test the pharmacy had, which was stupid of me. It's definitely not working properly. I probably left it out too long, and it gave me a false positive—even though I used a timer and followed the instructions. But maybe I read them wrong! I'll take another pregnancy test in a couple of days, and this whole mix-up will be behind me. I'll go to the doctor if I have to, just to prove to myself that the two blue lines on the test I took this morning are some kind of error. I can ask for a birth control prescription while I'm at it.

Everything will work out just fine.

I'm not pregnant. I'm just stressed and I need to eat more vegetables. My body is confused, that's all.

Just...don't ask me what vegetables have to do with anything. My brain is also confused.

But right now, I have work to do. I nod at the army of workers setting the tables, then duck out of the conservatory to head to the vast kitchen inside the Sorensens' home.

Rachael is in her element. She's wearing a black chef's uniform with a white apron, her hair tied back in a bandana. With one other line cook, she's busy prepping for the eight-course meal to come—one course for every five years of the Sorensens' marriage, plus a dessert to signify the sweet future they have ahead.

"Everything under control?" I ask, keeping well out of the way.

Rachael flashes me a smile. "Everything is great. Now go away."

Laughing, I do as I'm told. Despite what happened this morning, a pleasant buzz fills me up. It's the energy of all the workers coming together, the excitement of the final preparations before the guests arrive. I manage to push that pesky pregnancy test right out of my mind.

My life is going *well*. It's not going to implode because I decided the pull-out method was a good idea. No, sir-ee. Not me. I'm going to throw a fantastic event tonight, get that business deal, lift my family out of poverty, then ride off into the sunset with Leif. He'll give me millions of orgasms and the test I took this morning will just be a funny story I tell him in the very distant future.

My thought process is basically the equivalent of sticking my fingers in my ears and singing, "La-la-la-la!"

I'm halfway to the back door when I hear my name. "Layla!"

Turning to see Christine at the other end of the hallway, I head toward her. "Yes?"

"Did you get the sound system set up? My husband wants to make a speech once all the guests are here."

"It's set up and ready to go. I'm about to head to the conservatory, then out to the valet stand to make sure everyone is ready to welcome your guests."

She nods. "Good. You've done well. I look forward to working with you in the future. I'm excited about all we can accomplish together."

I paint a smile on my face while my brain screams, "LA-LA-LA-LA-LA!"

Miraculously, I manage to form coherent words. "I look forward to working with you too, Christine. I can't tell you how much I appreciate the opportunity."

Leif's mother stares at me for a moment, then dips her chin. "Good. You'd better get to the valet stand. Our guests will be arriving soon." Then she turns on her heels and clacks down the hallway and out of sight.

I let out a breath, then look down at my belly.

If that test wasn't a false positive, I'm in very, very big trouble.

LEFT OFF-BALANCE BY THE HOSTESS, I throw myself into my work for the next three hours. When Leif and Isla arrive, I greet them with a secret smile and a wink, but I'm immediately pulled away to put out one of the thousand fires that crop up during an event. I barely have time to think, let alone talk to anyone. Behind the scenes, it's chaos, but in the greenhouse, the delicate sounds of a string quartet float through the air as guests mill about, sipping drinks and laughing.

Every time I enter the space, a thrill of pride courses through me.

I did this. I pulled this event together, organized everything, thought of every detail. *Me.*

I can't think of a single time I've accomplished something like this. I'm proud of Emma, of course, and her success is in part due to the support I've given her (as she likes to remind me), but this event... It was all *me.* Every little detail from the location to the menu to the lighting to the centerpieces. It looks effortless and elegant all at once—just like the Sorensens.

From the sidelines, I watch Leif's parents talk to their guests and each other, feeling a twinge in my chest. They've been married thirty-five years. Longer than I've been alive, and look at them! Mr. Sorensen still touches his wife's back every time he's close, and she always glances at him across the room. They love each other.

My eyes move to Leif. He has Isla in his arms, and she's talking to him while she fiddles with the hair on his forehead. His smile is soft and tender, and my heart gives another violent squeeze.

Leif is a good father. He's caring and present, he loves spending time with Isla, but he's not afraid to set boundaries. That little girl is the apple of his eye and he dotes on her like I've never seen before. I wonder where I would have ended up if I'd had a father like that in my life... Maybe I wouldn't be experiencing pride in my accomplishments today for the first time in my life.

My hand drifts over my stomach and a sneaky little thought worms its way to the front of my mind.

What if the test was accurate?

Watching Leif with Isla, it's easy to indulge in the fantasy of another kid in his arms—*our* kid. After everything I've been through, all the struggle and the dead-end jobs and the tears shed in the shower where no one could hear me, what if I could be happy? What if Leif chose me? What if we had a family together?

"Layla." A young woman wearing thick-rimmed glasses steps into my field of view. "We don't have any steak knives. Rachael said to come find you."

The fantasy shatters and I'm back in the present—where I'm not part of the Sorensen family. I just work for them.

Nodding to the young woman, I follow her across the back-yard, the path cleared of snow and lit by temporary lanterns, and head to the kitchen. There, I'm made aware of the problem—as the young woman said, there isn't a single steak knife on the premises. We need fifty, ASAP. Grabbing the keys to the van I rented for all the errands I had to run today, I head out into the cold.

A frantic Walmart shopping spree later, I'm back at the Sorensens' house and entering the side door closest to the kitchen—when I hear two male voices coming from a room in the opposite direction.

I don't know what makes me do what I do next. Maybe it's the daydream I had earlier, where all the struggles in my life were washed away by Leif's love and care. That foolish need to be taken care of, to feel safe—that's why I tiptoe toward the voices and listen.

Leif's low rumble makes my core tighten with want, but whether it's lust or some deeper need set off by my discovery this morning, I'm not sure. I turn a corner and stop short beside a door that's been left ajar, completely unaware that my fragile, hopeful heart is about to be shattered into a million pieces.

THIRTY-FIVE
LEIF

MY FATHER SWIRLS his glass of brandy and stares out at the cold February evening beyond the window. "Will you be able to break ground on the condominiums in Newark next week?"

"Demolition will start on time next week. The lawyers have organized a mediation meeting with the last couple who are holding out on selling their property. I'm hoping to get that wrapped up this week, have the sale pushed through, and keep the project on schedule. We're hoping to be out of the ground by May with the foundations complete and the first story starting."

My father lets out an appreciative grunt. "You've done more than I could have expected, Leif. When you quit your position in the family business, I thought you were making a mistake. After Isla's mother left, it seemed like you were being impulsive. Reckless. You've proved me wrong. The growth your company has gone through is nothing short of staggering." He turns to meet my gaze. "I'm proud of you, son."

I hold my father's gaze, warmth spreading through my chest. "Thanks, Dad."

"New Jersey offers a lot of fresh opportunities."

I nod. "I've seen at least six other sites that would be perfect for new developments. Even Layla's old building would be a good acquisition. It's falling apart, but the location has incredible potential. The current project location is really ideal to start, though."

"You just need to make sure that elderly couple takes the deal."

"They will," I say with more confidence than I feel. "The truth is, I'm feeling nervous about the mediation. Meeting the couple personally is not something I've done before, but both their lawyers and mine seem to think it's the best way forward. If I can look the couple in the eyes, we might be able to reach an agreement."

"And if they don't agree to sell?"

"We'll start the demolition works on the surrounding properties according to schedule. When they're surrounded by dust and heavy machinery, they'll be begging us to buy their place." My voice is hard. Businesslike. In a way, it feels foreign to speak this way after the last few weeks I've had—like I'm putting on a mask that isn't the real me.

"The more people understand that business is business, the better," my father says.

"Agreed. In any case, I'll start tightening the screws on this old couple. They'll buckle under the pressure. I've done it before."

A noise outside the door makes me frown. It sounds like a gasp or a sob, but it's so faint I wonder if I imagined it. Walking across the room, I poke my head out the door, but see nothing. Must have been in my head. Closing the door, I turn back to my father. "I want to talk to you about Layla."

My father takes a sip of his drink, then places it down on a coaster on his desk. "Nice girl."

I can almost hear the "but" hanging in the air between us.

"But are you sure she's ready to be part of your life?" Dad asks quietly, holding my gaze. "You trust her to be with Isla? To...stay?"

I won't run away, Leif. You know I won't. The words she whispered in my ear a couple of weeks ago come back to me, and a rush of emotion swells inside me.

"She's nothing like Abby."

"True," my father agrees. "She works hard, and from what your mother tells me, she takes care of her family. Abby never had that work ethic or devotion." He lets out a long sigh. "But I think of how you were after Abby left, Leif, and I don't want to see you like that again."

"I care about Layla, Dad," I say. "And I'm only telling you this because I'd appreciate it if you welcomed her into the family as more than one of mom's minions who happens to be an event planner. She's...special to me."

My father huffs, then lifts one shoulder in a shrug. "Your mother likes her, so what choice do I have?"

The last barrier in my heart falls at my father's words, and I can't help the smile that breaks across my face. I would have fought for Layla even if my parents disapproved. I love my parents, just like I love my daughter, and I realize that I don't want to keep Layla separate from any of them. I want Layla to be entrenched in every part of my life.

It's time for me to stop compartmentalizing. Layla makes me feel whole.

I love her.

The thought flashes through me like a shooting star. I blink at the realization.

I have to stop fighting it. My parents like Layla, my daughter adores her, and I want her to stand by my side for all the world to see.

"I have to go," I tell my dad, already heading for the door. "I have to find Layla."

I hear a chuckle behind me, right before I take off at a jog toward the conservatory. I feel so full I could burst. I need to see Layla, hold her, kiss her, and tell her how I feel.

I love her. I love her so much it feels like I wasn't living before she came into my life. I love her to the point of insanity, and I was a fool to listen to my own stupid reasons for pushing her away.

Layla knowing and loving Isla is a good thing. Her working for me is just how we met—it's not a reason we shouldn't be together.

There's literally no reason to fight these feelings any longer. I'm not going to dance in this strange limbo of the past month. I'm going to tell her how I feel, and she's going to be mine. Officially.

I head to the conservatory and am immediately mobbed by my parents' friends. I scan the room while trying to extricate myself from inane conversations, only to be cornered by Great-Aunt Hilda.

"That vein pulsing in your forehead looks like it's about to explode," she tells me, using a gnarled finger to point out the offending vessel.

"Have you seen Layla?"

Hilda lets out a laugh and pats my arm. "You finally realized what you had, did you?"

I stop scanning the room and look at the old woman in front of me. "What?"

"It was obvious to everyone but you that you'd found the right woman. Why do you think your mother hired her? She wanted to get to know Layla herself. As soon as your mother saw you making moon eyes at Layla for the entire duration of your daughter's party, she knew you were lost."

That stops me dead. I stare at my great-aunt, jaw hanging open. "What are you talking about?"

"Don't look so horrified," Hilda answers. "Christine likes Layla. I think she was surprised at how much. And I haven't seen Layla in over an hour. I'd check the kitchen if I were you." She hobbles away before I can answer.

My great-aunt's words thundering in my ears, I duck out of the conservatory and make my way to the kitchen. My lips curl into a smile, my heart bursting with joy.

I love Layla. I love her stubbornness and her pride and how hard she works. I love her genius creativity and her ideas for party planning. I love the way her hands move so deftly while she braids my daughter's hair. I love the way she sighs every time I wrap my arms around her. I love that she fits into my life like the final puzzle piece that brings everything together.

Right now, I need to wrap my arms around Layla and tell her that I'm done dancing around the subject. I want her to be mine. Officially. Forever.

But when I burst into the hive of activity and noise that is the kitchen, I don't see the golden hair of the woman I adore.

Rachael glances at me. "Something wrong?"

"Where's Layla?" My voice sounds harsh, even to my ears.

The chef glances at the clock on the wall, then back at me. "She left over an hour ago. Said she wasn't feeling well, so I offered to take care of cleanup."

My blood pounds in my ears. "She left? Without telling me?"

THIRTY-SIX
LAYLA

"EMMA!" I scream as soon as I enter the door. "Emma, are you here?" The wall rattles as I kick the door closed behind me.

"In the library," comes the faint reply.

I hurry down the hallway and burst into the room. "Pack your bags," I tell her. My heart is beating so loudly I can hardly hear myself think. "We need to go."

Emma frowns. "What?"

"We're not staying here tonight. We need to leave, *now.*"

She pushes away from the desk, her papers strewn all across it. Emma stands up and walks toward me with careful steps, like I'm an animal on the verge of panic.

Hell, that's how I feel.

I heard him. Leif. I *heard* him say those words, those horrible words, that made me spin out. He's not my knight in shining armor. He's not the man who's going to sweep me off my feet and fix all my problems.

He's the *source* of all my problems. Lying, evil, despicable man.

"Layla, slow down," Emma says, palms out. "What's going on?"

I don't have *time* for this. We need to leave *now* so that Leif doesn't barge in here and try...try... I'm not sure what he would try, but all I know is I need to get far away from him.

Despite the screeching noise echoing in my head, I manage to have a rational thought: I need to tell Emma what I heard so she understands why we can't stay in this penthouse. So I take a deep breath, willing my chest to stop heaving so I can speak in a quasi-normal voice. "Leif is the one trying to push Grandma and Grandpa out of their home. He's the developer that's been bullying them for months. We need to *go*." Panic edges the last word, and I extend a hand toward my sister.

Please, Emma, just listen to me for once. Just do what I say.

She puts a hand up, ink-stained fingers spread wide. "Wait." My sister's eyes widen. She stares at me mutely for a few moments, then puts both her hands to her temples, transferring faint ink blots onto her skin. She drops her arms, meeting my gaze head-on. "*What?* Did he plan this? Is that why he moved us here?" She whirls around. "Is this a bribe? A setup? How. What. When. Who—Layla, no. How could he do that? Did he know?"

"I don't know." My breath hitches on the last word, and I have to grip the doorjamb for support. "He had to have known. He met them—he knew their names. Surely he looked over contracts...negotiations..."

"So he was playing you?" Emma's brows lower. "That

doesn't make sense. If he wanted to pressure us into taking a bad deal, he wouldn't have let us stay here. He would have squeezed us and made us desperate. Instead, he made our lives easier."

"Just—pack your bags!" The words explode out of me. "I can't stay here, Em. I *can't*. I have to go to the mediation tomorrow with Grandma and Grandpa and I have to sit across the table from him and I can't be living in his apartment while I do it. I just can't. I—"

I'm carrying his child.

A sob rips through my throat, and Emma's arms are around me in an instant. "Okay," she soothes. "We'll pack. We'll be out of here in half an hour, okay? I'll call Grandma and ask her if we can stay on her couch for a couple of days. We can't go back to our building; they've kicked everyone out and planned to demolish it once it was inspected by the city officials. So we need to find somewhere new, but we can do that from Grandma's place." She takes a deep breath, and I cling onto the stability I see in the set of her shoulders. "Everything will be fine. I'll chain myself to the house if it comes to it. They won't make our grandparents homeless."

I let out a snorting, wet laugh and pull away, wiping my eyes. "Yeah. Okay. You're right. We've been through worse. I'm going to go pack."

I don't tell my sister about the pregnancy test. I don't tell her that this is all a thousand times more complicated than she thinks, because moving out of this apartment isn't the end of anything. It's only the start.

Fear and anger burn away the last wisps of my denial until all that's left is brutal, merciless clarity.

A false positive? Please. I haven't had my period in two months, I've been exhausted and nauseous and my boobs have been two hunks of soreness bolted onto my chest.

I'm pregnant. With Leif's child.

Leif, the man who wants to kick my grandparents out of their home. Who sees them as an *inconvenience* to his grand plans and fancy condos, not as people who have lived their lives in a home they love. He met them, welcomed them into his home, all with the intention of kicking them out of their own.

How could he look me in the eyes for a month? How could he make love to me, hold my hand, let me spend time with his daughter? Was it all some ploy to get me wrapped up in his life so I couldn't protest? Was he trying to trick me?

As I tear open my closet—no, not *my* closet. Leif's closet. As I tear open Leif's closet to grab my clothes, I can't think of any other explanation. He had to know, which means he's been planning this.

Can I really be with a man like that? Can I really look him in the eyes and see the tender, loving man I thought he was?

Of course not.

He's not loving or tender or kind. He's the cruel Viking king who sees new land and wants to pillage it for his own gain.

I throw things into my bags, not bothering to fold anything. I can hardly see past the tears burning in my eyes, and my breaths are short and staggered.

I *heard* him. I heard the hard, harsh words Leif said to his father. He was...*cold.*

That's the man who's made me laugh and blush and burn?

That's the man who teases his daughter? How could someone be so loving at home and so ruthless at work?

Nothing makes sense. I'll have to face Leif, but I can't do it from this apartment, surrounded by his things, feeling so very beholden to him.

I need to *leave*. I need to be out of here before he realizes I'm gone.

And when I grab my charger out of the wall, tossing it into my suitcase, I scan the room and see nothing of mine. Emma is already wheeling her suitcase to the door. She grabs her extra pairs of shoes sitting by the door, stuffing them into a reusable grocery bag. I watch her hesitate near the entryway closet before finally grabbing our two new Balenciaga puffer jackets. She sees me watching and lifts them up. "We can sell these," she explains.

My heart turns to ash. I nod. "Yeah. It'll pay for a deposit for a new place."

"Exactly." She balls the jackets up and shoves them in her suitcase, then stands up straighter. "Ready?" Emma asks, a determined set in her jaw.

I give her a sharp nod. "Let's go."

THIRTY-SEVEN
LEIF

THE APARTMENT IS EMPTY. I stare at the bedroom closet, feeling a black void open up inside me.

She *left*.

After she told me she wouldn't run away. After she *promised*.

Why? Where did she go? What the hell happened?

I pull out my phone and call her for the thousandth time, and I'm sent straight to voicemail once again. What the *fuck* is going on? What happened tonight?

She left she left she left.

My vision goes blurry, the past melding with the present. I gave Layla everything. My home. My heart. My family. And then *she walked away*.

No. I'm not going to let that happen.

Rushing back to the kitchen, I look for something—anything—

that will tell me what's going on. There's no note, no clue. My heart pounds and my hands shake as I open drawers and cupboards, not sure what I'm looking for. I lean against the counter, closing my eyes, trying to figure out what the hell happened tonight.

I spoke to my father.

I learned that my parents approve of Layla.

I realized that I love her...

And she left.

She *left*.

Just like Abby. She wormed her way into my life, made me care about her, and decided to smash my heart to pieces—why? Nothing makes sense.

Sucking in a hard breath, I stalk back to the hallway. I throw open her sister's room, seeing an unmade bed and an empty closet. The second bathroom has empty drawers and a distinct lack of potions and creams and female detritus that used to litter every horizontal surface.

The library is cold and empty.

By the time I'm back in the master bedroom, I can't hear myself think. I can barely breathe, and I can't make sense of any of this.

Why would Layla leave? Was she playing me this whole time? Was she stealing from me? Taking advantage of me? Is this some sort of elaborate joke?

But she didn't take anything.

Was she trying to make a fool of me? Of my parents? Was she spying for a competitor? What the *hell* is going on?

I call her again. No answer.

Swearing loudly, I throw the covers off the bed, open the nightstand drawers, toss the pillows and the mattress.

Nothing.

I scream, throwing a pillow against the window. I wish I could smash it to pieces and watch the shards fall down to the street below.

Whywhywhywhywhy?

When my phone rings, it startles me so badly I jump. My father's name is on the screen.

"Dad," I answer. "I can't talk."

"Where did you go? We're about to do speeches."

"Layla's gone. She..." I stare at the empty room, the bare hangers in the walk-in closet. This is a joke, right? She played some elaborate prank on me. This is some kind of payback for a crime I committed in my past.

"What do you mean, gone?"

"I mean my apartment is empty. She's not here."

"Where did she go?"

"I don't fucking know!" The words explode out of me, and I have to close my eyes and suck in a deep breath. "I have to go. I'm going to check her old apartment and her grandparents' place."

"Okay. I'll let your mother know. We'll do the speeches without you."

"I'm sorry, Dad. I just—I need to find her."

"You will." His voice is calm, and I try to inhale that feeling into my lungs.

It doesn't work.

I hang up, hands shaking, and gently close the door to the

closet. Resolve solidifies inside me, along with an anger so strong it makes me feel like I'm floating outside my body.

I'm going to find Layla, and I'm going to make her explain herself.

If she's punishing me for something, I want to know what it is. I'm not letting yet another woman walk away from me without explanation. I'm not going to be left out in the cold on my own. I'm not going to let someone do that to my daughter all over again—especially not when Isla is old enough to remember.

This is not going to happen again.

THIRTY-EIGHT
LAYLA

IT'S NOT until the cab drops us off outside our grandparents' house that the enormity of my discovery starts to settle in my mind.

Leif is the developer bullying my grandparents into selling their house. Leif isn't the haven of safety and security I thought he was. He's cold-blooded, money-hungry, despicable, capitalist scum. I can't believe I woke up in his bed all those mornings, feeling like I was protected from the world. The biggest villain in the city was housing me the whole time. Sleeping next to me when he could. I *cuddled* with him. I let him stroke my hair and kiss my temple, and I felt *safe*.

I sucked his cock on many occasions. I let him inside me. I let him put his lips on me, his tongue. I gave him my body and my heart and now, now...

Bewilderment. That's what I feel. Like a tornado just tore through my life and whipped me up into the air. I don't know which way is up or down. I can't make sense of any of it. All I know is at some point soon, I'm going to come crashing back down to earth.

And it's going to hurt.

What kind of man tries to force an elderly couple out of their home for the sake of a tower of luxury condos? Am I really so stupid as to not see what he was like? Was I so blinded by the new boots and new jacket and fucking penthouse apartment not to see what was right in front of me?

How did I not notice it was his company that was mentioned in all those legal documents?

The answer is clear in my mind: because he refused to talk about his business. He gave me some bullshit excuse about leaving work at the office and I cheerily tied a blindfold over my eyes and complied.

I am a *fool*. An idiot. A complete and utter nitwit.

A pregnant nitwit.

My grandmother opens the door and ushers us inside while the blood pounds in my ears.

Finally, after an entire day of denial, I let the truth ring in my mind loud and clear on repeat, like some twisted, awful recording.

I know I'm pregnant. It wasn't a false positive. I'm having a baby, and the father is the bully who's trying to make my grandparents homeless.

He's rich and powerful and well-known and he'll kick my grandparents out, and then he'll take my baby. Horror yawns open inside me as I think of the implications—all that could go wrong.

He told me Isla's mother left, but do I know if that's true? Can I take his word for it? What if he did the same to her? He could have bullied her and taken her child. He could be truly, awfully evil.

Isn't it only evil people that make elderly couples homeless?

"What's this all about?" Grandma takes my jacket and hangs it up in the foyer closet. It's the old jacket that I saved. I couldn't bear to put on my stupid Balenciaga designer puffer jacket when we left Leif's apartment, letting Emma stuff it into her suitcase alongside the white one.

My grandmother turns back to me. "Why the cloak and dagger? What happened to the nice apartment in the city?"

"It's Leif," I say, my voice a croak. "Leif owns the company that's trying to push you out of this house."

Grandma stares at me, her wrinkled face blank. She blinks once, twice, three times, opens her mouth then closes it again. "He... Are you sure?"

"I heard him." I clap a hand over my mouth to push back the sob mounting inside me. Once I can speak again, I meet my grandmother's eyes. "I heard him speaking to his father. He said he does this all the time. He'll start demolishing all the other buildings they've already bought, he'll tighten the screws and pressure you until you buckle. He sounded so...cruel. Calculating."

"That *bastard*." My grandfather's voice is a low rumble at the mouth of the living room, his eyes a dark flame. "I shared a meal with him, and the whole time..."

"I know." I close my eyes for a moment. "I know."

"But did *he* know?" Emma looks at the three of us. "Did Leif know whose house he was trying to purchase?"

"How could he not?" I answer, my voice faraway. "He's the owner and CEO of the company. He built it from the ground up. His life is his company and his daughter—how could he not realize who we were? Who Grandma and Grandpa were? He had his driver take them home one night!"

I look down at myself, at the same old clothes I've always worn. The same person I was before I met him. Clinging onto stability with my fingernails, trying to carve out an existence from the pummeling blows life dealt me.

"Why else would he be interested in me?" I ask, my voice sounding as small as I feel.

Screeching tires outside make me turn my head. Looking through the half-moon window at the top of the front door, I see a familiar silver Rolls-Royce double-parked on the street.

He followed me. He fucking followed me.

That stupid car. Who needs a car like that? Why does he need to drive around in a car that's worth as much as my grandparents' house?

It's pretentious and flashy and I can't *fucking* believe I was so attracted to someone so outrageously conceited. He marched into the restaurant when I was *on a date with another man*—and made the other guy leave! And then I slept with him!

What the hell is wrong with me?

A thick, bloody spear of anger rips through me, and I grip it with both hands. A pretentious, conceited, egotistical, Rolls-Royce-driving *asshole* is trying to ruin my fucking life and I will *not* allow it.

I grab my old jacket off the coat hanger again, throw it on, and rip the front door open.

If Leif Sorensen thinks he's going to bully my family—if he thinks he can buy me off with a fancy apartment and an over-priced jacket, pull the wool over my eyes with all the money he's pillaged from his victims—he has another thing coming.

No one fucks with my family and gets away with it.

Especially not Leif fucking Sorensen.

THIRTY-NINE
LEIF

I STARE AT THE HOUSE, not understanding.

Layla's apartment was still boarded up and I couldn't see any light from any of the windows, so I told Elton to take me to her grandparents' house. He remembered the address from the time he drove them home.

But... This can't be Layla's grandparents' house; this is the house I've been trying to purchase for months. This is the site of my future development. I'm planning on knocking the surrounding buildings down next week, and this house shortly after, as long as my lawyers do their job and the mediation goes well tomorrow.

The door opens and Layla exits the house with thunder on her brow. She's wearing that fucking rain jacket again, wrapping it around her torso like it'll save her from the late-winter chill. I want to throw her over my shoulder and take her home, where she belongs. I want to make sure she's warm and safe and *mine*.

I want to shake her until she explains herself, explains why she left in the middle of my parents' anniversary party, why she looks like she wants to stab me in the throat.

But this house is explanation in itself, isn't it? Realization dawns, and I understand why Layla ran.

She found out that my company was trying to buy this property—she must have found out sometime during the party. Those legal troubles she told me about, the ones she wouldn't discuss—they were the ones my lawyers have been dealing with for weeks.

Once she realized who I was, she ran. She thought... She must think I'm some sort of comic book villain, trying to push her into a corner to get her to drop her fight for this house.

A noxious brew of emotions stews inside me. Anger at Layla for leaving without speaking to me. Fury at finding her gone from the apartment. Hope and terror and confusion at the thought of losing the only woman I've ever truly loved. And most uncomfortable of all, something that feels a lot like shame when I look at the house in front of me.

I was comfortable pushing the condominium development through by any legal means necessary. I was happy to squeeze the couple who lived here until they decided to sell.

But that was before I knew they were Layla's family.

It shouldn't make a difference; I'm offering them a fair deal. The development is good for the community. The city is on my side.

I never thought about the couple who live here as anything but an obstacle in my way. I thought it was business...but it's not. It's Layla's family.

The last barrier inside me falls down. Business can't be separate from love and family—not in this case. If I'd only talked to Layla about my work, we could have discovered this weeks ago. We could have found a solution. She wouldn't have run away, she wouldn't think that I'm... That I'm...

Trying to push her grandparents out of their house.

Which is exactly what I've been doing.

Shame is an ugly, twisted thing inside me that I don't want to look at too closely. It shouldn't matter that I know the people who live here. It shouldn't matter that they're related to Layla, because it's a good deal—for everyone. If the deal is truly mutually beneficial, why do I feel like I just got punched in the gut?

But even as the thought enters my mind, I know it *does* matter. I've met Layla's grandparents. They're kind and loving and gentle, and they care about Emma and Layla with a depth I can relate to. It's how I feel about my own daughter.

I'm the big bad wolf trying to blow their house down...and that doesn't feel good. It feels a lot like I *am* a comic book villain.

Layla descends the three steps from the stoop to the path that leads to the front door, widens her stance, and crosses her arms. She sneers at the car, and even though I'm still sitting in the back seat, I feel exposed. Raw.

Ashamed.

"Elton..." I clear my throat. "You drove Layla's grandparents' home a month ago. Why didn't you tell me this was where they lived? You know this is the property I've been trying to buy."

Elton glances in the rearview, then turns around to frown at me. "You didn't know?"

"That Layla's grandparents were the elderly couple I've been fighting with for months? No! What the fuck!" I rip the door open and step out, only to see Layla's jaw clench, her chin lifting.

God, I love this woman. I love her fight and her fire. I love how fiercely she loves her family.

And I... I'm losing her.

We stand watching each other for a moment, the front yard separating us, until I can't take it anymore. I stride toward her and reach a hand out only to have it batted away.

"Don't touch me," she hisses. "You lying sack of shit."

"I didn't know," I answer.

"Bullshit."

"I didn't know," I repeat. I stare into the blue fire of her eyes, then glance at the house behind her. My fingers tunnel into my hair as I watch one of the curtains twitch, my breath a cloud of white in front of my face. "Layla, I didn't know your grandparents lived here."

"I don't believe you. How could you not know?"

"You think I've been pretending all these weeks?" I ask, a strange, stabbing pain in my chest. I reach for Layla again, only to have my hand batted away—again.

"I don't know what you've been doing, apart from bullying my grandparents into giving up their home."

The malignant mix of emotion inside me gives way to anger, and I clench my fists. I can't face the shame I feel—if I do, I'll break. I can't look at myself and see how badly I've acted, so I cling to the last thing I can: business. "I offered them more than enough money. Well over the value of the home."

It's true. I gave them a fair offer—but a voice in my head still screams that I'm a villain and I should be ashamed. I shove that voice aside. I'm not ashamed. It's business. Nothing more; nothing less. Business isn't personal. Those two spheres don't mix.

"You offered, and they refused," Layla counters. "But you didn't take no for an answer. The same way you barged in on my dinner date with someone else and wouldn't leave. The same way you carted me off to your apartment where you could keep an eye on me. You're so used to steamrolling everyone around you into getting your way that you don't realize how far you've overstepped, Leif."

My temper builds inside me like a demon, burning away all my good sense. "I didn't hear you complaining when I set you up in my penthouse, Layla. I didn't hear you complaining when Emma had a place to study and sleep that was closer to her college. When I took you out and spoiled you every fucking chance I got. But that doesn't fit your narrative, does it? You can just ignore how much you enjoyed my *steamrolling*." I spit the word, gratified when red sweeps across her cheekbones.

"You need to leave, or I'll call the police."

"The police?" I gape at her. "Layla."

She clenches her jaw. "Go away, Leif." Her hands bunch into fists, and the pulse in her neck flutters so fast I want to ask her to sit down. My hands itch to reach for her. But the house behind her looms in the dark, and the shame I've been trying to smother rears up.

Layla has fought for her family her entire life. She gave up her own ambitions, her future, for the sake of the people she loves. She told me about the struggles she went through when her mother left, how she's been supporting her family for as long as she's been able to work.

I don't deserve to take care of her. As much as I want to wrap my arms around Layla, I know that someone so pure and good shouldn't be touched by a man like me—someone who would push an elderly couple out of their home for the sake of his own selfish ambitions. Despicable. I am the lowest of the low, the scum of the earth.

I *am* the big bad wolf. I deserve to be treated like Layla is treating me, because the truth is, if I hadn't met Layla, I'd be more than happy to bully the old couple that live here for the sake of my business. I've built such thick walls between business and personal that I hadn't thought... I hadn't realized...

But it's just like the wall between my daughter and my love life, isn't it? Before Layla, I thought what I did with women needed to be kept separate from my life at home. I thought it didn't matter how much I slept around, as long as it didn't affect my daughter.

But it *did* affect Isla. The absence of a woman, of a relationship. Isla's been living without a mother figure her whole life, and I've been more than happy to deprive her. She hasn't had someone to bake with her and braid her hair. She would have gone without a birthday party—a real, genuine, intimate birthday party that an eight-year-old girl deserves—if I still had those walls up. She hasn't had someone who will be able to be there to comfort her or, shit, I don't know. Explain how menstruation works.

I've kept everything separate because I thought it was the

right thing to do—but it's cost me everything. For the first time since Abby left, I realize what I've been missing. Life was better when Layla was there.

I should have known I should open up about my business, too.

Wouldn't life be better if I didn't feel like a horrible, immoral man when I look at the house behind Layla? If my business ambitions weren't so cleanly excised from my home life, my conscience?

Layla showed me how life should be. She showed me that I've been living a fragmented existence, that I haven't been honest about everything that's been missing.

Then I say the stupidest four words in existence and watch everything between us crumble to ash: "I love you, Layla."

She rears back as if I've struck her. "You *what?* Are you fucking kidding me?"

I grind my jaw. "I'm serious, Layla."

"How dare you? How dare you roll up here in your fancy car that you don't even deign to drive yourself, try to push me into a corner, then manipulate me with your professions of *love?* What's next, Leif? Are you going to tell me that you'll drop the project? That you'll dissolve your business because you finally realize you're harming the people who already live here? Please."

I'm losing her. A few hours ago, I realized I couldn't live without her, and now everything I say and do is wrong.

Layla lifts her chin. "I'm done. I can forgive a lot of things, Leif, but I can't forgive this." She points at the house behind her. "You think all that matters is money, but you're wrong. My grandparents have lived here for decades. This is their *home*. No amount of money will ever be enough to make them move. Ever. I can't be with a man who will intimidate vulnerable, elderly people just for the sake of a business deal—especially not when he pretends to be such a loving, doting father at home. You're a liar and a fraud, Leif."

In her eyes, I see only one thing: the end of us.

"Layla." My heart cracks in places I didn't know it was still whole.

She turns around and marches back inside. The door slams before I can think through the pain to find something to say.

FORTY
LAYLA

THREE PAIRS of wide eyes stare at me as soon as I enter.

"I need a shower," I announce. "And then I'm going to bed."

They watch me march past them to the bathroom, where I strip down and turn the water as hot as it will go. Maybe if I burn off the top layer of my skin, I'll feel clean. Stripping off the clothes that have become stuck to my body through stale sweat and panic, I step into the shower and wait for a revelation.

It doesn't come.

My life is still in shambles.

I'm pregnant with the child of a man who would throw an elderly couple out of the only home they know. I've lost the opportunity of a lifetime with his mother, because why the hell would she invest in me now?

Why the hell would I *agree*, even if she did want me to start a business with her? I can't work with people like that! People who have no moral fiber.

As the water sluices away the grime from my skin, I feel cleaner but no better. I wash until my skin is red and raw, stepping out into a steam-filled bathroom, grateful the mirror is too fogged up to see my reflection. I don't want to look at myself right now.

When I open the bathroom door, a scratchy old bath towel wrapped around my body, there's a neat stack of clothes just outside the door. Emma must have gotten my pajamas ready for me. Backing into the humid warmth of the bathroom, I tug the sleep shorts and old tee on, then run a wide-tooth comb through my hair.

I need to face Leif tomorrow, from the other side of a lawyer's boardroom table. It's too soon. I don't want to see him.

Except a small part of me does. The part that thought he could be my knight in a well-tailored suit. The one who believed him when he said he'd take care of me.

I must be a special kind of stupid. Women like me don't get scooped up out of the gutter by men like him. We grind and grind and grind until we're worn down and haggard. That's my lot in life. Has been since my mother walked away when I was sixteen years old.

I shuffle to the bedroom down the hall and see Emma on the air mattress on the floor. She's scrolling through her phone but puts it down when I enter.

"You take the bed," I tell her.

"Nope." She blinks.

Not in any mood to argue, I just shrug. "Your loss." I fall face-first onto the old mattress, feeling the familiar dip in the middle that will guarantee I wake up with a sore back. Turning onto my side, I see my sister watching me.

"Are you okay?" Her voice is quiet and so much older than it should be. She had to grow up quickly too, and it's my fault. I couldn't shield her from everything. Couldn't shield her from Leif.

My sister's words hang between us and I want to cry, but I won't let myself. I've been through worse. I lost The Job. I've been forgotten, ignored, groped, bullied, and pushed around before. This is nothing new. I may be broke, but I'm not broken.

I nod, my cheek rubbing against the soft cotton of the pillowcase. "Yeah, Emma. I'm okay."

"What are you going to do?"

"Sleep. Go to the mediation tomorrow. Beg my boss at the bar to put me on the schedule this week."

"I want to help."

"You can help by keeping your grades up so that scholarship money keeps coming," I answer.

Emma flops onto her back. "No, I want to *help*. You always take everything on your shoulders, but Layla, I'm older than you were when Mom left. I can handle it. Let me do something—anything. I'll look for a new apartment. I'll get a part-time job. You can't stop me. If I get a job and buy groceries for us, you'll have to eat them. You won't have a choice."

I huff, lips curling into a sad smile. "I don't want you to wear yourself down, Em. You need to graduate and become a doctor, remember?"

"And I will." She tucks her hands under her cheek, her

knees coming up on the air mattress. "I can do well in my classes and still contribute. School is easy for me."

"Even organic chemistry?" I arch a brow.

Emma's lips twitch. "Well, I did get an A on that midterm, so…"

I laugh, and it feels rusty in my throat. "Okay. Just let me get through tomorrow, and we'll talk about it after, okay? Maybe you can get a job on campus. Somewhere safe."

"Okay." My sister gives me a sad smile, then goes back to her phone.

I turn and look at the ceiling, wondering how it is that after a decade, I'm right back where I started. No richer. No wiser.

THE CHEAP POLYESTER of my thrift store suit scratches against my skin as I take a seat in the lawyer's boardroom. The skirt is a bit too tight around the thighs, the seams stretching as I shift in my chair. Grandma sits to my left, while Grandpa takes the seat on the other side of her. He puts his hand on her knee, and her back straightens. As if that simple touch buoyed her. Gave her the strength she needed to face this battle.

My heart gives a sharp twist.

I thought Leif's touch did that to me. I thought he had superpowers with how safe and strong he made me feel.

The clock's ticking sounds like gunshots in the small space. A young employee breezes in and offers us coffee, arranging cups and mugs and coffee-related accoutrements on the table in front of us. When she's gone, the stern-faced woman who's been dealing with our case enters.

I hear nothing of what she says. My heart is pounding too hard, my stomach yawning too far open. Just when I'm about to excuse myself to go hurl in the bathroom, the elevator doors slide open and Leif stalks out.

His face is a mask of brutality. The harsh line of his jaw tics when he sees me, his impossibly broad shoulders looming as he approaches the doorway.

For the first time, I wish he weren't so big. I wish his sheer physicality, his maleness, didn't feel so intimidating. It doesn't feel safe anymore.

But my body hasn't gotten the memo. My nipples turn to hard little pebbles in my bra as heat curls in the pit of my stomach. I remember all too well how it felt to have those huge hands on my skin, wrapped around my ribcage, teasing my breasts. I remember the rush of warmth when he cupped between my legs like that place belonged to him.

"Morning," he says with a curt nod to the room at large. "Should we get started?" He folds his big Viking's body into the chair across from mine, smoothing his tie in a move that fools no one. The veneer of civilization is thin enough to see through.

And his eyes. Those deep eyes, stormy as the ocean, stay glued on me.

Knowing he'll be able to spot my every weakness, I keep my spine rod-straight and let the lawyers start the formalities.

I hear very little of the meeting because I'm almost entirely consumed with withstanding the assault of Leif's presence. The room is much too small for him. He fills it from wall to wall, his energy pressing up against my skin, making me feel raw and exposed and turned on and angry and afraid.

"We have planning permission from the city," the Sorensen lawyer intones while Leif watches the pulse flutter in my neck. "All we can do is offer ten percent more."

"I don't want more money." My grandfather's hand slams the table, rattling glasses and mugs.

Leif clears his throat. "This discussion isn't going anywhere. Thank you for your time. We're done here."

I splutter. "You're not even going to *try?*"

Leif's gaze narrows. "I didn't say that. I merely pointed out that this mediation meeting is a waste of everyone's time." There's something in his eyes, some unspoken words he's trying to convey.

I can't read them. I don't *want* to read them. He's not the man I thought he was.

My grandfather harrumphs. "Well, do what you told Layla you'd do, then. Demolish everything around us. We'll deal with the noise and dust and disruption. We're not moving from that house." My grandfather pushes himself up to his feet, huffs, and hobbles to the door.

Meeting adjourned.

I stand and help my grandmother to her feet, only to feel Leif's eyes on me. My skin prickles, awareness in every pulse of my heart. It takes every ounce of self-control not to look at him, not to acknowledge how badly I wish things were different.

When I'm standing at the elevator bank, I feel him approach. His voice rumbles over my shoulder. "Layla. I need to speak with you."

"Speak to my lawyer."

A beat. Then, *"Please."*

Exchanging a glance with my grandmother, I turn slowly and lift my gaze up, up, up to meet Leif's. His jaw is clenched, hands fisted at his sides.

"Five minutes. That's all I ask."

"Go ahead, honey," my grandmother says. "We'll wait at the coffee shop downstairs."

The elevator doors open and my grandparents shuffle inside, along with three other fancy, lawyerly people in expensive-looking suits. My grandmother gives me a curt nod, and the doors close.

I hold my arms straight at my sides, trying to ignore the way Leif's gaze runs down my body, pausing on the stretched fabric cupping my thighs, then back up again. He reaches over and grips my elbow, guiding me back down the hallway we just exited.

Instead of heading for the conference room, though, he peeks inside a door and tugs me into a supply closet.

"Leif," I protest. "What are you doing?"

"I need to talk to you."

The fluorescent lights fizz when he hits the switch, closing the door in the same instant. I cross my arms, so keenly aware that we're alone.

I should have refused. Why am I here? I'm mad at him. He's despicable. He's a piece of shit developer who wants to make my grandparents homeless.

But he's the man who gave me a place to stay when my shower broke. He made sure my sister could come too. He celebrated with me when his mother offered to invest in me. He's a doting father. A loving son.

How can those be the same people? How can he be all of that, and still dismiss us from the mediation meeting like we're flies buzzing around his head?

"I didn't know your grandparents lived in that house," he says, eyes intent on mine. "I need you to understand that."

"It shouldn't matter. If they weren't my grandparents, they would be someone else's."

His lips pinch, eyes sliding away. A deep, shaking breath fills his lungs, then he brings his eyes back to mine. They look... tortured. It shouldn't bother me. It shouldn't make me want to fix whatever aches inside him.

But I'm weak, and I fell in love with him the moment he jogged toward me on the street and offered to walk me home.

He takes a step closer and it takes all my willpower not to move back. I turn my head to the side, pretending to be very, very interested in the reams of paper stacked neatly on the steel shelves.

"I don't want to fight. Please, Layla."

"That's twice you've said that," I spit. "'Please.' Didn't think you knew the word."

He takes another step closer. Despite my best efforts, a tremor courses through my body. He looms above me, and I can't help but remember the month of tangled sheets and panting breath and whispered filth we shared.

I should hate him. I *do* hate him! Except... I don't, really, do I? Leaving this room right now and telling him to go to hell should be the only option, but I find myself rooted to the floor when he takes another step closer. His hand skims the edge of my thigh, and heat rushes south.

"I like this skirt."

"I don't care what you like. Are we done here?"

"Not quite." Leif's voice gets lower, and I work up the courage to glance at him quickly. I don't like the look in his eyes. Not one bit.

"My grandparents are waiting for me." God, I wish my voice hadn't trembled.

"I meant what I said yesterday," he says quietly, dangerously.

I close my eyes. Yesterday, he told me he loved me. The words had hit me like bullets, piercing whatever mangled heap of flesh remained as my heart. It hasn't recovered.

How can he love me when he's about to take my grandparents' house?

"You don't know what you feel," I whisper. "You'll forget about me as soon as this is over."

He's close now, his chest brushing mine. My body strains to lean against him, blood rushing to the surface of my skin, nipples hard and aching.

This is wrong. I shouldn't want him. This won't fix anything between us. It'll make it worse.

But when Leif's hand slides along the side of my neck, when he curls his fingers around my nape and tilts it back, my legs turn to water and I know I can't leave.

Not now. Not when he's looking at me like no one else exists. Not when anger and hurt and lust form a caustic stew inside my stomach.

"You've forgotten something important, Layla," he says in that same low, dangerous voice. His fingers tighten on my nape as his other hand skims my hip, dipping back to smooth over my rear.

"What's that?" My voice is breathless, needy. His touch... How can I live without his touch? I already feel like all my aches are soothing. Like everything will be okay if he just keeps running his palms over my body just like that.

That hand slides down my curves to the back of my thigh, all the way to my knee where the skirt meets my skin. Slowly, torturously, while he crowds me against the shelves and holds onto the nape of my neck, Leif slides his hand up the inside of my thighs.

I widen my stance, because I'm weak-willed and horny and he's just...him.

And when his hand reaches the juncture of my thighs to cup the heat pulsing there, Leif leans in to rest his forehead against mine. "This is mine," he growls, the heel of his hand pressing against my clit. "You've forgotten that this belongs to me, and I'm not going to let it go."

"You're such an asshole." I mean for it to sound hard and biting, but it comes out in a pant.

"I'm going to fix this," he says, his breath coasting across my lips as that hand grinds and grinds against me. "Do you trust me?"

"Of course not," I answer, hands scrabbling back to grip the nearest shelf. Heat explodes down below, tightening and releasing as I clench around nothing. "Why would I trust you?"

He growls, deft fingers pulling my panties aside to run his middle finger through my sopping-wet seam.

I think this is a hormonal problem. That's why Leif's simple touch addles my brain so badly. I'm all messed up from unfamiliar hormones, and it's turning me into a needy, lusty, weak woman. That's what's going on here.

It's not that his shoulders are broad and strong and all I can see is Leif. All I can smell is Leif. All I *want* is Leif.

"I should leave you like this," he says in that low growl. "Wet and needy. I should leave you right here and walk away, because I've got shit to do, Layla. I've got a problem I need to fix, and you're in the center of it. I didn't end that meeting because I didn't want to try. I ended that meeting because it wasn't going to help me fix what's broken between us."

It sounds like he means it. Like he's not just going to make my grandparents homeless and build a big tower of fancy condos where I grew up. It sounds like he would do that... for me.

"I told you I loved you and you threw it back in my face," he grates. His finger slides up to rub against my clit and a whimper escapes me.

"You deserved it," I manage to croak, hands tightening on the shelves.

"God, you're sexy when you're mad," he says, lowering his lips to my neck. "All proud and angry and strong. I wanted to bend you over that conference room table and fuck you right there, Layla."

The image burns through my mind and I moan, no longer in control as my hips gyrate against him.

"My cock was so hard I couldn't think," he continues in a harsh rasp. "And then you stood up and twitched that ass at me as you walked out of the room and now..." He sucks in a hard breath, fingers gliding down to my opening. "Now I find out you're as wet as I imagined under that skirt of yours."

"Leif—"

His fingers surge inside me. I gasp, hands flying to his shoulders.

"I'm going to fix this," he growls. "Do you hear me?" His fingers pump harder.

I close my eyes. "This doesn't mean anything. I'm not in my right mind. You're—" A moan slips through. "This isn't fair."

A huff of laughter escapes from him as his teeth graze my neck. "I know that, baby. I don't fight fair. I hurt you, and that was wrong. But I'm going to make it better." His hands do something magic then. Curling his fingers inside me as his thumb grazes my clit. Pleasure surges inside me and I hold onto his shoulders for dear life.

"You can't fix this with an orgasm, Leif," I pant. At least, I don't think he can.

He doesn't answer. Instead, Leif drops to his knees, shoves my skirt up to my waist, tugs my panties down to my ankles, and hooks my knee over his shoulder. All in a matter of seconds.

Then his tongue is on me, flat and hot and oh, oh, it feels good. With both hands, I grip his hair and can't help but grind into him.

"That's it," he says against my flesh. "Use my mouth." He slides his fingers inside me again, swirling his wicked tongue around my clit. "Grind this pretty pussy all over my lips and let me do this for you."

I'm chanting, I realize. A low, steady pant that just says, *Leif, Leif, Leif.*

"You're going to make me explode in my pants, you taste so good." He gives me another long lick, moaning low in his throat.

I shouldn't say it, but I can't help it. He's on his knees in front of me, telling me he'll fix all my problems, making me feel like my feet have left the earth. "I want you," I whine. "I want your cock, Leif."

He chuckles, blowing a soft breath over my clit. "No. This is me making you feel good, Layla. This is my promise that everything that's wrong, I will make it right."

"But—"

He slides another finger inside me as his other hand moves to my rear, squeezing and kneading my ass before moving to tease my rear entrance. One knuckle. Two. And it's the feeling of fullness that does me in. That and the way his eyes meet mine, clear and blue and determined.

An orgasm ripples through me in slow, deep waves. I grip Leif's hair, riding through my orgasm. My hips buck, my inner muscles clench around his fingers, and all I can do is let it wash over me as I shatter into a million pieces.

Dazed, blind, deaf, and dumb, I lean limply against the shelves as Leif stands before me. He pulls my damp panties back up, tugs my skirt down, and smooths it over my hips and thighs. In a move that shouldn't be sexy but somehow is, Leif wipes his glistening mouth with his palm, then casually readjusts his cuffs.

"We should go before someone finds us," he says, tucking a strand of hair behind my ear.

"Yes," I answer, and I let him lead me out of the storeroom and back to the elevators. He keeps a possessive hand on the small of my back all the way to the coffee shop, where he gives me one last indecipherable look before walking away.

"Well," my grandmother says with false brightness, watching him leave. "That didn't exactly go to plan, now did it?"

FORTY-ONE
LAYLA

IT TAKES me three full days to figure out what the hell happened in that supply closet. Seventy-two hours of bewilderment, of putting on a mask and pretending life is normal, of mind-reeling, post-orgasmic distress.

Yes, distress.

I'm going to fix this, he said. *I'm going to make it better.*

That stubborn strand of hope in my heart apparently has a few threads left clinging on, because a part of me actually believes him.

And that's not okay.

When will I learn that any time I think things are going to get easier, I'm just setting myself up for a roundhouse kick to the head?

This time around, I don't even have to guess at what's going to happen. It was right there on the pregnancy test a few days ago. It's growing in my womb a little bit every day.

The roundhouse kick is my baby, and I'm pretty sure Leif hasn't figured *that* in his grand, *I'm-going-to-fix-everything* plans. When he finds out, how will he react?

I should have told him before he put his hands on me. I should have held up my palms and said, "Leif, I'm pregnant. It's yours and I'm keeping it. Please don't give me a mind-bending orgasm and rattle all my best-laid indignation before we figure this out."

Yeah. That would go over about as well as a snowball fight in hell.

Just when I'm coming to terms with what happened, I get a reminder of the reality of our situation.

Bright and early on the fourth morning after our failed mediation, huge, flat trailer trucks roll up outside my grandparents' house and start unloading machinery, fencing, scaffolding, traffic cones and signs, and all manner of construction implements. I watch them from my grandmother's dining room table, coffee cup halfway to my mouth, wondering how the hell this qualifies as "fixing" anything.

Stuffing my feet into old sneakers, I wrap a bathrobe around my shoulders and stomp outside. A gruff, bearded man in a plaid quilted jacket is waving his hand to back one of the trucks up. A huge, yellow excavator sits on the truck bed, waiting to be unloaded.

"Um, excuse me!"

The man turns. "Yeah?"

"What's going on here?"

"Unloadin' a digger."

"I can see that." It's the beginning of March and the early-morning wind has bite to it. I wrap my robe around me a little tighter, watching the truck back up.

The man keeps waving his hand then holds out his palm and the trucks stops. The driver jumps out and the two men start moving toward the trailer and sliding down the ramps that will allow the excavator to drive off.

"I thought this project was on hold," I call out, scurrying after the bearded man. "There was a mediation meeting only a few days ago."

The man sighs, then pulls a bunch of folded, scrunched-up papers from his back pockets. "You wanna check our permits, lady? Demolition is starting today. It ain't going to stop because you didn't know about it."

"I—you—what—" I splutter, taking the papers from him and glancing over them, sighing. They look official—not that I know what a freaking construction permit looks like.

A minute later, a convoy of pickup trucks drives up onto the front lawn of my grandparents' former neighbors and workers stream out by the hundreds. Okay, by the tens. But it feels like hundreds. One man takes the lead, calling everyone closer to start barking out orders. The workers scurry to do his bidding, grabbing temporary fencing from trailers, setting up cones and traffic signage around the entire block.

Things are happening too fast. Way, way too fast.

As a temporary fence goes up on the property line between my grandparents' house and the neighbors' place, a lump forms in my throat.

This is exactly what Leif said would happen. He said he'd make construction noisy and messy and in-our-faces, and force

Grandma and Grandpa to leave. This is his tactic to get us to fold.

I'm going to fix this, my ass.

Patting my pockets, I realize I didn't bring my phone out with me. I rush into the house, only to see my grandparents watching the proceedings from the living room window. They glance at me, then back at the workers setting up the fencing outside.

Finding my phone plugged into a charger on the kitchen counter, I rip the cord out and find Leif's number. He answers on the first ring.

"Layla," he says. "I've been waiting for you to call."

My spine stiffens. "What kind of game is this, Leif? What the hell is going on? There are dozens of workers here and they're saying they're demolishing all the neighbors' houses. I thought you said you were going to fix this. You said... You said..."

"I am fixing it." Leif's voice is calm. "I've been in meetings with town planners and architects and city officials every waking hour since I left you at the lawyers'."

"But they're knocking the houses down!"

"My company owns those houses, Layla," Leif answers quietly. "They need to be knocked down. They're falling apart, anyway."

I gulp. "What about our place?" My voice sounds thin and reedy, even to my ears.

Several beats pass. My heart hammers so hard I press a hand to my chest to make sure it won't burst through my ribcage. Then, quietly, he answers, "Your lawyers will get a notice by the end of the day. We're dropping your grandparents' property from the plans."

Light fills every inch of my body and that thread of hope grows brighter, stronger. "You're not going to pressure them to sell?"

"No, baby. I was wrong to try." His voice is soft, but firm.

"But... the demolition. You told your father... Noise and dust and..."

Another silence before Leif says, "I was on my knees in front of you when I told you I'd fix this, Layla. I meant it."

I should tell him about the baby. Right now. I should just blurt it out over the phone even if it comes out all wrong, because I believe Leif when he says my grandparents' place is safe. He really is trying to fix things, and all these construction workers aren't here to bully us into giving up this property, too.

But if I tell him about the baby, and he turns around and becomes that ruthless, uncaring businessman he was before... I'm not sure I can handle that. Not right now.

Maybe it's better to wait until I know what will happen with the land around my grandparents' place. I'll wait for the official letter from the lawyers, until I know what type of building will be going up beside us. Once I know that, I'll know my grandparents are safe.

Even if I'm not.

"Do you trust me, Layla?"

I open my mouth, but nothing comes up. What can I possibly answer? Despite my own reasoning, I trust that Leif is trying to do right by my grandparents. I trust that he's not going to bully them.

But do I trust him with the truth about the baby? Do I trust him with my heart?

"I don't know," I finally tell him.

A sigh comes through the phone. "That's probably better than I deserve."

"Yeah."

He huffs a laugh. "You wouldn't be willing to move back to my place in Midtown, would you? I'd feel much better if I knew you were somewhere safe."

"No," I answer. That's too much. I can't feel tied to Leif. Not right now. Not when I haven't told him the truth about my pregnancy.

Another sigh. "I expected that. I haven't had the guts to go back there, and I've forbidden my staff from going in and cleaning the place. It feels too much like it's yours."

Ouch, my heart. It squeezes into a tight, painful ball, and I'm not exactly sure why. Maybe because Leif is a complicated, caring man. Because he's trying to do right by me—he's trying to be better.

Maybe it hurts because I'm not doing the same for him. I'm hiding this huge, impossible secret... But don't I have a right to protect myself?

It's only been a few days. I need time to come to terms with it, to figure out what my next steps are.

If my grandparents' house is safe, that removes a huge weight from my shoulders. Maybe I can try to figure out what to do next. I need a doctor, and money, and a place to stay, and, and, and...

"I need to get ready for work," I choke out. "I'll talk to you later."

"I hope so," he says, voice strained.

When I hang up, I turn to see my grandparents and Emma staring at me with wide eyes. I wave my phone at them. "He says he's not going to try to buy your house," I tell my grandparents. "The official word should come by the end of the day. He's working on what will be built next door with the city officials and his architects." I clear my throat. "Your home is safe, Grandma. Grandpa."

My grandmother lets out a long sigh, turning to wrap her arms around Grandpa. Everyone's eyes are glassy, and I feel so unsteady I might as well be on a ship's deck.

"I need to get ready for work," I repeat to the room at large, then I shuffle to the spare room to do exactly that.

MY FIRST SHIFT back at the sports bar feels like stepping back in time. It's only been a couple of weeks since I was last here, but everything about it feels...dated. The dark-colored walls with chips in the paint where the chairs have bumped into it, the old bar polished to a high shine, the dusty memorabilia tacked onto every surface. It feels like a part of my past.

And yet, I'm still here.

I wrap my apron around my hips and cast an eye around the room, giving a start when I see Joe sitting in a section that isn't mine. An uncomfortable feeling churns in my gut, but I manage to square my shoulders.

If Leif can change his plans for an entire condo development just for me, I can face Joe.

Walking up to him as he wipes his hot sauce-covered fingers on a wet wipe, I drop his favorite beer on the table. "On me," I tell him.

"Layla," he says, wiping his mouth with the same wet wipe. "Hey."

With a deep breath, I say what needs to be said. "Joe, I'm so sorry about what happened between us. When I agreed to go out with you, things were already complicated between me and Leif, and I should have been upfront about that. I didn't expect him to show up, but the way I acted when he did... I should have told him to leave. I'm sorry."

To my surprise, Joe lets out a laugh. "It's all good, Layla."

It sounds like he means it, but I shake my head. "I was a jerk to you."

"Hey, Layla," Kylie says, slipping onto the chair next to Joe's. She's not wearing her waitress's uniform, and her hair and makeup are done up to the nines.

I blink. "Hi, Kylie."

Joe slides his arm around the back of her chair. "After I stormed out of La Trattoria, I ran into Kylie."

"Right there on the doorstep," she cuts in, making moon eyes at the man beside her.

"She saw I was in a bad mood and offered to go for a drink." His arm slides onto her shoulder, thumb sweeping over her skin. "And the rest is history."

Kylie's cheeks flush. "I've been meaning to call you," she tells me. "If you hadn't had such a disastrous date, we never would have run into each other that night. I would have kept admiring him from a distance every shift." She gives him a secret smile, as if they've joked about this often.

"I reckon we owe you a thank you, Layla," Joe finishes, eyes on Kylie. He leans in to give her a kiss, and the two of them slip into their own little world for a moment.

"Oh, well... You're welcome? And I'm sorry."

"No hard feelings," Joe says. "And thanks for the beer."

I nod, then head back to my section, mind reeling. I work until closing and make my way back to my grandparents' place on sore feet, exhaustion making it impossible to think.

Then I collapse into bed and do it all over again the next day.

FORTY-TWO
LEIF

I PROMISED myself I wouldn't call Layla until I could prove to her that I would keep my word, but as the days drag on, it becomes harder and harder to keep my distance.

After yet another round of meetings with architects and town planners and real estate agents, I start to wonder if I can actually pull this off.

Maybe I lied to her, after all. I won't be able to fix any of it. I went too far with the initial project, and now I can't back out. I really am the piece of shit developer who makes elderly couples homeless. I'm irredeemable.

Shaking my head to clear those thoughts, I stare at the updated architects' plans in front of me. Without the footprint where the Reynolds' house sits, we can't dig the right foundations for the tower of condos. We're limited to either a smaller building, townhouses, or single-family dwellings.

None of which will come close to breaking even financially.

But if I have to take a loss on this project, isn't that worth it? It means I get to see Layla smile, get to prove to her that I'm not the evil developer she thought I was. I'm not the kind of man who bullies elderly couples into selling their home—and I never will be again.

That's worth a couple million dollars' loss on a single project, isn't it?

Sighing, I roll up the plans and push them aside. It still doesn't feel right. Putting up a small apartment building would be the most lucrative option, but it would crowd the Reynolds' house and reduce the amount of natural light they have. Their house would feel hemmed in. I can't be the man who bullied them into selling their house, only to drop it and proceed to make their home unpleasant to live in. Putting up townhouses would be fine, but I just...

I can't put my finger on why it all feels so wrong.

Grabbing my wallet and phone, I call out a goodbye to my assistant Regina and head home. Elton is waiting for me outside, and instead of asking him to take me to the townhouse, I decide on a whim to head to the Midtown penthouse.

My heart hammers as I ride the elevator up, remembering that first night Layla and I spent here together, after the jazz bar. I felt so frantic, so out of control, on edge. It's like my body knew what my brain couldn't process—that having her here, in my space, would change everything.

I could have driven her home that night and that would have been the end. She might have worked with my mother, but I would have forced myself to keep my distance. All my boxes would have stayed nice and separate—family, women, work.

Now, though...

The elevator opens and I cross the gleaming marble floors to the apartment door. Unlocking it and stepping inside feels like entering a time capsule. Wisps of Layla's scent wrap around me, ghosts of her presence. My steps echo in the space, and it all feels so...cold. Empty. Sterile.

I don't have that reckless laugh of hers or get to see the light shining in her eyes. As I walk to the refrigerator and open it up to see a Tupperware of old, stale brownies Emma must have made, my chest squeezes.

It's been two weeks since that mediation meeting—and all that happened after. Two endless weeks without Layla to come home to, when all that's kept me together is the sheer determination to make things right.

And I will.

Once I figure out how.

I walk through the space, noting the mussed sheets in Emma's room—then start at the realization that I called it Emma's room. It's not the spare room anymore. It's Layla's sister's space.

No one has been in here since the night of my parents' anniversary party. I tore through the apartment in a panic, cupping in my two hands the realization that I loved Layla without knowing what to do with it.

Now I know. I'll use my love for Layla to become a better man. I'll take the love I have for her and Isla and let it imbibe every aspect of my life—from family to business to relationships. I'm a good father because I'm firm, fair, and I love my daughter unconditionally. Why can't I be a good businessman as well?

Why do I have to leave my heart at the door every time I enter the office?

My feet pause at the threshold to Layla's room. *Our* room. I grip the doorjamb, memories of our month together stacking on top of each other.

When this is over, I won't let her sleep here while I stay at the townhouse. She'll be woven into every aspect of my life. I want her to braid Isla's hair in the morning and go to her ballet performances with me. She'll eat with us, laugh with us. She and Emma will be part of my family.

Stepping into the room, I cross to the bed and bring Layla's pillow to my face. I inhale the scent of her, closing my eyes to gulp it down in long, trembling breaths.

Yes, I'll do anything for her. I'll figure out what to do with the property next to the Reynolds' place, and I'll prove to Layla that I'm worthy of her.

The light in the ensuite is on, so I tear myself away from the bed and cross the space to turn it off.

Then I immediately flick it back on.

There's something in the trash can.

Frowning, I cross the space and peer inside at the cardboard box, the blue cylindrical wrapper...and the pregnancy test hidden underneath.

LAYLA ISN'T AT HER GRANDPARENTS' house. Her sister stands in the doorway, staring at me suspiciously, and I know I haven't done enough to win her family over. They probably see the construction site next door, listen to the sounds of demolition all day long, and wonder if I'm going to keep my promise.

I will. Now, more than ever, I will.

"You can't tell me where she is?" I know I sound frantic, but I can't help it. My heart has been thumping violently for over an hour.

"I'll tell her you stopped by," Emma responds.

"This is important. I need to talk to her."

"And you can. When she calls you. After I've told her you stopped by."

I resist the urge to pinch the bridge of my nose. "Emma."

"Leif."

Huffing, I shake my head. "I can tell you two are related. Stubborn as mules."

"I'll let her know you think so."

Holding up my palms, I know I'm not going to win this argument. I glance at my phone for the millionth time, but she hasn't answered my texts or calls. I call out to Emma right before she closes the door, throat suddenly tight. "Layla hasn't mentioned anything..."

Emma arches a brow. "Anything...?"

"Anything big?"

Emma blinks. "Look, Leif, I have to go study. Can you just ask what you want to ask? I'll relay it to Layla."

"You were a lot more helpful the last time I was trying to find her."

"Last time you hadn't threatened to make my grandparents homeless."

I flinch. "Point taken."

The door closes, and my heart rises all the way up to my throat. I walk down the pathway but instead of getting in the back of my car, I wave Elton off and walk along the temporary fencing encircling my newly acquired property. I hook my fingers into the fence, staring at the rubble, the piles of steel and concrete and soil. Among the debris, the excavator looks almost sleepy sitting in the middle of the site, motionless.

It means nothing. The development, the plans, the money I could have made here—it means absolutely nothing to me.

I whirl around and head to the car. When Elton turns down a familiar street, I glance out the window, then grip the back of the seat in front of me. "Stop," I command.

Elton pulls the vehicle into an available space and I scramble out to stare at the crooked, worn building where Layla used to live.

And it comes to me.

I laugh, my breath puffing in the night air, feeling a new lightness steal over me as my idea solidifies like a ship appearing over misty waters.

I know what I'm going to do, and I won't let architects or city councilors or town planners change my mind.

I'm going to prove to Layla—once and for all—that she can trust me. That I'm worthy of her.

And worthy of our child.

FORTY-THREE
LAYLA

FOR THE FOUR-HUNDRED-THOUSANDTH time since we last spoke on the phone, I delete the draft of a text message and toss my phone away. I don't have the guts to text Leif, not even after Emma tells me he stopped by last night.

"He looked all panicked and disheveled," she tells me, biting into her toast.

"What did he say?"

"He asked if you'd mentioned anything important." She tilts her head, frowning. "What do you think that means?"

I resist the urge to curl my hands over my stomach. He couldn't... Leif doesn't know about the baby... Does he?

"I'm not sure, Em."

"Well, did you call him back?"

"Nope."

She giggles. "He's probably shitting his pants right now."

"Language, honey," my grandmother says, swanning into

the kitchen as she hums. Ever since we got the notice from the lawyers about Leif's company backing off, my grandmother looks ten years younger.

Leif did that for her. For *me*.

Would he have done it if he knew about the baby? If he knew how much more complicated things will become? Sure, he's already a dad, but he never mentioned wanting more kids. Plus, he might like me and all—or even say he loves me—but starting a family together is a whole other proposition.

Starting a family.

Oh, God. I am so not ready for this. I can hardly take care of myself and Emma, let alone a new baby. I close my eyes and try to stop myself from hyperventilating when I hear my sister shift.

Her arms appear around my shoulders and I bury my head in her shoulder, squeezing her tight.

"What's wrong, Layla?"

"I..." I shake my head. "Nothing. It's fine."

My grandmother stares at me from across the kitchen, eyes narrowed.

I turn to Emma. "How'd your assignment go?"

As expected, Emma lets out a dramatic groan and flops down on her chair. "It was impossible."

I hide my grin. "So impossible you'll probably get 100% on it?"

Emma's eyes twinkle. "I can't help it if I'm an overachiever."

We settle back into familiar patterns and conversations, and I push aside all thoughts of Leif. If he wants to talk to me so badly, he'll call today. If I'm not at work, I'll answer—but I'm not going to go chasing after him. No way.

. . .

LEIF DOESN'T CALL, as it turns out, and as I wipe down the last of the tables after the bar closes, I try not to let that sting.

He doesn't call for a whole week. Then another. The demolition of the buildings next door is progressing at a crazy-fast pace, and pretty soon the whole area is cleared. Where a bunch of buildings existed before, a flat patch of dirt remains.

Being a responsible pregnant woman, I've already been to the doctor once and have an appointment for four weeks from now, when I'll be sixteen weeks along.

Sixteen weeks out of forty. Nearly halfway. I'll probably have a visible bump by then.

I close my eyes, willing myself to calm down.

It's a beautiful spring day in early April now and I'm drinking a cup of herbal tea as I look at the lot next to my grandparents' place. The sun rises behind me, warming my shoulder blades. So many things have changed in the past few months and so many more things will change in a few more.

Buildings were razed and now nothing remains in their place but flat brown dirt. Maybe, by the time my baby arrives, there will be something new on this lot.

There's something poignant in that idea. A never-ending cycle of creation and evolution. Life charges forward, no matter how much I wish it would slow down and let me breathe once in a while.

The purr of an engine makes me spin around in time to see a beautiful, expensive silver car pull up next to the curb. Elton doesn't even have time to open his door before Leif is getting out, hauling a bunch of big, rolled-up papers out of the back seat.

His eyes lift to meet mine, and I suddenly wish I were wearing something other than my pajama pants and an old hoodie.

"Layla," he says, and it sounds like sheer relief. "You're here."

I nod. "Yeah," is the only response I can manage.

Leif doesn't look like he just rolled out of bed. He looks tall and powerful and male, and despite everything that happened, all I want to do is crawl into his arms and ask him to make everything better.

But...

There's still space between us. The looming memory of my anger, of his anger, the flat plot of land beside me as evidence of all that has happened to keep us apart.

He stalks forward, pausing a few feet away in a jerky motion that makes me think he wanted to come straight to me and wrap his strong arms around my body. Instead of giving in to the urge to leap into his embrace, I take a sip of tea.

"Have you figured out what you're going to build here?" I nod to the empty lot.

Leif sets down most of the rolls of paper and grabs one of them, unfurling it in a dramatic motion. He spins around, arms spread wide, to show me the plans.

I gape.

There are no fancy condos. No luxury building that will crowd every inch of space around my grandparents' house. No big mansions that will drive up property values and gentrify the neighborhood.

He's building a park.

The architect's render includes massive green space with trees lining a winding path, benches and lighting and a children's playground. But not just any children's playground. There are rolling mounds of green grass surrounding swings, slides, a freaking small *zipline*, something that looks like a *Ninja Warrior* obstacle course...

It's basically the coolest, most badass playground I've ever seen in my life. And it's going to be right beside my grandparents' house.

My mouth dries up completely. I can't stop staring at it, and it's not until my cheek bumps into his arm that I realize I've moved closer.

"Leif..."

"It took a lot to convince the city of my plan. They need more housing, and I had promised them sixty-two apartments." He gives me a wry grin, rolling up the image of the playground to grab another one from his pile. Leif unfurls it to show a new building—more modest than the plans I'd seen of the condos he was planning to build here. "I had my architects design something that provides the same number of apartments, although they're quite a bit smaller. It took a lot of convincing, because these apartments are more geared toward young couples or people downsizing, instead of the wealthier, established demographics we were targeting with the condos here. But I had my team put together a report showing a gap in the market for affordable housing in this area."

I blink. He's not plonking down luxury condos I'll never be able to afford in the middle of my neighborhood. He's thinking of young and old couples. A spiky ball lodges itself in my throat. "Where's that going to be built?"

"I bought your old apartment building," he says, and a bit of redness sweeps over his cheekbones. "It was condemned anyway, so I got a good deal. I was driving by it when I got the idea."

A good deal. Right. As if people can just up and buy whole apartment buildings.

"And the park?" I croak.

"Well, when I told the city council I'd donate the land, they weren't going to say no."

"Donate?" I blink, my breaths growing shallower by the minute.

"Yeah." He rolls up the plan and drops it next to the others, then combs his fingers through his hair, fusses with the lapels of his jacket, readjusts his collar. When his eyes lift up to mine, there's something infinitely tender in his expression. Something that terrifies me with how badly I want it to be true.

"You're putting in a children's playground next to my grand-parents' place," I say, my voice nothing more than a hoarse whisper.

Leif is quiet for a beat, his pulse thudding violently in his neck. "The night I called you, I had just gone to the Midtown apartment." He gulps. "I... I found something in the trash can."

I suck in a breath, my hand moving to my stomach.

Leif's eyes track the movement, then flick up to mine. "Is it true, Layla?"

I take a step back, but Leif just takes one forward.

"Layla," he says softly, reaching a hand toward me.

"I'm keeping it," I say, jutting my chin out. "You can't make me change my mind."

His eyes widen, hand still suspended between us.

"And I'm not asking anything of you, okay? I know it's probably throwing a wrench in your plans and whatever was happening between us is way too new, so I get it if you just want to back off. You can be part of the baby's life, of course, but I'm going to fight for custody. I'm not like your ex, Leif. I'm not going to walk away from my baby."

His breath is coming short and fast, his eyes glued on mine. "I know you're not."

"Good. So that's settled."

"Nothing is settled, Layla."

There's a bird trapped in my chest and it's flapping its wings far, far too violently. "It's not?"

"No, because you still think I'm going to back off." He takes a step forward. When I try to retreat, the fence encircling the empty lot hits my shoulder blades.

"You're not?" I squeak.

"If you think I just spent weeks negotiating for our child to have a playground next to his or her great-grandparents' house and then I'm going to walk away from you, Layla, you need to get your head checked."

Our child. He said those words, they rolled right off his tongue like he liked the way they sounded.

"You can't be so romantic and so damn arrogant at the same time, Leif. It doesn't work that way."

Leif's lips kick up at the corners and he erases the distance between us. His warm, broad hand slides over my cheek and he tilts my head up so all I can do is stare into those fathomless eyes. "Listen to me, Layla. I'll say this as many times as needed for you to understand. I love you. I love you so much I'm lost without you. This past month has been the hardest of my life, because you weren't beside me. The only reason I survived was because I knew I was fighting for you. I knew I needed to show you that I'm serious." His face inches closer, those sapphire eyes the only thing I can see. "You showed me that I was living a lie. I thought my life was perfect and orderly and set up in neat little boxes, but I was using that as an excuse to hide from the things that scared me. I was terrified when I realized I loved you. Scared shitless of the way you barreled into my life and made me see all the cracks in my walls. I wanted to fight it, but I couldn't. Because you're you, and you're meant for me."

A shuddering breath leaves my lips, but I can't find the words to reply.

"I love you so much I feel like I'm coming apart at the seams." Leif's other palm covers my hand, still resting against my belly. "And the thought of adding a new son or daughter to my family..." He closes his eyes and rests his forehead against mine. "Layla, I know I don't deserve you or the baby—not with the way I've acted and the mistakes I've made—but I'm a selfish bastard, and I'm not going to let you run away from me. Not when you've got my heart stitched up inside your chest where it belongs."

"Oh, Leif." Ceramic shatters against concrete as I drop my

mug, my arms flying around Leif's neck as I pull him in for a kiss.

His mouth angles over mine, and the world rights itself. His arms are strong and warm and safe when they wrap around my waist, his chest is broad and strong and fits perfectly against mine. His mouth tastes like heaven, lips moving in sweet seduction as his words sink into my skin like raindrops.

He loves me. He wants the baby. He's building a playground for our child instead of a multi-million-dollar condo tower.

A moan rattles his chest as he deepens the kiss, sliding his tongue over mine in a way that makes my head spin. His hands grip me tight and it feels so, so right to be in his arms.

"If you weren't pregnant already, I'd put a baby in you right now," he growls, nipping my jaw, my neck. "I've missed you so much."

Oh, that shouldn't turn me on as much as it does. "Me too," I pant, clinging onto Leif's shoulders—shoulders that can share all my burdens. "I've been miserable without you."

He pulls back to look me in the eyes, smile widening. "I shouldn't be happy to know you were miserable, but I kind of am."

"That's the arrogant jerk in you making an appearance."

He laughs, then in one swift move, hauls me into his arms, bride-style. "Elton," he barks. "Take a walk for a while."

"Sir." Elton nods before turning down the street, whistling to himself with his hands in his pockets.

My heart flutters as Leif rips open the back door of his car, shoves me inside, then comes to join me. Before I know what's happening, Leif's got my pajama pants off. There's a center console in the back seat and Leif sits my bare ass down on top of it, spreads my knees wide, kneels in front of me, then runs his tongue over every inch of me.

Leif moans like a man starved. Starved for *me*.

I'm no better. I'm whimpering and moaning and writhing against his mouth. For once, I'm glad he has a fancy, expensive car, because there's enough room back here for him to do *this* to me. He devours me until my vision goes dark and stars explode behind my eyes. Vaguely, I hear Leif grunt in approval. When I'm still loose-limbed from my trip to outer space, Leif tugs me down to one of the seats, pulls me to the edge, and shoves inside me in one hard thrust.

I gasp, clawing at his shoulders, bringing him down to my lips. It feels better than the first time. Better than anything before, because now I know we belong together.

"You're mine, Layla," he growls, breath hot against my neck. "Say it."

"I'm yours," I pant, clinging onto him for dear life.

He growls in response. "And you know I'm yours, don't you?"

"Yes," I answer. "Yes, I know."

That seems to please him more than anything. We find ecstasy together in the back of his car and as I slowly float back down to earth, I realize that thin thread of hope has turned into a blazing light inside me.

For the first time in my life, I know for sure that everything will be okay.

EPILOGUE

LAYLA

MY LAST SHIFT at the sports bar lasts an eternity, but I refuse to just quit. I've worked here long enough to know that I don't want to leave my coworkers in the lurch. Plus, it feels like the end of something. A new beginning.

I've been having a lot of those. Last week, Leif went with me to my first doctor's appointment. Then, he persuaded me to let his lawyers look over the contract his mother had drafted. They negotiated for more control for me, as well as clear delineation of what Christine could and couldn't dictate.

Yesterday, I signed the contract. Reynolds Events is about to become official.

As I carry a tray of drinks to a table in my section, I feel a prickling ghost over my skin. It doesn't surprise me to see Leif in the doorway, his regal, powerful demeanor drawing everyone's gaze.

Then he looks at me, and he looks thunderstruck.

Quickly, I dish the drinks out and slide my tray on a nearby table, just in time for Leif to wrap one arm around my waist, his other hand coming to rest on my cheek.

"It's you," he rasps. "You're the other splinter."

I frown. "What?"

"Six years ago, I met a waitress at a club. I never learned her name because I was thrown out for punching the creep who groped her."

My heart thuds as my breaths grow shallow.

Leif pulls me close, pressing my soft body against his hard one. His voice is harsh, ripped from his throat. "I went back every day for two weeks until I finally asked someone about you. They told me you didn't work there anymore. Wouldn't tell me your name or number or anything."

"You remembered me?" My voice sounds like it's coming from somewhere far away.

After everything, this is the thing that nearly breaks me. All the times I told myself to keep Leif at arm's length because he'd forget about me... I was wrong. He didn't forget.

"Of course I fucking remembered you," he says, his laugh sounding bitter. He closes his eyes and rests his forehead against mine. "That's why you looked familiar. Because it was you all along."

Wrapping my arms around Leif's neck, I tilt my chin until my lips touch his. Warmth glides through my body as everything settles into place. I was never forgotten or forgettable. I was Leif's.

"Let's get out of here," he says, pulling back enough to brush his thumb over my cheekbone. "I know you're trying to be noble and work out the rest of your shift, but just come home with me, Layla."

"Just do it!" Kylie calls out. "It's dead in here anyway."

Biting back my smile, I glance at the floor manager who's watching me from his perch at the bar. He gives me a flat stare, then shrugs and waves me off.

"Give me five minutes. I need to cash out."

But Leif just growls, and I feel a bubbly, effervescent laugh take over. Untying my apron, I shove it into Kylie's hands. "Cash out for me and keep the tips. As a thank you for not hating me."

She blinks three or four times, then grins. "Works for me."

Running to the back to grab my jacket and purse, I meet Leif outside and let him bundle me into his waiting car. We speed through the darkened streets, kissing and touching fervently until he pulls up outside the townhouse. Inside, Isla runs toward me with a squeal.

"We made cake!" she tells me, tugging me toward the kitchen. "Emma said it was her favorite recipe. Come eat it with us!"

My sister had to babysit tonight since Harriet needed a night off to take care of her husband. And it looks like she needed a study break, because the kitchen looks like it just went through a baking extravaganza. My sister grins at me from the kitchen as she loads up the dishwasher.

Laughing, I let Isla lead me to a seat, glancing over my shoulder at Leif. His eyes are soft, his hand pressed against his chest.

He mouths the words *I love you*, and I feel them all the way down to my toes.

I love you too, I tell him, and he comes to stand behind me to steal the first bite of cake. He hums in appreciation as I try to bat his hand away from my slice, but then I feel both hands settle onto my shoulders.

"Isla," he says in a tone that makes me sit up. "Layla and I have news for you."

My heart thumps. We've talked about this, about telling Isla about the baby, but as Leif's daughter twirls in the kitchen and comes to a stop in front of us, leaning her hands on the island counter that separates us, my heart suddenly starts to thud.

What if Isla gets jealous? What if she likes me enough to let me hang out here, but she doesn't want me to stay? What if more problems, more complications start to heap themselves on my plate and Leif decides it's all too complicated?

"What?" Isla says, licking a bit of frosting off the edge of the cake.

"You know how you always said you wanted a sibling?" Leif starts.

Isla freezes. She blinks at her father, then drops her eyes to meet mine.

Leif clears his throat. "Well, you're going to have one in a few months."

Isla is still for a beat. Two. Three. Then she vaults into the air, squealing, and comes sprinting around the counter to throw herself against her father's legs. "Really? Reallyreallyreally? I'm going to be a big sister like Talia?" She looks at me as I spin around in my chair, her little hands coming to rest on my thighs. "The baby is in there?" She points at my stomach.

Throat tight, all I can do is nod.

Isla's eyes grow bright, and she inches forward, lifting a hand. Her eyes flick to mine in question and I nod. Gently, she places her hand on my stomach. With Leif's fingers curled around my shoulders and Isla's acceptance right there in her touch, I let out a long breath, meeting my sister's gaze across the kitchen.

I told her and my grandparents about the baby a couple of weeks ago, when Leif told me he was building a park beside their place.

But now, as my sister comes around to wrap me in a side hug, my heart does a funny kind of flip right there in my chest. The four of us hug each other, tears shining in everyone's eyes. The future is bright. For the first time in my life, I'm not afraid of what will happen next. I'm excited.

Leif kisses the top of my head, then lets out a long-suffering sigh that sounds suspiciously like the ones Isla makes. "The baby better be a boy. I'm starting to feel a bit outnumbered here."

Laughing through my tears, I give him a sideways glance.

Isla just dances away. "I hope it's a girl. Then Layla can teach me how to do fancy braids and I can braid my sister's hair!"

The doorbell rings and my grandparents walk in without waiting for anyone to answer—like this is their home as much as Leif's. As much as mine.

Heart so full it's about to burst, I smile as they lift up trays of food and tell me they're here to celebrate the end of my career as a waitress—and the start of my future as an event planner.

I MOVE INTO THE TOWNHOUSE. Emma moves into the Midtown penthouse to be closer to college. Everyone—including Leif's parents, most weeks—meets at my grandparents' house for a weekly family dinner. We all watch the progress of the playground, and I can't help but feel insanely lucky that my child will get to play there and know his or her father created it.

When the cold weather rolls around again, I pull out my almost-four-thousand-dollar jacket (which I didn't have the heart to sell after the supply closet incident), put it on, and feel warm all the way down to my toes at the way Leif looks at me. It feels good to be taken care of.

Leif changes the direction of his business slightly. Instead of focusing on luxury properties, he includes a chunk of more affordable housing as well. He tells me about his projects as he works on them, no longer keeping business separate from other aspects of his life.

Leif doesn't get his wish, because on November 15, right on schedule, I give birth to a baby girl. By the way tears roll down his cheeks and he holds her like she's the most precious thing in the world, I know he doesn't mind that she's not a boy.

After the hubbub of birth and tests and cleaning, a day goes by, and I still feel high. I'm in the hospital room with Leif, Isla, Emma, my grandparents, and Baby Madeline, finally showered and feeling half-normal.

Leif rocks the baby, looking down at her with stars in her eyes. "Isla will have a partner in crime now," he says, voice rough. "I'll never be able to control anything."

"Were you ever?" his mother quips from the doorway. She congratulates me, then hands me a stack of five business cards.

"What's this?" I ask, sitting up in bed, eyes drifting to my daughter every few seconds.

"Five people who want to hire you for baby showers. They saw the pictures you posted of your own. All of them were at Isla's birthday party and the anniversary party, too."

Throat dry, I look through the business cards, then up at Christine. "Really?"

She smiles. "Mama, you're going to be busier than you ever imagined possible this year."

When I look at Leif, he shifts the baby into my arms, then places a kiss on my forehead. "You're going to do great," he says.

I settle into the comfort of his words, hearing the truth in them. He believes in me, and all these people around me will be there to support me. I'm no longer lost in a turbulent ocean on my own. I'm not carrying my family on my shoulders.

"I want to make it official," Leif says, catching my eyes.

"Make what official?" I ask, then squeak when he kneels beside the hospital bed.

He pulls out a velvet box, opening it up to reveal a marquise-cut diamond flanked by two smaller diamonds on a white-gold band. His hands tremble slightly, and I realize that last time he was in a hospital room with a new baby daughter, he was going through a very different time.

"Layla," he says in front of our entire family, "I love you so much I can hardly think whenever you're around. Make me the happiest man in Manhattan and tell me you'll marry me."

Tears budding in my eyes, I can't find my voice to tell him he's as high-handed, arrogant, and bossy as ever. Instead, I just let the tears roll down my cheeks and nod. I can't extend my hand toward him though, because I'm still holding our baby.

He slips the ring on my finger right there beside the swaddled bundle of love, then leans over and lays a soft kiss on my lips. When he pulls back, I know this moment has soothed the last of the hurts on his soul.

I'm not leaving him behind. I'm not walking away from him. We're going to live this life together—forever at each other's side.

Exactly where we belong.

EXTENDED EPILOGUE
LAYLA

THE EIFFEL TOWER thrusts up from the ground as tiny people mill all around the base. I press my nose up against our private jet's window, excitement shivering through every part of my body.

"Did French people invent French braids?" Isla asks, her own face pressed up against the window next to mine.

"I'm not sure," I answer. "Probably."

"We can look it up," Leif answers, shutting down his laptop as we circle the city. "Maybe they have a French Braid Museum right there beside the Louvre."

I give him a flat stare, and Leif just grins.

The baby fusses and Leif is there, leaning over the bassinet, shushing her and making her giggle in an instant. I settle back in my seat, unable to keep the smile off my face.

The past seven months have been like a dream—and not because I was sleep-deprived for the first few. My new life with

Leif has been easy to adjust to because he's made sure that everything is taken care of. I don't have to worry about a thing when he's around, and it's impossible to describe how good it feels not to be the sole bearer of responsibility in my family.

I feel *supported*. Loved. Cherished.

It took over a year for us to get here after my initial tiff in the store when Leif bought me my now-favorite jacket, but we're here. Flying over Paris. Going on my dream vacation.

We land a short while later and are bundled up and hauled to a nice hotel in the center of Paris. Isla is over the moon, awed by the wrought-iron balconies, the history imbibed in the beautiful city. My heart flutters, and I can't help but reach over to hold Leif's hand in the back seat of the car.

Our suite is massive, with separate bedrooms for Isla, a small nursery for Madeline, and a spare room for Harriet and her husband, who were delighted to come along with us.

"Emma would love this," I say, walking over to the windows to glance out. A wrought-iron balcony gives us a view of the busy Paris streets, with the top of the Arc de Triomphe visible in the distance.

Leif's hands slide over my hips. "We'll bring her next time."

I smile, leaning against his shoulder, listening to the hubbub behind us as Harriet corrals Isla toward the kitchen to feed her ever-growing body. Harriet's husband holds baby Madeline, cooing at her, laughing at everything she does.

I'm so, so lucky. There are so many people in my network to rely on, and I'll never forget what a privilege that is. Now when I need help, I only have to ask for it and half a dozen people are there to listen.

"Come on," Leif says. "I want to show you something."

His palm is warm against mine as he takes me through the suite to the master bedroom. Sitting on top of the bed is a garment bag. Leif drops my hand and crosses the vast room to grab it, unzipping it slowly to reveal the edge of the ivory fabric.

I gasp when he pulls out a gorgeous gown.

Leif grins at me. "You told me you wanted a designer gown to clean my toilets in, but I hope you'll settle for the ballet with me and Isla, then a late dinner with your future husband."

"Leif." I let my fingers drift over the delicate silk. "This is incredible."

The bodice consists of two straps that meet at the waist in the front and back, covered with delicate silver embroidery. At the waist, the dress explodes in a riot of feathers all the way down to the floor. It's dramatic and beautiful and so not something I've ever touched, let alone worn.

"It's Elie Saab," Leif says. "I saw it in black and asked them to make it custom for you."

"You—" I gape at my fiancé, unable to speak.

"We're going out tonight." He smiles, tugging me closer. "You're going to love it."

THE DRESS FITS like it was made for me. Which...it was, I guess. I twirl in front of the floor-length mirror in our suite, my hair professionally styled in loose waves, my feet clad in simple white heels. I look elegant and classy and oh my goodness, I can't even believe it.

Then Leif walks into the bedroom looking positively delicious in a crisp tux, and Isla is already twirling in her own pink dress. She has elbow-length gloves, and she looks so happy she could burst.

I turn to Harriet. "Do you have everything you need? She didn't eat much today, so try to feed her a bit. And she's had that weird cough, and…"

She gives me a wry smile. "I know it's your first evening away from the baby, but believe me, Layla, everything will be fine. It's only a couple of hours. Enjoy yourself."

"It's just…" I move to where Madeline crawls on her play mat, picking her up to nuzzle her soft, soft skin. "I'll miss you, baby girl."

She babbles and grabs my hair, planting a sloppy kiss on my cheek. Reluctantly, I pass Madeline over to Harriet, who smiles at my daughter, then at me. "We'll have fun this evening, won't we, Maddy?"

My daughter giggles, and I let out a breath. "Fine. I know. I'm being ridiculous."

"You're being a mother. It's normal. Go out, enjoy yourself. You look beautiful." Harriet smiles at me, then goes to sit next to her husband.

Squaring my shoulders, I nod, then turn to Isla and Leif. Isla jumps up and twirls, too excited to sit still. My heart flutters at the sight of the two of them, at my baby left in good hands, at the fact that my fiancé brought me to Paris just because I said I wanted to go.

"Ready?" Isla asks, beaming.

I nod. "Let's go."

A limousine waits outside to take us to the ballet, and the

next couple of hours are spent in awe of the dancers on stage. Isla watches with rapt attention, hands folded in her lap, feet kicking every once in a while in her seat. Leif, sitting on the other side of me, puts his arm around my shoulders and lets me settle into his warmth.

Surrounded by the old-world glamour of the ballet, I sink into my seat and let myself be transported to another world. When the show ends, Isla lets out a sigh, her eyes shining.

"Thank you, Daddy," she says quietly. "That was amazing."

My heart is so full it could burst. We take Isla back to the hotel, I check in on the baby, and then I finally let Leif take me out for our first dinner-date since the baby was born.

It's late, but Paris seems alive. Restaurants are full, streets are teeming with people, and there's an electric energy in the air that I can't help but inhale. Leif takes me to an elegant hotel where we share food and wine in a private dining room.

I feel like a princess. When the last plates have been cleared and we have half a glass of wine each to finish, Leif reaches across the table to take my hand. He brushes his thumb over my knuckles, smiling softly at me.

"Thank you, Layla."

I start. "For what? You're the one who planned the perfect evening."

"For being happy to have Isla come along with us to the ballet. For opening your heart not only to me but to my daughter and Harriet and my parents and everyone else who's important to my life."

"I could say the same to you." I smile, turning my hand so

our palms touch. "You've been housing Emma and doting on my grandparents for over a year."

His eyes hold mine, and I know there's something he's not telling me.

"What?" I ask softly. "What's wrong?"

"I want to marry you, Layla."

I laugh. "I'm still wearing your ring, aren't I?"

He squeezes my hand. "I want to marry you now, I mean. And I know you probably want to plan the perfect event, but I just... I don't know. Seeing you in that dress tonight just made me realize that I want this to be official. I want you to be mine forever."

My heart does a somersault. "I am yours forever, Leif."

His throat bobs, big hand curling around mine. "Let's fly our families over to France. We can meet them in Marseilles, get married on the edge of the Mediterranean."

My eyes widen, heart doing another funny kind of flip. As Leif stares at me, a soft vulnerability in his gaze, I realize that I've been stressed about planning a wedding. I've felt immense pressure to make it perfect, and I haven't been able to commit to a date or a venue or a theme or anything.

Once again, Leif *sees* me. He sees what I need and he's right there to catch me when I stumble. I don't need to plan the perfect event. I don't need a fairytale wedding. All I need are my loved ones beside me and this man at the altar with me.

"I love you," I blurt.

His lips curl. "Is that a yes?"

A tear escapes down my cheek. "It's a hell yes."

In a flash, Leif has me in his arms, twirling me around

before setting me down and kissing me senseless. My body goes boneless as he bands his strong arms around me, his lips devouring mine while he murmurs words of love and adoration and devotion.

I don't remember the drive home. All I know is when we get back to the hotel, everyone is asleep, and Leif carries me across the threshold to the bedroom like a bride. He undresses me with brisk efficiency, then lays me down on the bed completely naked.

I watch him take his jacket and bowtie off, curling onto my side as my fingers drift down my bare skin. He growls, then, forgetting the rest of his clothes as he kneels between my legs and presses my thighs apart. I gasp at the feel of his tongue on me, pleasure spearing through my core.

"Can't wait to call you my wife," he says against my intimate flesh. His tongue circles my clit as I shiver, tunneling my fingers into his hair. One finger enters me, then two, and his mouth does something magic to me.

I'll never get enough of this man. I'll never grow tired of him. And I can't wait to be his wife.

As pleasure winds tighter in the pit of my stomach, Leif's hands keep driving in and out of me, his lips suckling on my bud.

"Leif," I gasp. "I'm going to... I'm..."

"Give me this one," he says. "Let me taste it."

His dark, deep voice is what pushes me over the edge. I come apart, back arching, knees falling apart as Leif devours me.

In a haze, I hear the rustle of clothes against skin. I slit my eyes open to see Leif undressing, his erection jutting proud and thick at a ninety-degree angle from his body. He tosses his clothing aside, eyes coasting up and down the length of my body.

This man. This man is something special. Already, even though I'm wrung out from my first orgasm, I feel desire sparking between my legs again.

He must see something in my gaze, because Leif doesn't hesitate. He grabs my ankles, tugging me roughly toward him as he positions himself on the bed. "Cross your ankles behind my neck, baby," he says, lifting my legs up. "I want you to feel me deep. I want you to know what your husband will be giving you the rest of your life."

Whimpering, I place my legs on his shoulders. He runs his fingers in the wetness between my legs, growling in satisfaction at my arousal. And how could I not be aroused? How could I ever resist a man like this, saying dirty, beautiful things in my ear, promising me pleasure beyond anything I've ever had?

We both watch him pump his fingers inside me, then grab his thick cock in his fist to position it at my entrance. He teases me for long, interminable seconds, brushing his swollen cockhead against my flesh.

"Leif," I whine.

"My girl is greedy for my cock," he says. "Isn't she?"

"Yes." I grab at his legs, his ass, needing him inside me now. Now now now.

I'm dripping wet, so turned on I can't think or speak, but I'm still not ready for the feel of him. He thrusts inside me in one hard roll of his hips, bracing his hands against my thighs until he's buried to the hilt.

I pull in a hard breath, back bowing off the bed. I see stars. I touch the stratosphere. I lose my ever-loving *mind*.

Then Leif fucks me so hard I forget my own name, muffling my screams with his palm as he shows me exactly how hard my future husband will love his wife.

Pleasure is too small a word for what I feel when I come. It doesn't come close to describing what I feel for this beautiful, dirty, domineering, arrogant man. He wrings an orgasm out of me, then leans down to let me feel all his weight, his lips coasting over my sweat-dappled skin as his hands brand every inch of my body.

And when I feel him stiffen, his cock throbbing inside me, another wave of pleasure drags me under.

"I love you so much," he says, panting against my neck. "So fucking much, Layla."

THEN, a week later, I wear my custom Elie Saab dress to marry the man of my dreams on the edge of the Mediterranean Sea. My toes are in the sand, grounded in his love for me, as all my friends and family watch us vow to love and cherish each other for the rest of our lives.

Our wedding is unrefined and barely planned and completely spontaneous.

In other words, it's perfect.

WANT MORE?

KEEP READING FOR AN EXCLUSIVE
PREVIEW OF BIG BOSSY PROBLEM

ONE
PENNY

THE CLICK of a dog's claws on polished concrete greets me
when I enter my boss's house. As soon as my rain jacket is on
the hook by the front door, I drop to my knees and spread my
arms. "Bear!"

The dog launches himself at me, tackling me to the ground.
His wet snout touches my neck, followed by the rough scrape of
his tongue. "Ahh!" I squirm, laughing, scrubbing his fur. I try to
catch my breath while sixty pounds of dog plants itself on my
chest. "Ack! Get off!"

There's nothing like a pup greeting you like you've been off
at war for months, no matter how long it's been since he last saw
you. In my case, it's been about eighteen hours. Walking in my
employer's front door is my favorite part of my day, because I
get tackled by a furry bullet every single time.

Bear's a good boy. Always has been. He's some kind of

German shepherd mix, judging by his dark coloring and size, but his hair is quite a bit longer than a full-breed German shepherd, and those pointed ears flop down in the most adorable way. I've loved him since his very first greeting, which was a lot more wary than today's enthusiastic hello.

"Do you know what today is, Bear?" I get to my knees and give him scratches behind those big, floppy ears, just the way he likes.

The dog snuffles.

In the stillness of my employer's empty house, I don't mind talking to the dog like he's a person. Sometimes, I feel like animals are the only creatures worth talking to. Dogs never let you down the way people do.

I stroke Bear's snout and give him a kiss right between the eyes. "Today is our one-year anniversary. I've been walking you twice a day, five days a week for an entire year!"

Bear sits down on his haunches and tilts his head.

"Yep. I've been your dog walker for a whole year." Kneeling in front of him, I bring my crossbody bag to rest on my thighs before sliding the zipper open. Bear follows the movement with great interest.

"Your human said it was fine for me to bring you a T-R-E-A-T to celebrate," I explain, reaching into my bag for Bear's favorite type of dog bone. I pause, arching a brow. "Well, your human's assistant said so. Your actual human doesn't speak to me."

As soon as the treat emerges from the confines of my purse, Bear turns into a vibrating mass of excited doggy energy. "I also made you a special bow tie, fresh off the sewing machine an hour ago. But it looks like you much prefer this part of your present."

I lift the bone, a movement which Bear's gaze traces with laser-like precision. He stays still as long as I ask him to, until I finally take pity on him and let him take the treat. He carries it off to his dog bed by the back door, chewing contentedly.

I love my job. For the past year, five days a week, twice a day, I've done the same thing. This SoHo bachelor pad has become somewhat familiar, even though I haven't seen much more than the foyer and the open-plan living space. Marcus Walsh is in the news every so often, being the handsome, single tech genius he is, so I know he's mega-wealthy. But apart from a few expensive-looking pieces of art on two of the living room walls—and the fact that his home isn't the size of an airplane bathroom like mine—there isn't much evidence that Mr. Walsh is a billionaire.

The front door opens onto a big, open-plan room with the kitchen in the far right corner, complete with double ovens and a big island/breakfast bar area. Cushioned barstools line the island, with a funky, curvy light fixture hanging above. On the other side of the space, the living room wall is exposed brick, with an absolutely enormous television mounted in the center. Speakers and subwoofers halo the television, and a comfy-looking couch faces it all. I say comfy-*looking*, because in the hundreds of times I've been here, I've never actually sat down on the sofa.

I know I'm on camera, after all. I'm sure Mr. Tech Billionaire wouldn't take too kindly to me making myself at home.

Between the kitchen and living spaces, a hallway leads to

the bedrooms and living spaces beyond. I've never stepped foot past that threshold. There's an invisible wall keeping me out.

My entry into this billionaire's world has clear boundaries. I get a tiny sliver of a peek into how the other half lives. I have access to the big pantry where Bear's food is kept. I can use the kitchen to replenish his water, and I have permission to use the small powder room beside the kitchen. Once, I snooped through the door beside the powder room because I was looking for Bear's spare leash and saw that it leads into a garage. Yes, a private garage in New York City. The other half never has to circle the block for street parking or take the subway, apparently.

All other areas of this place are off-limits, and that's perfectly fine by me. Boundaries are good. I've spent most of my adult life building my own boundaries back up to healthy levels just to feel safe. I'm more than happy to respect someone else's.

While Bear celebrates with his treat, I do the various small tasks I've gotten used to completing for Bear and his owner. I check the dog's bowl and replenish it with fresh water, tidy a few stray toys, and make sure I have doggy bags and a leash ready for our first walk of the day.

As soon as I jingle it, Bear comes running.

"Last thing," I tell him, kneeling in front of him with his spiffy new bow tie. It clips to his collar with a special clasp I designed myself. The pattern is red with white polka dots, and it looks extremely dashing, if I do say so myself.

I'm probably biased. My dog clothing business has exploded recently, to the point that Bear is the only dog-walking client

I've kept. A year ago, I had about a dozen dogs I'd walk every day, but I had to drop all of them to make time for the new business. But Bear's owner pays a *lot* better than most people, so it seemed like a good safety net to keep this particular job.

Also, Bear is my favorite. Don't tell the others.

When I'm not walking Bear, my time is spent hunched over my sewing machine, coming up with new patterns and styles for bow ties, sweaters, rain jackets, and all kinds of pet clothing and costumes. Thank goodness for Brian, my best friend. He's the one who handles the technology side of things. Without him, I wouldn't have gotten very far with the business at all.

"Did you know," I tell Bear, "that I used to sell my wares at farmers' markets, until Brian convinced me to try doing things online? That was about a year ago, around the time we met." Bear sits while I adjust his bow tie. "I have to say, Brian was right. The internet is like a mystical fairyland I don't understand. I just give Brian the dog clothes, and he gets his little furball to model them, uploads the pictures, and runs the online store. We split the profits fifty-fifty."

Bear listens patiently, and I pretend he understands every word.

My arrangement with Brian works perfectly, because technology has a way of malfunctioning when I'm nearby. My body must be made of magnets. Or maybe I emit low-level electromagnetic pulses every time my heart beats. Screens go blue and freeze, computers start smoking, car alarms go off in my wake.

I'm kidding. Mostly.

The twenty-first century has been tough. Without Brian, I'd

still be walking a dozen dogs and barely scraping by. I'm happy to split the business's profits with him equally.

"Another fun fact," I say to Bear, "is that *your* human owns the website where I sell my products! That's right. Marcus Walsh created the online marketplace that made it possible for me and Brian to start this business together. Your human started Sellzy, and that website is the whole reason I was able to start sewing dog clothes full-time. Isn't that cool?" I straighten the red-and-white polka-dot bow tie and give Bear an extra little scratch behind the ears. "This is going to be a bestseller. I can already tell."

Bear sneezes. He agrees.

"Let's show your human," I tell the dog, leading him over to the nanny cam on the shelf by the door. Mr. Walsh's assistant made sure to show it to me and let me know that his security was top-notch when he hired me. I could have guessed that by the military-grade background check he required and the fact that his front door has a fingerprint scanner in place of a regular lock.

Little did my employer know that my fingers don't enjoy being scanned.

When the scanner malfunctioned for the tenth time in my second week of working for him, Marcus Walsh finally gave me a physical key. Unsurprising to me, considering my storied history with electronics, but apparently it was very unusual to my boss. He made a point to come check me out himself instead of sending the assistant I'd been dealing with up until that point.

I still remember the way his green eyes narrowed on me. I felt like a bug on a microscope slide, inspected down to a cellular level. He stared at me like he was trying to figure out if I was lying, if there was some subterfuge with the key. Not a man who trusts easily—but then again, I'm the same way. I can't blame him for being suspicious. Mr. Walsh takes good care of Bear, and that's good enough for me.

Still, the interaction was...unsettling. I don't like it when people—men especially, and *attractive* men like Marcus Walsh doubly so—pay that kind of close attention to me. I learned my lesson in college, *thankyouverymuch*. Male attention is not something I go out and seek on purpose. Not anymore.

But Mr. Walsh finally gave me the key, and that was that. It was the last time I saw my boss in person.

Even so, Bear and I still have a little daily ritual involving the nanny cam, and part of me likes to think Mr. Walsh appreciates it. In reality, he probably doesn't even notice—or he thinks I'm a total dork.

But a dork is better than a victim. A dork is way, *way* better than a target.

I bring Bear to the camera and kneel beside him, slinging my arm around the dog's body. "Smile!" We both look at the camera. I smile brightly, and Bear just gives a great big yawn, complete with lolling tongue.

"Okie dokie," I say, attaching Bear's leash to his collar and leading him to the door. "Let's go! It's a bit wet outside, so I left a towel by the door for when we come back. We'll have to wipe you down before we ruin all this nice furniture, okay?"

I point to the towel. Bear doesn't care; he's completely still, staring at the front door. His ears point forward, fur bristling. Tension turns his body to stone. While I'm busy frowning at his strange reaction, the door flies open.

A young teenage girl careens through the open doorway, sobbing, while an older woman stands on the porch looking like thunder and lightning personified.

"Stay here if you like it so much, you little slut," the woman sneers. I jump at the word. I've been called it, too, and it's a highly unpleasant feeling.

Bear growls while I wrap my hand around the leash to keep him by my side.

The woman finally notices me. She turns the storm clouds in my direction. "What the hell are you looking at?" Without waiting for me to answer, the woman slams the door closed. It rattles for a moment.

Silence crashes down around me, and I stand rooted to the spot, eyes wide. Slowly, I spin around, only to see the girl disappear down the hallway. The sounds of her cries and sniffles echo off the walls, and another door slams.

Bear tugs at the leash, but not in direction of the door. He wants to follow the girl.

I bite my lip, glancing at the dog, then at the hallway, and finally at the camera. "Mr. Walsh, I know I'm not allowed anywhere else in the house, but this seems like an emergency. I need to check on that girl."

For some reason, speaking to a camera in a silent apartment seems infinitely weirder than speaking to a dog, so I pull out my phone and find the phone number I haven't used once in the entire year I've been employed by him. It was given to me for emergencies only, of which I've had none. But this seems like a bad situation. The girl obviously knows my boss, but the way the woman spoke to her...

I have to tell him. He probably doesn't even check the nanny camera. He'd want to know a young girl just ran into his home. I would want to know if that happened in my house. Surely billionaires aren't *that* different from the rest of us?

I have an old flip phone because smartphones are the devil. If they don't malfunction, I usually end up accidentally dropping them in the toilet or down a sewer drain, like they're doing their best to get away from me even if it means diving into a dirty, watery grave. But with an old flip phone, texting isn't exactly easy. I try to keep texts short and sweet, if I send them at all.

Penny: Bear OK. Girl came crying. Please txt/call. Ty.

I wait a few seconds, staring at the scratched screen of my flip phone, waiting for it to vibrate with a response. I'd know a message was incoming anyway, because one of those expensive-looking speakers on the wall would start beeping and buzzing if a text message was on its way to my phone. They remain silent, though, and for the first time in my life, I wish I had a smartphone to tell me if my message made it to its recipient.

Nothing happens, so I snap the phone closed and slide it

into my purse. Then I unclip Bear's leash and follow him down the hallway toward the sounds of a very upset teenager.

Penny is about to come face to face with her big, bad boss...
Read BIG BOSSY PROBLEM:
https://geni.us/bigbossyproblem

ABOUT THE AUTHOR

Lilian Monroe adores writing swoonworthy heroes and the women who bring them to their knees. She loves making people laugh and is eternally grateful to have found people who share her sense of humor.

When she's not writing, she's reading (or rereading) a book, walking, lifting weights, or attempting to play the guitar with very limited success.

She grew up in Canada but now lives in Australia with her Irish husband. He frequently asks to be used as a cover model for her books, and she's not quite sure whether or not he's joking.

ALSO BY LILIAN MONROE

For all books, visit:

www.lilianmonroe.com

<u>Manhattan Billionaires</u>

Big Bossy Mistake

Big Bossy Trouble

Big Bossy Problem

Big Bossy Surprise

Forbidden Boss

The Wrong Boss

Dirty Boss

<u>More surprise babies!</u>

Knocked Up by the CEO

Knocked Up by the Single Dad

Knocked Up...Again!

Knocked Up by the Billionaire's Son

Yours for Christmas

Bad Prince

Heartless Prince

Cruel Prince

Broken Prince

Wicked Prince

Wrong Prince

Lone Prince

Ice Queen

Rogue Prince

Small Towns are the Best Towns

Four Steps to the Perfect Revenge

Four Steps to the Perfect Fake Date

Working with the Enemy

Faking It with the Firefighter

Conquest

Craving

Combat

Calamity

Small Town + Later-in-Life Romance

Dirty Little Midlife Crisis

Dirty Little Midlife Mess

Dirty Little Midlife Mistake

Dirty Little Midlife Disaster

Dirty Little Midlife Debacle

Dirty Little Midlife Secret

Dirty Little Midlife Dilemma

Dirty Little Midlife Drama

Dirty Little Midlife (fake) Date

Filthy Little Midlife Fling

Merry Little Midlife Matchmaker

Forty and Fighting Dirty

Brother's Best Friend Romance

Shouldn't Want You

Can't Have You

Don't Need You

Won't Miss You

He'll do anything to protect his woman

His Vow

His Oath

His Word

Enemies to Lovers/Workplace Romance

Hate at First Sight

Loathe at First Sight

Despise at First Sight

Fake Engagement Romance

Engaged to Mr. Right

Engaged to Mr. Wrong

www.ingramcontent.com/pod-product-compliance
Lightning Source LLC
Chambersburg PA
CBHW031743180726

48283CB00005B/1648